CRIERS & KIBITZERS, KIBITZERS & CRIERS

STANLEY ELKIN

AFTERWORD BY HAROLD BRODKEY
NEW PREFACE BY THE AUTHOR

THUNDER'S MOUTH PRESS

Copyright 1965, 1963, 1962, 1961, 1960, 1959 by Stanley Elkin.
Preface copyright 1990 by Stanley Elkin.
Afterword copyright 1990 by Harold Brodkey.

Published by Thunder's Mouth Press
54 Greene Street, Suite 4S
New York, N.Y. 10013

First Thunder's Mouth Press edition.
First printing, 1990.

These stories have appeared in *Accent*, *Chicago Review*, *Esquire*,
Paris Review, *Perspective*, and *Saturday Evening Post*.

Library of Congress Cataloging-in-Publication data:

Elkin, Stanley, 1930–
    Criers and kibitzers, kibitzers and criers: stories / by Stanley
Elkin ; with an afterword by Harold Brodkey ; and a new preface by the author. — 1st Thunder's Mouth Press ed.
        p.   cm. — (Classic reprint series)
    ISBN 1-56025-005-4 : $12.95
    I. Title.   II. Series
PS3555.L47C7   1990
813'.54 — dc20   90-10913
                                                                        CIP

Manufactured in the United States of America.

For

JERRY BEATY

HERB BOGART

BOB BROWN

DAN CURLEY

DAVE DEMAREST

BILL GASS

IRWIN GOLD

BILL GUGGENHEIM

AL LEBOWITZ

KERKER QUINN

HARRY RICHMAN

GEORGE SCOUFFAS

and

JARVIS THURSTON

Contents

PREFACE

For reasons not in the least clear to me, *Criers and Kibitzers, Kibitzers and Criers* has turned out to be my most enduring work, if by "enduring" one refers not to a time scheme encompassing geological epochs, or, for that matter, scarcely even to calendrical ones, but to those few scant handfuls — twenty-four since it was first published by Random House in hardback in 1966 — of years barely wide enough to gap a generation. Not counting down-time, when it was out-of-print, or the peculiar half-life when it was in that curious publisher's limbo, known to the trade (but never entirely understood, at least by this prefacer) as "out-of-stock," it has been in print under sundry imprimaturs (Berkley Medallion, Plume, Warner Books and, until I actually looked it up in *Books in Print* where I couldn't find it, I had thought Dutton's Obelisk editions, and, now, Thunder's Mouth Press), oh, say, eighteen or nineteen years. Set against the great timelines of history this ain't, of course, much — not in the same league with astronomy's skippy-stony'd light years certainly, or even, for that matter, the same ballpark as the universe, but we're talking very fragile book years, mind, which are to life span approximately what dog years are to the birthdays of humans. At a ratio of seven-to-one (seven doggie years equalling forty-nine bookie years), that would make my criers and kibitzers, depending on how the actuaries count that half-life, either eight-hundred-and-eighty-two, or nine-hundred-and-eleven-years old. A classic, antique as Methuselah — the test, as the saying goes, of time.

In addition — more new math — two of these stories, "Criers and Kibitzers, Kibitzers and Criers" and "The Guest," were adapted for and produced on the stage. "Criers" has been a radio play on the Canadian Broadcasting System, and one, "I Look Out for Ed Wolfe," was bought for the movies, though it never made the cut. ("Ed Wolfe," published in *Esquire* in 1962, was my first mass-market sale and put me, quite literally, on the map. Well, at least on *Esquire*'s rigged 1963 chart about America's "Literary Establishment," where I found myself in shameless scarlet, short-listed among a small, arbitrary bundle of real writers — realer, in any event, than me — in what that magazine deemed to be "The Red Hot Center." [Just Rust Hills and Bob Brown kidding around.] It thrilled me then, it embarrasses me now. Had I had more sense it would have embarrassed me then, too. God knows it angered a lot of important critics who wrote letters to the editor, columns, even essays about it, a short-lived tempest in a tea bag not unlike the one old John Gardner provoked when he made his pronouncements about moral fiction. Not art for art's sake but hype for hype's — like the PENs and Pulitzers, NBAs and National Book Critics Circle Awards, and all those other Masterpieces of the Minute that might not last the night.) "A Poetics for Bullies" was recorded on an LP by Jackson Beck, the radio actor and famous voice of Bluto in the Popeye cartoons, and somewhere loose in the world is a cassette tape of "The Guest" which I recorded for an outfit called the Printed Word. Oh, and eight of the nine stories in *C & K* — "Cousin Poor Lesley and the Lousy People" is the exception — have been anthologized, a few of them — the "Criers," "Guest," "Ed Wolfe" and "Bully" stories — several times, almost often.

"Criers" and "Ed Wolfe" were in *The Best American Short Stories* annuals back in the days when Martha Foley was Martha Foley. Indeed, for many years during the late sixties, the decade of the seventies, and into the eighties (it's starting to fall off), the stories have provided me and my family with a kind of widow's mite, a small annuity — "sky money," I like to call it. (I regard myself as a serious writer, even a professional one, but deep in my heart I think of most of the money I receive from my writing as essentially unearned. This isn't, as you may suppose, a poetic wimp factor kicking in — I'm no art jerk — so much as the heart's negotiated *quid pro quo*, all ego's driving power trip, the rush many writers get out of their almost sybaritic wallow in the unfettered luxury of their indulged imaginations. (What, they'll pay for this? I may be a badass, but I'm an honorable badass.) Anyway it — the money from the stories, all sources — never amounted to *that* much. I come cheap, after all. Maybe, top-of-the-head, all-told, thirty or thirty-five thousand dollars since 1966, my going rate for having passed the test of time. Nothing solid as a fortune, I admit, but tighter than loose change — something like the cumulative yield on a small CD, say.

What isn't clear to me, though, is why. Why this book, why these stories? Surely I've written better books. Surely I'm a better writer now than I was when I wrote these stories. (Five of them, including the title story, one of my favorites, were written when I was still back in graduate school, for Christ's sake, and only three, "The Guest," "A Poetics for Bullies" and "Perlmutter at the East Pole," were published after I'd published my first novel and before I'd written a second one.) So why? Why, really? I'd like to know.

One thing, certainly, is the accessibility of their style and (not behind that — indeed, quite the opposite — in absolute hand/glove relationship to the relative simplicity of the style) plain speaking's package deal with realism, time's honored literary arrangement between ease and verisimilitude. Here, for example, is Feldman, the butcher, returning to his store after a quick trip to the bank for change for his cash drawer. (In the story, had I been a better stylist in the realistic tradition, I would have used the word "silver" instead of "change.")

> The street was quiet. It looks like a Sunday, he thought. There would be no one in the store. He saw his reflection in a window he passed and realized he had forgotten to take his apron off. It occurred to him that the apron somehow gave him the appearance of being very busy. An apron did that, he thought. Not a business suit so much. Unless there was a brief-case. A briefcase and an apron, they made you look busy. A uniform wouldn't. Soldiers didn't look busy, policemen didn't. A fireman did, but he had to have that big hat on. Schmo, a man your age walking in the street in an apron. He wondered if the vice-presidents at the bank had noticed his apron. He felt the heaviness again.

There's something comforting, almost soothing, about realism, and it's nothing to do with shocks of recognition — well it wouldn't, would it, since shocks never console — or even with the familiarity that breeds content, so much as with the fact that the realistic world, in literature, at least, is one that, from a certain perspective, always makes sense, even its bum deals and trage-dies, inasmuch as it plays — even showboats and grandstands — to our passion for reason. The realistic tradition presumes to deal, I mean, with cause and effect, with some deep need in readers — in all of us — for justice, with the demand for the explicable reap/sow benefits (or punishments), with the law of just desserts — with all God's and Nature's organic bookkeeping. And since form fits and follows function, style is instructed not to make waves but merely to tag along, easy as pie, taking in everything that can be seen along the way but not much more and nothing at all of what isn't immediately available to the naked eye.

My point, then, is that the stories in *Criers and Kibitzers, Kibitzers and Criers* are right bang smack dab in the middle of realism.

I may get things wrong, or even silly — as I do in the improbable scene in "In the Alley" when my protagonist, top-heavy with incurable cancer, checks himself out of the hospital to wander the city and goes into a bar to die in an unfamiliar neighborhood; or in red-hot centered "I Look Out for Ed Wolfe," where — ending the story, as stories never should end, with a gesture — I have Ed throw his money away. But most of the stories have conventional, realistic sources. Only "On a Field, Rampant" and "A Poetics for Bullies" owe less to the syllogistic, rational world (though they're not experimental, none of my writing is; I don't care for experimental writing and, in my case at least, experimental writing would be if I did it in German or French) than they do to some conjured, imaginary one — and, sure enough, only in those stories am I more preoccupied with language than I am with realism's calmer tropes. I offer the battle of the headlines from "On a Field, Rampant":

" 'Docker Would Be King,' " a man said, reading an imaginary headline. " 'Immigrant Cargo Handler Says He's Nation's Rightful Majesty!' "

" 'Pretender Has Medallion Which Traces Lineage to Ancient Days of Kingdom.' "

" ' "Amazing Resemblance to Duke" Says Duke's Own Gateman.' "

" 'Dockman Defies Duke.' "

" 'Dockman Defies Duke, Dares Duke to Duel!' "

" 'Make-Believe Monarch.' "

" 'Cargo Con Man Claims Kingdom!' "

" 'Khardov Creates Kingdom for Cargo King.' "

" 'Who Is Khardov?' "

I offer, also, the abrasive, brassy up-frontiness of the opening paragraph in "A Poetics for Bullies":

I'm Push the bully, and what I hate are new kids and sissies, dumb kids and smart, rich kids, poor kids, kids who wear glasses, talk funny, show off, patrol boys and wise guys and kids who pass pencils and water the plants—and cripples, *especially* cripples. I love nobody loved.

The point here is that a "higher" or more conscious—if not conscientious—style is not only less realistic than the sedate and almost passive linears of the butcher's quiet street, but also much more aggressive and confrontational. (Only consider the two operative words in the titles of those two stories—"rampant" with all its up-in-your-face forepawardlies and dug-in hind-leggedness, and "bullies"—and you'll take my meaning.) In fiction and style not formed by the shared communal linkages between an author and the compacts, struck bargains, and done deals of a reasonable, recognizable morality—my law of just desserts—it's always the writer's service. Whatever spin, whatever "English" he puts on the ball is his. It's his call. He leads, you follow. He leads, you play catch-up. (It's that wallow in the ego again, the self's flashy mud wrassle.) Obviously this makes for difficulties that most readers—don't kid yourself, me too—don't much care to spend the time of day with, let alone hang out with long enough to pass any tests of time.

Who's afraid of the big bad wolf?

Damn near everyone.

Now I don't know how true this next part is, but it's a little true I should think. I'm trying to tell what turned me. Well, delight in language as language certainly (I'd swear to that part). But something less delightful, too. It was that nothing very bad had happened to me yet. (I was a graduate student, protected up to my ass in the ivy.) My daddy's rich and my mama's good lookin'. Then my father died in 1958 and my mother couldn't take three steps without pain. Then a heart attack I could call my own when I was thirty-seven years old. Then this, then that. Most of it uncomfortable, all of it boring. I couldn't run, I couldn't hop, I couldn't jump. Because, as the old saying *should* go, as long as you've got your health you've got your naïveté.

I lost the one, I lost the other, and maybe that's what led me toward revenge—a writer's revenge, anyway; the revenge, I mean, of style.

One final word about the stories in this collection and I'm done. I'm particularly fond of at least four of them: "Perlmutter at the East Pole" for its main character and the curses he invents, "The Guest" for its situation and humor, "Criers and Kibitzers, Kibitzers and Criers" for its situation and humor, and the truth, I think, of its perceptions and characters, and "A Poetics for Bullies," for its humor and energy and style. I like the "Ed Wolfe" story a bit less, but I like it—for the imagery in the opening paragraph, for a lot of its dialogue, and for one reason no one could ever possibly guess. Remember Polish jokes? I could be absolutely wrong about this, but I think I may have contributed to the invention of them in this story. It was published in the September 1962 issue of *Esquire*. In August of that I year I went off to Europe to write my first novel. Up to that time I'd never heard a Polish joke, but when I returned to America in June 1963, they were all the rage. Everyone was telling them. I think I invented the stereotype they are built on. A complete serendipity, of course, like penicillin or certain kinds of clear plastic, but *my* serendipity. What a claim to fame—to have invented the Polish joke. But it proves my point, I think, the one about the distance to which a writer's ego will stoop to have, whatever the cost, to him or to others, its own way.

STANLEY ELKIN
1990

CRIERS
AND
KIBITZERS,
KIBITZERS
AND
CRIERS

Greenspahn cursed the steering wheel shoved like the hard edge of someone's hand against his stomach. Goddamn lousy cars, he thought. Forty-five hundred dollars and there's not room to breathe. He thought sourly of the smiling salesman who had sold it to him, calling him Jake all the time he had been in the showroom: Lousy *podler*. He slid across the seat, moving carefully as though he carried something fragile, and eased his big body out of the car. Seeing the parking meter, he experienced a dark rage. They don't let you live, he thought. *I'll put your nickels in the meter for you, Mr. Greenspahn*, he mimicked the Irish cop. Two dollars a week for the lousy grubber. Plus the nickels that were supposed to go into the meter. And they talked about the Jews. He saw the cop across the street writing out a ticket. He went around his car, carefully pulling at the handle of each door, and he started toward his store.

"Hey there, Mr. Greenspahn," the cop called.

He turned to look at him. "Yeah?"

"Good morning."

"Yeah. Yeah. Good morning."

The grubber came toward him from across the street. Uniforms, Greenspahn thought, only a fool wears a uniform.

"Fine day, Mr. Greenspahn," the cop said.

Greenspahn nodded grudgingly.

"I was sorry to hear about your trouble, Mr. Greenspahn. Did you get my card?"

"Yeah, I got it. Thanks." He remembered something with flowers on it and rays going up to a pink Heaven. A picture of a cross yet.

"I wanted to come out to the chapel but the brother-in-law was up from Cleveland. I couldn't make it."

"Yeah," Greenspahn said. "Maybe next time."

The cop looked stupidly at him, and Greenspahn reached into his pocket.

"No. No. Don't worry about that, Mr. Greenspahn. I'll take care of it for now. Please, Mr. Greenspahn, forget it this time. It's okay."

Greenspahn felt like giving him the money anyway. Don't mourn for me, *podler*, he thought. Keep your two dollars' worth of grief.

The cop turned to go. "Well, Mr. Greenspahn, there's nothing anybody can say at times like this, but you know how I feel. You got to go on living, don't you know."

"Sure," Greenspahn said. "That's right, Officer." The cop crossed the street and finished writing the ticket. Greenspahn looked after him angrily, watching the gun swinging in the holster at his hip, the sun flashing brightly on the shiny handcuffs. *Podler*, he thought, afraid for his lousy nickels. There'll be an extra parking space sooner than he thinks.

He walked toward his store. He could have parked by his own place but out of habit he left his car in front of a rival grocer's. It was an old and senseless spite. Tomorrow he would change. What difference did it make, one less parking space? Why should he walk?

He felt bloated, heavy. The bowels, he thought. I got to move them soon or I'll bust. He looked at the street vacantly, feeling none of the old excitement. What did he come back for, he wondered suddenly, sadly. He missed Harold. Oh my God. Poor Harold, he thought. I'll never see him again. I'll never see my son again. He was choking, a big pale man beating his fist against his chest in grief. He pulled a handkerchief from his pocket and blew his nose. That was the way it was, he thought. He would go along flat and empty and dull, and all of a sudden he would dissolve in a heavy, choking grief. The street was no place for him. His wife was crazy, he thought, swiftly angry. "Be busy. Be busy," she said. What was he, a kid, that because he was making up somebody's lousy order everything would fly out of his mind? The bottom dropped out of his life and he was supposed to go along as though nothing had happened. His wife and the cop, they had the same psychology. Like in the movies after the horse kicks your head in you're supposed to get up and ride him so he can throw you off and finish the job. If he could get a buyer he would sell, and that was the truth.

Mechanically he looked into the windows he passed. The displays seemed foolish to him now, petty. He resented the wooden wedding cakes, the hollow watches. The manikins were grotesque, giant dolls. Toys, he thought bitterly. Toys. That he used to enjoy the displays himself, had even taken a peculiar pleasure in the complicated tiers of cans, in the amazing pyramids of apples and oranges in his own window, seemed incredible to him. He remembered he had liked to look at the little living rooms in the window of the furniture store, the wax models sitting on the couches offering each other tea. He used to look at the expensive furniture and think, *Merchandise.* The word had sounded rich to him, and mysterious. He used to think of camels on a desert, their bellies slung with heavy ropes. On their backs they carried *merchandise.* What did it mean, any of it? Nothing. It meant nothing.

He was conscious of someone watching him.

"Hello, Jake."

It was Margolis from the television shop.

"Hello, Margolis. How are you?"

"Business is terrible. You picked a hell of a time to come back."

A man's son dies and Margolis says business is terrible. Margolis, he thought, jerk, son of a bitch.

"You can't close up a minute. You don't know when somebody might come in. I didn't take coffee since you left," Margolis said.

"You had it rough, Margolis. You should have said something, I would have sent some over."

Margolis smiled helplessly, remembering the death of Greenspahn's son.

"It's okay, Margolis." He felt his anger tug at him again. It was something he would have to watch, a new thing with him but already familiar, easily released, like something on springs.

"Jake," Margolis whined.

"Not now, Margolis," he said angrily. He had to get away from him. He was like a little kid, Greenspahn thought. His face was puffy, swollen, like a kid about to cry. He looked so meek. He should be holding a hat in his hand. He couldn't stand to look at him. He was afraid Margolis was going to make a speech. He didn't want to hear it. What did he need a speech? His son was in the ground. Under all that earth. Under all that dirt. In a metal box. Airtight, the funeral director told him. Oh my God, *airtight. Vacuum-sealed.* Like a can of coffee. His son was in the ground and on the street the models in the windows had on next season's dresses. He would hit Margolis in his face if he said one word.

Margolis looked at him and nodded sadly, turning his palms out as if to say, "I know. I know." Margolis continued to look at him and Greenspahn thought, He's taking into account, that's what he's doing. He's taking into account the fact that my son has died. He's figuring it in and making apologies for me, making an allowance, like he was doing an estimate in his head what to charge a customer.

"I got to go, Margolis."

"Sure, me too," Margolis said, relieved. "I'll see you, Jake."

The man from R.C.A. is around back with a shipment. What do I need it?"

Greenspahn walked to the end of the block and crossed the street. He looked down the side street and saw the *shul* where that evening he would say prayers for his son.

He came to his store, seeing it with distaste. He looked at the signs, like the balloons in comic strips where they put the words, stuck inside against the glass, the letters big and red like it was the end of the world, the big whitewash numbers on the glass thickly. A billboard, he thought.

He stepped up to the glass door and looked in. Frank, his produce man, stood by the fruit and vegetable bins taking the tissue paper off the oranges. His butcher, Arnold, was at the register talking to Shirley, the cashier. Arnold saw him through the glass and waved extravagantly. Shirley came to the door and opened it. "Good morning there, Mr. Greenspahn," she said.

"Hey, Jake, how are you?" Frank said.

"How's it going, Jake?" Arnold said.

"Was Siggie in yet? Did you tell him about the cheese?"

"He ain't yet been in this morning, Jake," Frank said.

"How about the meat? Did you place the order?"

"Sure, Jake," Arnold said. "I called the guy Thursday."

"Where are the receipts?" he asked Shirley.

"I'll get them for you, Mr. Greenspahn. You already seen them for the first two weeks you were gone. I'll get last week's."

She handed him a slip of paper. It was four hundred and seventy dollars off the last week's low figure. They must have had a picnic, Greenspahn thought. No more though. He looked at them, and they watched him with interest. "So," he said. "So."

"Nice to have you back, Mr. Greenspahn," Shirley told him, smiling.

"Yeah," he said, "yeah."

"We got a shipment yesterday, Jake, but the *schvartze* showed up drunk. We couldn't get it all put up," Frank said.

Greenspahn nodded. "The figures are low," he said.

"It's business. Business has been terrible. I figure it's the strike," Frank said.

"In West Virginia the miners are out and you figure that's why my business is bad in this neighborhood?"

"There are repercussions," Frank said. "All industries are affected."

"Yeah," Greenspahn said, "yeah. The pretzel industry. The canned chicken noodle soup industry."

"Well, business has been lousy, Jake," Arnold said testily.

"I guess maybe it's so bad, now might be a good time to sell. What do you think?" Greenspahn said.

"Are you really thinking of selling, Jake?" Frank asked.

"You want to buy my place, Frank?"

"You know I don't have that kind of money, Jake," Frank said uneasily.

"Yeah," Greenspahn said, "yeah."

Frank looked at him, and Greenspahn waited for him to say something else, but in a moment he turned and went back to the oranges. Some thief, Greenspahn thought. Big shot. I insulted him.

"I got to change," he said to Shirley. "Call me if Siggie comes in."

He went into the toilet off the small room at the rear of the store. He reached for the clothes he kept there on a hook on the back of the door and saw, hanging over his own clothes, a woman's undergarments. A brassiere hung by one cup over his trousers. What is it here, a locker room? Does she take baths in the sink? he thought. Fastidiously he tried to remove his own clothes without touching the other garments, but he was clumsy, and the underwear, together with his trousers, tumbled in a heap to the floor. They looked, lying there, strangely obscene to him, as though two people, desperately in a hurry, had dropped them quickly and were somewhere near him even now, perhaps behind the very door, making love. He picked up his trousers and changed his clothes. Taking a hanger from a pipe under the

sink, he hung the clothes he had worn to work and put the
hanger on the hook. He stooped to pick up Shirley's underwear.
Placing it on the hook, his hand rested for a moment on the brassiere. He was immediately ashamed. He was terribly tired. He
put his head through the loop of his apron and tied the apron
behind the back of the old blue sweater he wore even in summer.
He turned the sink's single tap and rubbed his eyes with water.
Bums, he thought. Bums. You put up mirrors to watch the customers so they shouldn't get away with a stick of gum, and in the
meanwhile Frank and Arnold walk off with the whole store. He
sat down to try to move his bowels and the apron hung down
from his chest like a barber's sheet. He spread it across his knees.
I must look like I'm getting a haircut, he thought irrelevantly.
He looked suspiciously at Shirley's underwear. My movie star.
He wondered if it was true what Arnold told him, that she used
to be a 26-girl. Something was going on between her and that
Arnold. Two bums, he thought. He knew they drank together
after work. That was one thing, bad enough, but were they
screwing around in the back of the store? Arnold had a family.
You couldn't trust a young butcher. It was too much for him.
Why didn't he just sell and get the hell out? Did he have to look
for grief? Was he making a fortune that he had to put up with it?
It was crazy. All right, he thought, a man in business, there were
things a man in business put up with. But this? It was crazy.
Everywhere he was beset by thieves and cheats. They kept pushing him, pushing him. What did it mean? Why did they do it?
All right, he thought, when Harold was alive was it any different? No, of course not, he knew plenty then too. But it didn't
make as much difference. Death is an education, he thought.
Now there wasn't any reason to put up with it. What did he
need it? On the street, in the store, he saw everything. Everything. It was as if everybody else were made out of glass. Why
all of a sudden was he like that?

Why? he thought. Jerk, because they're hurting *you*, that's
why.

He stood up and looked absently into the toilet. "Maybe I need a laxative," he said aloud. Troubled, he left the toilet.

In the back room, his "office," he stood by the door to the toilet and looked around. Stacked against one wall he saw four or five cases of soups and canned vegetables. Against the meat locker he had pushed a small table, his desk. He went to it to pick up a pencil. Underneath the telephone was a pad of note paper. Something about it caught his eye and he picked up the pad. On the top sheet was writing, his son's. He used to come down on Saturdays sometimes when they were busy; evidently this was an order he had taken down over the phone. He looked at the familiar writing and thought his heart would break. Harold, Harold, he thought. My God, Harold, you're dead. He touched the sprawling, hastily written letters, the carelessly spelled words, and thought absently, He must have been busy. I can hardly read it. He looked at it more closely. "He was in a hurry," he said, starting to sob. "My God, *he* was in a hurry." He tore the sheet from the pad, and folding it, put it into his pocket. In a minute he was able to walk back out into the store.

In the front Shirley was talking to Siggie, the cheese man. Seeing him up there leaning casually on the counter, Greenspahn felt a quick anger. He walked up the aisle toward him.

Siggie saw him coming. "*Shalom*, Jake," he called.

"I want to talk to you."

"Is it important, Jake, because I'm in some terrific hurry. I still got deliveries."

"What did you leave me?"

"The same, Jake. The same. A couple pounds blue. Some Swiss. Delicious," he said, smacking his lips.

"I been getting complaints, Siggie."

"From the Americans, right? Your average American don't know from cheese. It don't mean nothing." He turned to go.

"Siggie, where you running?"

"Jake, I'll be back tomorrow. You can talk to me about it."

"Now."

He turned reluctantly. "What's the matter?"

"You're leaving old stuff. Who's your wholesaler?"

"Jake, Jake," he said. "We already been over this. I pick up the returns, don't I?"

"That's not the point."

"Have you ever lost a penny on account of me?"

"Siggie, who's your wholesaler? Where do you get the stuff?"

"I'm cheaper than the dairy, right? Ain't I cheaper than the dairy? Come on, Jake. What do you want?"

"Siggie, don't be a jerk. Who are you talking to? Don't be a jerk. You leave me cheap, crummy cheese, the dairies are ready to throw it away. I get everybody else's returns. It's old when I get it. Do you think a customer wants a cheese it goes off like a bomb two days after she gets it home? And what about the customers who don't return it? They think I'm gypping them and they don't come back. I don't want the *schlak* stuff. Give me fresh or I'll take from somebody else."

"I couldn't give you fresh for the same price, Jake. You know that."

"The same price."

"Jake," he said, amazed.

"The same price. Come on, Siggie, don't screw around with me."

"Talk to me tomorrow. We'll work something out." He turned to go.

"Siggie," Greenspahn called after him. "Siggie." He was already out of the store. Greenspahn clenched his fists. "The bum," he said.

"He's always in a hurry, that guy," Shirley said.

"Yeah, yeah," Greenspahn said. He started to cross to the cheese locker to see what Siggie had left him.

"Say, Mr. Greenspahn," Shirley said, "I don't think I have enough change."

"Where's the *schvartze?* Send him to the bank."

"He ain't come in yet. Shall I run over?"

Greenspahn poked his fingers in the cash drawer. "You got till he comes," he said.

"Well," she said, "if you think so."

"What do we do, a big business in change? I don't see customers stumbling over each other in the aisles."

"I told you, Jake," Arnold said, coming up behind him. "It's business. Business is lousy. People ain't eating."

"Here," Greenspahn said, "give me ten dollars. I'll go myself." He turned to Arnold. "I seen some stock in the back. Put it up, Arnold."

"I should put up the stock?" Arnold said.

"You told me yourself, business is lousy. Are you here to keep off the streets or something? What is it?"

"What do you pay the *schvartze* for?"

"He ain't here," Greenspahn said. "When he comes in I'll have him cut up some meat, you'll be even."

He took the money and went out into the street. It was lousy, he thought. You had to be able to trust them or you could go crazy. Every retailer had the same problem; he winked his eye and figured, All right, so I'll allow a certain percentage for shrinkage. You made it up on the register. But in his place it was ridiculous. They were professionals. Like the Mafia or something. What did it pay to aggravate himself, his wife would say. Now he was back he could watch them. *Watch* them. He couldn't stand even to be in the place. They thought they were getting away with something, the *podlers.*

He went into the bank. He saw the ferns. The marble tables where the depositors made out their slips. The calendars, carefully changed each day. The guard, a gun on his hip and a white carnation in his uniform. The big safe, thicker than a wall, shiny and open, in the back behind the sturdy iron gate. The tellers behind their cages, small and quiet, as though they went about barefooted. The bank officers, gray-haired and well dressed, comfortable at their big desks, solidly official behind their engraved name-plates. That was something, he thought. A bank. A bank was something. And no shrinkage.

He gave his ten-dollar bill to a teller to be changed.

"Hello there, Mr. Greenspahn. How are you this morning? We haven't seen you lately," the teller said.

"I haven't been in my place for three weeks," Greenspahn said.

"Say," the teller said, "that's quite a vacation."

"My son passed away."

"I didn't know," the teller said. "I'm very sorry, sir."

He took the rolls the teller handed him and stuffed them into his pocket. "Thank you," he said.

The street was quiet. It looks like a Sunday, he thought. There would be no one in the store. He saw his reflection in a window he passed and realized he had forgotten to take his apron off. It occurred to him that the apron somehow gave him the appearance of being very busy. An apron did that, he thought. Not a business suit so much. Unless there was a briefcase. A briefcase and an apron, they made you look busy. A uniform wouldn't. Soldiers didn't look busy, policemen didn't. A fireman did, but he had to have that big hat on. Schmo, he thought, a man your age walking in the street in an apron. He wondered if the vice-presidents at the bank had noticed his apron. He felt the heaviness again.

He was restless, nervous, disappointed in things.

He passed the big plate window of "The Cookery," the restaurant where he ate his lunch, and the cashier waved at him, gesturing that he should come in. He shook his head. For a moment when he saw her hand go up he thought he might go in. The men would be there, the other business people, drinking cups of coffee, cigarettes smearing the saucers, their sweet rolls cut into small, precise sections. Even without going inside he knew what it would be like. The criers and the kibitzers. The criers, earnest, complaining with a peculiar vigor about their businesses, their gas mileage, their health; their despair articulate, dependably lamenting their lives, vaguely mourning conditions, their sorrow something they could expect no one to understand. The kibitzers, deaf to grief, winking confidentially at the others, their voices high-pitched in kidding or lowered in conspiracy to tell of triumphs, of men they knew downtown, of tickets fixed, or languishing goods moved suddenly and unexpectedly, of the windfall that was life; their fingers sticky, smeared with the sugar from their rolls.

What did he need them, he thought. Big shots. What did they know about anything? Did they lose sons?

He went back to his place and gave Shirley the silver.

"Is the *schvartze* in yet?" he asked.

"No, Mr. Greenspahn."

I'll dock him, he thought. I'll dock him.

He looked around and saw that there were several people in the store. It wasn't busy, but there was more activity than he had expected. Young housewives from the university. Good shoppers, he thought. Good customers. They knew what they could spend and that was it. There was no monkey business about prices. He wished his older customers would take lessons from them. The ones who came in wearing their fur coats and who thought because they knew him from his old place that entitled them to special privileges. In a supermarket. Privileges. Did A&P give discounts? The National? What did they want from him?

He walked around straightening the shelves. Well, he thought, at least it wasn't totally dead. If they came in like this all day he might make a few pennies. A few pennies, he thought. A few dollars. What difference does it make?

A salesman was talking to him when he saw her. The man was trying to tell him something about a new product, some detergent, ten cents off on the box, something, but Greenspahn couldn't take his eyes off her.

"Can I put you down for a few trial cases, Mr. Greenspahn? In Detroit when the stores put it on the shelves . . ."

"No," Greenspahn interrupted him. "Not now. It don't sell. I don't want it."

"But, Mr. Greenspahn, I'm trying to tell you. This is something new. It hasn't been on the market more than three weeks."

"Later, later," Greenspahn said. "Talk to Frank, don't bother me."

He left the salesman and followed the woman up the aisle, stopping when she stopped, turning to the shelves, pretending to adjust them. One egg, he thought. She touches one egg, I'll throw her out.

It was Mrs. Frimkin, the doctor's wife. An old customer and a chiseler. An expert. For a long time she hadn't been in because of a fight they'd had over a thirty-five-cent delivery charge. He had to watch her. She had a million tricks. Sometimes she would sneak over to the eggs and push her finger through two or three of them. Then she would smear a little egg on the front of her dress and come over to him complaining that he'd ruined her dress, that she'd picked up the eggs "in good faith," thinking they were whole. "In good faith," she'd say. He'd have to give her the whole box and charge her for a half dozen just to shut her up. An expert.

He went up to her. He was somewhat relieved to see that she wore a good dress. She risked the egg trick only in a housecoat.

"Jake," she said, smiling at him.

He nodded.

"I heard about Harold," she said sadly. "The doctor told me. I almost had a heart attack when I heard." She touched his arm. "Listen," she said. "We don't know. We just don't know. Mrs. Baron, my neighbor from when we lived on Drexel, didn't she fall down dead in the street? Her daughter was getting married in a month. How's your wife?"

Greenspahn shrugged. "Something I can do for you, Mrs. Frimkin?"

"What am I, a stranger? I don't need help. Fix, fix your shelves. I can take what I need."

"Yeah," he said, "yeah. Take." She had another trick. She came into a place, his place, the A&P, it didn't make any difference, and she priced everything. She even took notes. He knew she didn't buy a thing until she was absolutely convinced she couldn't get it a penny cheaper some place else.

"I only want a few items. Don't worry about me," she said.

"Yeah," Greenspahn said. He could wring her neck, the lousy *podler*.

"How's the fruit?" she asked.

"You mean confidentially?"

"What else?"

"I'll tell you the truth," Greenspahn said. "It's so good I don't like to see it get out of the store."

"Maybe I'll buy a banana."

"You couldn't go wrong," Greenspahn said.

"You got a nice place, Jake. I always said it."

"So buy something," he said.

"We'll see," she said mysteriously. "We'll see."

They were standing by the canned vegetables and she reached out her hand to lift a can of peas from the shelf. With her palm she made a big thing of wiping the dust from the top of the can and then stared at the price stamped there. "Twenty-seven?" she asked, surprised.

"Yeah," Greenspahn said. "It's too much?"

"Well," she said.

"I'll be damned," he said. "I been in the business twenty-two years and I never did know what to charge for a tin of peas."

She looked at him suspiciously, and with a tight smile gently replaced the peas. Greenspahn glared at her, and then, seeing Frank walk by, caught at his sleeve, pretending he had business with him. He walked up the aisle holding Frank's elbow, conscious that Mrs. Frimkin was looking after them.

"The lousy *podler*," he whispered.

"Take it easy, Jake," Frank said. "She could be a good customer again. So what if she chisels a little? I was happy to see her come in."

"Yeah," Greenspahn said, "happy." He left Frank and went toward the meat counter. "Any phone orders?" he asked Arnold.

"A few, Jake. I can put them up."

"Never mind," Greenspahn said. "Give me." He took the slips Arnold handed him. "While it's quiet I'll do them."

He read over the orders quickly and in the back of the store selected four cardboard boxes with great care. He picked the stock from the shelves and fit it neatly into the boxes, taking a kind of pleasure in the diminution of the stacks. Each time he put something into a box he had the feeling that there was that much less to sell. At the thick butcher's block behind the meat counter, bloodstains so deep in the wood they seemed almost a part of its grain, he trimmed fat from a thick roast. Arnold, beside him, leaned heavily against the paper roll. Greenspahn was conscious that Arnold watched him.

"Bernstein's order?" Arnold asked.

"Yeah," Greenspahn said.

"She's giving a party. She told me. Her husband's birthday."

"Happy birthday."

"Yeah," Arnold said. "Say, Jake, maybe I'll go eat."

Greenspahn trimmed the last piece of fat from the roast before he looked up at him. "So go eat," he said.

"I think so," Arnold said. "It's slow today. You know?"

Greenspahn nodded.

"Well, I'll grab some lunch. Maybe it'll pick up in the afternoon."

He took a box and began filling another order. He went to the canned goods in high, narrow, canted towers. That much less to sell, he thought bitterly. It was endless. You could never liquidate. There were no big deals in the grocery business. He thought hopelessly of the hundreds of items in his store, of all the different brands, the different sizes. He was terribly aware of each shopper, conscious of what each put into the shopping cart. It was awful, he thought. He wasn't selling diamonds. He wasn't selling pianos. He sold bread, milk, eggs. You had to have volume or you were dead. He was losing money. On his electric, his refrigeration, the signs in his window, his payroll, his specials, his stock. It was the chain stores. They had the parking. They advertised. They gave stamps. Two percent right out of the profits—it made no difference to them. They had the tie-ins. Fantastic. Their own farms, their own dairies, their own bakeries, their own canneries. Everything. The bastards. He was committing suicide to fight them.

In a little while Shirley came up to him. "Is it all right if I get my lunch now, Mr. Greenspahn?"

Why did they ask him? Was he a tyrant? "Yeah, yeah. Go eat. I'll watch the register."

She went out, and Greenspahn, looking after her, thought, Something's going on. First one, then the other. They meet each other. What do they do, hold hands? He fit a carton of eggs carefully into a box. What difference does it make? A slut and a bum.

He stood at the checkout counter, and pressing the orange key, watched the *No Sale* flag shoot up into the window of the register. He counted the money sadly.

Frank was at the bins trimming lettuce. "Jake, you want to go eat I'll watch things," he said.

"Not yet," Greenspahn said.

An old woman came into the store and Greenspahn recognized her. She had been in twice before that morning and both times had bought two tins of the coffee Greenspahn was running on a special. She hadn't bought anything else. Already he had lost twelve cents on her. He watched her carefully and saw with a quick rage that she went again to the coffee. She picked up another two tins and came toward the checkout counter. She wore a bright red wig which next to her very white, ancient skin gave her the appearance of a clown. She put the coffee down on the counter and looked up at Greenspahn timidly. He made no effort to ring up the sale. She stood for a moment and then pushed the coffee toward him.

"Sixty-nine cents a pound," she said. "Two pounds is a dollar thirty-eight. Six cents tax is a dollar forty-four."

"Lady," Greenspahn said, "don't you ever eat? Is that all you do is drink coffee?" He stared at her.

Her lips began to tremble and her body shook. "A dollar forty-four," she said. "I have it right here."

"This is your sixth can, lady. I lose money on it. Do you know that?"

The woman continued to tremble. It was as though she were very cold.

"What do you do, lady? Sell this stuff door-to-door? Am I your wholesaler?"

Her body continued to shake, and she looked out at him from behind faded eyes as though she were unaware of the terrible movements of her body, as though they had, ultimately, nothing to do with her, that really she existed, hiding, crouched, somewhere behind the eyes. He had the impression that, frictionless, her old bald head bobbed beneath the wig. "All right," he said finally, "a dollar forty-four. I hope you have more luck with the item than I had." He took the money from her and watched her as she accepted her package wordlessly and walked out of the store. He shook his head. It was all a pile of crap, he thought. He had a vision of the woman on back porches, standing silently at back doors open on their chains, sadly extending the coffee.

He wanted to get out. Frank could watch the store. If he stole, he stole.

"Frank," he said, "it ain't busy. Watch things. I'll eat."

"Go on, Jake. Go ahead. I'm not hungry, I got a cramp. Go ahead."

"Yeah."

He walked toward the restaurant. On his way he had to pass a National; seeing the crowded parking lot, he felt his stomach tighten. He paused at the window and pressed his face against the glass and looked in at the full aisles. Through the thick glass he saw women moving silently through the store. He stepped back and read the advertisements on the window. My fruit is cheaper, he thought. My meat's the same, practically the same.

He moved on. Passing the familiar shops, he crossed the street and went into "The Cookery." Pushing open the heavy glass door, he heard the babble of the lunchers, the sound rushing to his ears like the noise of a suddenly unmuted trumpet. Criers and kibitzers, he thought. Kibitzers and criers.

The cashier smiled at him. "We haven't seen you, Mr. G. Somebody told me you were on a diet," she said.

Her too, he thought. A kibitzer that makes change.

He went toward the back. "Hey, Jake, how are you?" a man in a booth called. "Sit by us."

He nodded at the men who greeted him, and pulling a chair from another table, placed it in the aisle facing the booth. He sat down and leaned forward, pulling the chair's rear legs into the air so that the waitress could get by. Sitting there in the aisle, he felt peculiarly like a visitor, like one there only temporarily, as though he had rushed up to the table merely to say hello or to tell a joke. He knew what it was. It was the way kibitzers sat. The others, cramped in the booth but despite this giving the appearance of lounging there, their lunches begun or already half eaten, somehow gave him the impression that they had been there all day.

"You missed it, Jake," one of the men said. "We almost got Traub here to reach for a check last Friday. Am I lying, Margolis?"

"He almost did, Jake. He really almost did."

"At the last minute he jumped up and down on his own arm and broke it."

The men at the table laughed, and Greenspahn looked at Traub sitting little and helpless between two big men. Traub looked down shame-faced into his Coca-Cola.

"It's okay, Traub," the first man said. "We know. You got all those daughters getting married and having big weddings at the same time. It's terrible. Traub's only got one son. And do you think he'd have the decency to get married so Traub could one time go to a wedding and just enjoy himself? No, *he's* not *old* enough. But he's old enough to turn around and get himself bar mitzvah'd, right, Traub? The lousy kid."

Greenspahn looked at the men in the booth and at many-daughtered Traub, who seemed as if he were about to cry. Kibitzers and criers, he thought. Everywhere it was the same. At every table. The two kinds of people like two different sexes that had sought each other out. Sure, Greenspahn thought, would a crier listen to another man's complaints? Could a kibitzer kid a kidder? But it didn't mean anything, he thought. Not the jokes, not the grief. It didn't mean anything. They were like birds making noises in a tree. But try to catch them in a deal. They'd murder you. Every day they came to eat their lunch and make their noises. Like cowboys on television hanging up their gun belts to go to a dance.

But even so, he thought, they were the way they pretended to be. Nothing made any difference to them. Did they lose sons? Not even the money they earned made any difference to them finally.

"So I was telling you," Margolis said, "the guy from the Chamber of Commerce came around again today."

"He came to me too," Paul Gold said.

"Did you give?" Margolis asked.

"No, of course not."

"Did he hit you yet, Jake? Throw him out. He wants contributions for decorations. Listen, those guys are on the take from the paper-flower people. It's fantastic what they get for organizing the big stores downtown. My cousin on State Street told me about it. I told him, I said, 'Who needs the Chamber of Commerce? Who needs Easter baskets and colored eggs hanging from the lamppost?' "

"Not when the ring trick still works, right, Margolis?" Joe
Fisher said.

Margolis looked at his lapel and shrugged lightly. It was the
most modest gesture Greenspahn had ever seen him make. The
men laughed. The ring trick was Margolis' invention. "A business promotion," he had told Greenspahn. "Better than Green
Stamps." He had seen him work it. Margolis would stand at the
front of his store and signal to some guy who stopped for a min-
nute to look at the TV sets in his window. He would rap on the
glass with his ring to catch his attention. He would smile and say
something to him, anything. It didn't make any difference; the
guy in the street couldn't hear him. As Greenspahn watched,
Margolis had turned to him and winked slyly as if to say,
"Watch this. Watch how I get this guy." Then he had looked
back at the customer outside, and still smiling broadly had said,
"Hello, schmuck. Come on in, I'll sell you something. That's
right, jerk, press your greasy nose against the glass to see who's
talking to you. Shade your eyes. That-a-jerk. Come on in, I'll sell
you something." Always the guy outside would come into the
store to find out what Margolis had been saying to him. "Hello
there, sir," Margolis would say, grinning. "I was trying to tell
you that the model you were looking at out there is worthless.
Way overpriced. If the boss knew I was talking to you like this
I'd be canned, but what the hell? We're all working people. Come
on back here and look at a real set."

Margolis was right. Who needed the Chamber of Commerce?
Not the kibitzers and criers. Not even the Gold boys. Criers.
Greenspahn saw the other one at another table. Twins, but they
didn't even look like brothers. Not even they needed the paper
flowers hanging from the lamppost. Paul Gold shouting to his
brother in the back, "Mr. Gold, please show this gentleman
something stylish." And they'd go into the act, putting on a thick
Yiddish accent for some white-haired old man with a lodge
button in his lapel, giving him the business. Greenspahn could
almost hear the old man telling the others at the Knights of Co-

lumbus Hall, "I picked this suit up from a couple of Yids on Fifty-third, real greenhorns. But you've got to hand it to them. Those people really know material."

Business was a kind of game with them, Greenspahn thought. Not even the money made any difference.

"Did I tell you about these two kids who came in to look at rings?" Joe Fisher said. "Sure," he went on, "two kids. Dressed up. The boy's a regular *mensch*. I figure they've been downtown at Peacock's and Field's. I think I recognized the girl from the neighborhood. I say to her boy friend—a nice kid, a college kid, you know, he looks like he ain't been bar mitzvah'd yet—'I got a ring here I won't show you the price. Will you give me your check for three hundred dollars right now? No appraisal? No bringing it to Papa on approval? No nothing?'

" 'I'd have to see the ring,' he tells me.

"Get this. I put my finger over the tag on a ring *I* paid eleven hundred for. *A big ring.* You got to wear smoked glasses just to look at it. Paul, I mean it, this is some ring. I'll give you a price for your wife's anniversary. No kidding, this is some ring. Think seriously about it. We could make it up into a beautiful cocktail ring. Anyway, this kid stares like a big dummy, I think he's turned to stone. He's scared. He figures something's wrong a big ring like that for only three hundred bucks. His girl friend is getting edgy, she thinks the kid's going to make a mistake, and she starts shaking her head. Finally he says to me, listen to this, he says, 'I wasn't looking for anything that large. Anyway, it's not a blue stone.' Can you imagine? Don't tell me about shoppers. I get prizes."

"What would you have done if he said he wanted the ring?" Traub asked.

"What are you, crazy? He was strictly from wholesale. It was like he had a sign on his suit. Don't you think I can tell a guy who's trying to get a price idea from a real customer?"

"Say, Jake," Margolis said, "ain't that your cashier over there with your butcher?"

Greenspahn looked around. It was Shirley and Arnold. He hadn't seen them when he came in. They were sitting across the table from each other—evidently they had not seen him either—and Shirley was leaning forward, her chin on her palms. Sitting there, she looked like a young girl. It annoyed him. It was ridiculous. He knew they met each other. What did he care? It wasn't his business. But to let themselves be seen. He thought of Shirley's brassiere hanging in his toilet. It was reckless. They were reckless people. All of them, Arnold and Shirley and the men in the restaurant. Reckless people.

"They're pretty thick with each other, ain't they?" Margolis said.

"How should I know?" Greenspahn said.

"What do you run over there at that place of yours, a lonely hearts club?"

"It's not my business. They do their work."

"Some work," Paul Gold said.

"I'd like a job like that," Joe Fisher said.

"Ain't he married?" Paul Gold said.

"I'm not a policeman," Greenspahn said.

"Jake's jealous because he's not getting any," Joe Fisher said.

"Loudmouth," Greenspahn said, "I'm a man in mourning."

The others at the table were silent. "Joe was kidding," Traub, the crier, said.

"Sure, Jake," Joe Fisher said.

"Okay," Greenspahn said. "Okay."

For the rest of the lunch he was conscious of Shirley and Arnold. He hoped they would not see him, or if they did that they would make no sign to him. He stopped listening to the stories the men told. He chewed on his hamburger wordlessly. He heard someone mention George Stein, and he looked up for a moment. Stein had a grocery in a neighborhood that was changing. He had said that he wanted to get out. He was looking for a setup like Greenspahn's. He could speak to him. Sure, he thought. Why not? What did he need the aggravation? What did he need

it? He owned the building the store was in. He could live on the
rents. Even Joe Fisher was a tenant of his. He could speak to
Stein, he thought, feeling he had made up his mind about something. He waited until Arnold and Shirley had finished their
lunch and then went back to his store.

In the afternoon Greenspahn thought he might be able to move
his bowels. He went into the toilet off the small room at the back
of the store. He sat, looking up at the high ceiling. In the smoky
darkness above his head he could just make out the small, square
tin-ceiling plates. They seemed pitted, soiled, like patches of war-
ruined armor. Agh, he thought, the place is a pigpen. The sink
bowl was stained dark, the enamel chipped, long fissures radi-
ating like lines on the map of some wasted country. The single
faucet dripped steadily. Greenspahn thought sadly of his water
bill. On the knob of the faucet he saw again a faded blue S. S, he
thought, what the hell does S stand for? H hot, C cold. What the
hell kind of faucet is S? Old clothes hung on a hook on the back
of the door. A man's blue wash pants hung inside out, the zipper
split like a peeled banana, the crowded concourse of seams at the
crotch like carelessly sewn patches.

He heard Arnold in the store, his voice raised exaggeratedly.
He strained to listen.

"*Forty-five,*" he heard Arnold say.

"*Forty-five, Pop.*" He was talking to the old man. Deaf, he
came in each afternoon for a piece of liver for his supper. "*I can't
give you two ounces. I told you. I can't break the set.*" He heard a
woman laugh. Shirley? Was Shirley back there with him? What
the hell, he thought. It was one thing for them to screw around
with each other at lunch, but they didn't have to bring it into the
store. "*Take eight ounces. Invite someone over for dinner. Take
eight ounces. You'll have for four days. You won't have to come
back.*" He was a wise guy, that Arnold. What did he want to do,
drive the old man crazy? What could you do? The old man liked
a small slice of liver. He thought it kept him alive.

He heard footsteps coming toward the back room and voices raised in argument.

"I'm sorry," a woman said, "I don't know how it got there. Honest. Look, I'll pay. I'll pay you for it."

"You bet, lady," Frank's voice said.

"What do you want me to do?" the woman pleaded.

"I'm calling the cops," Frank said.

"For a lousy can of salmon?"

"It's the principle. You're a crook. You're a lousy thief, you know that? I'm calling the cops. We'll see what jail does for you."

"Please," the woman said. "Mister, please. This whole thing is crazy. I never did anything like this before. I haven't got any excuse, but please, can't you give me a chance?" The woman was crying.

"No chances," Frank said. "I'm calling the cops. You ought to be ashamed, lady. A woman dressed nice like you are. What are you, sick or something? I'm calling the cops." He heard Frank lift the receiver.

"Please," the woman sobbed. "My husband will kill me. I have a little kid, for Christ's sake."

Frank replaced the phone.

"Ten bucks," he said quietly.

"What's that?"

"Ten bucks and you don't come in here no more."

"I haven't got it," she said.

"All right, lady. The hell with you. I'm calling the cops."

"You bastard," she said.

"Watch your mouth," he said. "Ten bucks."

"I'll write you a check."

"Cash," Frank said.

"Okay, okay," she said. "Here."

"Now get out of here, lady." Greenspahn heard the woman's footsteps going away. Frank would be fumbling now with his apron, trying to get the big wallet out of his front pocket. Green-spahn flushed the toilet and waited.

"Jake?" Frank asked, frightened.

"Who was she?"

"Jake, I never saw her before, honest. Just a tramp. She gave me ten bucks. She was just a tramp, Jake."

"I told you before. I don't want trouble," Greenspahn said angrily. He came out of the toilet. "What is this, a game with you?"

"Look, I caught her with the salmon. Would you want me to call the cops for a can of salmon? She's got a kid."

"Yeah, you got a big heart, Frank."

"I would have let you handle it if I'd seen you. I looked for you, Jake."

"You shook her down. I told you before about that."

"Jake, it's ten bucks for the store. I get so damned mad when somebody like that tries to get away with something."

"*Podler*," Greenspahn shouted. "You're through here."

"Jake," Frank said. "She was a tramp." He held the can of salmon in his hand and offered it to Greenspahn as though it were evidence.

Greenspahn pushed his hand aside. "Get out of my store. I don't need you. Get out. I don't want a crook in here."

"Who are you calling names, Jake?"

Greenspahn felt his rage, immense, final. It was on him at once, like an animal that had leaped upon him in the dark. His body shook with it. Frightened, he warned himself uselessly that he must be calm. A *podler* like that, he thought. He wanted to hit him in the face.

"Please, Frank. Get out of here," Greenspahn said.

"Sure," Frank screamed. "Sure, sure," he shouted. Green-spahn, startled, looked at him. He seemed angrier than even himself. Greenspahn thought of the customers. They would hear him. What kind of a place, he thought. What kind of a place? "Sure," Frank yelled, "fire me, go ahead. A regular holy man. A saint! What are you, God? He smells everybody's rottenness but his own. Only when your own son—may he rest—when your own son slips five bucks out of the cash drawer, that you don't see."

Greenspahn could have killed him. "Who says that?"

Frank caught his breath.

"Who says that?" Greenspahn repeated.

"Nothing, Jake. It was nothing. He was going on a date probably. That's all. It didn't mean nothing."

"Who calls him a thief?"

"Nobody. I'm sorry."

"My dead son? You call my dead son a thief?"

"Nobody called anybody a thief. I didn't know what I was saying."

"In the ground. Twenty-three years old and in the ground. Not even a wife, not even a business. Nothing. He had nothing. He wouldn't take. Harold wouldn't take. Don't call him what you are. He should be alive today. You should be dead. You should be in the ground where he is. *Podler. Mumser*," he shouted. "*I saw the lousy receipts, liar*," he screamed.

In a minute Arnold was there and was putting his arm around him. "Calm down, Jake. Come on now, take it easy. What happened back here?" he asked Frank.

Frank shrugged.

"Get him away," Greenspahn pleaded. Arnold signaled Frank to get out and led Greenspahn to the chair near the table he used as a desk.

"You all right now, Jake? You okay now?"

Greenspahn was sobbing heavily. In a few moments he looked up. "All right," he said. "The customers. Arnold, please. The customers."

"Okay, Jake. Just stay back here and wait till you feel better."

Greenspahn nodded. When Arnold left him he sat for a few minutes and then went back into the toilet to wash his face. He turned the tap and watched the dirty basin fill with water. It's not even cold, he thought sadly. He plunged his hands into the sink and scooped up warm water, which he rubbed into his eyes. He took a handkerchief from his back pocket and unfolded it and patted his face carefully. He was conscious of laughter outside the door. It seemed old, brittle. For a moment he thought of the woman with the coffee. Then he remembered. The porter, he thought. He called his name. He heard footsteps coming up to the door.

"That's right, Mr. Greenspahn," the voice said, still laughing. Greenspahn opened the door. His porter stood before him in torn clothes. His eyes, red, wet, looked as though they were bleeding. "You sure told that Frank," he said.

"You're late," Greenspahn said. "What do you mean coming in so late?"

"I been to Harold's grave," he said.

"What's that?"

"I been to Mr. Harold's grave," he repeated. "I didn't get to the funeral. I been to his grave cause of my dream."

"Put the stock away," Greenspahn said. "Some more came in this afternoon."

"I will," he said. "I surely will." He was an old man. He had no teeth and his gums lay smooth and very pink in his mouth. He was thin. His clothes hung on him, the sleeves of the jacket rounded, puffed from absent flesh. Through the rents in shirt and trousers Greenspahn could see the grayish skin, hairless, creased, the texture like the pit of a peach. Yet he had a strength Greenspahn could only wonder at, and could still lift more stock than Arnold or Frank or even Greenspahn himself.

"You'd better start now," Greenspahn said uncomfortably.

"I tell you about my dream, Mr. Greenspahn?"

"No dreams. Don't tell me your dreams."

"It was about Mr. Harold. Yes, sir, about him. Your boy that's dead, Mr. Greenspahn."

"I don't want to hear. See if Arnold needs anything up front."

"I dreamed it twice. That means it's true. You don't count on a dream less you dream it twice."

"Get away with your crazy stories. I don't pay you to dream."

"That time on Halsted I dreamed the fire. I dreamed that twice."

"Yeah," Greenspahn said, "the fire. Yeah."

"I dreamed that dream twice. Them police wanted to question me. Same names, Mr. Greenspahn, me and your boy we got the same names."

"Yeah. I named him after you."

"I tell you that dream, Mr. Greenspahn? It was a mistake. Frank was supposed to die. Just like you said. Just like I heard you say it just now. And he will. Mr. Harold told me in the dream. Frank he's going to sicken and die his own self." The porter looked at Greenspahn, the red eyes filling with blood. "If you want it," he said. "That's what I dreamed, and I dreamed about the fire on Halsted the same way. Twice."

"You're crazy. Get away from me."

"That's a true dream. It happened just that very way."

"Get away. Get away," Greenspahn shouted.

"My name's Harold, too."

"You're crazy. Crazy."

The porter went off. He was laughing. What kind of a madhouse? Were they all doing it on purpose? Everything to aggravate him? For a moment he had the impression that this was what it was. A big joke, and everybody was in on it but himself. He was being *kibitzed* to death. Everything. The cop. The receipts. His cheese man. Arnold and Shirley. The men in the restaurant. Frank and the woman. The *schvartze*. Everything. He wouldn't let it happen. What was he, crazy or something? He reached into his pocket for his handkerchief, but pulled out a piece of paper. It was the order Harold had taken down over the phone and left on the pad. Absently he unfolded it and read it again. Something occurred to him. As soon as he had the idea he knew it was true. The order had never been delivered. His son had forgotten about it. It couldn't be anything else. Otherwise would it still have been on the message pad? Sure, he thought, what else could it be? Even his son. What did he care? What the hell did he care about the business? Greenspahn was ashamed. It was a terrible thought to have about a dead boy. Oh God, he thought. Let him rest. He was a boy, he thought. Twenty-three years old and he was only a boy. No wife. No business. Nothing. Was the five dollars so important? In helpless disgust he could see Harold's sly wink to Frank as he slipped the money out of the register. Five dollars, Harold, *five dollars*, he thought, as though he were admonishing him. "Why didn't you come to me, Harold?" he sobbed. "Why didn't you come to your father?"

He blew his nose. It's crazy, he thought. Nothing pleases me. Frank called him God. Some God, he thought. I sit weeping in the back of my store. The hell with it. The hell with everything. Clear the shelves, that's what he had to do. Sell the groceries. Get rid of the meats. Watch the money pile up. Sell, sell, he thought. That would be something. Sell everything. He thought of the items listed on the order his son had taken down. Were they delivered? He felt restless. He hoped they were delivered. If they weren't they would have to be sold again. He was very weary. He went to the front of the store.

It was almost closing time. Another half hour. He couldn't stay to close up. He had to be in *shul* before sundown. He had to get to the *minion*. They would have to close up for him. For a year. If he couldn't sell the store, for a year he wouldn't be in his own store at sundown. He would have to trust them to close up for him. Trust who? he thought. My Romeo, Arnold? Shirley? The crazy *schvartze?* Only Frank could do it. How could he have fired him? He looked for him in the store. He was talking to Shirley at the register. He would go up and talk to him. What difference did it make? He would have had to fire all of them. Eventually he would have to fire everybody who ever came to work for him. He would have to throw out his tenants, even the old ones, and finally whoever rented the store from him. He would have to keep on firing and throwing out as long as anybody was left. What difference would one more make?

"Frank," he said. "I want you to forget what we talked about before."

Frank looked at him suspiciously. "It's all right," Greenspahn reassured him. He led him by the elbow away from Shirley. "Listen," he said, "we were both excited before. I didn't mean it what I said."

Frank continued to look at him. "Sure, Jake," he said finally. "No hard feelings." He extended his hand.

Greenspahn took it reluctantly. "Yeah," he said.

"Frank," he said, "do me a favor and close up the place for me. I got to get to the *shul* for the *minion*."

"I got you, Jake."

Greenspahn went to the back to change his clothes. He washed his face and hands and combed his hair. Carefully he removed his working clothes and put on the suit jacket, shirt and tie he had worn in the morning. He walked back into the store.

He was about to leave when he saw that Mrs. Frimkin had come into the store again. That's all right, he told himself, she can be a good customer. He needed some of the old customers now. They could drive you crazy, but when they bought, they bought. He watched as she took a cart from the front and pushed it through the aisles. She put things in the cart as though she were in a hurry. She barely glanced at the prices. That was the way to shop, he thought. It was a pleasure to watch her. She reached into the frozen-food locker and took out about a half-dozen packages. From the towers of canned goods on his shelves she seemed to take down only the largest cans. In minutes her shopping cart was overflowing. That's some order, Greenspahn thought. Then he watched as she went to the stacks of bread at the bread counter. She picked up a packaged white bread, and first looking around to see if anyone was watching her, bent down quickly over the loaf, cradling it to her chest as though it were a football. As she stood, Greenspahn saw her brush crumbs from her dress, then put the torn package into her cart with the rest of her purchases.

She came up to the counter where Greenspahn stood and unloaded the cart, pushing the groceries toward Shirley to be checked out. The last item she put on the counter was the wounded bread. Shirley punched the keys quickly. As she reached for the bread, Mrs. Frimkin put out her hand to stop her. "Look," she said, "what are you going to charge me for the bread? It's damaged. Can I have it for ten cents?"

Shirley turned to look at Greenspahn.

"Out," he said. "Get out, you *podler*. I don't want you coming in here any more. You're a thief," he shouted. "A thief."

Frank came rushing up. "Jake, what is it? What is it?"

"Her. That one. A crook. She tore the bread. I seen her."

The woman looked at him defiantly. "I don't have to take that," she said. "I can make plenty of trouble for you. You're crazy. I'm not going to be insulted by somebody like you."

"Get out of here," Greenspahn shouted, "before I have you locked up."

The woman backed away from him, and when he stepped forward she turned and fled.

"Jake," Frank said, putting his hand on Greenspahn's shoulder. "That was a big order. So she tried to get away with a few pennies. What does it mean? You want me to find her and apologize?"

"Look," Greenspahn said, "she comes in again I want to know about it. I don't care what I'm doing. I want to know about it. She's going to pay me for that bread."

"Jake," Frank said.

"No," he said. "I mean it."

"Jake, it's ten cents."

"*My* ten cents. No more," he said. "I'm going to *shul*."

He waved Frank away and went into the street. Already the sun was going down. He felt urgency. He had to get there before the sun went down.

That night Greenspahn had the dream for the first time.

He was in the synagogue waiting to say prayers for his son. Around him were the old men, the *minion*, their faces brittle and pale. He recognized them from his youth. They had been old even then. One man stood by the window and watched the sun. At a signal from him the others would begin. There was always some place in the world where the prayers were being said, he thought, some place where the sun had just come up or just gone down, and he supposed there was always a *minion* to watch it and to mark its progress, the prayers following God's bright bird, going up in sunlight or in darkness, always, everywhere. He knew the men never left the *shul*. It was the way they kept from dying. They didn't even eat, but there was about the room the foul lemony smell of urine. Sure, Greenspahn thought in the dream, stay in the *shul*. That's right. Give the *podlers* a wide berth. All they have to worry about is God. Some worry, Greenspahn thought. The man at the window gave the signal and they all started to mourn for Greenspahn's son, their ancient voices betraying the queer melody of the prayers. The rabbi looked at Greenspahn and Greenspahn, imitating the old men, began to rock back and forth on his heels. He tried to sway faster than they did. I'm younger, he thought. When he was swaying so quickly that he thought he would be sick were he to go any faster, the rabbi smiled at him approvingly. The man at the window shouted that the sun was approaching the danger point in the sky and that Greenspahn had better begin as soon as he was ready.

He looked at the strange thick letters in the prayer book. "Go ahead," the rabbi said, "think of Harold and tell God."

He tried then to think of his son, but he could recall him only as he was when he was a baby standing in his crib. It was unreal, like a photograph. The others knew what he was thinking and frowned. "Go ahead," the rabbi said.

Then he saw him as a boy on a bicycle, as once he had seen him at dusk as he looked out from his apartment, riding the gray sidewalks, slapping his buttocks as though he were on a horse. The others were not satisfied.

He tried to imagine him older but nothing came of it. The rabbi said, "Please, Greenspahn, the sun is almost down. You're wasting time. Faster. Faster."

All right, Greenspahn thought. All right. Only let me think. The others stopped their chanting.

Desperately he thought of the store. He thought of the woman with the coffee, incredibly old, older than the old men who prayed with him, her wig fatuously red, the head beneath it shaking crazily as though even the weight and painted fire of the thick, bright hair were not enough to warm it.

The rabbi grinned.

He thought of the *schvartze*, imagining him on an old cot, on a damp and sheetless mattress, twisting in a fearful dream. He saw him bent under the huge side of red, raw meat he carried to Arnold.

The others were still grinning, but the rabbi was beginning to look a little bored. He thought of Arnold, seeming to watch him through the *schvartze's* own red, mad eyes, as Arnold chopped at the fresh flesh with his butcher's axe.

He saw the men in the restaurant. The criers, ignorant of hope, the *kibitzers*, ignorant of despair. Each with his pitiful piece broken from the whole of life, confidently extending only half of what there was to give.

He saw the cheats with their ten dollars and their stolen nickels and their luncheon lusts and their torn breads.

All right, Greenspahn thought. He saw Shirley naked but for her brassiere. It was evening and the store was closed. She lay with Arnold on the butcher's block.

"The boy," the rabbi said impatiently, "*the boy.*"

He concentrated for a long moment while all of them stood by silently. Gradually, with difficulty, he began to make something out. It was Harold's face in the coffin, his expression at the very moment of death itself, before the undertakers had had time to tamper with it. He saw it clearly. It was soft, puffy with grief; a sneer curled the lips. It was Harold, twenty-three years old, wifeless, jobless, sacrificing nothing even in the act of death, leaving the world with his life not started.

The rabbi smiled at Greenspahn and turned away as though he now had other business.

"No," Greenspahn called, "wait. Wait."

The rabbi turned and with the others looked at him.

He saw it now. They all saw it. The helpless face, the sly wink, the embarrassed, slow smug smile of guilt that must, volitionless as the palpitation of a nerve, have crossed Harold's face when he had turned, his hand in the register, to see Frank watching him.

I
LOOK
OUT
FOR
ED
WOLFE

He was an orphan, and, to himself, he seemed like one, looked like one. His orphan's features were as true of himself as are their pale, pinched faces to the blind. At twenty-seven he was a neat, thin young man in white shirts and light suits with lintless pockets. Something about him suggested the ruthless isolation, the hard self-sufficiency of the orphaned, the peculiar dignity of men seen eating alone in restaurants on national holidays. Yet it was this perhaps which shamed him chiefly, for there was a suggestion, too, that his impregnability was a myth, a smell not of the furnished room which he did not inhabit, but of the three-room apartment on a good street which he did. The very excellence of his taste, conditioned by need and lack, lent to him the odd, maidenly primness of the lonely.

He saved the photographs of strangers and imprisoned them behind clear plastic windows in his wallet. In the sound of his own voice he detected the accent of the night school and the correspondence course, and nothing of the fat, sunny ring of the word's casually afternooned. He strove against himself, a supererogatory enemy, and sought by a kind of helpless abrasion, as one rubs wood, the gleaming self beneath. An orphan's thinness, he thought, was no accident.

Returning from lunch, he entered the office building where he worked. It was an old building, squat and gargoyled, brightly patched where sandblasters had once worked and then, for some reason, quit before they had finished. He entered the lobby, which smelled always of disinfectant, and walked past the wide, dirty glass of the cigarette-and-candy counter to the single elevator, as thickly barred as a cell.

The building was an outlaw. Low rents and a downtown address and the landlord's indifference had brought together from the peripheries of business and professionalism a strange band of entrepreneurs and visionaries, men desperately but imaginatively failing: an eye doctor who corrected vision by massage; a radio evangelist; a black-belt judo champion; a self-help organization for crippled veterans; dealers in pornographic books, in paper flowers, in fireworks, in plastic jewelry, in the artificial, in the artfully made, in the imitated, in the copied, in the stolen, the unreal, the perversion, the plastic, the *schlak*.

On the third floor the elevator opened and the young man, Ed Wolfe, stepped out.

He passed the Association for the Indians, passed Plasti-Pens, passed *Coffin & Tombstone*, passed Soldier Toys, passed Prayer-a-Day. He walked by the open door of C. Morris Brut, Chiropractor, and saw him, alone, standing at a mad attention, framed in the arching golden nimbus of his inverted name on the window, squeezing handballs.

He looked quickly away, but Dr. Brut saw him and came toward him, putting the handballs in his shirt pocket, where they bulged awkwardly. He held him by the elbow. Ed Wolfe looked down at the yellowing tile, infinitely diamonded, chipped, the floor of a public toilet, and saw Dr. Brut's dusty shoes. He stared sadly at the jagged, broken glass of the mail chute.

"Ed Wolfe, take care of yourself," Dr. Brut said.

"Right."

"Regard your position in life. A tall man like yourself looks terrible when he slumps. Don't be a *schlump*. It's not good for the organs."

"I'll watch it."

"When the organs get out of line the man begins to die."

"I know."

"You say so. How many guys make promises. Brains in the brainpan. Balls in the strap. The bastards downtown." Dr. Brut meant doctors in hospitals, in clinics, on boards, non-orphans with M.D. degrees and special license plates and respectable patients who had Blue Cross, charts, died in clean hospital rooms. They were the bastards downtown, his personal New Deal, his neighborhood Wall Street banker. A disease cartel. "They won't tell you. The white bread kills you. The cigarettes. The whiskey. The sneakers. The high heels. They won't tell you. Me, *I'll* tell you."

"I appreciate it."

"Wise guy. Punk. I'm a friend. I give a father's advice."

"I'm an orphan."

"I'll adopt you."

"I'm late to work."

"We'll open a clinic. 'C. Morris Brut and Adopted Son.' "

"It's something to think about."

"Poetry," Dr. Brut said and walked back to his office, his posture stiff, awkward, a man in a million who knew how to hold himself.

Ed Wolfe went on to his own office. The sad-faced telephone girl was saying, "Cornucopia Finance Corporation." She pulled the wire out of the board and slipped her headset around her neck, where it hung like a delicate horse collar. "Mr. La Meck wants to see you. But don't go in yet. He's talking to somebody."

He went toward his desk at one end of the big main office. Standing, fists on the desk, he turned to the girl. "What happened to my call cards?"

"Mr. La Meck took them," she said.

"Give me the carbons," Ed Wolfe said. "I've got to make some calls."

The girl looked embarrassed. Her face went through a weird change, the sadness taking on an impossible burden of shame, so that she seemed massively tragic, like a hit-and-run driver. "I'll get them," she said, moving out of the chair heavily. Ed Wolfe thought of Dr. Brut.

He took the carbons and fanned them out on the desk, then picked one in an intense, random gesture like someone drawing a number on a public stage. He dialed rapidly.

As the phone buzzed brokenly in his ear he felt the old excitement. Someone at the other end greeted him sleepily.

"Mr. Flay? This is Ed Wolfe at Cornucopia Finance." (Can you cope, can you cope? he hummed to himself.)

"Who?"

"Ed Wolfe. I've got an unpleasant duty," he began pleasantly. "You've skipped two payments."

"I didn't skip nothing. I called the girl. She said it was okay."

"That was three months ago. She meant it was all right to miss a few days. Listen, Mr. Flay, we've got that call recorded, too. Nothing gets by."

"I'm a little short."

"Grow."

"I couldn't help it," the man said. Ed Wolfe didn't like the cringing tone. Petulance and anger he could meet with his own petulance, his own anger. But guilt would have to be met with his own guilt, and that, here, was irrelevant.

"Don't con me, Flay. You're a troublemaker. What are you, Flay, a Polish person? Flay isn't a Polish name, but your address . . ."

"What's that?"

"What are you? Are you Polish?"

"What's that to you? What difference does it make?" That's more like it, Ed Wolfe thought warmly.

"That's what you are, Flay. You're a Pole. It's guys like you who give your race a bad name. Half our bugouts are Polish persons."

"Listen. You can't . . ."

He began to shout. "*You* listen. You wanted the car. The refrigerator. The chintzy furniture. The sectional you saw in the funny papers. And we paid for it, right?"

"Listen. The money I owe is one thing, the way . . ."

"We paid for it, right?"

"That doesn't . . ."

"Right? *Right?*"

"Yes, you . . ."

"*Okay*. You're in trouble, Warsaw. You're in terrible trouble. It means a lien. A judgment. We've got lawyers. You've got nothing. We'll pull the furniture the hell out of there. The car. Everything."

"Wait," he said. "Listen, my brother-in-law . . ."

Ed Wolfe broke in sharply. "He's got money?"

"I don't know. A little. I don't know."

"Get it. If you're short, grow. This is America."

"I don't know if he'll let me have it."

"Steal it. This is America. Good-by."

"Wait a minute. Please."

"That's it. There are other Polish persons on my list. This time it was just a friendly warning. Cornucopia wants its money. Cornucopia. Can you cope? Can you cope? Just a friendly warning, Polish-American. Next time we come with the lawyers and the machine guns. Am I making myself clear?"

"I'll try to get it to you."

Ed Wolfe hung up. He pulled a handkerchief from his drawer and wiped his face. His chest was heaving. He took another call card. The girl came by and stood beside his desk. "Mr. La Meck can see you now," she mourned.

"Later. I'm calling." The number was already ringing.

"Please, Mr. Wolfe."

"Later, I said. In a minute." The girl went away. "Hello. Let

me speak with your husband, madam. I am Ed Wolfe of Cornucopia Finance. He can't cope. Your husband can't cope."

The woman made an excuse. "Put him on, goddamn it. We
know he's out of work. Nothing gets by. Nothing."

There was a hand on the receiver beside his own, the wide
male fingers pink and vaguely perfumed, the nails manicured.
For a moment he struggled with it fitfully, as though the hand
itself were all he had to contend with. Then he recognized La
Meck and let go. La Meck pulled the phone quickly toward his
mouth and spoke softly into it, words of apology, some ingenious
excuse Ed Wolfe couldn't hear. He put the receiver down beside
the phone itself and Ed Wolfe picked it up and returned it to its
cradle.

"Ed," La Meck said, "come into the office with me."

Ed Wolfe followed La Meck, his eyes on La Meck's behind.

La Meck stopped at his office door. Looking around, he shook
his head sadly, and Ed Wolfe nodded in agreement. La Meck let
him enter first. While La Meck stood, Ed Wolfe could discern a
kind of sadness in his slouch, but once the man was seated behind his desk he seemed restored, once again certain of the
world's soundness. "All right," La Meck began, "I won't lie to
you."

Lie to me. Lie to me, Ed Wolfe prayed silently.

"You're in here for me to fire you. You're not being laid off.
I'm not going to tell you that I think you'd be happier some place
else, that the collection business isn't your game, that profits
don't justify our keeping you around. Profits are terrific, and if
collection isn't your game it's because you haven't got a game. As
far as your being happier some place else, that's bullshit. You're
not supposed to be happy. It isn't in the cards for you. You're a
fall-guy type, God bless you, and though I like you personally
I've got no use for you in my office."

I'd like to get you on the other end of a telephone some day,
Ed Wolfe thought miserably.

"Don't ask me for a reference," La Meck said. "I couldn't give you one."

"No, no," Ed Wolfe said. "I wouldn't ask you for a reference." A helpless civility was all he was capable of. If you're going to suffer, *suffer*, he told himself.

"Look," La Meck said, his tone changing, shifting from brutality to compasssion as though there were no difference between the two, "you've got a kind of quality, a real feeling for collection. I'm frank to tell you, when you first came to work for us I figured you wouldn't last. I put you on the phones because I wanted you to see the toughest part first. A lot of people can't do it. You take a guy who's already down and bury him deeper. It's heart-wringing work. But you, you were amazing. An artist. You had a real thing for the deadbeat soul, I thought. But we started to get complaints, and I had to warn you. Didn't I warn you? I should have suspected something when the delinquent accounts started to turn over again. It was like rancid butter turning sweet. So I don't say this to knock your technique. Your technique's terrific. With you around we could have laid off the lawyers. But Ed, you're a gangster. A gangster."

That's it, Ed Wolfe thought. I'm a gangster. Babyface Wolfe at nobody's door.

"Well," La Meck said, "I guess we owe you some money."

"Two weeks' pay," Ed Wolfe said.

"And two weeks in lieu of notice," La Meck said grandly.

"And a week's pay for my vacation."

"You haven't been here a year," La Meck said.

"It would have been a year in another month. I've earned the vacation."

"What the hell," La Meck said. "A week's pay for vacation."

La Meck figured on a pad, and tearing off a sheet, handed it to Ed Wolfe. "Does that check with your figures?" he asked.

Ed Wolfe, who had no figures, was amazed to see that his check was so large. After the deductions he made $92.73 a week. Five $92.73's was evidently $463.65. It was a lot of money. "That seems to be right," he told La Meck.

La Meck gave him a check and Ed Wolfe got up. Already it was as though he had never worked there. When La Meck handed him the check he almost couldn't think what it was for. There should have been a photographer there to record the ceremony: ORPHAN AWARDED CHECK BY BUSINESSMAN.

"Good-by, Mr. La Meck," he said. "It has been an interesting association," he added foolishly.

"Good-by, Ed," La Meck answered, putting his arm around Ed Wolfe's shoulders and leading him to the door. "I'm sorry it had to end this way." He shook Ed Wolfe's hand seriously and looked into his eyes. He had a hard grip.

Quantity and quality, Ed Wolfe thought.

"One thing, Ed. Watch yourself. Your mistake here was that you took the job too seriously. You hated the chiselers."

No, no, I loved them, he thought.

"You've got to watch it. Don't love. Don't hate. That's the secret. Detachment and caution. Look out for Ed Wolfe."

"I'll watch out for him," he said giddily, and in a moment he was out of La Meck's office, and the main office, and the elevator, and the building itself, loose in the world, as cautious and as detached as La Meck could want him.

He took the car from the parking lot, handing the attendant the two dollars. The man gave him back fifty cents. "That's right," Ed Wolfe said, "it's only two o'clock." He put the half-dollar in his pocket, and, on an impulse, took out his wallet. He had twelve dollars. He counted his change. Eighty-two cents. With his finger, on the dusty dashboard, he added $12.82 to $463.65. He had $476.47. Does that check with your figures? he asked himself and drove into the crowded traffic.

Proceeding slowly, past his old building, past garages, past bar-and-grills, past second-rate hotels, he followed the traffic further downtown. He drove into the deepest part of the city, down and downtown to the bottom, the foundation, the city's navel. He watched the shoppers and tourists and messengers and men with appointments. He was tranquil, serene. It was something he could be content to do forever. He could use his check to buy gas, to take his meals at drive-in restaurants, to pay tolls. It would be a pleasant life, a great life, and he contemplated it thoughtfully. To drive at fifteen or twenty miles an hour through eternity, stopping at stoplights and signs, pulling over to the curb at the sound of sirens and the sight of funerals, obeying all traffic laws, making obedience to them his very code. Ed Wolfe, the Flying Dutchman, the Wandering Jew, the Off and Running Orphan, "Look Out for Ed Wolfe," a ghostly wailing down the city's corridors. What would be bad? he thought.

In the morning, out of habit, he dressed himself in a white shirt and light suit. Before he went downstairs he saw that his check and his twelve dollars were still in his wallet. Carefully he counted the eighty-two cents that he had placed on the dresser the night before, put the coins in his pocket, and went downstairs to his car.

Something green had been shoved under the wiper blade on the driver's side.

YOUR CAR WILL NEVER BE WORTH MORE THAN IT IS WORTH RIGHT NOW! WHY WAIT FOR DEPRECIATION TO MAKE YOU AUTOMOTIVELY BANKRUPT? I WILL BUY THIS CAR AND PAY YOU CASH! I WILL NOT CHEAT YOU!

Ed Wolfe considered his car thoughtfully a moment and then got in. That day he drove through the city, playing the car radio softly. He heard the news on the hour and half-hour. He listened to Art Linkletter, far away and in another world. He heard Bing Crosby's ancient voice, and thought sadly, Depreciation. When his tank was almost empty he thought wearily of having to have it filled and could see himself, bored and discontented behind the bug-stained glass, forced into a patience he did not feel, having to decide whether to take the Green Stamps the attendant tried to extend. Put money in your purse, Ed Wolfe, he thought. Cash! he thought with passion.

He went to the address on the circular.

He drove up onto the gravel lot but remained in his car. In a moment a man came out of a small wooden shack and walked toward Ed Wolfe's car. If he was appraising it he gave no sign. He stood at the side of the automobile and waited while Ed Wolfe got out.

"Look around," the man said. "No pennants, no strings of electric lights." He saw the advertisement in Ed Wolfe's hand. "I ran the ad off on my brother-in-law's mimeograph. My kid stole the paper from his school."

Ed Wolfe looked at him.

"The place looks like a goddamn parking lot. When the snow starts falling I get rid of the cars and move the Christmas trees in. No overhead. That's the beauty of a volume business."

Ed Wolfe looked pointedly at the nearly empty lot.

"That's right," the man said. "It's slow. I'm giving the policy one more chance. Then I cheat the public just like everybody else. You're just in time. Come on, I'll show you a beautiful car."

"I want to sell my car," Ed Wolfe said.

"Sure, sure," the man said. "You want to trade with me. I give top allowances. I play fair."

"I want you to buy my car."

The man looked at him closely. "What do you want? You want me to go into the office and put on the ten-gallon hat? It's my only overhead, so I guess you're entitled to see it. You're paying for it. I put on this big frigging hat, see, and I become Texas Willie Waxelman, the Mad Cowboy. If that's what you want, I can get it in a minute."

It's incredible, Ed Wolfe thought. There are bastards everywhere who hate other bastards downtown everywhere. "I don't want to trade my car in," he said. "I want to sell it. I, too, want to reduce my inventory."

The man smiled sadly. "You want me to buy *your* car. You run in and put on the hat. I'm an automobile *salesman*, kid."

"No, you're not," Ed Wolfe said. "I was with Cornucopia Finance. We handled your paper. You're an automobile *buyer*. Your business is in buying up four- and five-year-old cars like mine from people who need dough fast and then auctioning them off to the trade."

The man turned away and Ed Wolfe followed him. Inside the shack the man said, "I'll give you two hundred."

"I need six hundred," Ed Wolfe said.

"I'll lend you the hat. Hold up a goddamn stagecoach."

"Give me five."

"I'll give you two-fifty and we'll part friends."

"Four hundred and fifty."

"Three hundred. Here," the man said, reaching his hand into an opened safe and taking out three sheaves of thick, banded bills. He held the money out to Ed Wolfe. "Go ahead, count it."

Absently Ed Wolfe took the money. The bills were stiff, like money in a teller's drawer, their value as decorous and untapped as a sheet of postage stamps. He held the money, pleased by its weight. "Tens and fives," he said, grinning.

"You bet," the man said, taking the money back. "You want to sell your car?"

"Yes," Ed Wolfe said. "Give me the money," he said hoarsely.

He had been to the bank, had stood in the patient, slow, money-conscious line, had presented his formidable check to the impassive teller, hoping the four hundred and sixty-three dollars and sixty-five cents she counted out would seem his week's salary to the man who waited behind him. Fool, he thought, it will seem two weeks' pay and two weeks in lieu of notice and a week for vacation for the hell of it, the three-week margin of an orphan.

"Thank you," the teller said, already looking beyond Ed Wolfe to the man behind him.

"Wait," Ed Wolfe said. "Here." He handed her a white withdrawal slip.

She took it impatiently and walked to a file. "You're closing your savings account?" she asked loudly.

"Yes," Ed Wolfe answered, embarrassed.

"I'll have a cashier's check made out for this."

"No, no," Ed Wolfe said desperately. "Give me cash."

"Sir, we make out a cashier's check and cash it for you," the teller explained.

"Oh," Ed Wolfe said. "I see."

When the teller had given him the two hundred fourteen dollars and twenty-three cents, he went to the next window, where he made out a check for $38.91. It was what he had in his checking account.

On Ed Wolfe's kitchen table was a thousand dollars. That day he had spent one dollar and ninety cents. He had twenty-seven dollars and seventy-one cents in his pocket. For expenses. "For attrition," he said aloud. "The cost of living. For streetcars and newspapers and half-gallons of milk and loaves of white bread. For the movies. For a cup of coffee." He went to his pantry. He counted the cans and packages, the boxes and bottles. "The three weeks again," he said. "The orphan's nutritional margin." He looked in his icebox. In the freezer he poked around among white packages of frozen meat. He looked brightly into the vegetable tray. A whole lettuce. Five tomatoes. Several slices of cucumber. Browning celery. On another shelf four bananas. Three and a half apples. A cut pineapple. Some grapes, loose and collapsing darkly in a white bowl. A quarter-pound of butter. A few eggs. Another egg, broken last week, congealing in a blue dish. Things in plastic bowls, in jars, forgotten, faintly mysterious leftovers, faintly rotten, vaguely futured, equivocal garbage. He closed the door, feeling a draft. "Really," he said, "it's quite cozy." He looked at the thousand dollars on the kitchen table. "It's not enough," he said. "It's not enough," he shouted. "It's not enough to be cautious on. La Meck, you bastard, detachment comes higher, what do you think? You think it's cheap?" He raged against himself. It was the way he used to speak to people on the telephone. "Wake up. Orphan! Jerk! Wake up. It costs to be detached."

He moved solidly through the small apartment and lay down on his bed with his shoes still on, putting his hands behind his head luxuriously. It's marvelous, he thought. Tomorrow I'll buy a trench coat. I'll take my meals in piano bars. He lit a cigarette. "*I'll never smile again*," he sang, smiling. "All right, Eddie, play it again," he said. "Mistuh Wuf, you don' wan' ta heah dat ol' song no maw. You know whut it do to you. She ain' wuth it, Mistuh Wuf." He nodded. "Again, Eddie." Eddie played his black ass off. "The way I see it, Eddie," he said, taking a long, sad drink of warm Scotch, "there are orphans and there are orphans." The overhead fan chuffed slowly, stirring the potted palmetto leaves.

He sat up in the bed, grinding his heels across the sheets. "There are orphans and there are orphans," he said. "I'll move. I'll liquidate. I'll sell out."

He went to the phone, called his landlady and made an appointment to see her.

It was a time of ruthless parting from his things, but there was no bitterness in it. He was a born salesman, he told himself. A disposer, a natural dumper. He administered severance. As detached as a funeral director, what he had learned was to say goodby. It was a talent of a sort. And he had never felt quite so interested. He supposed he was doing what he had been meant for—what, perhaps, everyone was meant for. He sold and he sold, each day spinning off little pieces of himself, like controlled explosions of the sun. Now his life was a series of speeches, of nearly earnest pitches. What he remembered of the day was what he had said. What others said to him, or even whether they spoke at all, he was unsure of.

Tuesday he told his landlady, "Buy my furniture. It's new. It's good stuff. It's expensive. You can forget about that. Put it out of your mind. I want to sell it. I'll show you bills for over seven hundred dollars. Forget the bills. Consider my character. Consider the man. Only the man. That's how to get your bargains. Examine. Examine. I could tell you about inner springs; I could talk to you of leather. But I won't. I don't. I smoke, but I'm careful. I can show you the ashtrays. You won't find cigarette holes in *my* tables. Examine. I drink. I'm a drinker. I drink. But I hold it. You won't find alcohol stains. May I be frank? I make love. Again, I could show you the bills. But I'm cautious. My sheets are virginal, white.

"Two hundred fifty dollars, landlady. Sit on that sofa. That chair. Buy my furniture. Rent the apartment furnished. Deduct what you pay from your taxes. Collect additional rents. Realize enormous profits. Wallow in gravy. Get it, landlady? Get it, landlady! Two hundred fifty dollars. Don't disclose the figure or my name. I want to remain anonymous."

He took her into his bedroom. "The piece of resistance, landlady. What you're really buying is the bedroom stuff. This is where I do all my dreaming. What do you think? Elegance. *Elegance!* I throw in the living-room rug. That I throw in. You have to take that or it's no deal. Give me cash and I move tomorrow."

Wednesday he said, "I heard you buy books. That must be interesting. And sad. It must be very sad. A man who loves books doesn't like to sell them. It would be the last thing. Excuse me. I've got no right to talk to you this way. You buy books and I've got books to sell. There. It's business now. As it should be. My library—" He smiled helplessly. "Excuse me. Such a grand name. Library." He began again slowly. "My books, my books are in there. Look them over. I'm afraid my taste has been rather eclectic. You see, my education has not been formal. There are over eleven hundred. Of course, many are paperbacks. Well, you can see that. I feel as if I'm selling my mind."

The book buyer gave Ed Wolfe one hundred twenty dollars for his mind.

On Thursday he wrote a letter:

American Annuity & Life Insurance Company,
Suite 410,
Lipton-Hill Building,
2007 Beverly Street, S.W.,
Boston 19, Massachusetts

Dear Sirs,

I am writing in regard to Policy Number 593-000-34-78, a $5,000, twenty-year annuity held by Edward Wolfe of the address below.

Although only four payments have been made, and sixteen years remain before the policy matures, I find I must make application for the immediate return of my payments and cancel the policy.

I have read the "In event of cancellation" clause in my policy, and realize that I am entitled to only a flat three percent interest on the "total paid-in amount of the partial amortizement." Your records will show that I have made four payments of $198.45 each. If your figures check with mine this would come to $793.80. Adding three percent interest to this amount ($23.81.), your company owes me $817.61.

Your prompt attention to my request would be gratefully appreciated, although I feel, frankly, as though I were selling my future.

On Monday someone came to buy his record collection. "What do you want to hear? I'll put something comfortable on while we talk. What do you like? Here, try this. Go ahead, put it on the machine. By the edges, man. By the edges! I feel as if I'm selling my throat. Never mind about that. Dig the sounds. Orphans up from Orleans singing the news of chain gangs to café society. You can smell the freight trains, man. Recorded during actual performance. You can hear the ice cubes clinkin' in the glasses, the waiters picking up their tips. I have jazz. Folk. Classical.

Broadway. Spoken word. Spoken word, man! I feel as though
I'm selling my ears. The stuff lives in my heart or I wouldn't sell.
I have a one-price throat, one-price ears. Sixty dollars for the
noise the world makes, man. But remember, I'll be watching. By
the edges. *Only by the edges!*"

On Friday he went to a pawnshop in a Checker cab.
"*You?* You buy gold? You buy clothes? You buy Hawaiian
guitars? You buy pistols for resale to suicides? I wouldn't have
recognized you. Where's the skullcap, the garters around the
sleeves? The cigar I wouldn't ask you about. You look like anybody. You look like everybody. I don't know what to say. I'm
stuck. I don't know how to deal with you. I was going to tell you
something sordid, you know? You know what I mean? Okay, I'll
give you facts.
"The fact is, I'm the average man. That's what the fact is.
Eleven shirts, 15 neck, 34 sleeve. Six slacks, 32 waist. Five suits
at 38 long. Shoes 10-C. A 7½ hat. You know something? Those
marginal restaurants where you can never remember whether
they'll let you in without a jacket? Well, the jackets they lend
you in those places always fit me. That's the kind of guy you're
dealing with. You can have confidence. Look at the clothes. Feel
the material. And there's one thing about me. I'm fastidious. Fastidious. Immaculate. You think I'd be clumsy. A fall guy falls
down, right? There's not a mark on the clothes. Inside? Inside
it's another story. I don't speak of inside. Inside it's all Band-
Aids, plaster, iodine, sticky stuff for burns. But outside—fastidi-
ousness, immaculation, reality! My clothes will fly off your racks.
I promise. I feel as if I'm selling my skin. Does that check with
your figures?
"So now you know. It's me, Ed Wolfe. Ed Wolfe, the orphan?
I lived in the orphanage for sixteen years. They gave me a name.
It was a Jewish orphanage, so they gave me a Jewish name. Almost. That is, they couldn't know for sure themselves, so they
kept it deliberately vague. I'm a foundling. A lostling. Who

needs it, right? Who the hell needs it? I'm at loose ends, pawn-broker. I'm at loose ends out of looser beginnings. I need the money to stay alive. All you can give me.

"Here's a good watch. Here's a bad one. For good times and bad. That's life, right? You can sell them as a package deal. Here are radios. You like Art Linkletter? A phonograph. Automatic. Three speeds. Two speakers. One thing and another thing, see? And a pressure cooker. It's valueless to me, frankly. No pressure. I can live only on cold meals. Spartan. Spartan.

"I feel as if I'm selling—this is the last of it, I have no more things—I feel as if I'm selling my things."

On Saturday he called the phone company: "Operator? Let me speak to your supervisor, please.

"Supervisor? Supervisor, I am Ed Wolfe, your subscriber at TErrace 7-3572. There is nothing wrong with the service. The service has been excellent. No one calls, but you have nothing to do with that. However, I must cancel. I find that I no longer have any need of a telephone. Please connect me with the business office.

"Business office? Business office, this is Ed Wolfe. My telephone number is TErrace 7-3572. I am closing my account with you. When the service was first installed I had to surrender a twenty-five-dollar deposit to your company. It was understood that the deposit was to be refunded when our connection with each other had been terminated. Disconnect me. Deduct what I owe on my current account from my deposit and refund the rest immediately. Business office, I feel as if I'm selling my mouth."

When he had nothing left to sell, when that was finally that, he stayed until he had finished all the food and then moved from his old apartment into a small, thinly furnished room. He took with him a single carton of clothing—the suit, the few shirts, the socks, the pajamas, the underwear and overcoat he did not sell. It was in preparing this carton that he discovered the hangers. There were hundreds of them. His own, previous tenants'. Hundreds. In each closet, on rods, in dark, dark corners, was this anonymous residue of all their lives. He unpacked his carton and put the hangers inside. They made a weight. He took them to the pawnshop and demanded a dollar for them. They were worth more, he argued. In an A&P he got another carton for nothing and went back to repack his clothes.

At the new place the landlord gave him his key.

"You got anything else?" the landlord asked. "I could give you a hand."

"No," he said. "Nothing."

Following the landlord up the deep stairs he was conscious of the $2,479.03 he had packed into the pockets of the suit and shirts and pajamas and overcoat inside the carton. It was like carrying a community of economically viable dolls.

When the landlord left him he opened the carton and gathered all his money together. In fading light he reviewed the figures he had entered in the pages of an old spiral notebook:

Pay	$463.65
Cash	12.82
Car	300.00
Savings	214.23
Checking	38.91
Furniture (& bedding)	250.00
Books	120.00
Insurance	817.61
Records	60.00
Pawned:	
Clothes	110.00
2 watches	18.00
2 radios	12.00
Phonograph	35.00
Pressure cooker	6.00

Phone deposit (*less bill*)	*19.81*
Hangers	*1.00*

Total   **$2,479.03**

So, he thought, that was what he was worth. That was the going rate for orphans in a wicked world. Something under $2,500. He took his pencil and crossed out all the nouns on his list. He tore the list carefully from top to bottom and crumpled the half which inventoried his ex-possessions. Then he crumpled the other half.

He went to the window and pushed aside the loose, broken shade. He opened the window and set both lists on the ledge. He made a ring of his forefinger and thumb and flicked the paper balls into the street. "Look out for Ed Wolfe," he said softly.

In six weeks the season changed. The afternoons failed. The steam failed. He was as unafraid of the dark as he had been of the sunlight. He longed for a special grief, to be touched by anguish or terror, but when he saw the others in the street, in the cafeteria, in the theater, in the hallway, on the stairs, at the newsstand, in the basement rushing their fouled linen from basket to machine, he stood, as indifferent to their errand, their appetite, their joy, their greeting, their effort, their curiosity, their grime, as he was to his own. No envy wrenched him, no despair unhoped him, but, gradually, he became restless.

He began to spend, not recklessly so much as indifferently. At first he was able to recall for weeks what he spent on a given day. It was his way of telling time. Now he had difficulty remembering, and could tell how much his life was costing only by subtracting what he had left from his original two thousand four hundred seventy-nine dollars and three cents. In eleven weeks he had spent six hundred and seventy-seven dollars and thirty-four cents. It was almost three times more than he had planned. He became panicky. He had come to think of his money as his life. Spending it was the abrasion again, the old habit of self-buffing to come to the thing beneath. He could not draw infinitely on his credit. It was limited. Limited. He checked his figures. He had eighteen hundred and one dollars, sixty-nine cents. He warned himself, "Rothschild, child. Rockefeller, feller. Look out, Ed Wolfe. Look out."

He argued with his landlord and won a five-dollar reduction in his rent. He was constantly hungry, wore clothes stingily, realized an odd reassurance in his thin pain, his vague fetidness. He surrendered his dimes, his quarters, his half-dollars in a kind of sober anger. In seven more weeks he spent only one hundred and thirty dollars and fifty-one cents. He checked his figures. He had sixteen hundred seventy-one dollars, eighteen cents. He had spent almost twice what he had anticipated. "It's all right," he said. "I've reversed the trend. I can catch up." He held the money in his hand. He could smell his soiled underwear. "Nah, nah," he said. "It's not enough."

It was not enough, it was not enough, it was not enough. He had painted himself into a corner. Death by *cul-de-sac*. He had nothing left to sell, the born salesman. The born champion, long-distance, Ed Wolfe of a salesman lay in his room, winded, wounded, wondering where his next pitch was coming from, at one with the ages.

He put on his suit, took his sixteen hundred seventy-one dollars and eighteen cents and went down into the street. It was a warm night. He would walk downtown. The ice which just days before had covered the sidewalk was dissolved to slush. In darkness he walked through a thawing, melting world. There was something on the edge of the air, the warm, moist odor of the change of the season. He was touched despite himself. "I'll take a bus," he threatened. "I'll take a bus and close the windows and ride over the wheel."

He had dinner and some drinks in a hotel. When he finished he was feeling pretty good. He didn't want to go back. He looked at the bills thick in his wallet and went over to the desk clerk. "Where's the action?" he whispered. The clerk looked at him, startled. He went over to the bell captain. "Where's the action?" he asked and gave the man a dollar. He winked. The man stared at him helplessly.

"Sir?" the bell captain said, looking at the dollar.

Ed Wolfe nudged him in his gold buttons. He winked again. "Nice town you got here," he said expansively. "I'm a salesman, you understand, and this is new territory for me. Now if I were in Beantown or Philly or L.A. or Vegas or Big D or Frisco or Cincy—why, I'd know what was what. I'd be okay, know what I mean?" He winked once more. "Keep the buck, kid," he said. "Keep it, keep it," he said, walking off.

In the lobby a man sat in a deep chair, *The Wall Street Journal* opened wide across his face. "Where's the action?" Ed Wolfe said, peering over the top of the paper into the crown of the man's hat.

"What's that?" the man asked.

Ed Wolfe, surprised, saw that the man was a Negro.

"What's that?" the man repeated, vaguely nervous. Embarrassed, Ed Wolfe watched him guiltily, as though he had been caught in an act of bigotry.

"I thought you were someone else," he said lamely. The man smiled and lifted the paper to his face. Ed Wolfe stood before the opened paper, conscious of mildly teetering. He felt lousy, awkward, complicatedly irritated and ashamed, the mere act of hurting someone's feelings suddenly the most that could be held against him. It came to him how completely he had failed to make himself felt. "Look out for Ed Wolfe, indeed," he said aloud. The man lowered his paper. "Some of my best friends are Comanches," Ed Wolfe said. "Can I buy you a drink?"

"No," the man said.

"Resistance, eh?" Ed Wolfe said. "That's good. Resistance is good. A deal closed without resistance is no deal. Let me introduce myself. I'm Ed Wolfe. What's your name?"

"Please, I'm not bothering anybody. Leave me alone."

"Why?" Ed Wolfe asked.

The man stared at him and Ed Wolfe sat suddenly down beside him. "I won't press it," he said generously. "Where's the action? Where *is* it? Fold the paper, man. You're playing somebody else's gig." He leaned across the space between them and took the man by the arm. He pulled at him gently, awed by his own boldness. It was the first time since he had shaken hands with La Meck that he had touched anyone physically. What he was risking surprised and puzzled him. In all those months to have touched only two people, to have touched *even* two people! To feel their life, even, as now, through the unyielding wool of clothing, was disturbing. He was unused to it, frightened and oddly moved. Bewildered, the man looked at Ed Wolfe timidly and allowed himself to be taken toward the cocktail lounge.

They took a table near the bar. There, in the alcoholic dark, within earshot of the easy banter of the regulars, Ed Wolfe seated the Negro and then himself. He looked around the room and listened for a moment, then turned back to the Negro. Smoothly boozy, he pledged the man's health when the girl brought their drinks. He drank stolidly, abstractedly. Coming to life briefly, he indicated the men and women around them, their suntans apparent even in the dark. "Pilots," he said. "All of them. Airline pilots. The girls are all stewardesses and the pilots lay them." He ordered more drinks. He did not like liquor, and liberally poured ginger ale into his bourbon. He ordered more drinks and forgot the ginger ale. "*Goyim*," he said. "White *goyim*. American *goyim*." He stared at the Negro. He leaned across the table. "Little Orphan Annie, what the hell kind of an orphan is that with all her millions and her white American *goyim* friends to bail her out?"

He watched them narrowly, drunkenly. He had seen them before—in good motels, in airports, in bars—and he wondered about them, seeing them, he supposed, as Negroes or children of the poor must have seen him when he had sometimes driven his car through slums. They were removed, aloof—he meant it—a different breed. He turned and saw the Negro, and could not

think for a moment what the man was doing there. The Negro
slouched in his chair, his great white eyes hooded. "You want to
hang around here?" Ed Wolfe asked him.

"It's your party," the man said.

"Then let's go some place else," Ed Wolfe said. "I get nervous
here."

"I know a place," the Negro said.

"*You* know a place. You're a stranger here."

"No, man," the Negro said. "This is my home town. I come
down here sometimes just to sit in the lobby and read the newspapers. It looks good, you know what I mean? It looks good for
the race."

"*The Wall Street Journal?* You're kidding Ed Wolfe. Watch
that."

"No," the Negro said. "Honest."

"I'll be damned," Ed Wolfe said. "I come for the same reasons."

"Yeah," the Negro said. "No shit?"

"Sure, the same reasons." He laughed. "Let's get out of here."
He tried to stand, but fell back again in his chair. "Hey, help me
up," he said loudly. The Negro got up and came around to Ed
Wolfe's side of the table. Leaning over, he raised him to his feet.
Some of the others in the room looked at them curiously. "It's all
right," Ed Wolfe said. "He's my man. I take him with me everywhere. It looks good for the race." With their arms around each
other's shoulders they stumbled out of the bar and through the
lobby.

In the street Ed Wolfe leaned against the building, and the
Negro hailed a cab, the dark left hand shooting up boldly, the
long black body stretching forward, raised on tiptoes, the head
turned sharply along the left shoulder. Ed Wolfe knew that he
had never done it before. The Negro came up beside him and
guided Ed Wolfe toward the curb. Holding the door open, he
shoved him into the cab with his left hand. Ed Wolfe lurched
against the cushioned seat awkwardly. The Negro gave the

driver an address and the cab moved off. Ed Wolfe reached for
the window handle and rolled it down rapidly. He shoved his
head out the window of the taxi and smiled and waved at the
people along the curb.

"Hey, man, close the window," the Negro said after a moment.
"Close the window. The cops, the cops."

Ed Wolfe laid his head on the edge of the taxi window and
looked up at the Negro, who was leaning over him, smiling; he
seemed to be trying to tell him something.

"Where we going, man?" Ed Wolfe asked.

"We're there," the Negro said, sliding along the seat toward
the door.

"One ninety-five," the driver said.

"It's your party," Ed Wolfe told the Negro, waving away responsibility.

The Negro looked disappointed, but reached into his pocket.

Did he see what I had on me? Ed Wolfe wondered anxiously.
Jerk, drunk, you'll be rolled. They'll cut your throat and leave
your skin in an alley. Be careful.

"Come on, Ed," the Negro said. He took Ed Wolfe by the arm
and got him out of the taxi.

Fake. Fake, Ed Wolfe thought. Murderer. Nigger. Razor
man.

The Negro pulled him toward a doorway. "You'll meet my
friends," he said.

"Yeah, yeah," Ed Wolfe said. "I've heard so much about
them."

"Hold it a second," the Negro said. He went up to the window
and pressed his ear against the opaque glass.

Ed Wolfe watched him without making a move.

"Here's the place," the Negro said proudly.

"Sure," Ed Wolfe said. "Sure it is."

"Come on, man," the Negro urged him.

"I'm coming, I'm coming," Ed Wolfe said. "But my head is
bending low," he mumbled.

The Negro took out a ring of keys, selected one and put it in the door. Ed Wolfe followed him through.

"Hey, Oliver," somebody called. "Hey, baby, it's Oliver. Oliver looks good. He looks *good*."

"Hello, Mopiani," the Negro said to a short black man.

"How is stuff, Oliver?" Mopiani said to him.

"How's the market?" a man next to Mopiani asked, with a laugh.

"Ain't no mahket, baby. It's a *sto'*," somebody else said.

A woman stopped, looked at Ed Wolfe for a moment, and asked, "Who's the ofay, Oliver?"

"That's Oliver's broker, baby."

"Oliver's broker looks good," Mopiani said. "He looks *good*."

"This is my friend, Mr. Ed Wolfe," Oliver told them.

"Hey there," Mopiani said.

"Charmed," Ed Wolfe said.

"How's it going, man," a Negro said indifferently.

"Delighted," Ed Wolfe said.

He let Oliver lead him to a table.

"I'll get the drinks, Ed," Oliver said, leaving him.

Ed Wolfe looked at the room glumly. People were drinking steadily, gaily. They kept their bottles under their chairs in paper bags. He watched a man take a bag from beneath his chair, raise it and twist the open end of the bag carefully around the neck of the bottle so that it resembled a bottle of champagne swaddled in its toweling. The man poured liquor into his glass grandly. At the dark far end of the room some musicians were playing and three or four couples danced dreamily in front of them. He watched the musicians closely and was vaguely reminded of the airline pilots.

In a few minutes Oliver returned with a paper bag and some glasses. A girl was with him. "Mary Roberta, Ed Wolfe," he said, very pleased. Ed Wolfe stood up clumsily and the girl nodded.

"No more ice," Oliver explained.

"What the hell," Ed Wolfe said.

Mary Roberta sat down and Oliver pushed her chair up to the table. She sat with her hands in her lap and Oliver pushed her as though she were a cripple.

"Real nice little place here, Ollie," Ed Wolfe said.

"Oh, it's just the club," Oliver said.

"Real nice," Ed Wolfe said.

Oliver opened the bottle, then poured liquor into their glasses and put the paper bag under his chair. Oliver raised his glass. Ed Wolfe touched it lamely with his own and leaned back, drinking. When he put it down empty, Oliver filled it again from the paper bag. Ed Wolfe drank sluggishly, like one falling asleep, and listened, numbed, to Oliver and the girl. His glass never seemed to be empty any more. He drank steadily, but the liquor seemed to remain at the same level in the glass. He was conscious that someone else had joined them at the table. "Oliver's broker looks good," he heard somebody say. Mopiani. Warm and drowsy and gently detached, he listened, feeling as he had in barbershops, having his hair cut, conscious of the barber, unseen behind him, touching his hair and scalp with his warm fingers. "You see, Bert? He looks good," Mopiani was saying.

With great effort Ed Wolfe shifted in his chair, turning to the girl.

"Thought you were giving out on us, Ed," Oliver said. "That's it. That's it."

The girl sat with her hands folded in her lap.

"Mary Roberta," Ed Wolfe said.

"Uh huh," the girl said.

"Mary Roberta."

"Yes," the girl said. "That's right."

"You want to dance?" Ed Wolfe asked.

"All right," she said. "I guess so."

"That's it, that's it," Oliver said. "Stir yourself."

Ed Wolfe rose clumsily, cautiously, like one standing in a stalled Ferris wheel, and went around behind her chair, pulling it far back from the table with the girl in it. He took her warm, bare arm and moved toward the dancers. Mopiani passed them with a bottle. "Looks good, looks good," Mopiani said approvingly. He pulled her against him to let Mopiani pass, tightening the grip of his pale hand on her brown arm. A muscle leaped beneath the girl's smooth skin, filling his palm. At the edge of the dance floor he leaned forward into the girl's arms and they moved slowly, thickly across the floor. He held the girl close, conscious of her weight, the life beneath her body, just under her skin. Sick, he remembered a jumping bean he had held once in his palm, awed and frightened by the invisible life, jerking and hysterical, inside the stony shell. The girl moved with him in the music, Ed Wolfe astonished by the burden of her life. He stumbled away from her deliberately. Grinning, he moved ungently back against her. "Look out for Ed Wolfe," he crooned.

The girl stiffened and held him away from her, dancing self-consciously. Brooding, Ed Wolfe tried to concentrate on the lost rhythm. They danced in silence for a while.

"What do you do?" she asked him finally.

"I'm a salesman," he told her gloomily.

"Door to door?"

"Floor to ceiling. Wall to wall."

"Too much," she said.

"I'm a pusher," he said, suddenly angry. She looked frightened. "But I'm not hooked myself. It's a weakness in my character. I can't get hooked. Ach, what would you *goyim* know about it?"

"Take it easy," she said. "What's the matter with you? Do you want to sit down?"

"I can't push sitting down," he said.

"Hey," she said, "don't talk so loud."

"Boy," he said, "you black Protestants. What's that song you people sing?"

"Come on," she said.

"*Sometimes I feel like a motherless child*," he sang roughly.

The other dancers watched him nervously. "That's our national anthem, man," he said to a couple that had stopped dancing to look at him. "That's our song, sweethearts," he said, looking around him. "All right, *mine* then. I'm an orphan."

"Oh, come on," the girl said, exasperated, "an orphan. A grown man."

He pulled away from her. The band stopped playing. "Hell," he said loudly, "from the beginning. Orphan. Bachelor. Widower. Only child. All my names scorn me. I'm a survivor. I'm a goddamned survivor, that's what." The other couples crowded around him now. People got up from their tables. He could see them, on tiptoes, stretching their necks over the heads of the dancers. No, he thought. No, no. Detachment and caution. The La Meck Plan. They'll kill you. They'll kill you and kill you. He edged away from them, moving carefully backward against the bandstand. People pushed forward onto the dance floor to watch him. He could hear their questions, could see heads darting from behind backs and suddenly appearing over shoulders as they strained to get a look at him.

He grabbed Mary Roberta's hand, pulling her to him fiercely. He pulled and pushed her up onto the bandstand and then climbed up beside her. The trumpet player, bewildered, made room for him. "Tell you what I'm going to do," he shouted over their heads. "Tell you what I'm going to do."

Everyone was listening to him now.

"Tell you what I'm going to do," he began again.

Quietly they waited for him to go on.

"I don't *know* what I'm going to do," he shouted. "I don't *know* what I'm going to do. Isn't that a hell of a note?

"*Isn't* it?" he demanded.

"Brothers and sisters," he shouted, "and as an only child bachelor orphan I use the term playfully, you understand. Brothers and sisters, I tell you what I'm *not* going to do. I'm no consumer. Nobody's death can make me that. I won't consume. I mean, it's a question of identity, right? Closer, come up closer, buddies. You don't want to miss any of this."

"Oliver's broker looks good up there. Mary Roberta looks good. She looks good," Mopiani said below him.

"Right, Mopiani. She looks good, she looks *good*," Ed Wolfe called loudly. "So I tell you what I'm going to do. What am I bid? What am I bid for this fine strong wench? Daughter of a chief, masters. Dear dark daughter of a dead dinge chief. Look at those arms. Those arms, those arms. What am I bid?"

They looked at him, astonished.

"What am I bid?" he demanded. "Reluctant, masters? Reluctant masters, masters? Say, what's the matter with you darkies? Come on, what am I bid?" He turned to the girl. "No one wants you, honey," he said. "Folks, folks, I'd buy her myself, but I've already told you. I'm not a consumer. Please forgive me, miss."

He heard them shifting uncomfortably.

"Look," he said patiently, "the management has asked me to remind you that this is a living human being. This is the real thing, the genuine article, the goods. Oh, I told them I wasn't the right man for this job. As an orphan I have no conviction about the product. Now, you should have seen me in my old job. I could be rough. *Rough!* I hurt people. Can you imagine? I actually caused them pain. I mean, what the hell, I was an orphan. I *could* hurt people. An orphan doesn't have to bother with love. An orphan's like a nigger in that respect. Emancipated. But you people are another problem entirely. That's why I came here tonight. There are parents among you. I can feel it. There's even a sense of parents behind those parents. My God, don't any of you folks ever die? So what's holding us up? We're not making any money. Come on, what am I bid?"

"Shut up, mister." The voice was raised hollowly some place in the back of the crowd.

Ed Wolfe could not see the owner of the voice.

"He's not in," Ed Wolfe said.

"Shut up. What right you got to come down here and speak to us like that?"

"He's not in, I tell you. I'm his brother."

"You're a guest. A guest got no call to talk like that."

"He's out. I'm his father. He didn't tell me and I don't know when he'll be back."

"You can't make fun of us," the voice said.

"He isn't here. I'm his son."

"Bring that girl down off that stage!"

"Speaking," Ed Wolfe said brightly.

"Let go of that girl!" someone called angrily.

The girl moved closer to him.

"She's mine," Ed Wolfe said. "I danced with her."

"Get her down from there!"

"Okay," he said giddily. "Okay. All right." He let go of the girl's hand and pulled out his wallet. The girl did not move. He took out the bills and dropped the wallet to the floor.

"Damned drunk!" someone shouted.

"That whitey's crazy," someone else said.

"Here," Ed Wolfe said. "There's over sixteen hundred dollars here," he yelled, waving the money. It was, for him, like holding so much paper. "I'll start the bidding. I hear over sixteen hundred dollars once. I hear over sixteen hundred dollars twice. I hear it three times. Sold! A deal's a deal," he cried, flinging the money high over their heads. He saw them reach helplessly, noiselessly toward the bills, heard distinctly the sound of paper tearing.

He faced the girl. "Good-by," he said.

She reached forward, taking his hand.

"Good-by," he said again, "I'm leaving."

She held his hand, squeezing it. He looked down at the luxuriant brown hand, seeing beneath it the fine articulation of bones, the rich sudden rush of muscle. Inside her own he saw, indifferently, his own pale hand, lifeless and serene, still and infinitely free.

AMONG
THE
WITNESSES

The hotel breakfast bell had not awakened him. The hotel social
director had. The man had a gift. Wherever he went buzzers
buzzed, bells rang, whistles blew. He's a fire drill, Preminger
thought.

Preminger focused his eyes on the silver whistle dangling
from the neck of the man leaning over him, a gleaming, tooting
symbol of authority, suspended from a well-made, did-it-himself,
plastic lanyard. "Camp Cuyhoga?" he asked.

"What's that?" the man said.

"Did you go to Camp Cuyhoga? Your lanyard looks like Cuyhoga '41. Purple and green against a field of white plastic."

"Come on, boy, wake up a minute," the man said.

"I'm awake."

"Well," he began, "you probably think it's funny, the social
director coming into the room of a guest like this."

"We're all Americans," Preminger muttered.

"But the fact is," he went on, "I wanted to talk to you about
something. Now first of all I want you to understand that Bieberman doesn't know I'm here. He didn't put me up to it. As a matter of fact he'd probably fire me if he knew what I was going to
say, but, well, Jesus, Richard, this is a family hotel, if you know

what I mean." Preminger heard him say "well, Jesus, Richard," like a T-shirted YMCA professional conscious and sparing of his oaths. "That thing yesterday, to be frank, a thing like that could murder a small hotel like this. In a big place, some place like Grossinger's, it wouldn't mean a thing. It would be swallowed up in a minute, am I right? Now you might say this is none of my business, but Bieberman has been good to me and I don't want to see him get hurt. He took me off club dates in Jersey to bring me up here. I mean, I ain't knocking my trade but let's face it, a guy could get old and never get no higher in the show business than the Hudson Theater. He caught me once and liked my material, said if I came up with him maybe I could work up some of the better stuff into a musical, like. He's been true to his word. Free rein. Carte blanche. Absolutely blanche, Richard. Well, you know yourself, you've heard some of the patter songs. It's good stuff, am I telling a lie? You don't expect to hear that kind of stuff in the mountains. Sure, it's dirty, but it's clever, am I right? That crazy Estelle can't sing, she's got no class, we both know that, but the material's there, right? It's there."

People were always recruiting him, he thought. "So?" he asked carefully.

"Well," the social director said, embarrassed, "I'll get out of here and let you get dressed. But I just wanted to say, you know, how I feel about this guy, and warn you that there might be some talk. Mrs. Frankel and that crowd. If you hear anything, squash it, you know? Explain to them." He turned and went toward the door.

Preminger started to ask, "Explain what?" but it was too late. The social director had already gone out He could hear him in the hall knocking at the room next to his own. He heard a rustling and a moment later someone padding toward the door. He listened to the clumsy rattle of knobs and hinges, the inward sigh of wood as the door swung open, and the introductory murmurs of the social director, hesitant, explanatory, apologetic. Trying to make out the words, he heard the social director's voice shift, take on a loud assurance, and finally settle into the cheap conspiracy that was his lingua franca. "Between us," he would be saying now, winking slyly, perhaps even touching his listener's chest with his finger.

Preminger leaned back against his pillow, forgetting the social director. In a few minutes he heard the long loud ring of the second breakfast bell. It was Bieberman's final warning, and there was in it again the urgency of a fire alarm. He had once told Norma that if the hotel *were* to catch fire and they sounded that alarm, the guests would go by conditioned response into the dining hall. Well, he would not be with them at any rate. Richard Preminger, he thought, hotel hold-out. They moved and played and ate in a ferocious togetherness, eying with suspicion and real fear those who stood back, who apologized and excused themselves. They even went to town to the movies in groups of a dozen. He had seen them stuff themselves into each other's station wagons, and in the theater had looked on as they passed candy bars, bags of peanuts, sticks of gum to each other down the wide row of seats. With Norma he had watched them afterward in the ice cream parlor, like guests of honor at a wedding banquet, at the tables they had made the waiter push together. If they could have worked it out they would have all made love in the same big bed, sighing between climaxes, "Isn't this nice? Everybody, isn't this nice?"

He decided, enjoying the small extravagance, to ignore the bell's warning and forfeit breakfast. He was conscious of a familiar feeling, one he had had for several mornings now, and he was a little afraid of dissipating it. It was a feeling of deep, real pleasure, like waking up and not having to go to the bathroom. At first he had regarded it suspiciously, like some suddenly recurring symptom from an old illness. But then he was able to place it. It was a sensation from childhood; it was the way boys woke, instantly, completely, aware of some new fact in their lives. He was—it reduced to this—excited.

Now he began his morning inventory of himself. It was his

way of keeping up with his geography. He first tried to locate the source of his new feeling, but except for the obvious fact that he was no longer in the army and had had returned to him what others would have called his freedom, he didn't really understand it. But he knew that it was not simply a matter of freedom, or at any rate of that kind of freedom. It was certainly not his prospects. He had none. But thinking this, he began to see a possible reason for his contentment. His plans for himself were vague, but he was young and healthy. (At the hotel old men offered, only half jokingly, to trade places with him.) He had only to let something happen to himself, to let something turn up. Uncommitted, he could simply drift until he came upon his fate as a lucky victim of a shipwreck might come upon a vagrant spar. It was like being once again on one of those trips he used to take to strange cities. He had never admired nature. He would bear a mountain range if there was a city on the other side, water if it became a port. In cities he would march out into the older sections, into slums, factory districts, past railroad yards, into bleak neighborhoods where the poor stared forlornly out of windows. He would enter their dingy hallways and study their names on their mailboxes. Once, as he wandered at dusk through a skid row, meeting the eyes of bums who gazed listlessly at him from doorways, he had felt a hand grab his arm. He turned and saw an old man, a bum, who stared at him with dangerous eyes. "Give me money," the man wheezed from a broken throat. He hesitated and saw the man's fist grope slowly, threateningly, toward him. He thought he would be hit but he stood, motionless, waiting to see what the man would do. Inches from his face, the hand opened, turned, became a palm. "Money," the old man said. "God bless you, sir. Help a poor old man. Help me. Help me." He remembered looking into the palm. It was soft, incredibly flabby—the hand, weirdly, of a rich man. The bum began to sob some story of a wasted life, of chances missed, things lost, mistakes made. He listened, spellbound, looking steadily into the palm, which remained throughout just inches from his body. Finally it shook, reached still closer to him, and at last, closing on itself, dropped helplessly to the old man's side. Preminger was fascinated.

The talking in the other room had momentarily stopped. Then someone summed things up and a pleased voice agreed. A pact had been made. A door opened and the social director walked out, whistling, into the corridor.

In a little while he heard others in the corridor. Those would be the guests going to breakfast. He felt again a joy in his extravagance, and smiled at the idea of trying to be extravagant at Bieberman's (he thought of the shuffleboard court and the crack in the cement that snaked like a wayward S past the barely legible numbers where the paint had faded, of the frayed seams on the tennis nets and the rust on the chains that supported them, of the stucco main building that must always have looked obsolete, out of place in those green, rich mountains). It was a little like trying to be extravagant at Coney Island. Some places, he knew, commanded high prices for shabbiness; here you expected a discount.

He had seen the expressions on the guests' faces as they descended from the hotel station wagon. They came, traitors to their causes, doubtful, suspicious of their chances, their hearts split by some hope for change, some unlooked-for shift of fortune. Later they joked about it. What could you expect, they asked, from a mountain that had no Bronx, no Brooklyn on top of it? As for himself, he knew why he had come. He had heard the stories—comfortably illicit—of bored, hot mamas, people's eager aunts, office girls in virginity's extremis.

In the army he had known a boy named Phil, an amateur confidence man itching to turn pro, who, like a mystic, looked to the mountains. He remembered a conversation they'd had, sitting in the PX one night during basic training, solacing themselves with near-beer. Phil asked what he was going to do when he got out. He had to tell him he didn't know, and Phil looked doubtful for a moment. He could not understand how something so important had not been prepared for. Preminger asked him the same question, expecting to hear some pathetic little tale about night school, but Phil surprised him, reciting an elaborate plan he had worked out. All he needed was a Cadillac.

"A Cadillac?" he said. "Where would you get the money?"

"Listen to him. What do you think, I was always in the army?"

"What did you do before?"

"What did I do? I was a bellboy. In the mountains. In the mountains a bellboy is good for fifteen, sixteen hundred a season. If he makes book, add another five."

"You made book?"

"Not my own. I was an agent, sort of, for a guy. I was Bellboy five seasons. I was saving for the car, you understand. Well, now I've got enough. I've got enough for a wardrobe too. When you have a white Caddy convertible with black upholstery and gold fittings, you don't drive it in blue jeans. I must have about a thousand bucks just for the wardrobe part. When I get out I pick up my car and go back to the mountains. There must be a hundred hotels up there. All I do is just drive around until I see some girl who looks like she might be good for a couple of bucks. I'll pick her up. I'll make a big thing of it, do you follow me? We'll drive around with the top down to all the nice hotels, Grossinger's and the Concord, where all the bellboys know me, and we'll eat a nice lunch, and we make a date for the evening. Then when I pick her up that night we go out to the hotels again—they've got all this free entertainment in the mountains—but the whole time I'm with her I'm hanging back like, quiet, very sad. She's got to ask what's up, right? Well, I'll brush it off, but all the time I'll be getting more miserable, and she'll be all over me with questions about what's wrong, is it something she did, something she said— So finally I'll say, 'Look, dear, I didn't want to ruin your evening, but I see I'll have to tell you. It's the Cadillac. I've got just one payment to make on it and it's ours. Well, I'm broke this month. I lent money to a guy and I dropped a couple hundred on a nag last week. I missed the payment. They called me up today, they're going to repossess if they don't get the payment tomorrow. Hell, I wouldn't care, honey, but I like you and I know what a kick it gives you to ride in it.' Now you know yourself, a girl on vacation, she's got to have a few bucks in the suitcase, am I right? Sooner or later she's got to say, 'Maybe I could lend you some money toward it. How much do you need?' I tell her that it's crazy, she doesn't even know me, and anyway that I'd need about sixty bucks. Well, don't you see, she's so relieved it's not more she knocks herself out to get the dough to me. She's thinking I'm in to her for sixty bucks, we're practically engaged or something. The thing is, to close the deal, I've got to be able to make her. That's my insurance she won't try to find me later on. These girls make a big thing out of their reputation, and I could ruin her. It's easy. That's the whole setup. The next day I go to a new hotel. If I'm lucky it's good for the whole season. And then, in the winter, there's Miami."

Preminger smiled, recalling Phil's passion. It was a hell of an idea, and he would have to keep his eyes open for a white Cadillac convertible. But what was important was that somewhere in the outrageous plan there was sound, conservative thinking, the thinking of a man who knew his geography, who saw his symbols in the true white lights of a Cadillac's headlamps. The plan could work. It was, in its monstrous way, feasible, and he cheered Phil on. And while he had not himself come for the money, of course, he hoped to shake down a little glory from the skies. He wanted, in short, to get laid in Jewish, to get laid and laid, to abandon himself. Abandon was a new thing in his life, however, and he was not as yet very good at it. All he could be sure of was that he approved of it.

Well, anyway, he thought, playing his pleasant morning game, I'm in a new place, and there's Norma, at least.

Thinking of Norma, he felt some misgivings. It was too easy to make fun of her desperation. She was, after all, something like the last of her race—vacationing secretary, overripe vestal, the only girl in the whole damned family who had not walked down some flower-strewn aisle in The Bronx, amidst a glory going at four dollars a plate, toward the ultimate luck, a canopy of flowers, to plight what she might call her troth. Beauty is troth and troth beauty, that is all ye know on earth and all ye need to know. And Norma, he thought, on the edge of age, having tried all the other ways, having gone alone to the dances in the gymnasium of the Hebrew school, having read and mastered the *Journal of the American Medical Association* for April so that she might hold intelligent conversation with the nephew of her mother's friend, a perspiring intern at Bellevue, and having ceased to shave her underarms because of the pain, had abandoned herself to Bieberman's and to him.

He stretched in bed. Under the sheet he moved his toes and watched the lumps, like suddenly shifting mountain ranges, change shape. The sun lay in strips across his chest. He got out of the sun-warmed bed, and slices of light from the Venetian blinds climbed up and across his body.

He began to dress but saw that his ground-level window was open. He moved up to it cautiously and started to pull the string on the Venetian blinds to slant the sunlight downward. Seeing some of the guests standing in a large group beside the empty swimming pool, he paused. He remembered the cryptic warnings of the social director and shivered lightly, recalling against his will the confused and angry scene which yesterday had sickened them all. Was that the new excitement he had awakened with, he wondered.

He had even known the child slightly; she and her mother had sat at the table next to his in the dining hall. He had once commented to Norma that she was a pretty little girl. Her death and her mother's screams (the cupped hands rocking back and forth in front of her, incongruously like a gambler's shaking dice) had frightened him. He had come up from the tennis court with his

racket in his hand. In front of him were the sun-blistered backs
of the guests. He pushed through, using his racket to make a
place for himself. He stood at the inner edge of the circle, but
seeing the girl's blue face ringed by the wet yellow hair sticking
to it, he backed off, thrusting his racket before his face, defend-
ing his eyes. The people pushing behind him would not let him
through and helplessly he had to turn back, forced to watch as
Mrs. Goldstone, the girl's mother, asked each of them why it had
happened, and then begged, and then accused, and then turned
silently back to the girl to bend over her again and slap her.
He heard her insanely calm voice scolding the dead girl: "Wake
up. Wake up. Wake up." He watched the mother, squatting on
her heels over the girl, obscene as someone defecating in the
woods. She struggled hopelessly with the firemen who came to
remove the girl, and after they had borne her off, her body jounc-
ing grotesquely on the stretcher, he saw the mother try to hug
the wet traces of the child's body on the cement. When the others
put out their hands and arms to comfort her, crowding about her,
determined to make her recognize their sympathy, he looked
away.

Now he stood back from the window. Several of the people
from yesterday were there again. My God, he thought, they're
acting it out.

He recognized Mrs. Frankel among them. She was wearing
her city clothes and looked hot and uncomfortable standing beside Bieberman's empty pool. She seemed to be arguing ferociously, in her excitement unconscious of the big purse that followed weirdly the angry arcs of her arms. The sun caught the
faces of some stones on her heavy bracelet and threw glints of
light into Preminger's eyes as she pointed in the direction of the
pool. He did not know what she was saying, but he could imagine it easily enough. He had heard her bullying before. She was
like a spokesman for some political party forever in opposition.

In a moment he noticed something else. Beyond the excited

crowd gathered about Mrs. Frankel, he saw Bieberman, who stood, hanging back, his head cocked to one side, his expression one of troubled concentration. He looked like a defendant forced to listen in a foreign court to witnesses whose language he can not understand. Beside him was the social director, scowling like an impatient advocate.

He turned and began again to dress.

When he approached the main building the others had finished their breakfasts and were already in the positions that would carry them through until lunch. On the long shaded porch in front of Bieberman's main building people sat in heavy wicker rockers playing cards. They talked low in wet thick voices. Occasionally the quiet murmur was broken by someone's strident bidding. Preminger could feel already the syrupy thickness of the long summer day. He climbed the steps and was about to go inside to get some coffee when he saw Mrs. Frankel. She was talking to a woman who listened gravely. He tried to slip by without having to speak to her, but she had already seen him. She looked into his eyes and would not turn away. He nodded. She allowed her head to sway forward once slowly as though she and Preminger were conspirators in some grand mystery. "Good morning, Mrs. Frankel," he said.

She greeted him solemnly. "It won't be long now, will it, Mr. Preminger?"

"What won't?"

She waved her hand about her, taking in all of Bieberman's in a vague gesture of accusation. "Didn't they tell you I was leaving?" she asked slowly.

He was amazed at the woman's egotism. "Vacation over, Mrs. Frankel?" he asked, smiling.

"Some vacation," she said. "Do you think I'd stay with that murderer another day? I should say not! Listen, I could say plenty. You don't have to be a Philadelphia lawyer to see what's happening. Some vacation. Who needs it? Don't you think when my son heard, he didn't say, 'Mama, I'll be up to get you whenever you want?' The man's a fine lawyer, he could make plenty of trouble if he wanted."

For a moment as the woman spoke he felt the shadow of a familiar panic. He recognized the gestures, the voice that would take him into the conspiracy, that insisted he was never out of it. Mrs. Frankel could go to hell, he thought. He'd better not say that; it would be a gesture of his own. He would not go through life using his hands.

Mrs. Frankel still spoke in the same outraged tones Preminger did not quite trust. "The nerve," she said. "Well, believe me, he shouldn't be allowed to get away with it."

Bieberman suddenly appeared at the window behind Mrs. Frankel's chair. His huge head seemed to fill the whole window. His face was angry but when he spoke his voice was soft. "Please, Mrs. Frankel. Please," he said placatingly. Preminger continued toward the dining room.

Inside, the bus boys were still clearing the tables. He went up to one of the boys and asked for some coffee and sat down at one of the cleared tables. The boy nodded politely and went through the large brown swinging doors into the kitchen. He pushed the doors back forcefully and Preminger saw for a moment the interior of the bright kitchen. He looked hard at the old woman, Bieberman's cook, sitting on a high stool, a cigarette in her mouth, shelling peas. The doors came quickly together, but in a second their momentum had swung them outward again and he caught another glimpse of her. She had turned her head to watch the bus boy. Quickly the doors came together again, like stiff theatrical curtains.

He turned and saw Norma across the dining hall. She was holding a cigarette and drinking coffee, watching him. He went over to her. "Good morning," he said, sitting down. "A lot of excitement around here this morning."

"Hello," she said.

He leaned across to kiss her. She moved her head and he was able only to graze her cheek. In the instant of his fumbling movement he saw himself half out of his chair, leaning over the cluttered table, like a clumsy, bad-postured diver on a diving board. He sat back abruptly, surprised. He shrugged. He broke open a roll and pulled the dough from its center. "Mrs. Frankel's leaving," he said after a while.

"Yes," she said. "I know."

"The Catskillian Minute Man," he said, smiling.

"What's so funny about Mrs. Frankel?"

Preminger looked at her. "Nothing," he said. "You're right. One of these days, after this Linda Goldstone affair had blown over, she would have gotten around to us."

"She couldn't say anything about us."

"No," he said. "I guess not."

" 'Goldstone affair,' " she said. "The little girl is dead."

"Yes," he said.

"Affair," she said. "Some affair."

He looked at her carefully. Her face was without expression. What did she want from him—a *statement?*

"All right," he said. "Okay. The Goldstone affair—excuse me, the Goldstone tragedy—was just the Goldstone drowning. Norma, it was an accident. Everyone around here carries on as though it has implications. Even you. I suppose the thing I feel worst about—well, the parents, of course—is Bieberman. He's the only one who still has anything to lose. It could hurt him in the pocketbook and to a man like him that must be a mortal wound."

Norma looked as if he had slapped her. It was a dodge, her shock; it was a dodge, he thought. Always, fragility makes its demands on bystanders. The dago peddler whose apples have been spilled, the rolled drunk, the beat-up queer, the new widow shrieking at an open window—their helplessness strident, their despair a prop. What did they want? They were like children rushing to their toys, the trucks, the tin armies, manipulating them, making sounds of battle in their throats, percussing danger and emergency.

He was in his bathing trunks. On his feet were the "low-quarters" he had been discharged in. He had not had time, so anxious was he to get away, to buy other shoes, not even the sneakers appropriate for afternoon climbs like this one on the high hill behind Bieberman's.

He had lost interest in the hike. He turned his back on the sandy, rock-strewn path that continued on up the hill and into the woods he had promised himself to explore, and he looked down to see where he had come from. Below him was the resort. He had never seen the place from this vantage point, and its arrangement in the flat green valley struck him as comic. It looked rather like a giant fun house in an amusement park. He had the impression that if he were to return to his room he would find, bracketed in heavy yellow frames, mirrors that gave back distorted images. In the trick rooms, constructed to defy gravity, he would have to hang onto the furniture to keep from falling. He looked at the fantastic spires that swirled like scoops of custard in cups too small for them, and he pictured Bieberman climbing at sunset to the top of these minarets to bellow like a clownish muezzin to the wayward guests. He saw the beach umbrellas, bright as lollipops, on the hotel lawn. They were like flowers grown grossly out of proportion in a garden.

He grinned, shifting his gaze from the hotel grounds and letting it fall on his own body. It rested there a moment without any recognition and then, gradually conscious of himself, he stared, embarrassed, at his thighs, which exposure to the sun had failed to tan deeply. He traced his legs down past bony kneecaps and hairless shins and mocked in silence their abrupt disappearance into the formal shoes. Why, he was like someone come upon in the toilet. The fat thighs, the shiny pallor of the too-smooth legs, like the glaucous sheen on fruit, betrayed him. He seemed to himself clumsy and a little helpless, like old, fat women in camp chairs on the beach, their feet swollen in the men's shoes they have to leave untied, the loose strings like the fingers they lace protectively across their busts.

Just what was he really doing at Bieberman's, he wondered. He could write off his disappointment as an experience of travelers who, having left the airport in their hired cars, and spoken to clerks about reservations, and made arrangements for the delivery of bags, at last find themselves alone in strange cities, bored, depressed, sleepless in their rented beds, searching aimlessly for familiar names in the telephone directory. But what, finally, was he doing there at all? He thought of the other people who had come to the hotel and had to remind himself that they did not live there always, had not been hired by the hotel as a kind of folksy background, a monumental shill for his benefit. They were there, he supposed, for the access it gave them to the tennis court, the pool, the six-hole golf course, the floor show "nitely," the card tables, the dining room, each other. And he, fat-thighed lover, abandon bent, was there to lay them. Fat chance, Fat Thigh, he thought.

He wondered whether to start up the path once more, and turned to estimate the distance he had yet to travel. He looked again below him. He saw the drained pool. A little water, like a stain on the smooth white tile, still remained at the bottom. Some reflected light flashed against his eyes and he turned, instinctively shielding them with one cupped palm.

"I didn't think you'd see me," someone said.

Preminger stepped back. He hadn't seen anyone, but assumed that the boy who was now coming from within the trees that bordered the path had mistaken his gesture as a wave and had responded to it.

"If you're trying to hide," Preminger said, "you shouldn't wear white duck trousers. Law of the jungle." The bare-chested boy, whom he recognized as the lifeguard, came cautiously onto the path where Preminger stood. Preminger thought he seemed rather shamefaced, and looked into the green recess from which the boy had come, to see if perhaps one of the girls from the hotel was there.

"I wasn't hiding," the boy said defensively. "I come up here often when I'm not on duty. I've seen you down there."

"I've seen you too. You're the lifeguard." The boy looked down. They were standing in a circle of sunlight that seemed, in the woodsy arena, to ring them like contenders for a title of little note. He noticed uncomfortably that the boy was looking at his shoes. Preminger shuffled self-consciously. The boy looked up and Preminger saw that his eyes were red.

"Have they been talking about me?" the boy asked.

"Has who been talking about you?"

The boy nodded in the direction of the hotel.

"No," he said. "Why?" He asked without meaning to.

"Mr. Bieberman said I shouldn't hang around today. I didn't know anywhere to come until I remembered this place. I was going all the way to the top when I heard you. I thought Mr. Bieberman might have sent you up to look for me."

Preminger shook his head.

The boy seemed disappointed. "Look;" he said suddenly, "I want to come down. I'm not used to this. How long do they expect me to stay up here?" For all the petulance, there was real urgency in his voice. He added this to the boy's abjectness, to his guilt at being found, and to the terror he could not keep to himself. It wasn't fair to let the boy continue to reveal himself in the mistaken belief that everything had already been found out about him. He didn't want to hear more, but already the boy was talking again. "I'm not used to this," he said. "I told Mr. Bieberman at the beginning of the summer about my age. He knew I was sixteen. That's why I only get two hundred. It was okay then."

"Two hundred?"

The boy stopped talking and looked him over carefully. He might have been evaluating their relative strengths. As though he had discovered Preminger's weakness and was determined to seize upon it for his own advantage, he looked down at Preminger's knees. Preminger felt his gaze keenly.

"Does anyone else know?" Preminger asked abruptly.

"Mrs. Frankel, I think," he said, still not looking up.

Preminger shifted his position, moving slightly to one side. "She'll be going home today," he said. "I saw her this morning. She didn't say anything." He did not enjoy the cryptic turn in the conversation. It reminded him vaguely of the comical communication between gangsters in not very good films. A man leans against a building. Someone walks past. The man nods to a loitering confederate. The confederate lowers his eyes and moves on.

He made up his mind to continue the walk. "Look," he said to the boy, "I'm going to go on up the path." Having said this, he immediately began to move down toward Bieberman's. He realized his mistake but felt the boy staring at him. He wondered if he should make some feint with his body, perhaps appear to have come down a few steps to get a better look at some nonexistent activity below them and then turn to continue back up the path. The hell with it, he thought wearily. He could hear the boy following him.

Some pebbles that the boy dislodged struck Preminger's ankles. He watched them roll down the hill. The boy caught up with him. "I'm going down too," he said, as though Preminger had made a decision for both of them. The path narrowed and Preminger took advantage of the fact to move ahead of the boy. He moved down quickly, concentrating on the steep angle of the descent. Just behind him the boy continued to chatter. "He needed someone for the season. It was the Fourth of July and he didn't have anyone. I got a cousin who works in the kitchen. He told me. Mr. Bieberman knew about my age. I told him myself. He said, 'What's age got to do with it? Nobody drowns.' I had to practice the holds in my room." The path widened and the boy came abreast of him. He timed his pace to match Preminger's and they came to the bottom of the hill together.

He began to jog ahead of the boy but, soon tiring, he stopped and resumed walking. Though the boy had not run after him, Preminger knew he was not far behind and that he was still following him. He went deliberately toward one of the tables on Bieberman's lawn, thinking that when he reached it he would turn to the boy and ask him to bring him a drink. He did not notice until too late that it was Mrs. Frankel's table he was heading for. The wide, high-domed beach umbrella that stood over it had hidden her from him. He saw that the only way to take himself out of her range was to veer sharply, but remembering the boy behind him and the mistake he had made on the hill, he decided that he could not risk another dopey movement. What if the kid turned with him, he thought. They would wind up alone together on the golf course. He would never get away from him. He considered between Frankel and the kid and chose Frankel because she didn't need advice.

Mrs. Frankel, in her hot, thick city clothing, looked to him like a woman whose picture has just been taken for the Sunday supplements. ("Mrs. Frankel, seated here beneath a two-hundred-pound mushroom she raised herself, has announced . . .") But when he came closer he saw that she would not do for the supplements at all. Her legs, thrown out in front of her, gave her the appearance of an incredibly weary shopper whose trip downtown has failed. Her expession was disconsolate and brooding. It was an unusual attitude for Mrs. Frankel and he stood beside her for a moment. She stared straight ahead toward the useless pool.

"It's funny," she said, turning to him. "A little girl." He had never heard her talk so softly. "Did you see her? Like she was just some piece of cardboard that had been painted like a child. It's too terrible," she said. "To happen here? In the mountains? Just playing like that? All right, so a child is sick, it's awful, but a little child gets sick and sometimes there's nothing you can do and the child dies." He was not sure she was talking to him. "But here, in the mountains where you come for fun, for it to happen here? It's awful—terrible. A thing like that." She looked directly at Preminger but he could not be certain that she saw him. "Did you see the mother? Did you see the fright in the woman's eyes? Like, 'No, it couldn't be.' I was there. The child wanted an ice cream and the mother told her that her lips were blue, she should come out. She looked around for a second, for a *second*, and when she turned around again . . ." Mrs. Frankel shrugged. "How long could she have been under—five seconds, *ten?* Is the pool an ocean, they had to search for her? No, it's more important the lifeguard should be talking to his girl friends so when he hears the screaming he should look up and holler 'What? What? Where? Where?' Who's to blame?" she asked him. "God? We're not savages. Let's fix the blame a little close to home."

He shifted under her direct stare. She had recovered her stentorian coloratura and for this he was grateful. She was running true to form again and her elegy or whatever it had been was only a kind of interlude, as though the woman caught her breath not by ceasing to talk but by lowering her voice. However, her question still hung in the air. He didn't want to answer it but that didn't seem to make any difference to these people. At least, then, he could give his testimony on the side he believed in.

"All right, Mrs. Frankel," he said. "What is it? All morning you've been hinting at some dark secret. Is it that the lifeguard wasn't old enough?" His voice sounded louder than he had intended. He heard it as though he were listening to a recording he could not remember having made. "Is that what's bothering you? Is that the little secret you're determined to let everyone in on? Well, relax, it's no secret. Everybody knows about it. It's too bad, but even if the kid had been eighteen instead of sixteen the little girl would still have drowned."

"The lifeguard was only sixteen?" the woman asked. It was impossible that she didn't know. She must have guessed, must have suspected it. That had to be the reason for her outrage.

"The lifeguard was only sixteen?" she repeated. It was too much; he couldn't be the one she learned it from. "Only *sixteen?*" she insisted.

"I don't know how old he is," he said, reneging. "That's not the point. It was an accident. What difference does it make how old he is?" Only now was he conscious that the boy had not left them. He was standing about twenty feet away, listening. Preminger remembered seeing Bieberman stand in the same attitude just that morning, his head bowed low under the weight of his embarrassment, buffered from his enemies by the social director. He was waiting for Preminger to go on with the defense.

Blithely, however, he changed the subject. For no apparent reason he began to tell Mrs. Frankel of the walk he had just taken, of his vague plans for the future. She listened politely and even nodded in agreement once or twice to things he said. He remained with her in this way for about ten minutes, but when he started to leave he caught for a moment Mrs. Frankel's angry stare. "It's better we should all get out," she said.

He lay beside Norma beyond the closed-in tennis court. He watched the moon's chalk-silver disintegrate and drift icily to the lawn. They had not spoken for a quarter of an hour. He did not know whether she was asleep. The ground was damp. He could feel, beneath the blanket, the evening's distillation like a kind of skin. He raised himself on one elbow and looked at Norma's face. Her eyes were closed and he lay back down again and watched the sky.

The lawn was deserted; the exodus of late that afternoon had ended; the last cars from the city had gone back. He thought of Bieberman, alone beside the pool, and could still see the old man's awful face as he waved at the departing guests, pretending it was only the natural end of their vacation that took them back.

He pulled a blade of grass from beside the blanket.

"The slob," he said.

Norma stirred, made a small sound.

Preminger only half heard her. "He stood in the driveway and waved at them. He shook their hands and said he'd save their rooms. He even told the bellboy where to put everything." He tore the grass in half and threw one piece away. "The slob. I was ashamed for him."

He rolled the grass between his fingers. Feeling its sticky juice, he threw it away in disgust. "Even the social director. Did you hear him? 'I'm sorry, Bieberman, but I've got to have people. I've got to have people, right?' And Bieberman told him, 'You're a fine actor. You give a professional performance.' It made me sick. And Mrs. Frankel didn't say a word. She didn't have to. He gave himself away."

"The poor thing," Norma said. Her voice was low and cool, not sleepy at all. He turned to her and smiled.

"*Bieberman?*"

"I meant the little girl," she said. Her voice was flat. He studied her pale face and the skin, which looked cooler and softer than he remembered ever having seen it. She seemed smaller somehow, and, in a way he did not mind, older. It's the moon, he thought.

He touched her cheek with his fingers. "You would have gone with them, wouldn't you?" he asked softly. "You would have gone with them if I hadn't asked you to stay." She didn't answer. She turned her head and his hand dropped to the blanket. "You've done that twice today," he said.

"Have I?"

He looked at her body. She lay straight back, her arms at her sides. He rolled toward her quickly and his arm fell across her breast. She tried to move away from him, but he grabbed her arms and pinned them to her sides and kissed her on the mouth. In a few minutes, he thought, my vacation begins. A nice abandoned Jewish girl in a nice abandoned Jewish hotel. She shook her head ferociously. His face fell on top of hers and he forced it with his weight toward the blanket. He felt her body stiffen, her arms go rigid. Then her arms shook in a rage against him and he was helpless to hold them at her sides. She was very strong, and with a sudden convulsive movement she threw him off. She sprang up quickly and stood looking down at him. She seemed unsure of herself.

"Get away from me," he said.

"Richard . . ."

"Get away from me."

"Richard, I didn't want to go back."

"Get away."

"All right," she said quietly. She turned and started away.

"There she goes," he called after her. "Don't touch her, she's in mourning." His anger rose in him. "Hey, come back, I've got an idea. We'll have a lynching. We'll string the kid up to the diving board and hang Bieberman from a beach umbrella."

She was moving from him quickly, back to the hotel. He got up and ran after her. He put out his hand to stop her but she eluded him and he saw himself stumble forward, his empty hand reaching toward her. He recovered his balance and walked along a little behind her, talking to her. He felt like a peddler haggling, but he couldn't help himself. "The drowning loused things up, didn't it? It killed a stranger, but nobody around here knows from strangers." She broke into a run. From the way she ran he could tell she was crying. He ran after her, hearing her sobbing. "Let's blame someone. The lifeguard. Bieberman. *Me*. You want to know what to blame? Blame cramps and lousy Australian crawl." As he approached the hotel Preminger halted. Norma walked into the hotel and Preminger slumped on the steps. He clapped his palms together nervously in raged applause. That kid, that lousy kid, he thought. He thought of his tantrum as of a disease which recurs despite its cure.

When the world had quieted again he knew that he was not alone. He realized that he had been aware of someone on the porch when he turned from Norma and let her go inside. He looked around and saw in the shadows about twenty feet away the silhouette of a man propped against the side of the porch. In the dark he could not make out his face.

"Bieberman?"

The man came toward him from the dark recesses of the porch. He walked slowly, perhaps uncertainly, and when he passed in front of the hotel entrance he was caught in the light slanting down from the interior like a gangplank secured to the building.

"Ah, Preminger." The voice was deep and mocking.

"Mr. Bieberman," he said softly.

The man stayed within the light. Preminger rose and joined him there nervously. "It's about time for bed," he said. "I was just going up."

"Sure," Bieberman said. "So this will be your last night with us, hah, Preminger?"

Preminger looked at him, feeling himself, as they stood together within the close quarters of the light, somehow under attack. "I hadn't planned for it to be."

"*Planned?*" The old man laughed. "The girl will be going in the morning. What will there be to keep you? The food?" He laughed again. "You'll leave tomorrow. But I thank you for staying the extra day. It will make me a rich man, and I can go myself to a hotel." He noticed the bottle in Bieberman's hand. The old man followed his glance and looked up, smiling broadly. "Schnapps," he said, holding up the bottle. "A little schnapps. I've been sitting here on my porch and I'm on a deck chair on the *Queen Mary*, which in honor of my first voyage over is keeping a kosher kitchen. The only thing wrong is that once in a while someone falls overboard and it upsets me. If we weren't three days out, I would call my wife she should swim up from the city and we would go back."

Preminger smiled and Bieberman offered him the bottle. He took it and, unconsciously wiping off the neck, began to drink.

"I guess I will be going," he said.

"I guess you will."

"I shouldn't be here," Preminger said. "It was supposed to be a lark. I didn't come slumming, don't think that. But it didn't work out. I guess I just wanted to fool around."

"Yeah," Bieberman said. "I know you guys. You've got a suitcase filled with contraceptives. Fooey."

"I just wanted to fool around," Preminger repeated.

"Nobody fools. Never," Bieberman said.

"You said it," Preminger said.

Bieberman went back into the dark wing of the porch. Preminger followed him. "I don't want you to think I'm leaving for the same reason as the others. *I* don't blame you." The old man didn't answer. "I really don't," he said.

Preminger almost lost him in the shadows. "A boy who likes to fool around doesn't blame me," the old man said.

Preminger paused. "Well," he said lamely, "good night." He went toward the door.

"Preminger, tell me, you're an educated person," Bieberman said suddenly. "Do you really think they could sue me?"

He turned back to Bieberman. "I don't see how," he said.

"But the lifeguard—the boy. If I knew he was a boy? If I knew he was sixteen? If they could prove that, couldn't they sue?"

"How could they find that out?" Preminger said uncomfortably.

"Well, I wouldn't tell them. I wouldn't run an ad in the *Times*, but if they knew it, could they sue me?"

"I suppose they could try, I don't know. I'm no lawyer. I don't see how they could find you responsible."

"My guests did."

"They'll forget."

"Ah," the old man said.

"Next year your place will be full again."

"Yes, I suppose so," he said sadly.

"Wait a minute, it *wasn't* your fault."

"It made them sick," Bieberman said so softly Preminger

thought he was talking to himself. "All they could do was get away. Some of the women couldn't even look at me. Sure, that's why the Catskills and Miami Beach and Las Vegas and all those places are so important. That's why a man named Bieberman can have his name written across a hotel, and on towels." Preminger couldn't follow him. "I mean, what the hell," he said, suddenly talking to Preminger again. "Does Spinoza get his name written on towels?"

"Why don't you come inside?" Preminger said, offering him his arm.

"When a little girl drowns in such a place where nobody must drown, where you pay good money just to keep everybody on top of the water, it's a terrible thing. I understand that. You're not safe anywhere," Bieberman said. "Not anywhere. You go to a football game and all of a sudden the man on the loudspeaker calls for a doctor it's an emergency. Not during a holiday, you think. You think so? You think not during a holiday? You think so? In a forest even, by yourself, one day you notice how the deer are diseased or how the rivers are dried up—something."

"Come on inside, Mr. Bieberman," he said.

"Preminger, listen to me. Do me a favor, yeah? Tomorrow when you get back to the city, maybe you could call up those people and tell them what the lifeguard told you. You're the only one who knew about it."

The old man lighted a cigarette. He could see the glowing tip pulsating softly as Bieberman spoke. He tried to see his face but it was too dark.

"You're crazy," Preminger said finally.

"I'm responsible," he said sadly. "I just don't have the nerve."

"Well, I'm not responsible," Preminger said.

"You are, Preminger."

Preminger got up quickly. He walked across the darkened wing of the porch and came abruptly into the slanting yellow light. Bieberman called him and he turned around. "Preminger," he said. "I mean it, tell them you heard me brag once how I saved a couple hundred bucks." Preminger shook his head and started carefully down the steps, afraid he would stumble in the dark. "Preminger, I mean it," Bieberman called.

He took the rest of the steps quickly, forgetting the danger. He discovered, surprised, he was going toward the empty pool. So many times now, after he had already made them, he had discovered the pointlessness of his gestures, his un-willed movements. Ah, I *am* abandoned, he thought, surrendering. He turned around. A light was on in Norma's room. He could still hear Bieberman calling his name. He stood among the beach umbrellas on the wide dark lawn and listened to the old man's desperate voice. "Preminger, Preminger." It was as if he were hiding and the old man had been sent out to look for him. "Preminger, I mean it."

All right, he thought, all right, damn it, all right. He would wait until the morning and then he would go to Norma's room and apologize and they would go back to the city together and he might investigate some jobs and they might continue to see each other and, after a while, perhaps, he might ask her to marry him.

THE
GUEST

On Sunday, Bertie walked into an apartment building in St. Louis, a city where, in the past, he had changed trains, waited for buses, or thought about Klaff, and where, more recently, truckers dropped him, or traveling salesmen stopped their Pontiacs downtown just long enough for him to reach into the back seat for his trumpet case and get out. In the hallway he stood before the brass mailboxed wall seeking the name of his friend, his friends' friend really, and his friends' friend's wife. The girl had danced with him at parties in the college town, and one night—he imagined he must have been particularly pathetic, engagingly pathetic—she had kissed him. The man, of course, patronized him, asked him questions that would have been more vicious had they been less naïve. He remembered he rather enjoyed making his long, patient answers. Condescension always brought the truth out of him. It was more appealing than indifference at least, and more necessary to him now. He supposed he didn't care for either of them, but he couldn't go further. He had to rest or he would die.

He found the name on the mailbox—Mr. and Mrs. Richard Preminger—the girl's identity, as he might have guessed, swallowed up in the husband's. It was no way to treat women, he thought gallantly.

He started up the stairs. Turning the corner at the second landing, he saw a man moving cautiously downward, burdened by boxes and suitcases and loose bags. Only as they passed each other did Bertie, through a momentary clearing in the boxes, recognize Richard Preminger.

"Old man, old man," Bertie said.

"Just a minute," Preminger said, forcing a package aside with his chin. Bertie stood, half a staircase above him, leaning against the wall. He grinned in the shadows, conscious of his ridiculous fedora, his eye patch rakishly black against the soft whiteness of his face. Black-suited, tiny, white-fleshed, he posed above Preminger, dapper as a scholarly waiter in a restaurant. He waited until he was recognized.

"Bertie? Bertie? Let me get rid of this stuff. Give me a hand, will you?" Preminger said.

"Sure," Bertie said. "It's on my family crest. One hand washing the other. Here, wait a minute." He passed Preminger on the stairs and held the door for him. He followed him outside.

"Take the key from my pocket, Bertie, and open the trunk. It's the blue convertible."

Bertie put his hand in Preminger's pocket. "You've got nice thighs," he said. To irritate Preminger he pretended to try to force the house key into the trunk lock. Preminger stood impatiently behind him, balancing his heavy burdens. "I've been to Dallas, lived in a palace," Bertie said over his shoulder. "There's this great Eskimo who blows down there. Would you believe he's cut the best side ever recorded of 'Mood Indigo'?" Bertie shook the key ring as if it were a castanet.

Preminger dumped his load on the hood of the car and took the keys from Bertie. He opened the trunk and started to throw things into it. "Going somewhere?" Bertie asked.

"Vacation," Preminger said.

"Oh," Bertie said.

Preminger looked toward the apartment house. "I've got to go up for another suitcase, Bertie."

"Sure," Bertie said.

He went up the stairs behind Preminger. About halfway up he stopped to catch his breath. Preminger watched him curiously. He pounded his chest with his tiny fist and grinned weakly. "*Mea culpa*," he said. "Mea booze, Mea sluts. Mea pot. Me-o-mea."

"Come on," Preminger said.

They went inside and Bertie heard a toilet flushing. Through a hall, through an open door, he saw Norma, Preminger's wife, staring absently into the bowl. "If she moves them now you won't have to stop at God knows what kind of place along the road," Bertie said brightly.

Norma lifted a big suitcase easily in her big hands and came into the living room. She stopped when she saw Bertie. "Bertie! Richard, it's Bertie."

"We bumped into each other in the hall," Preminger said.

Bertie watched the two of them look at each other.

"You sure picked a time to come visiting, Bertie," Preminger said.

"We're leaving on our vacation, Bertie," Norma said.

"We're going up to New England for a couple of weeks," Preminger told him.

"We can chat for a little with Bertie, can't we, Richard, before we go?"

"Of course," Preminger said. He sat down and pulled the suitcase next to him.

"It's very lovely in New England." Bertie sat down and crossed his legs. "I don't get up there very regularly. Not my territory. I've found that when a man makes it in the Ivy League he tends to forget about old Bertie," he said sadly.

"What are you doing in St. Louis, Bertie?" Preminger's wife asked him.

"It's my Midwestern swing," Bertie said. "I've been down

South on the southern sponge. Opened up a whole new territory down there." He heard himself cackle.

"Who did you see, Bertie?" Norma asked him.

"You wouldn't know her. A cousin of Klaff's."

"Were you living with her?" Preminger asked.

Bertie shook his finger at him. The Premingers stared glumly at each other. Richard rubbed the plastic suitcase handle. In a moment, Bertie thought, he would probably say, "Gosh, Bertie, you should have written. You should have let us know." He should have written! Did the Fuller Brush man write? Who would be home? Who *wouldn't* be on vacation? They were commandos, the Fuller Brush man and he. He was tired, sick. He couldn't move on today. Would they kill him because of their lousy vacation?

Meanwhile the Premingers weren't saying anything. They stared at each other openly, their large eyes in their large heads on their large necks largely. He thought he could wait them out. It was what he *should* do. It should have been the easiest thing in the world to wait out the Premingers, to stare them down. Who was he kidding? It wasn't his forte. He had no forte. *That* was his forte. He could already hear himself begin to speak.

"Sure," he said. "I almost married that girl. Klaff's lady cousin. The first thing she ever said to me was, 'Bertie, they never build drugstores in the middle of the block. Always on corners.' It was the truth. Well, I thought, this was the woman for me. One time she came out of the ladies' john of a Greyhound bus station and she said, 'Bertie, have you ever noticed how public toilets often smell like bubble gum?' That's what it was like all the time. She had all these institutional insights. I was sure we could make it together. It didn't work out." He sighed.

Preminger stared at him, but Norma was beginning to soften. He wondered randomly what she would be like in bed. He looked coolly at her long legs, her wide shoulders. Like Klaff's cousin: institutional.

"Bertie, how are your eyes now?" she asked.

"Oh," he said, "still seeing double." He smiled. "Two for one. It's all right when there's something to look at. Other times I use the patch."

Norma seemed sad.

"I have fun with it," he said. "It doesn't make any difference which eye I cover. I'm ambidexterous." He pulled the black elastic band from his forehead. Instantly there were two large Richards, two large Normas. The Four Premingers like a troupe of Jewish acrobats. He felt surrounded. In the two living rooms his four hands fumbled with the two patches. He felt sick to his stomach. He closed one eye and hastily replaced the patch. "I shouldn't try that on an empty stomach," he said.

Preminger watched him narrowly. "Gee, Bertie," he said finally, "maybe we could drop you some place."

It was out of the question. He couldn't get into a car again. "Do you go through Minneapolis, Minnesota?" he asked indifferently.

Preminger looked confused, and Bertie liked him for a moment. "We were going to catch the Turnpike up around Chicago, Bertie."

"Oh, Chicago," Bertie said. "I can't go back to Chicago yet."

Preminger nodded.

"Don't you know anybody else in St. Louis?" Norma asked.

"Klaff used to live across the river, but he's gone," Bertie said.

"Look, Bertie . . ." Preminger said.

"I'm fagged," Bertie said helplessly, "locked out."

"Bertie," Preminger said, "do you need any money? I could let you have twenty dollars."

Bertie put his hand out mechanically.

"This is stupid," Norma said suddenly. "Stay *here*."

"Oh, well—"

"No, I mean it. Stay *here*. We'll be gone for two weeks. What difference does it make?"

Preminger looked at his wife for a moment and shrugged. "Sure," he said, "there's no reason you *couldn't* stay here. As a matter of fact you'd be doing us a favor. I forgot to cancel the newspaper, the milk. You'd keep the burglars off. They don't bother a place if it looks lived in." He put twenty dollars on the coffee table. "There might be something you need," he explained. Bertie looked carefully at them both. They seemed to mean it. Preminger and his wife grinned at him steadily, relieved at how easily they had come off. He enjoyed the idea himself. At last he had a real patron, a real matron. "Okay," he said.

"Then it's settled," Preminger said, rising.

"It's all right?" Bertie said.

"Certainly it's all right," Preminger said. "What harm could you do?"

"I'm harmless," Bertie said.

Preminger picked up the suitcase and led his wife toward the door. "Have a good time," Bertie said, following them. "I'll watch things for you. Rrgghh! Rrrgghhhfff!"

Preminger waved back at him as he went down the stairs. "Hey," Bertie called, leaning over the banister, "did I tell you about that crazy Klaff? You know what nutty Klaff did out at U.C.L.A.? He became a second-story man." They were already down the stairs.

Bertie pressed his back against the door and turned his head slowly across his left shoulder. He imagined himself photographed from underneath. "Odd man in," he said. He bounded into the center of the living room. I'll bet there's a lease, he thought. I'll bet there's a regular lease that goes with this place. He considered this respectfully, a little awed. He couldn't remember ever having been in a place where the tenants actually had to sign a lease. In the dining room he turned on the chandelier lights. "Sure there's a lease," Bertie said. He hugged himself. "How the fallen are mighty," he said.

In the living room he lay down on the couch without taking off his shoes. He sat up and pulled them off, but when he lay down again he was uneasy. He had gotten out of the habit, living the way he did, of sleeping without shoes. In his friends' leaseless basements the nights were cold and he wore them for warmth. He put the shoes on again, but found that he wasn't tired any more. It was a fact that dependence gave him energy. He was never so alert as when people did him favors. It was having to be on your own that made you tired.

"Certainly," Bertie said to the committee, "it's scientific. We've suspected it for years, but until our researchers divided up the town of Bloomington, Indiana, we had no proof. What our people found in that community was that the orphans and bastards were sleepy and run down, while the housewives and people on relief were wide awake, alert, raring to go. We can't positively state the link yet, but we're fairly certain that it's something to do with dependency—in league perhaps with a particularly virulent form of gratitude. Ahem. Ahem."

As he lectured the committee he wandered around the apartment, touring from right to left. He crossed from the living room into the dining room and turned right into the kitchen and then right again into Preminger's small study. "Here's where all the magic happens," Bertie said, glancing at the contour chair near Preminger's desk. He went back into the kitchen. "Here's where all the magic happens," he said, looking at Norma's electric stove. He stepped into the dining room and continued on, passing Norma's paintings of picturesque side streets in Mexico, of picturesque side streets in Italy, of picturesque side streets in Puerto Rico, until he came to a door that led to the back sun parlor. He went through it and found himself in a room with an easel, with paints in sexy little tubes, with brushes, with palettes and turpentine and rags. "Here's where all the magic happens," Bertie said and walked around the room to another door. He opened it and was in the Premingers' master bedroom. He looked at the bed. "Here's where all the magic happens," he said. Through a door at the other end of the room was another small hall. On the right was the toilet. He went in and flushed it. It was one of those toilets with instantly renewable tanks. He flushed it again. And again. "The only kind to have," he said out of the side of his mouth, imagining a rental agent. "I mean, it's like this. Supposing the missus has diarrhea or something. You don't want to have to wait until the tank fills up. Or suppose you're sick. Or suppose you're giving a party and it's mixed company. Well, it's just corny to whistle to cover the noise, know what I mean? 'S jus' corny. On the other hand, you flush it once suppose you're not through, then what happens? There's the damn noise after the water goes down. What have you accomplished? This way"—he reached across and jiggled the little lever and then did it a second time, a third, a fourth—"you never have any embarrassing interim, what we in the trade call 'flush lag.' "

He found the guest bedroom and knew at once that he would never sleep in it, that he would sleep in the Premingers' big bed.

"Nice place you got here," he said when he had finished the tour.

"Dooing de woh eet ees all I tink of, what I fahting foe," the man from the Underground said. "Here ees eet fahrproof, air-condizione and safe from Nazis."

"Stay out of Volkswagens, kid," Bertie said.

He went back into the living room. He wanted music, but it was a cardinal principle with him never to blow alone. He would drink alone, take drugs alone, but somehow for him the depths of depravity were represented by having to play jazz alone. He had a vision of himself in a cheap hotel room sitting on the edge of an iron bedstead. Crumpled packages of cigarettes were scattered throughout the room. Bottles of gin were on top of the Gideon Bible, the Western Union blanks. His trumpet was in his lap. "Perfect," Bertie said. "Norma Preminger could paint it in a picture." He shuddered.

The phonograph was in the hall between the dining room and living room. It was a big thing, with the AM and the FM and the short wave and the place where you plugged in the color television when it was perfected. He found records in Preminger's little room and went through them rapidly. "Ahmad Jamahl, for Christ's sake." Bertie took the record out of its sleeve and broke it across his knee. He stood up slowly and kicked the fragments of the broken recording into a neat pile.

He turned around and scooped up as many of Preminger's recordings as he could carry and brought them to the machine. He piled them on indiscriminately and listened with visible, professional discomfort. He listened to *The New World Symphony*, to Beethoven's *Fifth*, to *My Fair Lady*. The more he listened the more he began to dislike, the Premingers. When he could stand it no longer he tore the playing arm viciously away from the record and looked around him. He saw the Premingers' bookcase.

"I'll read," Bertie said.

He took down the Marquis de Sade and Henry Miller and Ronald Firbank and turned the pages desultorily. Nothing happened. He tried reading aloud in front of a mirror. He went back to the bookcase and looked for *The Egg and I* and *Please Don't Eat the Daisies*. The prose of a certain kind of bright housewife always made Bertie feel erotic. But the Premingers owned neither book. He browsed through Rachel Carson's *Silent Spring* with his fly unzipped, but he felt only a mild lasciviousness.

He went into their bedroom and opened the closet. He found a pair of Norma's shoes and put them on. Although he was no fetishist, he had often promised himself that if he ever had the opportunity he would see what it was like. He got into drag and walked around the apartment in Norma's high heels. All he experienced was a pain in his calves.

In the kitchen he looked into the refrigerator. There were some frozen mixed vegetables in the freezer compartment. "I'll starve first," Bertie said.

He found a Billie Holiday record and put it on the phonograph. He hoped that out in Los Angeles, Klaff was being beaten with rubber hoses by the police. He looked up at the kitchen clock. "Nine," he said. "Only seven in L.A. They probably don't start beating them up till later."

"Talk, Klaff," he snarled, "or we'll drag you into the Blood Room."

"Flake off, copper," Klaff said.

"That's enough of that, Klaff. Take that and that and that."

"*Bird lives!*" Bertie screamed suddenly, invoking the dead Charlie Parker. It was his code cry.

"Mama may have," Billie Holiday wailed, "Papa may have, but God Bless the child who's got his own, who—oo—zz—"

"Who—oo—zz," Bertie wailed.

"Got his own," Billie said.

"I'll tell him when he comes in, William," Bertie said.

He waited respectfully until Billie was finished and then turned off the music.

He wondered why so many people felt that Norman Mailer was the greatest living American novelist.

He sat down on the Premingers' coffee table and marveled at his being alone in so big and well-furnished an apartment. The Premingers were probably the most substantial people he knew. Though plenty of the others wanted to, Bertie thought bitterly, Preminger was the only one from the old crowd who might make it. Of course he was Jewish, and that helped. Some Jews swung pretty good, but he always suspected that in the end they would hold out on you. But then who wouldn't, Bertie wondered. Kamikaze pilots, maybe. Anyway, this was Bertie's special form of anti-Semitism and he cherished it. Melvin Gimpel, for example, his old roommate. Every time Melvin tried to kill himself by sticking his head in the oven he left the kitchen window open. One time he found Gimpel on his knees with his head on the oven door, oddly like the witch in Hansel and Gretel. Bertie closed the window and shook Gimpel awake.

"Mel," he yelled, slapping him. "*Mel.*"

"Bertie, go way. Leave me alone, I want to kill myself."

"Thank God," Bertie said. "Thank God I'm in time. When I found that window closed I thought it was all over."

"What, the window was closed? My God, was the *window* closed?"

"Melvin Gimpel is so simple
Thinks his nipple is a pimple,"

Bertie recited.

He hugged his knees, and felt again a wave of the nauseous sickness he had experienced that morning. "It's foreshadowing. One day as I am shoveling my walk I will collapse and die."

When the nausea left him he thought again about his situation. He had friends everywhere and made his way from place to place like an old-time slave on the Underground Railway. For all the pathos of the figure he knew he deliberately cut, there were always people to do him favors, give him money, beer, drugs, to nurse him back to his normal state of semi-invalidism, girls to kiss him in the comforting way he liked. This was probably the first time he had been alone in months. He felt like a dog whose master has gone away for the weekend. Just then he heard some people coming up the stairs and he growled experimentally. He went down on his hands and knees and scampered to the door, scratching it with his nails. "Rrrgghhf," he barked. "Rrgghhfff!" He heard whoever it was fumbling to open a door on the floor below him. He smiled. "Good dog," he said. "Good dog, goodog, gudug, gudugguduggudug."

He whined. He missed his master. A tear formed in the corner of his left eye. He crawled to a full-length mirror in the bathroom. "Ahh," he said. "Ahh." Seeing the patch across his eye, he had an inspiration. "Here, Patch," he called. "Come on, Patch." He romped after his own voice.

He moved beside Norma Preminger's easel in the sun parlor. He lowered his body carefully, pushing himself slightly backward with his arms. He yawned. He touched his chest to the wooden floor. He wagged his tail and then let himself fall heavily on one side. He pulled his legs up under him and fell asleep.

When Bertie awoke he was hungry. He fingered the twenty dollars in his pocket that Preminger had given him. He could order out. The light in the hall where the phone and phone books were was not good, so he tore "Restaurants" from the Yellow Pages and brought the sheets with him into the living room. Only two places delivered after one A.M. It was already one-thirty. He dialed the number of a pizza place across the city. "Pal, bring over a big one, half shrimp, half mushroom. And two six-packs." He gave the address. The man explained that the truck had just gone out and that he shouldn't expect delivery for at least another hour and a half.

"Put it in a cab," Bertie said. "While Bird lives Bertie spends." He took out another dozen or so records and piled them on the machine. He sat down on the couch and drummed his trumpet case with his fingers. He opened the case and fit the mouthpiece to the body of the horn. He put the trumpet to his lips and experienced the unpleasant shock of cold metal he always felt. He still thought it strange that men could mouth metal this way, ludicrous that his professional attitude should be a kiss. He blew a few bars in accompaniment to the record and then put the trumpet back in the case. He felt in the side pockets of the trumpet case and took out two pairs of dirty underwear, some handkerchiefs and three pairs of socks. He unrolled one of the pairs of socks and saw with pleasure that the drug was still there. He took out the bottle of carbon tetrachloride. This was what he cleaned his instrument with, and it was what he would use to kill himself when he had finally made the decision.

He held the bottle to the light. "If nothing turns up," he said, "I'll drink this. And to hell with the kitchen window."

The cab driver brought the pizza and Bertie gave him the twenty dollars.

"I can't change that," the driver said.

"Did I ask you to change it?" Bertie said.

"That's twenty bucks there."

"Bird lives. Easy come, easy go go go," Bertie said.

The driver started to thank him.

"Go." He closed the door.

He spread Norma Preminger's largest tablecloth over the dining-room table and then, taking china and silver from the big breakfront, laid several place settings. He found champagne glasses.

Unwrapping the pizza, he carefully plucked all the mushrooms from it ("American mushrooms," he said. "Very square. No visions.") and laid them in a neat pile on the white linen. ("Many mushloom," he said. "Mushloom crowd.") He poured some beer into a champagne glass and rose slowly from his chair.

"Gentlemen," he said, "to the absent Klaff. May the police in Los Angeles, California, beat his lousy ass off." He drank off all the beer in one gulp and tossed the glass behind him over his shoulder. He heard it shatter and then a soft sizzling sound. Turning around, he saw that he had hit one of Norma's paintings right in a picturesque side street. Beer dripped ignobly down a donkey's leg. "Goddamn," Bertie said appreciatively, "*action painting.*"

He ate perhaps a quarter of the pizza before rising from the table, wiping the corner of his lips with a big linen napkin. "Gentlemen," he said. "I propose that the ladies retire to the bedroom while we men enjoy our cigars and port and some good talk."

"I propose that we men retire to the bedroom and enjoy the ladies," he said in Gimpel's voice.

"Here, here," he said in Klaff's voice. "Here, here. Good talk. Good talk."

"If you will follow me, gentlemen," Bertie said in his own voice. He began to walk around the apartment. "I have often been asked the story of my life. These requests usually follow a personal favor someone has done me, a supper shared, a bed made available, a ride in one of the several directions. Indeed, I have become a sort of troubadour who does not sing so much as whine for his supper. Most of you—"

"Whine is very good with supper," Gimpel said.

"Gimpel, my dear, why don't you run into the kitchen and play?" Bertie said coolly. "Many of you may know the humble beginnings, the sordid details, the dark Freudian patterns, and those of you who are my friends—"

Klaff belched.

"Those of you who are my *friends*, who do not run off to mix it up with the criminal element in the far West, have often wondered what will ultimately happen to me, to 'Poor Bertie' as I am known in the trade."

He unbuttoned his shirt and let it fall to the floor. In his undershirt he looked defenseless, his skin pale as something seen in moonlight. "Why, you wonder, doesn't he do something about himself, pull himself up by his bootstraps? Why, for example, doesn't he get his eyes fixed? Well, I've tried."

He kicked off his shoes. "You have all admired my bushy mustache. Do you remember that time two years ago I dropped out of sight for four months? Well, let me tell you what happened that time."

He took off his black pants. "I had been staying with Royal Randle, the distinguished philologist and drunk. You will recall what Royal, Klaff, Myers, Gimpel and myself once were to each other. Regular Whiffenpoofs we were. Damned from here to eternity. Sure, sure." He sighed. "You remember Randle's promises: 'It won't make any difference, Bertie. It won't make any difference, Klaff. It won't make any difference, fellas.' He married the girl in the muu-muu."

He was naked now except for his socks. He shivered once and folded his arms across his chest. "Do you know why the girl in the muu-muu married Randle?" He paused dramatically. "*To get at me, that's why!* The others she didn't care about. She knew even before I did what they were like. Even what *Klaff* was like. She knew they were corrupt, that they had it in them to sell me out, to settle down—that all anyone had to do was wave their deaths in front of them and they'd come running, that reason and fucking money and getting it steady would win again. But in me she recognized the real enemy, the last of the go-to-hell-god-damn-its. Maybe the first.

"They even took me with them on their honeymoon. At the time I thought it was a triumph for dependency, but it was just a trick, that's all. The minute they were married, this girl in the muu-muu was after Randle to do something about Bertie. And it wasn't 'Poor' Bertie this time. It was she who got me the appointment with the mayor. Do you know what His Honor said to me? 'Shave your mustache and I'll give you a job clerking in one of my supermarkets.' Christ, friends, do you know I *did* it? Well, I'm not made of stone. They had taken me on their honeymoon, for God's sake."

He paused.

"I worked in that supermarket *for three hours*. Clean-shaved. My mustache sacrificed as an earnest to the mayor. Well, I'm telling you, you don't know what square *is* till you've worked in a supermarket for three hours. They pipe in Mantovani. Mantovani! I cleared out for four months to raise my mustache again and to forget. What you see now isn't the original, you understand. It's all second growth, and believe me it's not the same."

He drew aside the shower curtain and stepped into the tub. He paused with his hand on the tap. "But I tell you this, friends. I would rather be a mustached bum than a clean-shaved clerk. I'll work. Sure I will. When they pay anarchists! When they subsidize the hip! When they give grants to throw bombs! When they shell out for gainsaying!"

Bertie pulled the curtain and turned on the faucet. The rush of water was like applause.

After his shower Bertie went into the second bedroom and carefully removed the spread from the cot. Then he punched the pillow and mussed the bed. "Very clever," he said. "It wouldn't do to let them think I never slept here." He had once realized with sudden clarity that he would never, so long as he lived, make a bed.

Then he went into the other bedroom and ripped the spread from the big double bed. For some time, in fact since he had first seen it, Bertie had been thinking about this bed. It was the biggest bed he would ever sleep in. He thought invariably in such terms. One cigarette in a pack would suddenly become distinguished in his mind as the best, or the worst, he would smoke that day. A homely act, such as tying his shoelaces, if it had occurred with unusual ease, would be remembered forever. This lent to his vision an oblique sadness, conscious as he was that he was forever encountering experiences which would never come his way again.

He slipped his naked body between the sheets, but no sooner had he made himself comfortable than he became conscious of the phonograph, still playing in the little hall. He couldn't hear it very well. He thought about turning up the volume, but he had read somewhere about neighbors. Getting out of bed, he moved the heavy machine through the living room, pushing it with difficulty over the seamed, bare wooden floor, trailing deep scratches. Remember not to walk barefoot there, he thought. At one point one of the legs caught in a loop of the Premingers' shag rug and Bertie strained to free it, finally breaking the thick thread and producing an interesting pucker along one end of the rug, not unlike the pucker in raised theatrical curtains. At last he had maneuvered the machine into the hall just outside the bedroom and plugged it in. He went back for the Billie Holiday recording he had heard earlier and put it on the phonograph. By fiddling with the machine, he fixed it so that the record would play all night.

Bertie got back into the bed. "Ah," he said, "the *sanctum sanctorum*." He rolled over and over from one side of the bed to the other. He tucked his knees into his chest and went under the covers. "It makes you feel kind of small and insignificant," he said.

"Ladies and gentlemen, this is Graham Macnamee speaking to you from the Cave of the Winds. I have made my way into the heart of this darkness to find my friend, Poor Bertie, who, as you know, entered the bed eight weeks ago. Bertie is with me now, and while there isn't enough light for me to be able to see his condition, his voice may tell us something about his physical state. Bertie, just what *is* the official record?"

"Well, Graham, some couples have been known to stick it out for seventy-five years. Of course, your average is much less than that, but still—"

"Seventy-five years."

"Seventy-five, yes sir. It's amazing, isn't it, Graham, when you come to think? All that time in one bed."

"It certainly is," Graham Macnamee said. "Do you think you'll be able to go the distance, Bert?"

"Who, me? No, no. A lot of folks have misunderstood my purpose in coming here. I'm rather glad you've given me the opportunity to clear that up. Actually my work here is scientific. This isn't a stunt or anything like that. I'm here to learn."

"Can you tell us about it, Bert?"

"Graham, it's been a fascinating experience, if you know what I mean, but frankly there are many things we still don't understand. *I* don't know why they do it. All that licit love, that regularity. Take the case of Richard and Norma, for example—and incidentally, you don't want to overlook the significance of that name 'Norma.' Norma/Normal, you see?"

"Say, I never thought of that."

"Well, I'm trained to think like that, Graham. In my work you have to."

"Say," Graham Macnamee said.

"Sure. Well, the thing is this, buddy, when I first came into this bed I felt the aura, know what I mean, the *power*. I think it's built into the mattress or something."

"Say."

"Shut your face, Graham, and let me speak, will you please? Well, anyway, you feel surrounded. Respectable. Love is made here, of course, but it's not love as we know it. There are things that must remain mysteries until we have more facts. I mean, Graham, checks could be cashed in this bed, for Christ's sake, credit cards honored. It's ideal for family reunions, high teas. Graham, it's the kind of place you wouldn't be ashamed to take your mother."

"Go to sleep, Bert," Graham Macnamee said.

"Say," Bertie said.

Between the third and fourth day of his stay in the Premingers' apartment Bertie became restless. He had not been outside the house since the Sunday he arrived, even to bring in the papers Preminger had told him about. (Indeed, it was by counting the papers that he knew how long he had been there, though he couldn't be sure, since he didn't know whether the Premingers had taken the Sunday paper along with them.) He could see them on the back porch through the window of Norma's sun parlor. With the bottles of milk they made a strange little pile. After all, he was not a caretaker; he was a guest. Preminger could bring in his own papers, drink his own damn milk. For the same reasons he had determined not even to answer the phone when it rang.

One evening he tried to call Klaff at the Los Angeles County Jail, but the desk sergeant wouldn't get him. He wouldn't even take a message.

Although he had not been outside since Sunday, Bertie had only a vague desire to leave the apartment. He weighed this against his real need to rest and his genuine pleasure in being alone in so big a place. Like the man in the joke who does not leave his Miami hotel room because it is costing him thirty-five dollars a day, Bertie decided he had better remain inside.

With no money left he was reduced to eating the dry, cold remainder of the pizza, dividing it mathematically into a week's provisions, like someone on a raft. (He actually fancied himself, not on a raft perhaps, but set alone and drifting on, say, the *Queen Mary*.) To supplement the pizza he opened some cans of soup he found in the pantry and drank the contents straight, without heating it or even adding water. Steadily he drank away at the Premingers' modest stock of liquor. The twelve cans of beer had been devoured by the second morning, of course.

After the second full day in the apartment his voices began to desert him. It was only with difficulty that he could manage his imitations, and only for short lengths of time. The glorious discussions that had gone on long into the night were now out of the question. He found he could not do Gimpel's voice any more, and even Klaff's was increasingly difficult and largely confined to his low, caressing obscenities. Mostly he talked with himself, although it was a real strain to keep up his end of the conversation, and it always made him cry when he said how pathetic he was and asked himself where do you go from here. Oh, to be like Bird, he thought. Not to have to be a bum. To ask, as it were, no quarter.

At various times during the day he would call out "Bird lives" in seeming stunning triumph. But he didn't believe it.

He watched a lot of television. "I'm getting ammunition," he said. "It's scientific."

Twice a day he masturbated in the Premingers' bed.

He settled gradually, then, into restlessness. He knew, of course, that he had it always in his power to bring himself back up to the heights he had known in those wonderful first two days. He was satisfied, however, not to use this power, and thought of himself as a kind of soldier, alone in a foxhole, in enemy territory, at night, at a bad time in the war, with one bullet in his pistol. Oddly, he derived more pride—and comfort, and a queer security—from this single bullet than others might have from whole cases of ammunition. It was his *strategic* bullet, the one he would use to get the big one, turn the tide, make the difference. The Premingers would be away two weeks. He would not waste his ammunition. Just as he divided the stale pizza, cherishing each piece as much for the satisfaction he took from possessing it during a time of emergency as for any sustenance it offered, so he enjoyed his knowledge that at any time he could recoup his vanishing spirits. He shared with the squares ("Use their own weapons to beat them, Bertie") a special pride in adversity, in having to do without, in having to expose whatever was left of his character to the narrower straits. It was strange, he thought seriously, it was the paradox of the world and an institutional insight that might have come right out of the mouth of that slut in Dallas, but the most peculiar aspect of the squares wasn't their lack of imagination or their bland bad taste, but their ability, like the wildest fanatics, like the furthest out of the furthest out, to cling to the illogical, finally untenable notion that they must have and have in order to live, at the same time that they realized that it was better not to have. What seemed so grand to Bertie, who admired all impossible positions, was that they believed both things with equal intensity, never suspecting for a moment any inconsistency. And here was Bertie, Bertie thought, here was Bertie inside their capitol, on the slopes of their mountains, on their smooth shores, who believed neither of these propositions, who believed in not having and in not suffering too, who yet realized the very same pleasure that they would in having and not using. It was the strangest thing that would ever happen to him, he thought.

"Are you listening, Klaff, you second-story fink?" Bertie yelled. "Do you see how your old pal is developing what is called character?"

And so, master of himself for once, he resolved—feeling what someone taking a vow feels—not to use the last of his drugs until the strategic moment of strategic truth.

That was Wednesday evening. By Thursday morning he had decided to break his resolution. He had not yielded to temptation, had not lain fitfully awake all night—indeed, his resolution had given him the serenity to sleep well—in the sweaty throes of withdrawal. There had been no argument or rationalization, nor had he decided that he had reached his limit or that this was the strategic moment he had been waiting for. He yielded as he always yielded: spontaneously, suddenly, unexpectedly, as the result neither of whim nor of calculation. His important decisions were almost always reached without his knowledge, and he was often as surprised as the next one to see what he was going to do—to see, indeed, that he was already doing it. (Once someone had asked him whether he believed in Free Will, and after considering this for a moment as it applied to himself, Bertie had answered "Free? Hell, it's positively *loose*.")

Having discovered his new intention, he was eager to realize it. As often as he had taken drugs (he never called it anything but drugs, never used the cute or obscene names, never even said "dope"; to him it was always "drugs," medicine for his spirit), they were still a major treat for him. "It's a rich man's game," he had once told Klaff, and then he had leaned back philosophically. "You know, Klaff, it's a good thing I'm poor. When I think of the snobbish ennui of your wealthy junkies, I realize that they don't know how to appreciate their blessings. God keep me humble, Klaff. Abstinence makes the heart grow fonder, a truer word was never spoken."

Nor did a drug ever lose its potency for him. If he graduated from one to another, it was not in order to recover some fading jolt, but to experience a new and different one. He held in contempt all those who professed disenchantment with the drugs they had been raised on, and frequently went back to rediscover the old pleasures of marijuana, as a sentimental father might chew some of his boy's bubble gum. "Loyalty, Gimpel," he exclaimed, "loyalty, do you know what *that* is?"

Bertie would and did try anything, though currently his favorite was mescaline for the visions it induced. Despite what he considered his eclectic tastes in these matters, there were one or two things he would not do, however. He never introduced any drug by hypodermic needle. This he found disgusting and, frankly, painful. He often said he could stand anything but pain and was very proud of his clear, unpunctured skin. "Not a mark on me," he would say, waving his arms like a professional boxer. The other thing he would not do was take his drugs in the presence of other users, for he found the company of addicts offensive. However, he was not above what he called "seductions." A seduction for him was to find some girl and talk her into letting him share his drugs with her. Usually it ended in their lying naked in a bed together, both of them serene, absent of all desire and what Bertie called "unclean thoughts."

"You know," he would say to the girl beside him, "I think that if all the world's leaders would take drugs and lie down on the bed naked like this without any unclean thoughts, the cause of world peace would be helped immeasurably. What do you think?"

"I think so too," she would say.

Once he knew he was going to take the drug, Bertie made his preparations. He went first to his trumpet case and took out the last small packet of powder. He opened it carefully, first closing all the windows so that no sudden draft could blow any of it away. This had once happened to a friend of his, and Bertie had never forgotten the warning.

"I am not one on whom a lesson is lost," Bertie said.

"You're okay, Bertie," a Voice said. "Go save France."

He placed the packet on the Premingers' coffee table and carefully spread the paper, exactly like the paper wrapper around a stick of chewing gum, looking almost lustfully at the soft, flat layer of ground white powder. He held out his hand to see how steady it was, and although he was not really shaky he did not trust himself to lift the paper from the table. He brought a water tumbler from the kitchen and gently placed it upside down on top of the powder. He was not yet ready to take it. Bertie was a man who postponed his pleasures as long as he possibly could; he let candy dissolve in his mouth and played with the threads on his tangerine before eating the fruit. It was a weakness in his character perhaps, but he laid it lovingly at the feet of his poverty.

He decided to wait until sundown to take the drug, reasoning that when it wore off, it would be early next morning and he would be ready for bed. Sleep was one of his pleasures too, and he approved of regularity in small things, taking a real pride in being able to keep hours. To pass the time until sundown he looked for something to do. First he found some tools and busied himself by taking Norma's steam iron apart. There was still time left after that, so he took a canvas and painted a picture. Because he did not know how to draw he simply covered the canvas first with one color and then with another, applying layer after layer of the paint thickly. Each block of color he made somewhat smaller than the last, so that the finished painting portrayed successive jagged margins of color. He stepped back and considered his work seriously.

"Well, it has texture, Bertie," Hans Hoffman said.

"Bertie," the Voice said suddenly, "I don't like to interrupt when you're working, but it's sundown."

"So it is," he said, looking up.

He went back into the living room and removed the tumbler. Taking up the paper in his fingers and creasing it as if he were a cowboy rolling a cigarette, Bertie tilted his head far back and inhaled the powder deeply. This part was always uncomfortable for him. "Ooo," he said, "the bubbles." He stuffed the last few grains up his nose with his fingers. "Waste not, want not," he said.

He sat down to wait. After half an hour in which nothing happened, Bertie became uneasy. "It's been cut," he said. "Sure, depend upon friends to do you favors." He was referring to the fact that the mescaline had been a going-away present from friends in Oklahoma City. He decided to give it fifteen more minutes. "Nothing," he said at last, disappointed. "Nothing."

The powder, as it always did, left his throat scratchy, and there was a bitter taste in his mouth. His soft palate prickled. He seized the water tumbler from the coffee table and walked angrily into the kitchen. He ran the cold water, then gargled and spit in the sink. In a few minutes the bitter taste and the prickly sensation subsided and he felt about as he had before he took the drug. He was conscious, however, of a peculiar smell, unpleasant, unfamiliar, nothing like the odor of rotting flowers he associated with the use of drugs. He opened a window and leaned out, breathing the fresh air. But as soon as he came away from the window, the odor was again overpowering. He went to see if he could smell it in the other rooms. When he had made his tour he realized that the stench *must* be coming from the kitchen. Holding his breath, he came back to see if he could locate its source. The kitchen was almost as Norma had left it. He had done no cooking, and although there were some empty soup and beer cans in the sink he knew *they* couldn't be causing the odor. He shrugged. Then he noticed the partially closed door to Preminger's study.

"Of course," Bertie said. "Whatever it is must be in there." He pushed the door open. In the middle of the floor were two blackish mounds that looked like dark sawdust. Bertie stepped back in surprise.

"Camel shit," he said. "My God, how did *that* get in here?" He went closer to investigate. "That's what it is, all right." He had never seen it before but a friend had, and had described it to him. This stuff fitted the description perfectly. He considered what to do.

"I can't leave it there," he said. He found a dustpan and a broom, and propping the pan against the leg of Preminger's chair, began to sweep the stuff up. He was surprised at how remarkably gummy it seemed. When he finished he washed the spot on the floor with a foaming detergent and stepped gingerly to the back door. He lifted the lid of the garbage can and shoved the broom and the contents of the dustpan and the dustpan itself into the can. Then he went to the bathroom and washed his hands.

In the living room he saw the Chinaman. "Jesus," Bertie said breathlessly.

The Chinaman lowered his eyes in a shy, almost demure smile. He said nothing, but motioned Bertie to sit in the chair across from him. Bertie, too frightened to disobey, sat down.

He waited for the Chinaman to tell him what he wanted. After an hour (he heard the chime clock strike nine times and then ten times), when the Chinaman still had not said anything, he began to feel a little calmer. Maybe he was just tired, Bertie thought, and came in to rest. He realized that perhaps he and the China-man had more in common than had at first appeared. He looked at the fellow in this new light and saw that he had been foolish to fear him. The Chinaman was small, smaller even than Bertie. In fact, he was only two feet tall. Perhaps what made him seem larger was the fact that he was wrapped in wide, voluminous white silk robes. Bertie stared at the robes, fascinated by the del-icate filigree trim up and down their length. To see this closer he stood up and walked tentatively toward the Chinaman.

The Chinaman gazed steadily to the front, and Bertie, seeing no threat, continued toward him. He leaned down over the Chinaman, and gently grasping the delicate lacework between his forefinger and his thumb, drew it toward his eye. "May I?" Bertie asked. "I know a good deal about this sort of thing."

The Chinaman lowered his eyes.

Bertie examined the weird symbols and designs, and although he did not understand them, recognized at once their cabalistic origin.

"Magnificent," Bertie said at last. "My God, the man hours that must have gone into this. *The sheer craftsmanship!* That's really a terrific robe you've got there."

The Chinaman lowered his eyes still further.

Bertie sat down in his chair again. He heard the clock strike eleven and he smiled at the Chinaman. He was trying to be sym-pathetic, patient. He knew the fellow had his reasons for coming and that in due time they would be revealed, but he couldn't help being a little annoyed. First the failure of the drug and then the camel shit on the floor and now this. However, he remained very polite.

There was nothing else to do, so he concentrated on the Chinaman's face.

Then a strange thing happened.

He became aware, as he scrutinized the face, of some things he hadn't noticed before. First he realized that it was the oldest face he had ever seen. He knew that this face was old enough to have looked on Buddha's. It was only *faintly* yellow, really, and he understood with a sweeping insight that originally it must have been white, as it still largely was, a striking, flat white, naked as a sheet, bright as teeth, that its yellowness was an intrusion, the intruding yellowness of fantastic age, of pages in ancient books. As soon as he perceived this he understood the origin and mystery of the races. All men had at first been white; their different tints were only the shades of their different wisdoms. Of course, he thought. Of course. It's beautiful. Beautiful!

The second thing Bertie noticed was that the face seemed extraordinarily wise. The longer he stared at it the wiser it seemed. Clearly this was the wisest Chinaman, and thus the wisest man, in the history of the world. Now he was impatient for the Chinaman to speak, to tell him his secrets, but he also understood that so long as he was impatient the Chinaman would *not* speak, that he must become serene, as serene as the Chinaman himself, or else the Chinaman would go away. As this occurred to him the Chinaman smiled and Bertie knew he had been right. He was aware that if he just sat there, deliberately trying to become serene, nothing would happen. He decided that the best way to become serene was to ignore the Chinaman, to go on about his business as if the Chinaman weren't even there.

He stood up. "Am I getting warm?" Bertie asked.

The Chinaman lowered his eyes and smiled.

"Well, then," Bertie said, rubbing his hands, "let's see."

He went into the kitchen to see if there was anything he could do there to make him serene.

He washed out the empty cans of soup.

He strolled into the bedroom and made the bed. This took him an hour. He heard the clock strike twelve and then one.

He took a record off the machine, and starting from the center hole and working to the outer edge, counted all the ridges. This took him fourteen seconds.

He found a suitcase in one of the closets and packed all of Norma's underwear into it.

He got a pail of water and some soap and washed all the walls in the small bedroom.

It was in the dining room, however, that he finally achieved serenity. He studied Norma's pictures of side streets throughout the world and with sudden insight understood what was wrong with them. He took some tubes of white paint and with a brush worked over the figures, painting back into the flesh all their original whiteness. He made the Mexicans white, the Negroes white, feeling as he worked an immense satisfaction, the satisfaction not of the creator, nor even of the reformer, but of the restorer.

Swelling with serenity, Bertie went back into the living room and sat down in his chair. For the first time the Chinaman met his gaze directly, and Bertie realized that something important was going to happen.

Slowly, very slowly, the Chinaman began to open his mouth. Bertie watched the slow parting of the Chinaman's thin lips, the gleaming teeth, white and bright as fence pickets. Gradually the rest of the room darkened and the thinly padded chair on which Bertie sat grew incredibly soft. He knew that they had been transported somehow, that they were now in a sort of theater. The Chinaman was seated on a kind of raised platform. Meanwhile the mouth continued to open, slowly as an ancient drawbridge. Tiny as the Chinaman was, the mouth seemed enormous. Bertie gazed into it, seeing nothing. At last, deep back in the mouth, he saw a brief flashing, as of a small crystal on a dark rock suddenly illuminated by the sun. In a moment he saw it again, brighter now, longer sustained. Soon it was so bright that he had to force himself to look at it. Then the mouth went black. Before he could protest, the brightness was overwhelming again and he saw a

cascade of what seemed like diamonds tumble out of the Chinaman's mouth. It was the Chinaman's tongue.

Twisting, turning over and over like magicians' silks pulled
endlessly from a tube, the tongue continued to pour from the
Chinaman's mouth. Bertie saw that it had the same whiteness as
the rest of his face, and that it was studded with bright, beautiful
jewels. On the tongue, long now as an unfurled scroll, were thick
black Chinese characters. It was the secret of life, of the world,
of the universe. Bertie could barely read for the tears of gratitude
in his eyes. Desperately he wiped the tears away with his fists.
He looked back at the tongue and stared at the strange words,
realizing that he could not read Chinese. He was sobbing helplessly now because he knew there was not much time. The presence of the Chinaman gave him courage and strength and he
forced himself to read the Chinese. As he concentrated it became
easier, the characters somehow re-forming, translating themselves into a sort of decipherable Chinesey script, like the words
"Chop Suey" on the neon sign outside a Chinese restaurant. He
was breathless from his effort and the stunning glory of what
was being revealed to him. Frequently he had to pause, punctuat-
ing his experience with queer little squeals. "Oh," he said. "Oh.
Oh."

Then it was over.

He was exhausted, but his knowledge glowed in him like fire.
"So *that's* it" was all he could say. "So *that's* it. So *that's* it."

Bertie saw that he was no longer in the theater. The Chinaman was gone and Bertie was back in the Premingers' living
room. He struggled for control of himself. He knew it was urgent that he tell someone what had happened to him. Desperately
he pulled open his trumpet case. Inside he had pasted sheets with
the names, addresses and phone numbers of all his friends.

"Damn Klaff," he said angrily. "Damn Second-Story Klaff in
his lousy jail."

He spotted Gimpel's name and the phone number of his boarding house in Cincinnati. Tearing the sheet from where it was

pasted inside the lid, he rushed to the phone and placed the call. "Life and death," he screamed at Gimpel's bewildered landlady. "Life and death."

When Gimpel came to the phone Bertie began to tell him, coherently, but with obvious excitement, all that had happened. Gimpel was as excited as himself.

"Then the Chinaman opened his mouth and this tongue with writing on it came out."

"Yeah?" Gimpel said. "Yeah? Yeah?"

"Only it was in Chinese," Bertie shouted.

"Chinese," Gimpel said.

"But I could read it, Gimpel! *I could read it!*"

"I didn't know you could read Chinese," Gimpel said.

"It was the meaning of life."

"Yeah?" Gimpel said. "Yeah? What'd it say? What'd it say?"

"What?" Bertie said.

"What'd it say? What'd the Chink's tongue say was the meaning of life?"

"I forget," Bertie said and hung up.

He slept until two the next afternoon, and when he awoke he felt as if he had been beaten up. His tongue was something that did not quite fit in his mouth, and throughout his body he experienced a looseness of the bones, as though his skeleton were a mobile put together by an amateur. He groaned dispiritedly, his eyes still closed. He knew he had to get up out of the bed and take a shower and shave and dress, that only by making extravagant demands on it would his body give him any service at all. "You *will* make the Death March," he warned it ruthlessly.

He opened his eyes and what he saw disgusted him and turned his stomach. His eye patch had come off during the night and now there were two of everything. He saw one eye patch on one pillow and another eye patch on another pillow. Hastily he grabbed for it, but he had chosen the wrong pillow. He reached for the other eye patch and the other pillow, but somehow he had put out one of his illusory hands. It did not occur to him to shut one eye. At last, by covering all visible space, real or illusory, with all visible fingers, real or illusory—like one dragging a river—he recovered the patch and pulled it quickly over one of his heads.

He stood stunned in his hot shower, and then shaved, cutting his neck badly. He dressed.

"Whan 'e iz through his toilette, *Monsieur* will see how much better 'e feel," his valet said. He doubted it and didn't answer.

In the dining room he tried not to look at Norma's paintings, but could not help noticing that overnight many of her sunny side streets had become partial snow scenes. He had done that, he remembered, though he could not now recall exactly why. It seemed to have something to do with a great anthropological discovery he had made the night before. He finished the last of the pizza, gagging on it briefly.

Considering the anguish of his body, it suddenly occurred to him that perhaps he was hooked. Momentarily this appealed to his sense of the dramatic, but then he realized that it would be a terrible thing to have happen to him. He could not afford to be hooked, for he knew with a sense of calm sadness that his character could no more sustain the responsibility of a steady drug habit than it could sustain the responsibility of any other kind of pattern.

"Oh, what a miserable bastard I am," Bertie said.

In near-panic he considered leaving the Premingers' apartment immediately, but he knew that he was in no condition to travel. "You wouldn't make it to the corner," he said.

He felt massively sorry for himself. The more he considered it the more certain it appeared that he was hooked. It was terrible. Where would he get the money to buy the drugs? What would they do to his already depleted physical resources? "Oh, what a miserable bastard I am," he said again.

To steady himself he took a bottle of Scotch from the shelf in the pantry. Bertie did not like hard liquor. Though he drank a lot, it was beer he drank, or, when he could get them, the sweeter cordials. Scotch and bourbon had always seemed vaguely square to him. But he had already finished the few liqueurs that Preminger had, and now nothing was left but Scotch. He poured himself an enormous drink.

Sipping it calmed him—though his body still ached—and he considered what to do. If he *was* hooked, the first thing was to tell his friends. Telling his friends his latest failure was something Bertie regarded as a sort of responsibility. Thus his rare letters to them usually brought Bertie's intimates—he laughed at the word—nothing but bad news. He would write that a mistress had given him up, and, with his talent for mimicry, would set down her last long disappointed speech to him, in which she exposed in angry, honest language the hollowness of his character, his infinite weakness as a man, his vileness. When briefly he had turned to homosexuality to provide himself with funds, the first thing he did was write his friends about it. Or he wrote of being fired from bands when it was discovered how bad a trumpeter he really was. He spared neither himself nor his friends in his passionate self-denunciations.

Almost automatically, then, he went into Preminger's study and began to write all the people he could think of. As he wrote he pulled heavily at the whiskey remaining in the bottle. At first the letters were long, detailed accounts of symptoms and failures and dashed hopes, but as evening came on and he grew inarticulate he realized that it was more important—and, indeed, added to the pathos of his situation—for him just to get the facts to them.

"Dear Klaff," he wrote at last, "I am hooked. I am at the bottom, Klaff. I don't know what to do." Or "Dear Randle, I'm hooked. Tell your wife. I honestly don't know where to turn." And "Dear Myers, how are your wife and kids? Poor Bertie is hooked. He is thinking of suicide."

He had known for a long time that one day he would have to kill himself. It would happen, and even in the way he had imagined. One day he would simply drink the bottle of carbon tetrachloride. But previously he had been in no hurry. Now it seemed like something he might have to do before he had meant to, and what he resented most was the idea of having to change his plans.

He imagined what people would say.

"I let him down, Klaff," Randle said.

"Everybody let him down," Klaff said.

"Everybody let him down," Bertie said. "Everybody let him down."

Weeping, he took a last drink from Preminger's bottle, stumbled into the living room and passed out on the couch.

That night Bertie was awakened by a flashlight shining in his eyes. He threw one arm across his face defensively and struggled to sit up. So clumsy were his efforts that whoever was holding the flashlight started to laugh.

"Stop that," Bertie said indignantly, and thought, I have never been so indignant in the face of danger.

"You said they were out of town," a voice said. The voice did not come from behind the flashlight, and Bertie wondered how many there might be.

"Jesus, I thought so. Nobody's answered the phone for days. I never seen a guy so plastered. He stinks."

"Kill him," the first voice said.

Bertie stopped struggling to get up.

"Kill him," the voice repeated.

"What is this?" Bertie said thickly. "What is this?"

"Come on, he's so drunk he's harmless," the second voice said.

"Kill him," the first voice said again.

"You kill him," the second voice said.

The first voice giggled.

They were playing with him, Bertie knew. Nobody who did not know him could want him dead.

"Turn on the lights," Bertie said.

"Screw that," the second voice said. "You just sit here in the dark, sonny, and you won't get hurt."

"We're wasting time," the first voice said.

A beam from a second flashlight suddenly intersected the beam from the first.

"Say," Bertie said nervously, "it looks like the opening of a supermarket."

Bertie could hear them working in the dark, moving boxes, pulling drawers.

"Are you folks Negroes?" Bertie called. No one answered him. "I mean I dig Negroes, man—*men*. Miles. Jay Jay. Bird lives." He heard a closet door open.

"You *are* robbing the place, right? I mean you're actually *stealing*, aren't you? This isn't just a social call. Maybe you know my friend Klaff."

The men came back into the living room. From the sound of his footsteps Bertie knew one of them was carrying something heavy.

"I've got the TV," the first voice said.

"There are some valuable paintings in the dining room," Bertie said.

"Go see," the first voice said.

One of Norma's pictures suddenly popped out of the darkness as the man's light shone on it.

"Crap," the second voice said.

"You cats can't be all bad," Bertie said.

"Any furs?" It was a third voice, and it startled Bertie. Someone flashed a light in Bertie's face. "Hey, you," the voice repeated, "does your wife have any furs?"

"Wait a minute," Bertie said as though it were a fine point they must be made to understand, "you've got it wrong. This isn't *my* place. I'm just taking care of it while my friends are gone." The man laughed.

Now all three flashlights were playing over the apartment. Bertie hoped a beam might illuminate one of the intruders, but this never happened. Then he realized that he didn't want it to happen, that he was safe as long as he didn't recognize any of them. Suddenly a light caught one of the men behind the ear. "Watch that light. Watch that light," Bertie called out involuntarily.

"I found a trumpet," the second voice said.

"Hey, that's mine," Bertie said angrily. Without thinking, he got up and grabbed for the trumpet. In the dark he was able to get his fingers around one of the valves, but the man snatched it away from him easily. Another man pushed him back down on the couch.

"Could you leave the carbon tetrachloride?" Bertie asked miserably.

In another ten minutes they were ready to go. "Shouldn't we do something about the clown?" the third voice said.

"Nah," the second voice said.

They went out the front door.

Bertie sat in the darkness. "I'm drunk," he said after a while. "I'm hooked and drunk. It never happened. It's still the visions. The apartment is a vision. The darkness is. Everything."

In a few minutes he got up and wearily turned on the lights. Magicians, he thought, seeing even in a first glance all that they had taken. Lamps were gone, curtains. He walked through the apartment. The TV was gone. Suits were missing from the closets. Preminger's typewriter was gone, the champagne glasses, the silver. His trumpet was gone.

Bertie wept. He thought of phoning the police, but then wondered what he could tell them. The thieves had been in the apartment for twenty minutes and he hadn't even gotten a look at their faces.

Then he shuddered, realizing the danger he had been in. "Crooks," he said. "Killers." But even as he said it he knew it was an exaggeration. He had never been in any danger. He had the fool's ancient protection, his old immunity against consequence.

He wondered what he could say to the Premingers. They

would be furious. Then, as he thought about it, he realized that this too was an exaggeration. They would not be furious. Like the thieves they would make allowances for him, as people always made allowances for him. They would forgive him; possibly they would even try to give him something toward the loss of his trumpet.

Bertie began to grow angry. They had no right to patronize him like that. If he was a clown it was because he had chosen to be. It was a way of life. Why couldn't they respect it? He should have been hit over the head like other men. How dare they forgive him? For a moment it was impossible for him to distinguish between the thieves and the Premingers.

Then he had his idea. As soon as he thought of it he knew it would work. He looked around the apartment to see what he could take. There was some costume jewelry the thieves had thrown on the bed. He scooped it up and stuffed it in his pockets. He looked at the apartment one more time and then got the hell out of there. "Bird lives," he sang to himself as he raced down the stairs. "He lives and lives."

It was wonderful. How they would marvel! He couldn't get away with it. Even the far West wasn't far enough. How they hounded you if you took something from them! He would be back, no question, and they would send him to jail, but first there would be the confrontation, maybe even in the apartment itself: Bertie in handcuffs, and the Premingers staring at him, not understanding and angry at last, and something in their eyes like fear.

IN
THE
ALLEY

Four months after he was to have died, Mr. Feldman became
very bored. He had been living with his impending death for
over a year, and when it did not come he grew first impatient,
then hopeful that perhaps the doctors had made a mistake, and
then—since the pains stayed with him and he realized that he
was not, after all, a well man—bored. He was not really sure
what to do. When he had first been informed by the worried-
looking old man who was his physician that the disquieting thing
he felt in his stomach was malignant, he had taken it for granted
that some role had been forced upon him. He knew at once, as
though he had been expecting the information and had long since
decided his course, what shape that role had to assume, what
measures his unique position had forced him to. It was as if until
then his intuitions had been wisely laid by, and now, thriftlessly,
he might spend them in one grand and overwhelming indulgence.
As soon as the implications of the word "malignant" had settled
peaceably in his mind, Feldman decided he must (it reduced to
this) become a hero.

Though the circumstances were not those he might have
chosen had he been able to determine them, there was this, at
least: what he was going to do had about it a nice sense of

rounded finality. Heroism depended upon sacrifice, and that which he was being forced to sacrifice carried with it so much weight, was so monumental, that he could not, even if he were yet more critical of himself than he was, distrust his motives. Motives, indeed, had nothing to do with it. He was not motivated to die; he was motivated to live. His heroism was that he *would* die and did not want to.

The doctor, who would know of and wonder at Feldman's generous act, could serve as an emotional check to the whole affair. He could represent, in a way, the world; thus Feldman, by observing the doctor observing him, might be in a better position to determine whether or not he was going too far.

While Feldman had known with certainty the exact dimension of his heroism, it was almost a disappointment to understand that heroism, in his particular situation, demanded nothing, and therefore everything. It demanded, simply, acquiescence. He must, of course, tell no one. But this was not the drawback. It was, indeed, the one advantage he was sure of, since heroism, *real* heroism, like real treachery, was the more potent for being done in the dark. He knew that the hero who performed his services before an audience risked a surrender to pride, chanced a double vision of himself: a view of himself as he must appear before those who would judge him. All that frightened Feldman was his awareness that his peculiar situation allowed him the same opportunity for change that might come to ordinary men during the course of normal lifetimes—permitting it, moreover, to occur in the split second of his essentially unnatural act. His chance for heroism, then, stretched-out as it had to be by the doctor's pronouncement that he had still one year to live, was precariously and unfortunately timed. For a year he must go on as he had gone on, work for what he had worked for, talk to others as he had talked to others. In this way his heroism would be drawn out, but there would be the sustained temptation to self-awareness, to sweet but inimical self-consciousness. Since the essence of his role was to pretend that he was playing none, he would have to prevent any knowledge of the wonderful change wrought in himself, even at the moment of his death.

Feldman set upon his course and performed conscientiously everything he thought was required of him. That is, he did until the others found him out. They had, seeing signs of his physical discomfort, pressed the doctor for information. Urged from the beginning by his patient to say nothing, the doctor told them some elaborate lie about ulcers. So, on top of his other discomfitures, Feldman's family saw to it that he remained on a strict diet, directed toward dissolving a nonexistent ulcer. When his family saw that his pains continued, and the doctor refused to carry the joke to the uncomfortable extreme of operating on what did not in fact exist, the family realized that far graver things than they had been led to believe were wrong with Feldman.

The doctor, under pressure and understandably unwilling to invent further (and anyway he himself, though old, though experienced, though made accustomed by years of practice of his art to the melodramatic issue of his trade, had, despite his age, his experience, his familiarity with crises, still maintained a large measure of that sentimental attachment which the witness to tragedy has toward great rolling moments of life and death: an attachment which, indeed, had first attracted him to medicine and had given him that which in his superb flair for the dramatic would have been called in men of lesser talent their "bedside manner," but which, in him, soared beyond the bedside—beyond, in fact, the sickroom itself to the family in the waiting room, the nurses in the corridor, to the whole hospital, in fact), thought it best that others learn of Feldman's sacrifice, and so went back on his promise and told the anxious family everything. They were, of course, astounded, and misread Feldman's composure as a sign of solicitude lest he might hurt them. Feldman's anger at having been found out was badly translated into a magnificent display of unselfishness. They thought, in their innocence, that he had merely meant not to worry them. Had they had any insight, however, they would have realized, at some cost to their pride, that far from the secrecy of his suffering being unendurable to him, contemplation of it had provided him with his only source of comfort (he had gone back that quickly on his resolves), and that what they had mistaken for unselfishness was Feldman's last desperate attempt to exploit the self. But in a game where certain feelings, of necessity, masquerade as certain others, what is so is hardly to be distinguished from what is *not* so. What they, in their blindness, had forced upon Feldman was the one really unendurable feature of his illness. What had come to him gratuitously—his immediate, heroic reaction to the prospect of his own death—had now to be called back, reappraised, withdrawn.

Feldman had now to compose himself and deliberately scheme out what he was to do with the remainder of his life. He was now the prisoner of his freedom of choice. Further heroism (pretending that death meant nothing) would be ludicrous with all of them looking on, their eyes shielded by impossible lace handkerchiefs. It was almost better deliberately to impale himself upon their sympathies, to cry out for water in the middle of the night, to languish visibly before their frightened stares, to call to strangers in the street, "Look, look, I'm dying."

With their discovery of his situation, what he had hoped would be the dignified end of his life threatened in fact to become a stagey, circusy rout, rather like the disorganized, sentimental farewell of baseball fans to a team moving forever to another city. And since he would not soon die (the one year he had been given had already extended itself to sixteen months and there were no visible signs of any acceleration of his decay) he became rather annoyed with his position. He quickly discovered that planning one's death had as many attendant exigencies as planning one's life. Were he a youth, a mistake in planning could be neutralized, even changed perhaps to an unexpected asset; the simple fact was that he had no time. That he was still alive four months after his year of grace indicated only a mistake in calculation, not in diagnosis. Strangely, the additional four months served to make his expected end more imminent for him.

He found himself suddenly an object. On Sundays, distant cousins and their children would make pilgrimages to his home to see him. They meant no harm, he knew, but in a way they had come for a kind of thrill, and when they discovered this they grew uncomfortable in his presence. Ashamed of what they suddenly realized were their motives, they secretly blamed him for having forced their tastes into a debauch. Others, not so sensitive, made him a hero long after he himself had dismissed this as a possibility. A nephew of his, who consistently mistook in himself as legitimate curiosity what was only morbid necrophilism, would force him into ridiculous conversations which the boy considered somehow ennobling. On one occasion he had completely shocked Feldman.

"Do you find yourself believing in an after-life?"

"I think that's in poor taste," Feldman said.

"No, what I mean is that before it happens, lots of people who had never been particularly religious before suddenly find themselves slipping into a kind of wish-fulfillment they call faith."

"Stop that," Feldman told him angrily.

After his conversation with his nephew Feldman realized something he found very disturbing. He knew that he had not, after all, accepted his death as a very real possibility. Though he had made plans and changed them, though he had indulged in protean fantasies in which he had gone alone to the edge of sheer marble precipices, he had been playing merely. It was as if he had been toying with the idea of a "grim reaper," playing intellectual games with chalky skeletons and bogeymen; he had not in fact thought about his death, only about his dying: the preoccupied man of affairs casually scribbling last words on a telephone memorandum pad. His nephew's absolute acceptance of the likelihood that one day Feldman would cease to exist had offended him. He had considered the boy's proposition an indelicacy, the continuance of the familiar world after his own absence from it a gross insult. He knew the enormity of such vanity and he was ashamed. He thought for the first time of other dying men, and though he knew that each man's cancer was or should be a sacred circumstance of that man's existence, he felt a sudden urgency to know such men, to submerge himself in their presence. Because he could think of no other way of doing this, he determined to speak to his doctor about having himself committed to a hospital.

It was evening and the other patients had left the old man's office. They had gone, he knew, to drugstores to obtain prescriptions which would make them well. The doctor stood over the small porcelain sink, rubbing from his hands the world's germs.

"You've been lucky," the doctor said. "The year I gave you has turned out to be much more than a year. Perhaps your luck will continue longer, but it can't continue indefinitely. Get out of your mind that there's any cure for what you have. You've been mortally wounded."

"I didn't say anything about cures."

"Then what good would a hospital be? Surely you don't mean to die in a hospital? I can't operate. There's no chance." The doctor spoke slowly, his voice soft. Obviously, Feldman thought, he was enjoying the conversation.

"What I have, this imperfection in my side, is too private to remove," Feldman said, rising to the occasion of the other's rhetoric, engaging the old man's sense of drama, his conspicuous taste for the heavy-fated wheelings of the Great Moment. Looking at the doctor, Feldman was reminded of his nephew. He felt, not unpleasantly, like an actor feeding cues. "I thought that with the others . . ."

"You're wrong. Have you ever been in a hospital room with three old men who are dying, or who think they are? Each is jealous of the others' pain. Nothing's so selfish. People die hard. The death rattle, when it comes, is a terrored whine, the scream of sirens wailing their emergency."

"You're healthy," Feldman told him. "You don't understand them."

The doctor did not answer immediately. He remained by the porcelain bowl and turned on the hot-water tap. When it was so hot that Feldman could see steam film the mirror above the sink, the doctor plunged his hands into the water. "I'm old," he finally said.

Oh no, Feldman thought; really, this was too much. Even this ridiculous old man could not contemplate another's death without insisting on his own. "But you're not dying," Feldman said. "There is nothing imminent." He noted with unreasonable sadness that he had soiled the tissue paper which covered the examination table. He stood up self-consciously. "I want to be with the others. Please arrange it."

"What could you gain from it? I'm tired of this talk. It smells of voices from the other side. Disease has taught you nothing, Feldman. When you first knew, you behaved like a man. You continued to go to business. You weren't frightened. I thought, 'This is wonderful. Here's a man who knows how to die.'"

"I didn't know I would be stared at. The others watch me, as though by rubbing against it now they can get used to it."

"I had a patient," the doctor said, "who had more or less what you have. When I told him he was to die, his doom lifted from him all the restraints he had ever felt. He determined to have the most fun he could in the time he had left. He left here a dangerous, but a reasonably contented, man."

"Of course," Feldman said. "I've thought about this too. It's always the first thing that occurs to you after the earthquakes and the air raids, after the ice cream truck overturns. It's a strong argument. To make off with all you can before the militia comes. I feel no real compulsion to appease myself, to reward myself for dying. Had I been forced to this, I would have been forced to it long before I learned I must die. For your other patient, nothing mattered. To me, things matter very much. We're both selfish. Will you send me to the hospital?"

The ring of steam had thickened on the mirror. Feldman could see no reflection, only a hazy riot of light. The doctor told him he would make the arrangements.

At first the rituals of the hospital room strangely excited Feldman. He watched the nurses eagerly as they came into the four-bed ward to take temperatures and pulses. He studied their professional neutrality as they noted the results of blood pressure readings on the charts. When he could he read them. When they brought medication to the men in the other beds, Feldman asked what each thing was, what it could be expected to do. By casually observing the activity in the room, Feldman discovered that he could keep tabs on the health of the others, despite what even the men themselves might tell him when he asked how they were feeling.

He soon knew, though, that his was an outsider's view, a casualness that was the result of a life's isolation from disease, the residual prejudice of the healthy that somehow the sick are themselves to blame for what is wrong with them. Realizing this, he deliberately tried to negate those techniques which had come naturally to him while he was still the stranger in the room. He would have to acknowledge himself their diseased ally. If his stay in the hospital were to help him at all, he knew he had willfully to overcome all reluctance. Thus, he began to watch everything with the demanding curiosity of a child, as though only through a constant exercise of what once he might have considered bad taste could he gain important insight into the processes of life and death. He began, then, non-judiciously to observe everything. It was a palpable disappointment to him when a doctor or a nurse had occasion to place a screen around the bed of one of the other patients, and often he would ask the man after the nurse had gone what had been done for him.

Even the meals they ate together were a new experience for him. There was something elemental in the group feedings.

Everything about the eating process became familiar to him. He examined their trays. He studied the impressions their teeth made on unfinished pieces of bread. He stared at bones, bits of chewed meat; he looked for saliva left in spoons. Everything was pertinent. Processes he had before considered inviolate now all had a place in the design. When a nurse brought a bedpan for one of the men and he sat straight up in his bed and pulled the sheet high up over his chest, Feldman would not look away.

He asked them to describe their pain.

The others in the room with Feldman were not, as the doctor had predicted they would be, old men. Only one, the man in the bed next to his own, was clearly older than Feldman. But if they were not as aged as he had expected, they *were* as sick. The chronic stages of their illnesses—even the fetid patterns of the most coarse inroads of their decay—were somehow agreeable to Feldman and seemed to support his decision to come to the hospital. These men shared with him, if not his own unconditional surrender of the future, then certainly a partial disavowal of it; and if they counted on getting better, at least they did not make the claims on that future which Feldman had found (it came to this) so disagreeable in others. It had been suggested to them that they might not get well. They considered this seriously and acknowledged, once they understood the nature of their conditions, the unpleasant priority of doom. Only then did they hire their doctors, call in their specialists, retire from their businesses, and set themselves resolutely to the task of getting well. This much Feldman could accept as long as—and here he drew an arbitrary line—they behaved like gentlemen. He found in the sick what he had wanted to find: a group of people who knew their rights, but would not insist on them. Their calm was his own assurance that his instincts had been right, and so what little he said to them was to encourage them in that calm.

One morning the youngest of the four, a college boy who had been stricken with a severe heart attack, showed signs of rapid weakening. He had vomited several times and was in great pain. Someone called the nurse. Seeing the serious pallor of the suffering man, she called the intern. The intern, a nervous young doctor who gave the air of being at once supremely interested in the patient's convulsions and supremely incapable of rising to their occasion, immediately dispatched a call for the boy's doctor.

"It seems," the boy said, smiling weakly, "that I won't be able to die until all of them have examined me."

It was for Feldman precisely the right note. "Hang on," he said to him. "If you feel yourself going, ask for a specialist from Prague."

The boy laughed and did not die at all. Feldman attributed this to some superior element in this patient's character which fell halfway between resolutely dignified determination and good sportsmanship.

He had come, he knew, to a sort of clearing house for disease, and sometimes at night (he did not sleep much) he could visualize what seemed to him to be the tremendous forces of destruction at work in the room. His own cancer he saw as some horribly lethal worm that inched its way through his body, spraying on everything it touched small death. He saw it work its way up through the channels of his body and watched as pieces of it fell from his mouth when he spit into his handkerchief. He knew that inside the other men something like the same dark ugliness worked with a steady, persevering ubiquity, and supposed that the worm was pridefully aware that its must be the triumph.

One night as Feldman lay between sleep and wakefulness, there came a terrible groan from the next bed. He looked up quickly, not sure he had not made the sound himself. It came again, as if pushed out by unbearable pain. Feldman buried his head in the pillow to smother the sound, but the groan continued. It was a noise that started deep in the man's chest and became at last a gasping yell for breath. Feldman lay very still. He did not want the man to know he was awake. Such pain could not continue long. He would lie quietly and wait it out. When the noise did not stop, Feldman held his breath and bit his lips. There was such urgency in the screams, nothing of gentlemanly relinquishment. He was about to give in to the overbearing insistence of the man's pain, but before he could force himself to do something he heard the sick man push himself nearer. Feldman turned his face to watch, and in the glow from the red night lamp above the door he could see that the man lay half out of the bed. He was trying, with a desperate strength that came from somewhere deep inside, to reach Feldman. He watched as the man's hand clawed the air as though it were some substance by which he could sustain himself. He called to him, but Feldman could not answer.

"Mister, mister. You up?"

The hand continued to reach toward Feldman until the wild strength in it pulled the man off balance and the upper half of his body was thrust suddenly toward the floor. He was almost completely out of the bed.

"Mister. Mister. Please, are you up?"

Feldman forced himself to say yes.

The man groaned again.

"Do you want me to get the nurse?" Feldman asked him.

"Help me. Help me in the bed."

Feldman got out of bed and put his arms around the man's body. The other worked his arms around Feldman's neck and they remained for a moment in a crazy embrace. Suddenly all his weight fell heavily in Feldman's arms. Feldman feared the man was dead and half lifted, half pushed him back onto the bed. He listened carefully and heard at last, gratefully, spasms of breath. They sounded like sobs.

He was an old man. Whatever he had been like before, his contact and exchange with what Feldman had come to think of as a kind of poisoned, weathering rain, had left his skin limp, flaccid. (He had discovered that people die from the outside in.)

After a minute the man opened his eyes. He looked at Feldman, who still held him, leaning over his bed with his arms around his shoulders as though to steady them.

"It's gone now," the man said. His breath was sweetly sick, like garbage fouled by flies and birds. "I'm better."

The man closed his eyes and lowered his head on his chest. "I needed," he said after a while, "someone's arms to hold me. At the house my daughter would come when I cried. My wife couldn't take it. She's not so well herself, and my daughter would come to hold me when I cried from the pain. She's just a teen-ager." The man sobbed.

Feldman took his hands from the man's shoulders and sat on the edge of the bed.

"It's all right," the man said. "Nothing will happen now. I'm sorry I made a nuisance."

"You'll be all right?"

"Sure. Yes. I'm good now."

Feldman watched the man's hand draw the blanket up over him. He held the blanket as one would hold the reins of a horse. The man turned his face away, and Feldman got up and started to go back to his own bed. "Mister," the man called. Feldman turned quickly around. "Mister, would you ring the nurse? I think . . . I think I wet myself."

After that, in the last stages of the man's last illness, the disease multiplied itself; it possessed him, occupied him like an angry invader made to wait too long in siege beyond the gates. For Feldman it represented a stage in the process of decay he knew he might some day reach himself. When he spoke to the man he found that what he really wanted to say circled somewhere above them both like an unsure bird. It became increasingly difficult for him to speak to him at all. Instead, he lay quietly at night when in the urgency of his remarkable pain the man screamed, and pretended he was asleep. He could stand it only a week. Like the man's wife, Feldman thought, I am not so well myself. No, I

am not so very damned well myself. And one more thing, disso-
lution and death are not as inscrutable as they're cracked up to
be. They're scrutable as hell. I'm tired, Feldman thought, of all
this dying.

Once he had determined to leave he was impatient. He had
wasted too much time already. He had been, he realized, so in
awe of death that he had cut his own to his notions of it as a tailor
cuts cloth to his model.

He moved quickly. That morning, while the old man slept and
the two others were in private sections of the hospital for treat-
ment, Feldman dressed. He hoped that the nurse would not come
in. "Don't you groan. Be still," he silently addressed the sleeping
body in the next bed. In the closet he found his clothes where the
nurse had hung them. When he put them on he discovered that
though he had worn them into the hospital only a few weeks
before, they were now too big for him. They hung, almost without shape, over a body he did not remember until he began to
clothe it. He dressed quickly, but could not resist tying his tie
before the mirror in the bathroom. Knotting and reknotting it,
adjusting the ends, gave him pleasure, imposed a kind of happi-
ness.

He started to leave the room, but something held him. It was a
vase of flowers set carefully on the window sill. The flowers had
been a gift for the old man. They had been there for several days
and now were fading. He walked to the window, lifted the vase
and took it with him into the hospital corridor.

He waited until a student nurse came by. "Miss," Feldman
called after her softly. "Miss." The nurse did not recognize him.
"I want you to give these flowers to Feldman in Room 420." She
looked at the decayed blossoms. Feldman shrugged and said,
"Alas, poor man, he's dying. I did not want to offend him with
anything too bright." The nurse, bewildered, took the flowers he
pushed into her hands. Feldman walked to the elevator and
jabbed at the button. When the elevator did not come at once, he

decided he couldn't wait and took the four flights of steps down. At the main desk in the lobby he had an inspiration. "How is Feldman, Room 420?" he asked the receptionist.

The girl thumbed through the card file in front of her. When she found his card she said, "Feldman, sir? He's satisfactory."

"I understood he was very sick. Condemned."

The girl looked again at the card. "My card says 'Satisfactory.' "

"Oh," Feldman said.

"That only means he's comfortable. In these terminal cases that's all they ever say."

"Satisfactory? Comfortable? Why doesn't the hospital tell him? He'd be pleased."

"I beg your pardon?"

"Sure," Feldman said.

Outside, it occurred to him that since he had been partner to him in everything else, he would call his doctor. He went into a drugstore and dialed.

"It's me. It's Feldman. I'm out."

"Where are you, Feldman?" the doctor asked.

"In a phone booth. You've cured me. You've made me well. I wanted to thank you."

"What are you talking about? Where are you?"

"I told you. I've left the hospital. That idea of mine about a fraternity among the sick? It wasn't any good. I just blackballed myself. A man almost died in my room a few days ago and it paralyzed me. I couldn't help him. I held him away from me as though he were soiled linen."

"Get back to the hospital."

"What for?"

"What am I going to say, that you're cured? The charts still exist."

"So do I. I'm not going back. I'm going to business."

"You're in no condition to go to business. Do you want to aggravate an already untenable position?"

"You are maybe the world's all-time lousy doctor. You promised death. Now you threaten it. You said a year, and I sat down to wait. Well, I'm not waiting any more, that's all." He wondered if the old doctor's passion for rhetoric were still strong in him. He decided to try him. "On every occasion I am going to hit for the solar plexus of the solar system," Feldman said.

There was silence. Then the doctor, calmer, said, "I'll call your wife."

Outside the drugstore the sun was shining brightly and everything looked clean and new. Feldman was aware of the keenness of his impressions, but astonished more by the world itself than by his perception of it, he wondered at the absolute luminescence of the things about him. Objects seemed bathed in their own light. Things looked not new, he decided, so much as extraordinarily well kept up.

Across the street was a park, but between the park and Feldman was a boulevard where traffic raced by swiftly. He had to dodge the cars. It was an exciting game, having to dodge cars for one's life as though death were, after all, something that could be held off by an effort of the will. The idea that he could control death made him giddy, and once, in his excitement, he almost slipped and fell. He thought, even in the act of regaining his lost balance, how strange that the death that might have resulted from his misstep would have been an accident unrelated to his disease. I've cured cancer, he thought happily.

In the park he sat down on a bench to rest. His activity had made him tired. "Slowly, slowly," he cautioned himself. He had been aware of pain in his stomach since he left the hospital. Though it was not great, it was becoming gradually more severe, and he was afraid that it would become too much for him. He found that by holding his breath and remaining very still he could control the pain. Does it hurt? he asked himself. Only when I breathe, he answered. Nevertheless, he waited until he thought he could move without reawakening what he still thought of as the slothful parasite within himself, and then he looked around.

The world he had thought he was never to see again when he entered the hospital lay now around and before him in adjacent strata, disparate but contiguous planes in space. Because of his heightened awareness it seemed compartmentalized. He had the impression that he could distinguish where each section had been sewn onto the next. He saw the wide-arced slope of grass and trees—the park. Interrupting it—the busy boulevard like an uncalm sea. Beyond the angry roll and toss of traffic and black frozen asphalt like queer, dark ice in perpetual lap against the gutters of a foreign shore—an avenue. A commercial country of bank and shop where the billboards and marquees hung appended and unfurled, annexed like gaudily partisan consulate flags—almost, it seemed to Feldman in its smugly high-tariffed insularity, like a young and enterprising foreign power. Tall apartment buildings backstopped the planet, mountain ranges stacked against the world's last margins, precarious and unbalanced. He knew that over these and beyond the curve of his world there were many leftover worlds. And the sun shone on them all. It was remarkable to him that people and worlds should be dying beneath such a sun.

A young Negro girl came by, pushing a baby carriage. She sat down on Feldman's bench.

Feldman smiled at her. "Is your baby a boy or a girl?" he asked her.

The girl laughed brightly. "My baby an elevator operator downtown. This one here is a white child, mister."

"Oh," Feldman said.

"It's okay," she said.

Feldman wondered whether she would get up now, whether she had taken him for one of the old men who sit in parks and tamper with the healthy they meet there.

He got up to go. " 'Bye, mister," the girl said.

He looked to see if she was mocking him.

He started toward the corner. He could catch a bus there. With a panic that startled the worm sleeping in his stomach and made it lurch forward, bringing him pain, he realized that in leaving the hospital he had given no thought to where he would go. He understood for the first time that when he had gone into the hospital not to be cured but to die, he had relinquished a sort of citizenship. Now he had no rights in a place given over to life. People did not come back from the grave. Others wouldn't stand for it. He could not even stay in the park, unless he was to stay as one of the old men he had for a moment feared he had become.

He could go home, of course. He could kiss his wife and explain patiently to her what had happened to him. He could tell her that his disease had been a joke between the doctor and himself—not a joke in the sense that it didn't really exist, but merely a sort of pale irony in that while it *did* exist, it did not behave as it had in others; that he was going to die, all right, but that they must both be patient.

He saw a large green and yellow bus halted at the stop light. He did not recognize its markings, but when it came abreast of him he got on. He sat up front, near the driver. When the bus had made its circuit two times, the driver turned toward Feldman.

"Okay, mister, end of the line."

"What?"

"You should have slept it off by this time. End of the line. Far as we go."

"But there are still people on the bus."

"Sorry. Company rule."

"If I pay another fare?"

"Sorry."

"Look," he started to say, but he was at a loss as to how to complete his thought. "All right," he said. "Thank you."

He got off and saw that he had come to a part of the city with which he was unfamiliar. He could not remember ever having been there before. It was a factory district, and the smoke from many furnaces forced on the day, still in its early afternoon, a twilight haze. He walked down a block to where the bare, unpainted shacks of the workers led into a half-commercial, half-residential section. He saw that secured between the slate-colored homes was more than the usual number of taverns. The windows in all the houses were smudged with the opaque soot from the chimneys. The brown shades behind them had been uniformly pulled down almost to the sills. Feldman sensed that the neighborhood had a peculiar unity. Even the deserted aspect of the streets seemed to suggest that the people who lived there acted always in concert.

The porches, their peeling paint like dead, flaking skin, were wide and empty except for an occasional piece of soiled furniture. One porch Feldman passed, old like the rest, had on it a new card table and four brightly chromed, red plastic-upholstered chairs, probably the prize in a church bingo party. The self-conscious newness of the set, out of place in the context of the neighborhood, had been quickly canceled by the universal soot which had already begun to settle over it, and which, Feldman imagined, through that same silent consent to all conditions here, had not been wiped away.

Behind the window of each tavern Feldman passed was the sign of some brewery. They hung, suspended neon signatures, red against the dark interiors. He went into one of the bars. Inside it was almost dark, but the room glowed with weird, subdued colors, as though it were lighted by a juke box which was burning out. The place smelled of urine and beer. The floor was cement, the color of an overcast sky.

There were no other men in the tavern. Two women, one the barmaid, a coarse, thick-set woman whose dirty linen apron hung loosely from her big body, stood beside an electric bowling machine. She held the hands of a small boy who was trying to intercept the heavy silver disk that the other woman, probably his mother, aimed down the sanded wooden alley of the machine.

"Let me. Let me," the boy said.

The mother, a thin girl in a man's blue jacket, was wearing a red babushka. Under it, her blond hair, pulled tightly back on her head, almost looked wet. The child continued to squirm in the older woman's grasp. The mother, looking toward a glass of beer set on the edge of the machine, spoke to the woman in the apron. "Don't let him, Rose. He'll knock over the beer."

"He wants to play."

"I'll break his hands he wants to play. Where's his dime?"

Feldman sat down on a stool at the bar. The barmaid, seeing him, let go of the child and stepped behind the bar. "What'll you have?" she said.

"Have you sandwiches?"

"Yeah. Cheese. Salami. Ham and cheese."

"Ham and cheese."

She took a sandwich wrapped in wax paper from a dusty plastic pie bell and brought it to him. "You must be new around here. Usually I say 'What'll you have?' the guy answers 'Pabst Blue Ribbon.' It's a joke."

Feldman, who had not often drunk beer even before his illness, suddenly felt a desire to have some. "I'll have some 'Pabst Blue Ribbon.' "

The woman drew it for him and put it next to his sandwich. "You a social worker?" she asked.

"No," Feldman said, surprised.

"Rose thinks every guy wears a suit he's a social worker," the blond girl said, sitting down next to him. "Especially the suit don't fit too good." The child had run to the machine and was throwing the silver disk against its back wall. The machine, still activated, bounced the disk back to him.

"Don't scratch the surface," the woman behind the bar yelled at him. "Look, he scratches the surface, the company says I'm responsible. They won't give me a machine."

"Petey, come away from the machine. Rose is gonna break your hands." Looking again at Rose, she said, "He don't even carry a case."

"Could be he's a parole officer," Rose said.

"No," Feldman said.

"We ain't used up the old one yet," the blond woman said, grinning.

Feldman felt the uncomfortable justice of these speculations, made almost as though he were no longer in the room with them. He finished his beer and held up his glass to be refilled.

"You got people in this neighborhood, mister?"

"Yes," he said. "My old grandmother lives here."

"Yeah?" the woman behind the bar said.

"What's her name?" the blond girl asked suspiciously.

Feldman looked at the thin blonde. "Sterchik," he said. "Dubja Sterchik."

"Dubja *Finklestein*," the girl said. She took off her blue jacket. Feldman saw that her arms, though thin, were very muscular. She raised her hand to push some hair that had come loose back under the tight caress of the red babushka. He saw that the inside of her white wrist was tattooed. In thin blue handwriting, the letters not much thicker than ink on an ordinary envelope, was the name "Annie." He looked away quickly, as though inadvertently he had seen something he shouldn't have, as though the girl had leaned forward and he had looked down her blouse and seen her breasts.

"I don't know nobody named Dubja Sterchik," Rose said to him. "Maybe she drinks across the street with Stanley," she added.

He finished the second glass of beer and, getting used to the taste, asked for another. He wondered whether, had they known he was a dying man, they would have been alarmed at his outlandish casualness in strolling into a strange bar in a neighborhood where he had never been. He wondered whether they would be startled to realize that he had brought to them, strangers, the last pieces of his life, giving no thought now to reclamation, since one could not reclaim, ever, what one still had, no matter how fragile or even broken it might be. He held the beer in his mouth until it burned the soft skin behind his lips. It felt good to feel pain in an area where, for once, it was not scheduled. He felt peculiarly light-hearted.

He turned to the girl beside him. "Your husband work around here?"

"Al?"

"Yes, Al. Does Al work around here?"

She nodded. "When Al works, he works around here."

Feldman smiled. He felt stirrings which were now so unfamiliar to him he had to remember deliberately what they were. The death rattle is starting in my pants, he thought, dismissing what he could not take seriously. It would not be dismissed. Instead, the warmth he felt began to crowd him, to push him into unaccustomed corners. You've got the wrong man, he thought. He was not sure, however, which instincts he encouraged, which side he was on.

Feldman was surprised to discover that he really wanted to talk to her, to tell her that he had come with his disease into their small tavern to die for them. He thought jealously of the blond girl's husband, the man Al, with lunch pail and silk team bowling jacket. She rubs him with her wounded wrist, he thought, excited.

"Would you like another drink?" he asked the girl haltingly. "Would you?" he asked again. He looked at her shabby clothes. "I just got paid today," he added.

"Why not?" she said lightly. The little boy came over to her, drew her down and whispered something in her ear. The woman looked up at Feldman. "Excuse me," she said, "he needs to pee."

"Of course," Feldman said stiffly. She took the child through a little door at the back of the tavern. When the door swung open Feldman could see cases of beer stacked on both sides of the lidless toilet. He turned to the woman behind the bar. "I want to buy a bottle of whiskey," he said to her. "We'll sit in that booth over there."

"I don't sell by the bottle. This ain't no package store."

"I'll pay you," he said.

"What are you, a jerk, mister? I run a nice place. I don't want to have to throw you out."

"It's all right. I just want to talk."

"She's got a kid."

"I just want to talk to her," he said. "Here, here," he said quietly. He reached into his pocket and pulled out two loose bills and flung them on the counter. The woman laughed at him.

"I'll be damned," she said. She handed him a bottle.

Feldman took it and walked unsteadily to the booth. When the woman brought two glasses, he poured a drink and swallowed it quickly. He felt as though a time limit had been imposed upon him, that it was all right to do anything in the world he wanted so long as he did it quickly. He saw the door at the rear of the tavern open and the girl step out. She leaned over her son, buttoning his pants. Feldman bit his lips. She straightened and, seeing Feldman sitting in the booth, glanced quickly at the woman behind the bar. The woman shrugged and held up the two five-dollar bills. The girl took the boy to the bowling machine and put a dime into its slot for him. He watched her as she came slowly toward his table. He was sure she wore no underclothing. He motioned for her to sit down. "There's more room," he said apologetically, indicating the booth.

She sat down and Feldman nodded toward her drink. "That's yours," he said. "That's for you."

"Thanks," she said absently, but made no effort to drink it. Feldman raised his own glass and touched hers encouragingly in some mute toast. She continued to stare at him blankly.

"Look," he said, "I'm bad at this. I don't know what to say to you."

She smiled, but said nothing.

"I want you to understand," he went on stiffly, "I'm not trying to be funny with you."

"Better not," she said.

"I know," Feldman said. "That girl behind the bar said she'd throw me out of here."

"Rose could do it," the girl said. "I could do it."

"Anyone can do it," Feldman said glumly. "Look, do you want me to go? Do you want to forget about it?"

"No," she said, "Just be nice is all. What's the matter with you, Jack?"

"I'm dying." He had not meant to say it. It was out of his mouth before he could do anything about it. He thought of telling her a lie, of expanding his statement to something not so preposterously silly: that he was dying of boredom, of love for her, of fear for his job. Anything with more reason behind it than simply death. It occurred to him that dying was essentially ludicrous. In any real context it was out of place. It was not merely unwelcome; it was unthinkable. Then he realized that this was what he had meant to say all along. He had no interest in the girl; his body had played tricks on him, had made him believe for a moment that it was still strong. What he wanted now was to expose it. It was his enemy. Its sexlessness was a good joke on it. He could tell her that.

"I'm dying," he said again. "I don't know what to do." He could no longer hear himself speaking. The words tumbled out of his mouth in an impotent rage. He wondered absently if he was crying. "The doctor told me I'm supposed to die, only I don't do it, do you see?"

"Go to a different doctor," the girl said.

She joked with him. It was impossible that she didn't understand. He held the worm in his jaws. It was in his stomach, in the hollows of his armpits. Pieces of it stoppered his ears. "No, no. I'm really dying. There have been tests. Everything."

"Yeah?"

"Yes. You don't know what it's like."

"You married?"

"Yes."

"Got kids, I suppose, and a family?"

"Yes."

"They know about this?"

He nodded.

"Don't care, probably, right? Hey," she said, "look at me sitting and talking to you like this. You ain't got something contagious, have you?"

"No," he said. "Where are you going?" The girl was standing. "No, don't go. Please sit down."

"I'm sorry for your trouble, mister. Thanks for the drink."

"Have another. There's a whole bottle."

She was looking down at him. He wondered if she really meant to go, whether her standing up was merely a form, a confused deference to death. She leaned toward him unexpectedly. "What is it, mister?" she said. She came to his side of the booth and sat down. "What is it, mister? Do you want to kiss me?" He was sure he had not heard her correctly. She repeated her question. She was smiling. He saw now that she had made a decision, had determined to cheat him. He didn't care.

"Yes," he answered weakly. "Would you kiss me?"

"Sure," she said, her voice level, flat. Her eyes were nowhere. She sat closer. He put his hand on her warm thighs. They were hard and thin. She put one arm around Feldman and ground her lips against his. Her kid was staring at them. Feldman could taste the girl's breath. It was foul. He put his hand inside the girl's skirt and touched her thighs. He felt nothing inside himself. There was no urgency. The girl, incorrectly gauging Feldman's responses, took his hand in one of hers and began to squeeze it. She held his wrist. Her hands, as Feldman had known they would be, were powerful. She dug her nails into his wrist. He could not get free. He tried to pull his wrist away. "Stop it," he said. "Stop it, you're hurting me."

"See?" she said. "I'll break your wrist."

Under the table he kicked at her. She let go of him.

"You son of a bitch, I'll break your face for that." She started to scratch him. He struck her wildly and she began to cry. The little boy had rushed over and was pulling at Feldman's suit jacket. The woman behind the bar came over with a billy club she had taken from some hiding place, and began to hit Feldman on his neck and chest. The girl recovered and pulled him from the booth. She sat on his chest, her legs straddling his body as a jockey rides a horse, thighs spread wide, knees up. Her body was exposed to him. He smelled her cunt. He saw it. They beat him until he was unconscious.

The men from the factories lifted him from the floor where he lay and carried him into the street. It was dark now. Under the lamplight they marched with him. Children ran behind and chanted strange songs. He heard the voices even in his sleep, and dreamed that he was an Egyptian king awaking in the underworld. About him were the treasures, the artifacts with which his people mocked his death. He was betrayed, forsaken. He screamed he was not dead and for answer heard their laughter as they retreated through the dark passage.

Before he died Feldman awoke in an alley. The pains in his stomach were more severe than ever. He knew he was dying. On his torn jacket was a note, scribbled in an angry hand: STAY AWAY FROM WHITE WOMEN, it said.

He thought of the doctor's somber face telling him more than a year ago that he was going to die. He thought of his family and the way they looked at him, delicately anticipating in his every sudden move something breaking inside himself, and of the admiration in all their eyes, and the unmasked hope that it would never come to this for them, but that if it should, if it ever should, it would come with grace. But nothing came gracefully —not to heroes.

In the alley, before the dawn, by the waiting garbage, by the coffee grounds in their cups of wasted orange hemispheres, by the torn packages of frozen fish, by the greased, ripped labels of hollow cans, by the cold and hardened fat, by the jagged scraps of flesh around the nibbled bones, and the coagulated blood of cow and lamb, Feldman saw the cunt one last time and raised himself and crawled in the darkness toward a fence to sit upright against it. He tugged at his jacket to straighten it, tugged at the note appended to him like a price tag: STAY AWAY FROM WHITE WOMEN. He did not have the strength to pull the tag from his jacket. Smiling, he thought sadly of the dying hero.

ON A
FIELD,
RAMPANT

Long before he began to wonder about it in any important way, he felt the weight of it, the familiar tug of it against his chest as he moved forward, its heavy, gentle arc as it swung, pendent, from the golden chain about his throat. In bed he felt it like a warm hand pressing against his heart.

What surprised him later was that he had never questioned it, that it had always seemed a quite natural extension of his own body. It had not occurred to him to take it off even in the bath. He could recall lying back in the warm water, somnolent and comfortable, just conscious of its dull glint beneath the surface. Though he enjoyed the subtle shift of its weight in the water, its slow, careful displacements as he moved in the bath, he didn't really think about it, even as a toy. When he stood and reached for the towel hanging from the curtainless rod above the tub, the medallion, like a metal moon, would catch the light of the electric bulb, and sifting it in its complex corrugated surfaces, throw off thick rings of bright yellow which seemed to sear themselves into his outstretched, upraised hands.

He could not remember when it was he had first looked at it as a thing apart, having properties of its own. Once, as a child in the gymnasium, a classmate had grabbed it as they were running in a game and had held him by it. He felt the pressure of the golden links on the back of his neck. The boy pulled steadily on the medallion and he lurched forward clumsily. Then the boy, grasping the chain in his fists, drew him toward him, hand over hand, as one might draw a rope up a well. When he could feel the other's face, abrasive against his own, the boy released him suddenly and backed away, pointing at the spinning medallion unsnarling on his chest.

The figures on the medallion were as familiar to him as the features on his face, but for this reason he had been strangely unconscious of them, accepting them through long accommodation, nothing else. One night, shortly after the scene in the gymnasium, he took the medallion from beneath his pajama shirt, and holding it underneath the lamp by his bed, studied it. His finger traced the medallion's outline, a shield large as a man's hand. It was made of a thick, crusted gold, almost the color of leather, and its surface bristled with figures in sharp relief. At one edge an animal—perhaps a lion—reared, its body rampant, its front legs pawing the air fiercely, its head angry and turned strangely on its body in vicious confrontation. At the medallion's center a knight sat stiffly, canted crazily on a horse's back, and reached a mailed fist toward the thick-feathered legs of an eagle just above his head. The eagle's head, in profile, hung at a queer angle from the long, naked neck, distended in fright. Its wings seemed to beat the heavy air in a clumsy desperation. Its eye, almost human, and in proportion larger than anything else on the shield, seemed, unlike the dangerously clawed, enraged lion, or the thick-walled mail of the stiff, awkward knight, vulnerable, open to unendurable pain and fright. Its talons clutched a crown shape which somehow in its anguish the eagle appeared to have forgotten it held, as though it protected itself from its attackers absent-mindedly, still clutching some irrelevant baggage. The figures emerged from a field of gradually diminishing darkness, the background, a deep gold the color of old brass, finally exploding in a sunburst of yellow in the eagle's golden eye.

He had replaced it carefully inside his pajamas and from that time thought of it no longer as a part of his own body but rather as something merged with it, yet isolate: not part of him, but *his*, like a glass eye or an ivory limb.

He decided to ask his father about it. He and Khardov lived together at the back of Khardov's shop. He had been a craftsman in precious metals, but the wars and revolutions had ruined his trade and now he repaired watches. In the dark back room where Khardov ate his lunch, even there not out of earshot of the noisy watches, the old man chewed on the raw, doughy bread and spoke to him.

"Time," he said hoarsely. "Time, time, time," he said, shrugging, jerking his thumb in the direction of the watches.

The boy looked uneasily at the dark curtain that separated their apartment from the shop.

"Listen to them chattering." He drew the back of his hand across his cheek where a piece of moist bread had stuck to it. "Even the wars, even the wars, once leisurely and provisional with the news of battle a hard ride three days off, the capital always the last place to fall. Even the wars," he said, his voice trailing off. He looked at the boy. "Where are your sieges today?" he asked him. "Where are your pitched tents, your massive bivouacs like queer cities of the poor outside the walls? The terrible armies and the gentle, gentle soldiers? Who storms a summer palace now? Isn't that right, sir? Doesn't that strike you as right?"

The boy nodded, confused.

"It is to be understood then, sir, that the new national product is the pocket watch. A cheap, sturdy symbol of the times, isn't that right? And a practical symbol, too. More than the old icons, or the glazed four-color pictures of the dead presidents from the papers." As Khardov spoke he held in his lap a carved, heavy casket in which were still the last precious shavings from the great times. He had pushed back the lid which slid on smooth wooden rails and let one hand loll idly in the dark box, as a man in a boat trails his hand in cool water. The boy could not see it but he knew that in Khardov's fingers were the shapeless golden chips, the fragments of platinum and chunks of splintered silver, like the pebbled residuum of some lavish flood.

Khardov had almost finished eating and the boy still had not asked him about the medallion. "Khardov," he said—he had been told to call him Khardov, not Father—"Khardov, why do I have this?" He pointed to his shirt under which the flat, cool part of the medallion lay against his chest.

He thought for a moment that Khardov might not understand him. He could have been pointing at his heart.

"You have it because it is yours, sir," Khardov said softly.

This had been (though he could not understand now how naïve he had been; there should have been dozens of times when the subject of the medallion would have come up) the first time he could remember speaking to Khardov about it. Strangely, he had experienced a deep satisfaction in Khardov's answer. It seemed an absolute confirmation of his own discovery the night before when he had taken the medallion, like the heart from his chest, to examine it beneath the lamp.

Until then, like all children, he'd had no real sense of his own being. His self he had simply accepted with the other natural facts of the world, something which had always existed. But his father's answer, that he had the medallion because it was his, provided him with an insight into his own uniqueness. It was as if the center of the universe had suddenly and inexplicably shifted. No longer a part of it, he sensed irreconcilable differences between himself and it, but like a castaway who suddenly finds himself on an island to which he is bound only by the physics of geography, he felt an amused tolerance of customs and conditions arrived at through no consultation with himself, and for which he could never be made to answer. Relieved somehow of burdens he had been made to feel only when they had been lifted from him, he experienced a heady freedom. Of course. It was *his*. He was himself.

One afternoon, not long after his interview with Khardov, he returned from his classes to find a package on his bed. Inside were the richest, finest clothes he had ever seen. There were trousers of so deep a blue that they appeared black. Along the seams stitches were so closely set against each other that they seemed a single fat, stranded thread. "Tailors have gone blind making these," Khardov boasted to him. There were jackets with wool so thick he could not bunch it in his fist, and high black stockings with silk so sheer that his legs looked gray in them. The heavy shoes he found beneath the bed were of a rich, pungent leather, the color of horses' saddles on state occasions. He did not wonder where the clothes had come from, or even if they were for him. He put them on quickly and went to stand before the shard of mirror in the kitchen. By standing back far enough he could see, except for his face, his whole reflection. Pleased, he thought of the medallion settled comfortably, with himself inside the heavy clothes.

Behind him Khardov came up and placed himself against the kitchen door with his hands at his sides and his head slightly forward on his neck. "Do I look well, Khardov?" he asked without turning around.

"Yes, sir," the man replied. "You look splendid."

His awareness of himself was confused now with a new deep consciousness of the medallion he wore. It seemed to him that the medallion, even more than himself, had achieved an insular security beneath the fine clothes. It had become inviolate, immured, like the precious metal in Khardov's casket, not so much by the thickness of the covering as by the implicit delicacy of its surroundings. One ripped valuables from a paper bag, but did not touch the pearl at the throat of the great lady fallen in the street.

He discovered later that the packages he frequently found on his bed were paid for by the steady depletion of the gold and silver in Khardov's box. It was almost as if *it*, rather than Khardov, were his benefactor (as a young boy he thought of the power of the metals to transform themselves into visible symbols he could wear as somehow self-generative, an implicit condition built comfortably into the very premise of wealth), for as he grew and his needs multiplied, it was, as he by that time knew, only at the expense of the wealth that glittered beneath the ornate surfaces of the carved casket that they were met. Khardov no longer sat in the dark back room solacing his fingers in the rich depths of the box, stirring the opulent shards as he ate his lunch. One day, of course, their little treasury was empty and there were no more packages. As a child he had thought of the metals as fragments broken by main force from heavy sheets of silver and gold, and it saddened him to realize that even these were susceptible of a further and final depletion. He had become used to the silky luxury of the gifts and it was a disappointment to him that they should stop; but in a way, forced as he was to wear clothing that was still fine though no longer new, he was made aware of a subtle shift in his status which was not at all unpleasant to him. With use, the clothing, too substantial ever to become threadbare, gradually lost its gloss, its stiff novelty. An aura of respectable solidity settled over it. The jackets and suits were not old, but aged, and had about them now an aspect of classic and somewhat ancient fashionableness, and although Khardov still managed to find money for fresh and expensive linen—this, somehow, was perishable, like the brittle and yellowing paper notes Khardov traded to obtain it—its silken crispness seemed only to deepen the musty gentility of the rest of his clothing.

Thinking now of the clothes always in relation to the thick casket and its contents, he began to view his life as a syllogism proceeding with a calm deliberateness from the premise of the medallion. From the first the medallion had seemed to hint at some mystery about himself which sooner or later he would have to solve. Even the handsome clothes which had drained the box had gone, not so much to dress him, as to set off the medallion, as though all arrangements in his life were controlled finally by the eccentric object which hung about his neck. There was some-

thing curiously effeminate about his position, ludicrously not unlike a woman's commitment to a strangely colored handbag
which, accessory to nothing, makes ceaseless demands on her
wardrobe. He told Khardov about his feelings, and although the
old man laughed he had seemed angry. Later Khardov came to
him. "You were right, sir," he said. "It was perceptive in you to
see that. The poor man's rags are given outright, but golden rai-
ments are always lent. They are a responsibility. If this seems to
diminish you, remember they are a responsibility only the very
few can have."

Increasingly he enjoyed going out among the few people he
knew. It may have seemed to others that he glided too smoothly
among them. Like a man on ice skates nodding to friends who
stand by less sure of themselves, he went from one to the other,
asking of this one's health, desiring to be remembered to that
one's family. He sensed that others hung back from him and assumed at first that it was his dress, so different from their own,
which had made him seem somehow too forbidding and caused
their caution, forcing them apart from him, as one steps aside for
a man in a uniform one has never worn. He understood later,
however, that his interest must have seemed patronizing to them,
and he was hurt that they should misinterpret his sincere affection. Gradually, though, he concluded that their suspicion of him
was not entirely unjustified, that he *had* held something of himself in reserve. It was, he decided, a flaw in his character. He
resolved to correct it. But once, after he was a grown man, a
mistress of his, having had too much to drink, refused to use his
name in talking to him. Instead, she kept on calling him "Jeho-
vah." Finally, in some anger, he asked her why she did this. "Because," she said, "you show me only your behind."

In the evenings, even from the first, he read a good deal.
Khardov brought him the books—elaborate, heavy treatises on
government; heroic, copious histories of an older world; state-
ments of political philosophy; royalist tracts; the diaries and secret papers of personages in famous courts; and novels, many

novels. It was the novels which he read with an increasing absorption. Gradually he began to return more and more of the other books unread and to demand of Khardov that he bring him still more novels. These were always romances, books with involved, old-fashioned plots. He had no illusions about their art, but he experienced a never diminishing satisfaction and excitement in the stories of depressed but golden lovers whose difficulties were invariably that they lived in worlds of frozen status. He read with a double tension. Delighted with the tales of the sons of struggling merchants, of traveling circus performers, and the strong, tanned boys of gamekeepers, he sensed in them, in their careful language, in their unaccountable benevolence in worlds fraught with evil and terror, in their almost jejune resistance to temptation, what their petite, soprano-throated girl friends sensed in them—a quality, an essence which would not submerge, which popped like a cork to the surface in even the wildest storms and displacements of their condition. For him it was not the wart or mole or scarlet pimpernel which in the last act of their drama finally brought recognition even from the enemy who stood to lose because the prince was found. It was not the superficial deformity, scar of quality so important to others that was important to him. It was rather a concept, the validity of which he came increasingly to recognize as he raced through the novels—a concept of blood itself. He knew his man long before the dullard others did, spotting them their familiarity with the telltale wound inflicted on the inner thigh by ruffians at birth. A man's blood was his character, he knew. At the same time he experienced a real anxiety that for once the heroine would not find out in time, that the gypsy would be killed before things could work themselves out. But it was not the hero's marriage which he longed for; he did not yearn for the pale and distant princess. He wanted one thing for the hero, one thing only. He wanted restoration. To him it was a daring and delicious word. He said it under his breath.

It was a pleasant life, but he knew, even from the beginning,

that the sense of special condition he felt so deeply was not forever to be enjoyed passively. All right, he reasoned. I have
known for a long time that I am different. But I know no more
about myself than does a small child. I have no *facts*.

Instead of gratitude to Khardov he felt a growing resentment.
The quality, the essence he could identify so easily in the heroes
he read about, he recognized in himself. He was *something*—a
prince of the blood—something other than what he seemed. To
be grateful for a few fine clothes, for Khardov's open deference,
for the leisure he enjoyed, for the promise swinging on his chest,
was foolish. Like feeling gratitude toward the clerk who hands
out the money when one makes a withdrawal from the bank.
What he wanted now, *needed*, was not the small change of personal assurance, nor Khardov's blank checks on his specialness
—conspiratorial drafts on a vague but somehow splendid future.
He needed only what his blood demanded: restoration. If one
wanted it for stranger/heroes in foolish romances, one insisted
upon it for oneself.

Toward his twentieth year he went to Khardov.

"Look here, Khardov," he said. "You've been hinting at things
long enough. What is it you know?"

"Don't be angry, sir. Please."

"Angry? Of course I'm angry. You act more like a family re-
tainer than a father. *The things you know*. Who are you? What
am I to you?"

"Haven't I provided? I'm not rich, you know that. But I have
provided. You've never wanted."

"I know that. I know all that. You've been very kind. But there
are too many things I don't understand. Please, Khardov. What
do you know about me?"

"I know that you are worthy to be who you are."

"Who is that?"

"Please, sir. I can only give things. The other I have nothing
to do with."

"Am I a prince?" he asked suddenly. "Is there a plan, Khardov? A prince, Khardov? Am I a boy of the bulrushes?" He spoke feverishly, excitedly, his voice shrill and unseemly in the little room.

"The world has tired of princes," Khardov said sadly. He pointed in the direction of the watches, rioting, noisy and disorderly in his shop. "Listen. Listen, sir. Sundials on a green lawn were once enough. To know the hour, to distinguish, if need be, between morning and afternoon. That was all."

"I know all that. What have I to do with that?"

"The world has thrown away its princes. It ships them downstream in baskets. The gypsies hide them."

"Khardov, please," he said impatiently. He looked at the obedient old man, so different from himself. Then he had an insight which seemed to explain everything. "Is this my country?" he asked. Somehow it had never occurred to him that he might not be in his own country. "Is this my country?" he repeated.

"This is no man's country," Khardov said. Again he pointed to the watches. "It is their country," he said contemptuously. "This is no prince's country."

"Ah," he said. "Khardov, no more mystery, please. We are tired of mystery." He took Khardov's hand and brought it, unresisting, to his breast. "The medallion," he said. He released the hand. It fell swiftly, almost smartly, to Khardov's side and came to rest ritualistically against the seams of his trousers. "Often I feel its weight," he said. "That it will crush me." He smoothed his shirt where Khardov's hand had pressed against it. "At night," he said slowly, "when I am sick with wonder about myself, I can sometimes feel a throbbing, and I don't know if it is my heart or the medallion itself." He heard, unpleasantly, the excitement in his voice and was oddly conscious of his body. Queerly detached, he sensed that his pupils were dilating and the eyes faintly, redly filming. His breathing, under his words, was choppy and passionate, indelicate as a lover's. "I can't stay on here," he said, his voice rising. "I have my country to discover."

"Things happen as they will," Khardov said.

That night Khardov came to him in his room. He was not asleep. All the countries of the world jostled each other in his mind, their borders elastic, shifting endlessly, the continents tumbling from the globe like waxed fruits spilling from a basket. He was a conqueror, untried but powerful, seeing it all from the dizzying slopes of hope and expectation. Khardov stood patiently by the foot of the bed until he was noticed.

"Yes, Khardov, what is it?"

"For your journey," Khardov said, extending an envelope. "Some money for you, sir. You will need money."

He took the envelope and tore it open quickly. There was more money than Khardov could possibly have saved. The box, he thought, it wasn't all used up. He held this in reserve.

"Thank you, Khardov," he said. He watched the humble man still standing tentatively at the foot of his bed. Suddenly expansive, he got out of the bed and embraced Khardov warmly. "Thank you for many things," he said. "You are a loyal man. We'll not forget you."

In a month he had left Khardov and the country he had always lived in but had never known. He was outward bound, determined to choose his destinations as one picks one grape from a cluster rather than another. For a year, while his money held out, he reeled across the world, his itinerary open, himself uncommitted to plans, his own vague ideas of destination easily deflected by any chance overheard conversation of cabin boys, travel buffs, monied widows on journeys of solace. He steamed into strange ports, many of them merely names to him, but each time the tugs pulled the great lumbering vessel into the narrow slip, he found himself on the deck beside the other travelers, those coming home indistinguishable from those, like himself, who were only tourists. For him, however, there was the excited hope that this time perhaps he *had* come home, and with the others he stared down into the upturned faces of the waving, cheering crowds gathered at the pier to meet the boat. At these times his joy was uncontrollable. His neck prickling, he grinned and laughed at the brassy anthems. It was a year of splendid arrivals. Once on land he did what the other tourists did. Although he found it necessary to engage his rooms in increasingly less expensive hotels, he shuffled with them through the public buildings and sat beside them in the restaurants, picking experimentally at the strange food. Frequently, however, he traveled alone into the interior, stopping at the homes of farmers who eagerly rented their spare rooms to him, or finding a place in languishing rural inns. He accustomed himself to the sounds of many languages and was surprised at his facility of soon picking up enough of the local speech to hold reasonably complex conversations in almost any place he found himself. Soon, though, he began to feel a jarring uneasiness. It was not boredom, for he found that he could respond to everything that each country held out to him; it was rather a gradual conviction that his very freedom hindered him, that other places held what he mistakenly looked for in the country he was in. When this happened an old wild nervousness mounted in him again, and soon he was aboard another vessel, outward bound another time.

It was an exciting year, and he learned many things he had never known at home with Khardov. The dark back rooms he had grown up in came increasingly to seem more dingy, and he had despondent visions of himself lying alone in his room, naked, turning dissatisfied in the troubled bed, one hand clutching the medallion like a hope.

The more he traveled the more he came to resent Khardov's sly patronage. It was not enough to make seductive hints, carefully couched allusions, circumspectly to unreel information to him as one feeds slack to a fish. The old man's air, he realized now, had been meretricious, yet oddly professional, his casualness carefully arranged, like a dressing gown around a whore. He was sure now that the *medallion* was the truth about himself. Khardov should not have made him wait so long. He felt that it

was this, his difference from others, that counted. Even in the
foreign countries he visited he could feel the difference. He
looked at other young men, men his own age, who held down
their jobs, dissatisfied, restless, the average ones dulled, jaded,
surrender glowing dully in their eyes like the rheum of age, the
smarter ones impatient, somewhat too loud, too forward, just
looking for the chance to break free, and who would find the
chance, he knew, only on violent roads, in gas stations held up,
houses broken into, in the freely flowing blood of old men hit on
their heads with heavy instruments, the blood staining the crowns
of their Panama hats. He had seen them cruising on Saturday
nights in their open cars, shouting at girls or staggering from
bars, their arms around each other in a foolish, wasted camara-
derie. Sometimes, he had to admit, they frightened him, their
aims so different from his own, their faces clouded with a dissat-
isfaction they could not explain, which perhaps they even felt
was a part of the way things were supposed to be. At these
times he took a fierce pride in his medallion, felt it as a surety of
what he had learned from the old romances: that blood, blood
itself was the talisman, that it wheeled, despite submersion and
the tricks played upon it by villains, steady as a star toward its
ultimate fate.

He walked alone into quarters of the cities where other tourists did not dare to go, down narrow streets that twisted in a kind
of chaos, the buildings mismated, humped together like a string
of freight cars of different shapes winding about a curve in the
tracks. He stared at the bitter, wizened people he found there and
sensed the hardness of their lives. They wore despair like open,
unbandaged wounds upon their faces. But even as he nodded to
them, smiling patiently at their bewildered responses to his unexpected greetings, he felt ashamed. He knew he cheated them. He
was like a general from far behind the lines come forward to
review his troops during a lull in the fighting. It was safety he
felt like a sheet of thick armor, even its clumsy heaviness comfortable with use. It was immunity he experienced. He might em-

brace them, roll with them in the gutters, kiss their leprous sores, but their diseases would be helpless against him.

Once he was stopped by four young men. He recognized the fierceness in their eyes.

The leader grabbed his arm, sheathed in the heavy wool. He looked at it sneeringly, as if it were the flag of an enemy country. The others ringed themselves about him.

"What hour is it?" the leader asked.

He told him.

"That is late to be about these streets."

The one standing behind him said, "There are gangs. Don't you read the papers?" He felt the words, forced contemptuously from the fellow's chest, stir the hairs on the back of his neck.

"I fear no gangs," he said. "It is not late for me."

"A foreigner," the leader said, discovering the alien in the sound of his voice. "I've never killed a foreigner," he said seriously. "Have you boys ever killed a foreigner?"

The others laughed easily.

"Give us your money, foreigner," the leader said.

"I have no money," he said.

They came forward and were about to begin the gentle nudgings, the subtle insult of elbow and knee that would gain momentum slowly as they gathered courage until at last they would all be upon him, flailing him, caution abandoned, soiling him with their anger and hate. As the leader moved toward him he did not step back. "I am the prince of my country," he said distinctly, feeling a proud joy as he said the words.

The leader hesitated. "What's that?" he said.

He told him again. The leader looked to the others, questioning them. Already they stood uneasily, ready to run.

"You lie," the leader said.

With quick movements he pulled the medallion from beneath his shirt. Holding it in one hand, as far forward as the chain would allow it to reach, he thrust it toward the leader's face. With his heel and toes he made a series of quick right faces, pausing before each of the men positioned about him, letting them see. Again he faced the leader who now backed away from him deferentially. "Forgive us, your honor," he said. "We didn't know. Forgive us, your honor." He broke and ran. Instantly the others were with him.

He could not, of course, miss the ludicrous aspect of this encounter, but ludicrous or not, they had accepted his claim. It had been easy. The medallion had clinched things, but the assertion itself had been almost enough. Something he had missed before now occurred to him: there was a reputation to be made among the people. The implications startled him. There was a reputation to be made among them. What the boys felt, others could be made to feel. The simplicity of the truth amazed him. He had it in him to be a conqueror. It was not impossible, but he would not do it; he would not usurp where he felt he had no rights.

But the incident forced him into making a decision. He had been in the world a year. His money was almost gone, but he was still no closer to the truth about himself than he had been at home with Khardov. He could waste no more time. He had to invent some system less unwieldy than the random, capricious one he now followed.

The next day he purchased a large folding map of the world and a cheap, second-hand history book, outdated but for his purposes still usable. He sat on the bed in his room and systematically eliminated those countries which he knew would be valueless to him: the perpetual republics; nations which had long since abandoned royalty and where the traces of descendent kings were by this time so adulterated by alliances with ignoble stock that almost any man might claim some sort of tenuous kinship with authority; countries which though still living under the monarchical forms were made up of people obviously alien to his own racial strains. When he had done this he was surprised at the number of countries which had disqualified themselves; as he penciled through each eliminated possibility, he felt that even here, in the small, cramped room, he was somehow coming closer, making his presence felt, bringing about a restoration which would change things in the world.

He made a list of the countries left to him and was pleased at its wieldiness. Of course there were still problems. What would he do for money? He took stock of his resources and realized that he still had more than enough money for one more passage. The countries on his list were either on the continent or near it. Once he had established himself on the continent it would not be difficult to find jobs that would support him while he searched. And he did not need much. He had his medallion, his clothes; he had lived before in small, dark bedrooms. He had only to discover some procedure, some technique of pursuing seriously what before he had actually expected to come to him gratuitously.

He did not know how the occasion would arise, but he had suspected that when recognition came, it would come suddenly, unanticipated, except in the broadest sense: the result, perhaps, of his casual sunbathing on a public beach, the duke's yacht anchored a quarter mile off shore, the duke himself on deck scanning the beach with a high-power telescope, bored, absently lowering the glass to his chest, checking its magnification against what his own eye could see, lifting it slowly to his eye again—appearing to one beside him almost to fit it to his skull—once more swinging it slowly across the beach, the long tube suddenly catching the dazzle of the medallion; the duke momentarily blinded, muttering, "I say, what's that damned thing that lad's got about his neck?" as he slides the telescope back into position for another look, catching again the sudden flare of the medallion intensified in the long glass, stopping, refocusing on the medallion itself now —which to the duke seems ludicrously like a chunk of brilliant fire burning impossibly at the end of a golden chain—waiting patiently until a shadow can bring it to heel, rewarded suddenly by an unplanned sigh from the boy on the beach, who stretches expansively and leans forward as far as he can, placing one palm on the sand beside each ankle, the chest's forward arch angling the medallion into shadow; the duke excited now, remembering something he had seen once a long time ago, calling anxiously to the regal-looking woman in the deck chair, "Martha, look at this a moment, will you? I've the strangest thing trapped in my glass . . ."

So he crossed the sea again, like a lost Columbus retracing his steps, for the first time aware (since for the first time he understood that whatever it was he expected would have to come through his own efforts) of the possibility of failure. Certain resources were available to him, of course: the facilities of museums and great libraries in whose dark carrels he checked heraldic and armorial records and illustrations against the frieze figures of the medallion laid covertly on the corner of the study table toward the window. He found that the figures on his medallion—the lion, the knight, the eagle and the crown—were standard symbols on royal coats-of-arms; it was the combination which was unique and which he could find no duplicate for in the heavy, ancient books.

For a year his money had been gone. Finding that he was no longer able to present himself as a tourist to the countries he visited, he discovered that at some time during the year that had passed he had inexplicably become an immigrant while he was not looking. It was because he no longer had money, but he supposed that there was something else. The officials who met him now at the dock no longer smiled so warmly at him. That pleasure was gone from his traveling they somehow sensed immediately. Once necessity had been introduced into it, everything changed. Like the men checking his passport more carefully than they had ever done when he was still merely a tourist, he was now involved once more with the world, with the business of making a living, and men did not give their smiles so freely to such people. Even his health was now a matter of suspicion to the officials who peered closely at papers for subtle omissions which they, sneering when they found them, did not accept as accidents. Coming to live and work in countries where once he had come to play, he found himself quarantined for reasons which were never fully explained to him. Even to strangers it was somehow obvious that he was no tourist. They no longer took the time to explain expansively when he asked some question of them regarding a public building, its long history or some unusual feature of its construction, or to walk with him part of the way, talking happily to him, holding his arm, to the street he had asked about. Now when he asked a direction of them they mumbled it hurriedly and walked on. He was sensible for the first time that others were suspicious of his accent.

Many things had changed for him. He needed work. In a new country he no longer walked at leisure through the unfamiliar streets. Indeed, he seemed scarcely to notice that they *were* unfamiliar and fell into step quickly with those who had lived their lives there.

Usually he found work on the docks—heavy immigrant work. He took jobs as soon as they were offered, never promising to come back the next day, never telling some vague lie about a man he had to see that afternoon, careful always to avoid raising the suspicion in hiring agents that he shared the peculiar irresponsibility of the poor. Seasonal, subject to wildfire strikes, dependent even upon economic conditions elsewhere, his jobs had a temporary quality about them, a provisional aspect which he insisted upon. Otherwise, he demanded very little of a job, and even found a sort of satisfaction in dealing with time clocks, in seeing the purple, indelible evidence of his labors accumulate on the lined white cards.

He did his work steadily, but when the slack time came, he was laid off with the others. He even knew when it would come. He would feel a sudden chill in the air and he knew that in distant, northern countries the rivers and seas were blocked with ice. Nothing would get through. The men grumbled and slowed down, dragging out for as long as they could the little work that was left, but he continued to work steadily in a kind of desperate, clipped hurry. Often when the time came for him to be laid off, the foreman distributing the pay would hand him his and smile at him, and sometimes even put his arm about his shoulder, as if to say, "It's a tough thing, but what can we do? You're a good man." It was recognition he was neither grateful for nor understood. He always left quickly, and within a few days would find another job.

Once, after disembarking, he saw a sign advertising for men to unload cargo. He left his luggage in customs and went off to find the foreman. The foreman looked suspiciously at his fine clothes. "Look," he said. "I'm very strong. I'm a good worker and I'm used to the work." He called off the names of ports where he had worked. "Please," he said. "I need the job." For a moment he hesitated. He had heard the desperation in his voice and recognized that it was strained, forced, not accurately the fact of his condition. Why did he insist upon a helplessness so self-conscious? A despair which set aside in the very waver of his voice all the things he had before insisted to be true about himself? With a sense of all the wasted miles he had already come, he feared that perhaps relinquishment had become a new cause with him. No, he thought, interregnum is not exile. "I can do the work. It's nothing for a guy like me," he said more firmly. "Come on now, fellow. Use me or not. Don't keep me waiting."

The foreman suspected that the man before him in the fine clothes was some sort of rascal on a lark, a rich man's son, probably. He laughed and set him to work unloading the very ship he had a few moments before stepped down from himself.

There were some on the docks like himself, young men in whom he recognized a terrible transience. But most were older men, hard from heavy work, their movements cautious, almost stolid, as if they feared to rekindle the ache of old ruptures. Their faces were lined with the wounds of their expressions. Confused, they seemed trying to understand what had happened to them, like men stunned in awful automobile accidents. Endlessly they struggled with boxes too big for them, with crates marked "Fragile" which they came to hate for the cynical reminder of the fragility which somewhere they had lost. He remembered a man who one day had stumbled against such a crate, kicking it with his heavy shoes. Recovering, the man had taken his hammer and torn the nails from the thin wood wildly, like one pulling burs from his own flesh. From the open crate he had pulled handfuls of excelsior like the grotesque hair of a dowager, and ripping the green, tissuey paper had come at last to the bowl inside. He held it for a moment in his hands, examining it closely. Disappointed, he spit into it from deep in his chest and put it back.

He avoided such men. Their despair was earned too slowly; their dreams died daily, and one day's loss meant nothing, even to themselves. What he feared, of course, was that he might lose his own dream. It, more than the possibility that the dream was wild, irresponsible—which he recognized as more than possibility—was what tormented him, drove him to do anything, accept every job. He worked only at night, or, forced to it, in the afternoon and evening. These were the vulnerable shifts, he knew, but he had to keep the mornings open for his search, even though much of the time he was exhausted, could do nothing but strain to reach the bed in his small room, to fall upon it like a man impaling himself upon some terrible destruction.

At night, drugged with the endless labor of loading and unloading, it was not so bad. He'd sometimes stop, straining at a cigarette, and look at the boats, the light from the portholes outlining the ships. When he squinted his eyes, the lights seemed to come across the water like Japanese lanterns strung for some incredible entertainment. He would look up at the decks looming large and dark above him and see here and there members of the crew seated on chairs, a cook still in his white pants and jacket looking ghostly in the light from the dim stars, like someone dressed in silver, seeming to loll there in remarkable peace, at ease in deck chairs that he himself had *paid* to rest in and then known only the stare of the sun, or the air's sudden chill, or the sickening roll of the decks beneath him until he thought that he must surely slide into the sea. But the ship was truly the sailors' home. Perched so high above him, caught in the light from area- ways left casually open, they seemed gigantic, like gods, dimin- ished not at all by their distance from him or by a night which hid even the sea.

But once he had gone across the street from the piers into a shop for merchant seamen, a great bare wooden-floored room with open card tables on which were thrown together glass jew- elry, shiny plaster-of-Paris souvenirs, bottles of cheap wine, the liquid bright purple or red as artificial cherry candy in the clear bottles. On one table were scattered bundles of back-issue maga- zines tied with thin white strings, the faded pictures of burlesque dancers, insane, overdeveloped girls from the country, in obscene poses on the torn covers, their flesh bright pink, like a baby's, glittering silver stars on their nipples. Men from the docked ships crowded sullenly at the counter, turning the pages of a few loose issues torn from the bundles, one hand in the pockets of their raincoats holding down their erections, their faces set carefully without expression. He had stood in the doorway and known at once their longing and their sense of loss, intuited their over- whelming homelessness, like a great hole torn in their bodies. He had gone quickly back to his work, saddened, troubled for all who sailed at sea.

At night, under the heavy senseless strain of weights too great to be borne, he forgot the vision he'd had in the shop and thought bitterly of Khardov's box, grinding out wealth for him, but now perpetually stilled, more fragile than anything in the cargo he helped to unload.

He no longer wore his precious clothes, realizing that if some- thing happened to change his fortune it would not do to have them look too threadbare. At work he thought of ways to pre- serve them, steps he could take to restore them to their former handsomeness. Surely, he would think, moving a large crate into place on a platform, things which cost so much money must still have much of their usefulness left in them. He remembered the location of weavers' shops he had seen on his walks through the city, and tried to estimate the cost of resurrection to his clothing.

He had come to a country where the tradition of a ruling family stretched backward to the beginning of its history. In the low hills tribes and clans had made their camps, and in each had emerged, by dint of intelligence or force of arms or God's fiat, one who had been leader, king. It excited him to think about it. Barbarian, horn-helmeted, clothed in skin of tiger or of bear, he had yet embodied even in the placating gesture of hands that calmed the watchers of the lightning, the hearers of the thunder, some major principle of civilization.

The nation was still a provenance of empire, albeit a waning one (each year another governor was recalled). Because its long history had been neither placid nor uninterrupted, there seemed still to drift in the atmosphere claims and counter-claims, whispered conspiracy of pretender and fool. In towns near the capital each old inn had housed its would-be king. Ambition had even become a major theme in the national literature.

Here, he felt, if anywhere, something would turn up. On his free mornings he haunted the palace grounds. A custom made things easier for him. By tradition petitioners of the royal family were allowed to mill about outside the gates to await the arrival of the king's carriage. At the king's discretion he might extend one royal glove and the coachman would stop. Then the petitioners would come forward individually (in an order agreed upon among themselves) and standing, eyes lowered, beneath the high gilt sides of the carriage, address the king. He did not stop every day. There was no pattern. Everything was left to royal whim.

He had no desire himself to address the king and was, of course; suspicious of appeals made in this way. The hangers-on about the palace gates were almost always old people, or young hoodlums who came to tease them.

He had stood close enough to hear one old man's strange request: "Your Highness, I should like to propose myself for a postal stamp. I've a remarkable good-looking face. All think so. I've been to the authorities but they say it's your decision, sire, who gets on the postal stamps."

And the king's amused reply: "Oh, we've postage stamps enough, I think. And an endless supply of faces for them, what with the queen and the children and the war heroes. Wouldn't a statue suit you better? Think about it and let us know."

He didn't really know why he came to these audiences, unless it was because he felt that even this easily shared proximity to royalty somehow advanced his cause. At any rate, he continued to gather with the others outside the gates despite his own awareness of the king's disdain and scornful patronage of the mob he was a part of, and he was disappointed on those mornings when the carriage did not stop. Gradually he became familiar with the public habits of the royal family. There was the trip at the beginning of each week to open the parliament, and when it was warm the morning ride in the public park, or the shopping tour of the princess. He could even predict with some accuracy those periods in which the king's benevolence was running at full tide and he would be sure to stop.

One day he saw a new face in the royal carriage. He was so excited that he had to ask one of the regulars next to him who it was.

"Cousin of the queen. Duke somebody or other."

He thought he had seen a resemblance between himself and the duke. It was only a remote possibility but he had to follow it up.

"Excuse me, but would you say I look something like the duke? It seems a foolish thing, but as he rode by I thought I saw a resemblance."

The man looked at him carefully. "Oh, he's much older than you are."

"Older, of course, but is there a resemblance?"

"Well, that beard he's got. That covers him up pretty well. I don't know. It's hard to say. I didn't get a very good look at him. He's not here often."

"Yes, of course," he said, feeling foolish.

"You've the same builds now," the man said. "And maybe around the eyes, though I didn't get a good look."

The next morning he came again to the palace gates. In a short while he heard the clatter of the horses pulling the royal carriage. In a moment trumpets blew and the gates were pushed open smartly by the palace guard. The carriage lumbered through and he saw the royal hand go up. In the white glove it seemed flaccid, contemptuous of the crowd it had given the signal to stop for. He heard the wheels skid noisily as the coachman applied the brakes. The king smiled and whispered to the duke beside him, the white glove shielding the side of the king's mouth. Of course, he thought. He's mocking us.

He stared steadily at the duke, who was smiling, obviously enjoying himself. He was certain now he had not imagined the resemblance between them. It's real, he thought, I *do* look like him.

The man he had spoken to the day before came up beside him. "It's amazing," he whispered. "He could almost be your father."

"I know, *I know*," he said hoarsely.

An old woman curtsied at the side of the carriage, her ancient body shaking in the awkward position. She spoke rapidly and he could not hear what she said. At last he heard the king thank her and watched as, still bent in the stiff curtsy, she backed away from the carriage. When she stood, turning to face the crowd, he saw that her face and neck were flushed. Several in the crowd had gathered around her and were demanding in excited voices that she tell them what had been said.

Just then he saw a very tall, white-haired man begin to move forward slowly, approaching the carriage. Before he realized what he was doing he found himself pushing through the crowd urgently, roughly. Walking quickly, he was soon abreast and then ahead of the tall man, who, startled by his brusqueness and misinterpreting what had happened, thinking somehow he had made a mistake and had disgraced himself before his king, stepped back to lose himself in the crowd.

In the meantime he continued to advance, head downward, to the side of the carriage. He stopped when he saw before him, at the level of his chest, the high top of a yellow wheel. He was conscious of the odor of dung and felt a random, irrelevant anger. He stood by the side of the carriage, his eyes inadvertently falling on the small pile of manure flattened precisely at its center where the rim of the wheel pressed on it. He had no idea what he would say, nor why he had so precipitately come forward. His mind burned. He stood there for at least a minute, his head bowed, trying desperately to think of something to say. Finally he heard the king's voice above him. "Yes?" it said. He could think of nothing. He had no sensation, except for the consciousness of the medallion which hung from his bowed neck like a heavy weight. He could feel the sharp point of the shield shape prick uncomfortably against his flesh. He thought of the terrified eagle, impudent usurper, on its surface, and as he pressed his chin still tighter against his chest it seemed that surely the point of the shield would pierce the skin, as if the talons of the eagle itself might dig themselves into his bunched flesh. Again he heard the voice above him. "Yes? What is it you want?" it asked impatiently. He looked up quickly, jerking his neck, and saw the king's face looking down into his own. The quickness of the movement had startled the king, but he did not look away. Neither did he avert his own gaze, but stared directly into the king's face, the frightened eyes. His own eyes strained desperately, as though he were forcing them to see a great distance. He seemed to search for something in the king's face; he did not himself know what. It was as though he were trying to recognize something there, the horn-helmeted strength perhaps, or the ferocity he had predicated as a premise for kings. At last the king, his outrage mitigated by embarrassment at this stranger's stare, looked away; his eyes darted nervously to the guards, who came forward quickly. He shot his white glove toward the driver and the carriage lurched away.

A guard came up to him. "Here now, what's all this?" he said. He looked at the guard absently for a moment and then began to walk away.

"Wait a minute," the guard yelled, rushing after him. "Hold on, now. I asked you a question. What's all this about?"

"He's all right, Guardsman," the man said who had spoken to him before. He touched his temple familiarly, obscenely, and winked at the guard. The guard stopped, looked at the man, grinned and made no effort to go after him as he walked off.

During the long day, and then in the evening on the docks, his excitement did not wane. It was self-assertive, something true about himself, like the color of his hair. He went over each detail of his encounter, and though he could not forget that he had behaved stupidly, had stood, hulking and dumb, a great gaping baby, the odor of dung corrosive in the wings of his nose, he did not forget either that it had been the king who had finally averted his eyes. Thinking about the king, he saw him in a new light— pale, delicate, watery, committed not to the obligations of king- ship, but merely to its ceremonies, dressed not in the skins of animals he felt he would himself have worn, but in a neat blue uniform, vaguely naval—a king of peace and quiet in a country that kept the armistice, whose borders were historical and as fixed and final as a canceled stamp. He imagined lawn parties and the king—excusing himself, too tired to dance—in the static blue uniform, a banker's image of a king, the uniform merely a cloth against which one hung red and yellow ribbons, symbols of imaginary campaigns. For himself he eschewed even armor. Kings should ride forth naked into battle, panoplied only by their anger. They should still be what they had been once: leaders, recruiters for the kingdom who, sitting their horse in an open field, could tease a hero from each coward, could shout, "*The day is ours.*"

But this king had seen him that morning as a kind of enemy, had looked at him through those conceited eyes as he must have looked at all his subjects—as slightly mad. Yet there was a difference. He had elicited fear, had come forward to thrust an assassin's eyes into his face until, in confusion and terror, the king had been forced to look away. His presence had disturbed the bored placidity of even those hands, white-gloved agents of the royal will, had stiffened them in unfamiliar urgency and made them a real king's hands, if only for a moment, and if only a frightened king's. But it would not do, he thought angrily, to be remembered as a madman, and it would not do—he recalled the gesture of the man he had spoken to at the palace gates—to be dismissed as harmless. He was *not* harmless. If his claims were at all valid (and as yet he had made no claims) their validity was a threat. Made to wait so many years, thrust aside with only the medallion as a warrant for an insight into his condition, restoration would harm them all.

What he must do now, he thought, was to contact the duke. He did not know his name, nor even his formal title, but that was no real problem. There would be pictures in the newspapers and in the magazines. He even imagined one: a photograph of a man reclining in a lawn chair, the face in profile, the beard heaped in an awkward mound upon the neck.

Nevertheless it took him two weeks to find out the duke's name, and another week to get his address from the registry. On approaching a clerk in the registry office, he had been so secretive, not realizing that his was a normal request, that the clerk had hesitated, and then, sensing that he was dealing with a man merely unfamiliar with the procedures, had deliberately made him believe that his request had been quite out of the way, hinting to him that certain risks were involved, that he was only a clerk, that he was taking upon himself a terrible responsibility. It had ended by the clerk's extorting from him a small sum of money that it had not been necessary for him to pay at all.

He wrote a note, composing it several times in order to achieve the properly urgent tone, and sent it to the duke's home by messenger.

> Sir, may I speak with you? It is impossible to reveal anything in a note like this, but I have business which is of extreme importance to the State. You can arrange with the messenger a suitable time for our meeting.

He signed only his first name.

The messenger returned empty-handed.

"Didn't he get my message?" he asked him, bewildered.

"There was a man at the gate. He said he'd see that the duke got it. I told him there was supposed to be an answer and that I'd wait, but when he came back in a few minutes he tells me, 'Look, you, don't you pester your betters with a lot of foolishness.' "

He felt rage mount quickly in him. "All right," he said. "I want you to take another message tomorrow."

"Sir," the messenger said, "do you think I'd better? These are important people."

"I pay you, don't I?" he said angrily. "You'll take the message all right."

The messenger, aware of his own innocence, of his status as a go-between—he had not even read the first note—allowed himself to be coaxed by the promise of more money. He watched as the crazy fellow before him quickly scribbled a second note.

> Sir, evidently you did not trust my first communication to you. I appreciate that we are strangers to each other and that my advances are unorthodox, but I assure you that my business is real. Please advise my messenger when we may meet.

But when the messenger returned, again he had brought no answer.

He decided to go himself, and the next morning, dressed in the finest of the clothes remaining to him but conscious that his work on the docks had thickened his chest and arms so that the garments no longer hung loosely on him, he followed the messenger's complicated directions and appeared before the duke's estate. He went up to an old stone sentry box that stood beside the locked gate.

"Yes, sir?" a voice said within the dark box.

He peered inside but could not see the man who had spoken. "I'm to see the duke," he said finally, apparently to the low sloping eaves of the box.

"Have you an appointment, sir?"

He thought for a moment of lying, but realized that the fellow would probably ask his name and then call the house to check.

"I've sent messages."

"Oh, so you're the one," the voice said as a large, florid man stepped quickly from the recesses of the box. "Persistent, ain't you? Where's the little fellow?"

"I've come myself."

"His Grace *thought* you might show up today. It's the police for you, boy-o!"

"Give this message to the duke. He'll see me." He handed the man a note he had written that morning.

> Sir, I have twice sent communications petitioning for a meeting between us, and twice my messenger has been rebuffed. I am not at all sure you have seen my notes. Until I have some definite word from your Grace that you do not wish to meet with me, I'm afraid I must continue to harass you in this way. Today I have come myself and await an answer by your front gate."

"No more messages, lad. No more messages."

"All right," he shouted. "That's enough." He produced the medallion from beneath his shirt. "Now you go in there immediately and take this message to the duke. If he doesn't want to see me, let him write the word 'No' on the back of my note."

The gateman hesitated and looked closely at the man before him. He hadn't really noticed the clothes before; they were peculiar, foreign like, but he could tell they were expensive. And that badge he'd flashed. He reached his hand toward the folded note and took it quietly.

"Wait here, please," he said. "I'll find his Grace."

The gateman retreated into the sentry box, opened a door at its rear, flooding it with light, and emerged on the other side of the gate. Turning, he carefully closed the door and locked it from the outside. Instantly the box was black again. He watched the gateman mount a motorcycle with a wide sidecar attached to it and ride off in the direction of the main house.

He was elated. The day was bright and very clear; the air, for all the hard, sharp sunlight, was cool and smelled of the sea wide and clear and deep behind him. It was good to be in the handsome clothes again. His shoes, carefully polished that morning, glowed richly through a thin layer of dust from the road, but this came off easily as he buffed each shoe against a silken sock. Adjusting his clothing, he noticed that the medallion still hung outside his jacket. It was rich and golden against the brown background of the jacket, and for a moment he considered allowing it to remain there, exposed, mounted handsomely, a rich trophy of his identity. He was pleased that it had lost none of its power and remembered the other times it had served as his calling card, instantly melting the recalcitrance and resistance with which people chose to oppose him.

If the duke were to see him, he thought, he would come directly to the point. It would be good to have it all over with. This was a good country; he would not begin again in another.

A man went by him pushing a bicycle. He nodded warmly at the fellow and watched, amused, as the cyclist finally managed a shy reply to his greeting.

He returned his gaze to the house, one wing of which he could see through the tall leafy trees which guarded it. He stood very still, conscious again of the dead weight of the medallion, which he had carefully replaced inside his shirt, as one slips valuables inside an envelope.

In a moment he heard the guttural approach of the motorcycle and saw it emerge from the trees as the driveway curved into the gate by which he stood. He could see that someone sat in the sidecar, but annoyed that he should be seen staring through the bars like a curious child, he turned his back and looked out over the sea, tapping his foot like a busy man waiting for a door to open. He heard the motor stop and the gateman address the man in the sidecar. "He's right there, sir. I'll get him for you." It was probably the duke, then, whom the gateman had brought.

He turned casually, feigning surprise as the guard approached him from the other side of the gate. "I've brought someone to see you, sir," the man announced.

He looked past the gateman to the motorcycle and was surprised to see that it had been parked behind thick, high bushes about fifteen feet from him and to the side of the driveway. The motorcycle's front end canted around the bush, its large headlamp and wide handlebars incongruously resembling a quizzical animal looking out at him. If the man in the sidecar did not stand up it would be impossible to see him. "Is it the duke?" he asked the gateman, who by this time had disappeared too, retreating inside the sentry box. He remained at the gate, trying to see through the dappled shadows of the trees and the deceptive openings in the bushes. At last a voice, queerly muffled, addressed him. "Yes?" it said.

"Good morning," he said, his eyes fixed on the motorcycle's front tire.

"All that's all right," the voice said. "What do you want here?"

He heard a low laugh from inside the sentry box. He regarded it angrily for a moment and then looked back in the direction of the motorcycle. The leaves, stirred by a low wind, twinkled brightly. "Are you the duke, sir? My business is with the duke."

"Oh," the voice said, "your *business* again. We've heard a precious lot about your business lately. You write a rude, anarchist's prose, do you know that? And you've a good deal to learn about the art of the ultimatum." The man made a clicking sound with his tongue.

"*You're* here," he said slyly.

The man in the sidecar laughed, and the sound was echoed by a low chuckle from the sentry box. He walked to the box quickly and peered into the blackness. The gateman disparaged him with the same clicking sounds the man in the sidecar had made. "Here now. Here now. You've no *business* with me."

He went back to the gate and placed his hands, wide apart, on two of the iron bars. "Please," he said gently, "could you stand up a moment? I must be sure you're the duke."

"Oh, so that's it. You *are* an anarchist. Probably want to get a shot at me. Let me warn you, the gateman is armed. Now, what is it you want?"

He hesitated.

"All right. All right. *I'm* the duke. Isn't that right, gateman?"

"That's right, sir," said the gateman sepulchrally inside the dark sentry box.

"There. You see? Now go ahead with your business. I've got business too, you know."

It was ridiculous. If they chose to play with him he would be helpless. They would not care enough about his claims even to reject them. This was no disinterested duke on a yacht. Sick at heart, he thought wearily of the man who wanted to have his face on postage stamps.

"What is it, please?" the man in the sidecar said.

All he could do was to tell his story and hope it was the duke to whom he was talking. "Very well," he said. "I can only assume that so wise a man as the duke would not send a servant to hear business as urgent as my own." Again the gateman laughed, though this time the sound was muffled, as though he had put his wrist in his mouth.

It would be best to begin quickly, he thought. Addressing himself to the concealed man, he told him first of the medallion, then of Khardov's oblique hints, and finally of his own great expectations. Spoken aloud, it did not sound like very good evidence even to himself, but the man in the sidecar did not interrupt him and he hoped that he had struck some responsive chord. He finished by adding that he was satisfied that he had no legitimate claims in any of the other countries he had visited; it seemed to him that this added somehow to the force of his claim in this country. "There's one other thing," he said. "You see, there's a strong resemblance between myself and the duke." He waited for some response from the man in the sidecar. Finally there was a long, loud laugh. He stood in terrible confusion as the laughter of the man in the sidecar mingled with the laughter of the gateman. Soon both were laughing and coughing uncontrollably.

He turned to go. As he walked off, the laughter stopped and a voice called out clearly behind him. "No, no. Don't go. Let's have a look at you." He turned around. The man had stepped from the sidecar and come out into the open. He had a full beard.

The duke came up to the gate and stood there looking at him. "Well, well," he said finally. "There *is* a resemblance. Not as striking as all that, of course, but we'll see, we'll see. Let's have a look at that medallion."

He waited to see if it was a trick.

"Come on, come on," the duke urged.

He walked back to the gate and again took the medallion from beneath his shirt. He did not remove it, but standing very close to the gate and turning the medallion sideways, handed it through the bars to the duke. The duke held it in his palm, studying it, turning it over to look at its back. Finally he let it go and the medallion swung back, clanging against the bars. He slipped it back inside his clothes and buttoned his shirt wordlessly, finally adjusting his tie.

"This is marvelous," the duke said. "A pretender. Why, we haven't had a pretender in the family for over two hundred years. I wonder if we still know how to deal with them. We used to be very good, you know, very efficient in a crude sort of way. Stabbings, hangings, forest ambushes, that sort of thing. That will all have changed by now, of course, but we'll work something out. *A pretender*. I'm delighted, sir." The duke thrust his hand between the gateposts. He hesitated, then shook the outstretched hand. "Well, now," the duke said, "come inside. *Gateman*. We've much to talk about. This Khardov is quite a man."

He got into the sidecar with the duke and was driven by the gateman back to the main house, the duke talking animatedly to him all the way.

"Let's see now," the duke said when they were sitting together in the book-walled study, "you'll have to decide whose son you are. Have you thought much about that? Rupert's? Edward's? Eleanor's? My own, perhaps, had not an unfortunate hunting accident disqualified me from kingmaking. It's a delicate point in your scheme. You see, it would not have been worthwhile for anyone outside the immediate family to have done you in. A prince's boy, that would be the very thing. Earls have more children, of course, but standing so far down in the line of succession, they're rarely in anyone's way. We're all quite comfortable with earls, really. They make splendid, non-competitive cousins."

"I was wrong to come," he said. "I'm sorry to have troubled you."

"Not at all. I perfectly understand. You want to be a king. Or a prince. Or even a duke, eh? I know. It's very important. Blood is the one absolute left us."

"Please," he said.

"The World's Last Pretender. That's quite a title in itself. The one man so thoroughly detached from the way things are that he still aspires to a way of life which everyone else long ago dismissed as legitimately desirable. That's refreshing. Why, it's more—it's flattering. Thank you. Thank you very much."

"All right," he said. "I'm sorry to have troubled you."

He returned to the docks. It was not clear to him why he felt as he did but he was surprised to realize that he was not angry. He felt only weariness and a wish to be done with things. He had banked all these years neither on evidence, nor on manufacturing a case, nor on logic; blood itself was his case, the medallion its only sign. Nothing else had mattered. He had banked on recognition, had trusted in a consummation which would come about simply because there were no alternatives. His physiognomy was his scarlet pimpernel, his strawberry of quality on rosy backside. If there were to be resistance he would no longer put forward his claims. It was strange, but in all this time the duke's laughter had been the only valid argument against those claims. Had he been what he thought he was, there would have been no laughter; there would have been only the meeting of eyes, the swift joy of reclamation.

That evening a man asked to see him. He went wearily to the foreman's office, and as he stepped into the dim room he made out the forms of several men sitting around a cold and ancient stove. They spoke to each other in low tones. Seeing him, one looked up.

"Come over here, fellow, would you? There's a man," he said.

"Yes?" he asked.

"What's the story?" another said quietly. "You got anything on the duke?"

"What's that?"

"We've heard," someone else said.

"Let's have a look at that badge. How about it?"

"Who are you men?" he asked.

"Journalists."

"Reporters, fellow. Now what's it all about? You've got claims against the Crown? What's there to it?"

" 'DOCKER WOULD BE KING,' " a man said, reading an imaginary headline. " 'IMMIGRANT CARGO HANDLER SAYS HE'S NATION'S RIGHTFUL MAJESTY!' "

" 'PRETENDER HAS MEDALLION WHICH TRACES LINEAGE TO ANCIENT DAYS OF KINGDOM.' "

" ' "AMAZING RESEMBLANCE TO DUKE" SAYS DUKE'S OWN GATEMAN.' "

" 'DOCKMAN DEFIES DUKE.' "

" 'DOCKMAN DEFIES DUKE, DARES DUKE TO DUEL!' "

" 'MAKE-BELIEVE MONARCH.' "

" 'CARGO CON MAN CLAIMS KINGDOM!' "

" 'KHARDOV CREATES KINGDOM FOR CARGO KING.' "

" 'WHO IS KHARDOV?' "

"What is this?" he asked again. "How do you know about me?"

"Are you going all the way with this, mister, or did you just want some quick publicity?"

"Who are your backers?"

"Any influence with the people?"

Suddenly a bulb exploded in his face. It pierced the room with a bright, blue-white light, and he thrust his hands to his eyes defensively.

"Not used to having your picture taken, right, fellow?"

"The gateman said he keeps that medallion inside his shirt."

"Let's have a look at it, mister."

"No. Get out of here. Please."

"Come on, a shot of the medallion."

"It'll be good for your campaign."

"There's no campaign," he said. "Please. There's no campaign."

"Come on now, one shot and we'll get out of here."

"Grab his arms, someone."

"Come on. The shirt, the shirt. I've got him."

There were half a dozen pairs of hands on him. They closed about his mouth, his eyes. Someone held him by his throat. He felt hard fingers jabbing at his chest. Someone was trying to unbutton his shirt.

"Rip it off," somebody said. "We can't hold him all night."

He heard the anguished ripping of material like a quick, low scream. He struggled with somebody's hands, forcing his own hands toward his chest, trying to protect his medallion. His fingers closed around a loose button on his shirt. It came off convulsively and he felt it, something alien, in his hand. "Please," he screamed. "*Please.*" There was another sudden brightness flaring in the darkness and he struck out at the reporters. Strangely saddened, conscious of a peculiar loss, he dropped the button.

"I could use a few more shots but you'd better let him go."

" 'PRESS PUMMELS PRETENDER PRINCE,' " a man said, giggling nervously.

" 'MONARCH'S MEDAL MEDDLED!' "

Then, suddenly, he was free. They let him go and he stumbled backward, clumsily slumping into a chair. Someone took another photograph. Dazed, he thought of heat lightning on a summer night.

The photographers gathered in front of him in a half circle. On their knees they aimed their cameras at him as he sat, stunned and dulled, in the chair. One man, stooping slightly and holding his camera balanced carefully before him, backed away from him slowly. A final explosion of light filled the room. It was as though they had been striking matches under his eyes. "That's it," one called. "Let's get out of here." He could not see them clearly. They moved, blocks of greater and lesser darknesses, like huge, dimly seen, milky chunks of ice retreating slowly in some northern ocean.

"Wait," he called, not sure they were still in the room, "I have no claims." There was no answer. "*I have no claims,*" he shouted. They had not heard him. They would print their story and their pictures and he would appear, tattered and brawling, in their papers, like one deranged, his claims distorted, insisted upon. He would never be able to explain that it was all a harmless hunch that he had acted upon but once. He rubbed his eyes. Gradually he was conscious of the medallion which hung exposed, obscenely visible through the torn shirt, like the phallus of a careless old man.

For three days he lay on the cot in his work clothes, sick in his shabby room. He knew he was feverish. The medallion felt cold against his skin, and once he took it off. He removed the chain from his neck and wrapped it about the medallion; it was very heavy in his hand. He would have liked to throw it away, but at the last minute he found that he could not do it. He had had it too long—all his life. Even its shape, he thought. His very heart must have taken its shape by now. He thought of his heart, shield-shaped beneath his rib cage. He put the chain back around his throat, and again the medallion lay against his skin, a dead weight, useless and cold.

He wondered if Khardov was still alive. My father, he thought. My kingmaker. What a joke he had played. What a joke!

He would have liked to write him. It would be a very long letter. It was too bad he had no strength. The founder of kingdoms would have liked it. He could tell him how he had wasted his life, how it had been dissipated . . .

How had it? In disappointment? It was strange, but he knew that disappointment was not among the ruins of feelings lying about him like collapsed, dropped pants. Nor was failure. Nor frustration. Nor pity for his cause. Yet he knew a sense of dreadful, terrible waste. Nothing could be reclaimed, nothing, and he gnashed his teeth and ground his fist into his palm. That was it, he thought. It had been thrown away, dissipated in anger, in outrage at imagined affronts, his energy destroyed by a dubious righteousness. It was as though his life had been sliced thin by a daily, steady outrage, as real as pain. He took the medallion in his hands and looked at it. He had often wondered which of the figures was meant to represent himself. The knight, militant astride the horse, pledged to some unknown cause, his fury, like his loyalty, merely a technique? The lion, defiant, all its weight in the vicious arching outrage of its paws? The eagle, its legs and feet in queer, attenuated taper, as nude as spikes, its talons curved about the crown shape in the act of usurpation, fantastically appearing to perch on it in mid-air, like any canary on its toy swing?

He looked more closely at the figures. The hauberked knight was protected by his armor. He would not feel the blows of enemies. His cause was borrowed anyway, something not his own. The eagle, intimidated, bewildered in his adventitious majesty, had not meant to grasp the crown. The eagle bespoke accident. It was the lion then, rampant, the claws bursting from the furred paws, its rage, like his own, concentrated on no object, irrelevant but steady, just steady, spraying the air like spit. It was the lion, then, at the edge of the shield as at the edge of the jungle—loose, lost, peripheral, partner to nothing.

But there was something more than outrage. From the very beginning there was the hope, not tarnished even now, on the cot in the shabby room, in the broken house, in the wounded neighborhood, in the strange city, in the alien country, in the unfamiliar hemisphere, in, at last, the unresponsive world—the hope, conviction even, that in a real way he had been a prince. A real one. There had been no sports cars climbing the sides of hills along the Mediterranean, nor racquets stitched crisscross on a jacket, nor education at an American university, nor hilarious incognito revels, nor grandly formal balls where stag lines of princesses waited for him to choose among them for a dance. Although he had known none of the conditions of the prince, he had felt like one. He still did; he could feel it now. Precious. His identity. He would have to tell Khardov that too.

There was the question, of course, of what he was to do with his life now. He had not anticipated failure—his dream had been too wild. Yet failure had changed everything. It was one thing for the king, biding his time, awaiting his chance, to seek anonymity, to float on the oceans of the world, to hide behind the cargoes piled high on those oceans' docks; it was quite another thing for himself, the man of no hope, in whose heart no conviction burned steady as a painted flame. But he saw that it made no difference to him. His failure had been of gross proportions. To mitigate it, to settle for less, and so *much* less—to bargain, as it were, with his fate—would hardly do. He would not settle for less, but for least. He determined that when his fever went down he would return to the docks.

In three days he was well. It was painful for him to think of what the newspapers must have printed about him. Now there would be strange looks, perhaps words, from the other workers. He could imagine himself as he must seem to them. Quiet, sober, steady, the very man to nurse some wild, impossible dream. The gentle husband who one day slays his wife and small son, who rapes children, whose love nest is discovered. "Those quiet guys," they would say, "they're the ones to watch." "Still waters," they would say.

He dressed slowly. As he was tucking the medallion into his shirt he paused. There would be trouble. They would ask to see it. If he wore it exposed they would not say anything. It would shame them and they would avoid him. It was only the appearance of sanity that would drive them to ferret out the gauche detail, the unhealthy fact. Exposed, they would look away from it, or through it, pretending it was not there, as one looks away from a spastic in the street. He left the medallion on the dark denim shirt. It flared there like the sun in a night sky.

He returned to the docks. In the locker room the foreman looked at him peculiarly but said nothing. As he started outside the man called after him. "Hey," he said.

He turned slowly. "Yes?"

"Next time you're going to be out for a few days you'd better call in."

"I will," he said. "I certainly will."

"That was some story about you in the papers," the foreman said. "Well, just do your work and I got no complaint."

"I will," he said.

He worked quickly. From time to time he noticed some of the men watching him, but no one bothered him. The man he worked with worked as steadily as himself. At midnight it was time to quit. He heard the long, low whistle. "I guess that's it," he said to the man who worked beside him.

"That's right," the man said quietly.

He returned his gear to the locker room and went upstairs, coming out at the foot of an old wooden pier. A merchant vessel, its portholes blazing, was anchored at the pier. He looked up and saw some of the crew leaning against the railing. They were staring in his direction. As he walked along he was conscious of unusual activity on the dock. The shifts have changed, he thought. Women passed, looking at him. He saw small children huddled along the wharf. They looked like orphans. He walked on uneasily, tired.

Across the street, in front of a sailors' bar, a group of cripples had convened quietly. Standing there, maimed, their canes and crutches a complex of tangled wood, they looked strangely like a team of athletes before the beginning of a game. Next to them was a group of beggars. They held boxes of pencils and faded paper flowers in their caps. One extended a torn jeweler's card on which were mounted two red-glass earrings. A night clerk from one of the flophouses stared sullenly from beneath his green eye shade, a gaudy elastic sleeve band on each arm. A cook from the steamy kitchen of some restaurant, his apron stained with orange blood, leaned against a wall, smoking.

As he watched, the bars seemed to empty, the patrons—old sailors, whores, bums—filing silently into the street. They lined up in front of store fronts all the way down the block. They looked like people preparing to watch a parade. Here and there a tourist stood among them adjusting his camera lens, his empty case swinging at the ends of leather straps.

He heard a cry, triumphant, strong—clear and urgent in the silent street as a call for help. "There he is," it shouted. He heard it again and saw an old woman, lame, her neck and face covered with running sores, push herself with her crutch away from the group of cripples, as one in a rowboat shoves away from the shore with an oar. "There he is," she screamed again. The cry was amazingly strong in the old, wounded throat. It was delirious, transfixed. Others took it up and in their frenzy began to stumble forward, blindly shouldering each other out of the way. It was him they meant.

They crowded toward him, one wave after another coming down toward him from the high curb. He stood in the cobbled street wondering if he dared to run. He looked about him. Others were coming from behind. He stood very still and raised his arms defensively, thinking they would fall upon him. His movement checked them. The ones in front stopped where they were and petitioned silence from the ones behind who had not seen his gesture. He heard their warnings for silence retreating into the deep fringes of the crowd ringed about him.

He stood now, immobile, directly in their center. He thought they meant to kill him. "What do you want?" he asked finally.

No one answered. They stared stupidly. One pointed to the medallion about his throat and the others looked in the direction of the pointing finger. He heard them gasp, shocked, thrilled.

"*What do you want?*" he repeated, raising his voice.

"We *believe* you," the old crippled woman in the vanguard of the crowd called out.

"You're what you say you are," another said fiercely.

"You're one of us. Tell them. Tell them. *Tell them*," cried an old man.

"Tell them about us," a whore said ecstatically.

"It don't have to be this way. It don't have to be this way," a drunk was crying.

"Please, sir," a beggar urged.

"Prince," a cripple murmured.

"King," another whined.

"Lord!" a young woman, pregnant, drunk, whispered hoarsely.

He stared at them unbelievingly. Their broken faces, beatific, rapturous, were soft and stained with grief and love. They fixed their looks of patient ecstasy upon him, their weak sad freight of disease and despair and hope and love. He could feel their senseless love mounting steadily, building, bursting in upon him like waters that have split their banks. Feeling it, he knew that he would never be the same. It poisoned him, staining him like dirty, broken furniture in a room from which flood waters have retreated.

Suddenly an old man stepped tentatively forward. There was something familiar about his patient shuffle. It was the man he had stood next to outside the palace gates, the one who had wanted his face on the postage stamps. "Sir . . ." he began.

The rage, unfeigned, pure as poison, rattled in him. Instantly the chain of the medallion was in his hand and he was beating the man across his face, cutting him with the sharp shield shape. The man fell fragilely, sprawling at his feet in some final, terrible parody of petition. Helplessly he dropped the medallion, hearing the links and shield collapse goldenly in the silent street.

The mob seemed to undulate, to sway transfixed. Now they would kill him—now. Someone pressed forward. He heard the serene, leathery creak of wooden crutches. Now they would kill him. He waited, thinking irrelevantly of the fine wool woven from the precious shards in Khardov's box, of his heavy leather shoes, untenanted, gathering dust in the closet in his shabby room, of the places he had seen, of tips left on glass tables under beach umbrellas on golden shores, of dusty carrels in quiet libraries, big, heavy books open on the ancient desks, the faded colored pictures of escutcheons across the huge pages like panels in a comic strip.

"Please, sir. Please, sir." He looked down. The old woman, bent beneath him on her ruined legs, extended the medallion toward him.

He felt his rage, final, immense, filling him like fragments from a dropped glass spreading widely across a bare floor.

"Bastards. Bastards. *You bastards*," he roared.

On the medallion the lion; on the cobbled street himself: rampant, inflamed, enraged, furious with their golden hate.

A
POETICS
FOR
BULLIES

I'm Push the bully, and what I hate are new kids and sissies,
dumb kids and smart, rich kids, poor kids, kids who wear
glasses, talk funny, show off, patrol boys and wise guys and kids
who pass pencils and water the plants—and cripples, *especially*
cripples. I love nobody loved.

One time I was pushing this red-haired kid (I'm a pusher, no
hitter, no belter; an aggressor of marginal violence, I hate *real*
force) and his mother stuck her head out the window and
shouted something I've never forgotten. "*Push*," she yelled.
"*You, Push*. You pick on him because you wish you had his red
hair!" It's true; I *did* wish I had his red hair. I wish I were tall, or
fat, or thin. I wish I had different eyes, different hands, a mother
in the supermarket. I wish I were a man, a small boy, a girl in
the choir. I'm a coveter, a Boston Blackie of the heart, casing the
world. Endlessly I covet and case. (Do you know what makes me
cry? The Declaration of Independence. "All men are created
equal." That's beautiful.)

If you're a bully like me, you use your head. Toughness isn't
enough. You beat them up, they report you. Then where are
you? I'm not even particularly strong. (I used to be strong. I
used to do exercise, work out, but strength implicates you, and

often isn't an advantage anyway—read the judo ads. Besides, your big bullies aren't bullies at all—they're *athletes*. With them, beating guys up is a sport.) But what I lose in size and strength I make up in courage. I'm very brave. That's a lie about bullies being cowards underneath. If you're a coward, get out of the business.

I'm best at torment.

A kid has a toy bow, toy arrows. "Let Push look," I tell him. He's suspicious, he knows me. "Go way, Push," he says, this mama-warned Push doubter.

"Come on," I say, "come on."

"No, Push. I can't. My mother said I can't."

I raise my arms, I spread them. I'm a bird—slow, powerful, easy, free. I move my head offering profile like something beaked. I'm the Thunderbird. "In the school where I go I have a teacher who teaches me magic," I say. "Arnold Salamancy, give Push your arrows. Give him one, he gives back two. Push is the God of the Neighborhood."

"Go way, Push," the kid says, uncertain.

"Right," Push says, himself again. "Right. I'll disappear. First the fingers." My fingers ball to fists. "My forearms next." They jackknife into my upper arms. "The arms." Quick as bird-blink they snap behind my back, fit between the shoulder blades like a small knapsack. (I am double-jointed, protean.) "My head," I say.

"No, Push," the kid says, terrified. I shudder and everything comes back, falls into place from the stem of self like a shaken puppet.

"The arrow, the arrow. Two where was one." He hands me an arrow.

"*Trouble, trouble, double rubble!*" I snap it and give back the pieces.

Well, sure. There *is* no magic. If there were I would learn it. I would find out the words, the slow turns and strange passes, drain the bloods and get the herbs, do the fires like a vestal. I would look for the main chants. *Then* I'd change things. *Push* would!

But there's only casuistical trick. Sleight-of-mouth, the bully's poetics.

You know the formulas:

"Did you ever see a match burn twice?" you ask. Strike. Extinguish. Jab his flesh with the hot stub.

"Play 'Gestapo'?"

"How do you play?"

"What's your name?"

"It's Morton."

I slap him. "You're lying."

"Adam and Eve and Pinch Me Hard went down to the lake for a swim. Adam and Eve fell in. Who was left?"

"Pinch Me Hard."

I do.

Physical puns, conundrums. Push the punisher, the conundrummer!

But there has to be more than tricks in a bag of tricks.

I don't know what it is. Sometimes I think *I'm* the only new kid. In a room, the school, the playground, the neighborhood, I get the feeling I've just moved in, no one knows me. You know what I like? To stand in crowds. To wait with them at the airport to meet a plane. Someone asks what time it is. I'm the first to answer. Or at the ball park when the vendor comes. He passes the hot dog down the long row. I want *my* hands on it, too. On the dollar going up, the change coming down.

I am ingenious, I am patient.

A kid is going downtown on the elevated train. He's got his little suit on, his shoes are shined, he wears a cap. This is a kid going to the travel bureaus, the foreign tourist offices to get brochures, maps, pictures of the mountains for a unit at his school —a kid looking for extra credit. I follow him. He comes out of the Italian Tourist Information Center. His arms are full. I move from my place at the window. I follow for two blocks and bump into him as he steps from a curb. It's a *collision*—The pamphlets fall from his arms. Pretending confusion, I walk on his paper Florence. I grind my heel in his Riviera. I climb Vesuvius and sack his Rome and dance on the Isle of Capri.

The Industrial Museum is a good place to find children. I cut somebody's five- or six-year-old kid brother out of the herd of eleven- and twelve-year-olds he's come with. "*Quick*," I say. I pull him along the corridors, up the stairs, through the halls, down to a mezzanine landing. Breathless, I pause for a minute. "I've got some gum. Do you want a stick?" He nods; I stick him. I rush him into an auditorium and abandon him. He'll be lost for hours.

I sidle up to a kid at the movies. "You smacked my brother," I tell him. "After the show—I'll be outside."

I break up games. I hold the ball above my head. "You want it? Take it."

I go into barber shops. There's a kid waiting. "I'm next," I tell him, "understand?"

One day Eugene Kraft rang my bell. Eugene is afraid of me, so he helps me. He's fifteen and there's something wrong with his saliva glands and he drools. His chin is always chapped. I tell him he has to drink a lot because he loses so much water.

"Push? Push," he says. He's wiping his chin with his tissues. "Push, there's this kid—"

"Better get a glass of water, Eugene."

"No, Push, no fooling, there's this new kid—he just moved in. You've got to see this kid."

"Eugene, get some water, please. You're drying up. I've never seen you so bad. There are deserts in you, Eugene."

"All right, Push, but then you've got to see—"

"Swallow, Eugene. You better swallow."

He gulps hard.

"Push, this is a kid and a half. Wait, you'll see."

"I'm very concerned about you, Eugene. You're dying of thirst, Eugene. Come into the kitchen with me."

I push him through the door. He's very excited. I've never seen him so excited. He talks at me over his shoulder, his mouth flooding, his teeth like the little stone pebbles at the bottom of a fishbowl. "He's got this sport coat, with a patch over the heart. Like a king, Push. No kidding."

"Be careful of the carpet, Eugene."

I turn on the taps in the sink. I mix in hot water. "Use your tissues, Eugene. Wipe your chin."

He wipes himself and puts the Kleenex in his pocket. All of Eugene's pockets bulge. He looks, with his bulging pockets, like a clumsy smuggler.

"Wipe, Eugene. Swallow, you're drowning."

"He's got this funny accent—you could die." Excited, he tamps at his mouth like a diner, a tubercular.

"Drink some water, Eugene."

"No, Push. I'm not thirsty—really."

"Don't be foolish, kid. That's because your mouth's so wet. Inside where it counts you're drying up. It stands to reason. Drink some water."

"He has this crazy haircut."

"*Drink*," I command. I shake him. "*Drink!*"

"Push, I've got no glass. Give me a glass at least."

"I can't do that, Eugene. You've got a terrible sickness. How could I let you use our drinking glasses? Lean under the tap and open your mouth."

He knows he'll have to do it, that I won't listen to him until he does. He bends into the sink.

"Push, it's *hot*," he complains. The water splashes into his nose, it gets on his glasses and for a moment his eyes are magnified, enormous. He pulls away and scrapes his forehead on the faucet.

"Eugene, you touched it. Watch out, please. You're too close to the tap. Lean your head deeper into the sink."

"It's *hot*, Push."

"Warm water evaporates better. With your affliction you've got to evaporate fluids before they get into your glands."

He feeds again from the tap.

"Do you think that's enough?" I ask after a while.

"I do, Push, I really do," he says. He is breathless.

"Eugene," I say seriously, "I think you'd better get yourself a canteen."

"A canteen, Push?"

"That's right. Then you'll always have water when you need it. Get one of those Boy Scout models. The two-quart kind with a canvas strap."

"But you hate the Boy Scouts, Push."

"They make very good canteens, Eugene. *And wear it!* I never want to see you without it. Buy it today."

"All right, Push."

"Promise!"

"All right, Push."

"Say it out."

He made the formal promise that I like to hear.

"Well, then," I said, "let's go see this new kid of yours."

He took me to the schoolyard. "Wait," he said, "you'll see." He skipped ahead.

"Eugene," I said, calling him back. "Let's understand something. No matter what this new kid is like, nothing changes as far as you and I are concerned."

"Aw, Push," he said.

"Nothing, Eugene. I mean it. You don't get out from under me."

"Sure, Push, I know that."

There were some kids in the far corner of the yard, sitting on the ground, leaning up against the wire fence. Bats and gloves and balls lay scattered around them. (It was where they told dirty jokes. Sometimes I'd come by during the little kids' recess and tell them all about what their daddies do to their mommies.)

"There. See? Do you see him?" Eugene, despite himself, seemed hoarse.

"Be quiet," I said, checking him, freezing as a hunter might. I stared.

He was a *prince*, I tell you.

He was tall, tall, even sitting down. His long legs comfortable in expensive wool, the trousers of a boy who had been on ships, jets; who owned a horse, perhaps; who knew Latin—what *didn't* he know?—somebody made up, like a kid in a play with a beautiful mother and a handsome father; who took his breakfast from a sideboard, and picked, even at fourteen and fifteen and sixteen, his mail from a silver plate. He would have hobbies—stamps, stars, things lovely dead. He wore a sport coat, brown as wood, thick as heavy bark. The buttons were leather buds. His shoes seemed carved from horses' saddles, gunstocks. His clothes had once grown in nature. *What it must feel like inside those clothes,* I thought.

I looked at his face, his clear skin, and guessed at the bones, white as beached wood. His eyes had skies in them. His yellow hair swirled on his head like a crayoned sun.

"Look, look at him," Eugene said. "The sissy. Get him, Push."

He was talking to them and I moved closer to hear his voice. It was clear, beautiful, but faintly foreign—like herb-seasoned meat.

When he saw me he paused, smiling. He waved. The others didn't look at me.

"Hello there," he called. "Come over if you'd like. I've been telling the boys about tigers."

"Tigers," I said.

"Give him the 'match burn twice,' Push," Eugene whispered.

"Tigers, is it?" I said. "What do you know about tigers?" My voice was high.

"*The 'match burn twice,' Push.*"

"Not so much as a Master *Tugjah*. I was telling the boys. In India there are men of high caste—*Tugjahs*, they're called. I was apprenticed to one once in the Southern Plains and might

perhaps have earned my mastership, but the Red Chinese at-
tacked the northern frontier and . . . well, let's just say I had
to leave. At any rate, these *Tugjahs* are as intimate with the tiger
as you are with dogs. I don't mean they keep them as pets. The
relationship goes deeper. Your dog is a service animal, as is your
elephant."

"Did you ever see a match burn twice?" I asked suddenly.

"Why no, can you do that? Is it a special match you use?"

"No," Eugene said, "it's an ordinary match. He uses an ordinary match."

"Can you do it with one of mine, do you think?"

He took a matchbook from his pocket and handed it to me.
The cover was exactly the material of his jacket, and in the center was a patch with a coat-of-arms identical to the one he wore
over his heart.

I held the matchbook for a moment and then gave it back to
him. "I don't feel like it," I said.

"Then some other time, perhaps," he said.

Eugene whispered to me. "His accent, Push, his funny *accent.*"

"Some other time, perhaps," I said. I am a good mimic. I can
duplicate a particular kid's lisp, his stutter, a thickness in his
throat. There were two or three here whom I had brought close
to tears by holding up my mirror to their voices. I can parody
their limps, their waddles, their girlish runs, their clumsy jumps.
I can throw as they throw, catch as they catch. I looked around.
"Some other time, perhaps," I said again. No one would look at
me.

"I'm *so* sorry," the new one said, "we don't know each other's
names. You are?"

"I'm so sorry," I said. "You are?"

He seemed puzzled. Then he looked sad, disappointed. No one
said anything.

"It don't sound the same," Eugene whispered.

It was true. I sounded nothing like him. I could imitate only defects, only flaws.

A kid giggled.

"Shh," the prince said. He put one finger to his lips.

"Look at that," Eugene said under his breath. "He's a sissy." He had begun to talk to them again. I squatted, a few feet away. I ran gravel through my loose fists, one bowl in an hourglass feeding another.

He spoke of jungles, of deserts. He told of ancient trade routes traveled by strange beasts. He described lost cities and a lake deeper than the deepest level of the sea. There was a story about a boy who had been captured by bandits. A woman in the story —it wasn't clear whether she was the boy's mother—had been tortured. His eyes clouded for a moment when he came to this part and he had to pause before continuing. Then he told how the boy escaped—it was cleverly done—and found help, mountain tribesmen riding elephants. The elephants charged the cave in which the mo—the *woman*—was still a prisoner. It might have collapsed and killed her, but one old bull rushed in and, shielding her with his body, took the weight of the crashing rocks. Your elephant is a service animal.

I let a piece of gravel rest on my thumb and flicked it in a high arc above his head. Some of the others who had seen me stared, but the boy kept on talking. Gradually I reduced the range, allowing the chunks of gravel to come closer to his head.

"You see?" Eugene said quietly. "He's afraid. He pretends not to notice."

The arcs continued to diminish. The gravel went faster, straighter. No one was listening to him now, but he kept talking.

"—of magic," he said, "what occidentals call 'a witch doctor.' There are spices that induce these effects. The *Bogdovii* was actually able to stimulate the growth of rocks with the powder. The Dutch traders were ready to go to war for the formula. Well, you can see what it could mean for the Low Countries.

Without accessible quarries they've never been able to construct a permanent system of dikes. But with the *Bogdovii's* powder"— he reached out and casually caught the speeding chip as if it had been a ping-pong ball—"they could turn a grain of sand into a pebble, use the pebbles to grow stones, the stones to grow rocks. This little piece of gravel, for example, could be changed into a mountain." He dipped his thumb into his palm as I had and balanced the gravel on his nail. He flicked it; it rose from his nail like a missile and climbed an impossible arc. It disappeared. "The *Bogdovii* never revealed how it was done."

I stood up. Eugene tried to follow me.

"Listen," he said, "you'll get him."

"Swallow," I told him. "Swallow, you pig!"

I have lived my life in pursuit of the vulnerable: Push the chink seeker, wheeler dealer in the flawed cement of the personality, a collapse maker. But what isn't vulnerable, *who* isn't? There is that which is unspeakable, so I speak it, that which is unthinkable, which I think. Me and the devil, we do God's dirty work, after all.

I went home after I left him. I turned once at the gate, and the boys were around him still. The useless Eugene had moved closer. *He* made room for him against the fence.

I ran into Frank the fat boy. He made a move to cross the street, but I had seen him and he went through a clumsy retractive motion. I could tell he thought I would get him for that, but I moved by, indifferent to a grossness in which I had once delighted. As I passed he seemed puzzled, a little hurt, a little— this was astonishing—guilty. *Sure* guilty. Why *not* guilty? The forgiven tire of their exemption. Nothing could ever be forgiven, and I forgave nothing. I held them to the mark. Who else cared about the fatties, about the dummies and slobs and clowns, about the gimps and squares and oafs and fools, the kids with a mouthful of mush, all those shut-ins of the mind and heart, all those losers? Frank the fat boy knew, and passed me shyly. His wide, fat body, stiffened, forced jokishly martial when he saw me, had already become flaccid as he moved by, had already made one more forgiven surrender. Who cared? The streets were full of failure. Let them. Let them be. There was a paragon, a paragon loose. What could he be doing here, why had he come, what did he want? It was impossible that this hero from India and everywhere had made his home here; that he lived, as Frank the fat boy did, as Eugene did, as *I* did, in an apartment; that he shared our lives.

In the afternoon I looked for Eugene. He was in the park, in a tree. There was a book in his lap. He leaned against the thick trunk.

"Eugene," I called up to him.

"Push, they're closed. It's Sunday, Push. The stores are closed. I looked for the canteen. The stores are closed."

"Where is he?"

"Who, Push? What do you want, Push?"

"*Him.* Your pal. The prince. Where? Tell me, Eugene, or I'll shake you out of that tree. I'll burn you down. I swear it. Where is he?"

"No, Push. I was wrong about that guy. He's nice. He's really nice. Push, he told me about a doctor who could help me. Leave him alone, Push."

"Where, Eugene? *Where?* I count to three."

Eugene shrugged and came down the tree.

I found the name Eugene gave me—funny, foreign—over the bell in the outer hall. The buzzer sounded and I pushed open the door. I stood inside and looked up the carpeted stairs, the angled banisters.

"What is it?" She sounded old, worried.

"The new kid," I called, "the new kid."

"It's for you," I heard her say.

"Yes?" His voice, the one I couldn't mimic. I mounted the first stair. I leaned back against the wall and looked up through the high, boxy banister poles. It was like standing inside a pipe organ.

"Yes?"

From where I stood at the bottom of the stairs I could see only a boot. He was wearing boots.

"Yes? What is it, please?"

"*You*," I roared. "Glass of fashion, mold of form, it's me! It's Push the bully!"

I heard his soft, rapid footsteps coming down the stairs—a springy, spongy urgency. He jingled, the bastard. He had coins —I could see them: rough, golden, imperfectly round; raised, massively gowned goddesses, their heads fingered smooth, their arms gone—and keys to strange boxes, thick doors. I saw his boots. I backed away.

"I brought you down," I said.

"Be quiet, please. There's a woman who's ill. A boy who must study. There's a man with bad bones. An old man needs sleep."

"He'll get it," I said.

"We'll go outside," he said.

"No. Do you live here? What do you do? Will you be in our school? Were you telling the truth?"

"Shh. Please. You're very excited."

"Tell me your name," I said. It could be my campaign, I thought. His *name*. Scratched in new sidewalk, chalked onto walls, written on papers dropped in the street. To leave it behind like so many clues, to give him a fame, to take it away, to slash and cross out, to erase and to smear—my kid's witchcraft. "Tell me your name."

"It's John," he said softly.

"What?" ·

"It's John."

"John what? Come on now. I'm Push the bully."

"John Williams," he said.

"John Williams? John Williams? Only that? Only John Williams?"

He smiled.

"Who's that on the bell? The name on the box?"

"She needs me," he said.

"Cut it out."

"I help her," he said.

"You stop that."

"There's a man that's in pain. A woman who's old. A husband that's worried. A wife that despairs."

"You're the bully," I said. "Your John Williams is a service animal," I yelled in the hall.

He turned and began to climb the stairs. His calves bloomed in their leather sheathing.

"*Lover*," I whispered to him.

He turned to me at the landing. He shook his head sadly.

"We'll see," I said.

"We'll see what we'll see," he said.

That night I painted his name on the side of the gymnasium in enormous letters. In the morning it was still there, but it wasn't what I meant. There was nothing incantatory in the huge letters, no scream, no curse. I had never traveled with a gang, there had been no togetherness in my tearing, but this thing on the wall seemed the act of vandals, the low production of ruffians. When you looked at it you were surprised they had gotten the spelling right.

Astonishingly, it was allowed to remain. And each day there was something more celebrational in the giant name, something of increased hospitality, lavish welcome. John Williams might have been a football hero, or someone back from the kidnapers. Finally I had to take it off myself.

Something had changed.

Eugene was not wearing his canteen. Boys didn't break off their conversations when I came up to them. One afternoon a girl winked at me. (Push has never picked on girls. *Their* submissiveness is part of their nature. They are ornamental. Don't get me wrong, please. There is a way in which they function as part of the landscape, like flowers at a funeral. They have a strange cheerfulness. They are the organizers of pep rallies and dances. They put out the Year Book. They are *born* Gray Ladies. I can't bully them.)

John Williams was in the school, but except for brief glimpses in the hall I never saw him. Teachers would repeat the things he had said in their other classes. They read from his papers. In the gym the coach described plays he had made, set shots he had taken. Everyone talked about him, and girls made a reference to him a sort of love signal. If it was suggested that he had smiled at one of them, the girl referred to would blush or, what was worse, look aloofly mysterious. (*Then* I could have punished her, *then* I could.) Gradually his name began to appear on all their notebooks, in the margins of their texts. (It annoyed me to remember what *I* had done on the wall.) The big canvas books, with their careful, elaborate J's and W's, took on the appearance of ancient, illuminated fables. It was the unconscious embroidery of love, hope's bright doodle. Even the administration was aware of him. In Assembly the principal announced that John Williams had broken all existing records in the school's charity drives. She had never seen good citizenship like his before, she said.

It's one thing to live with a bully, another to live with a hero. Everyone's hatred I understand, no one's love; everyone's grievance, no one's content.

I saw Mimmer. Mimmer should have graduated years ago. I saw Mimmer the dummy.

"Mimmer," I said, "you're in his class."

"He's very smart."

"Yes, but is it fair? You work harder. I've seen you study. You spend hours. Nothing comes. He was born knowing. You could have used just a little of what he's got so much of. It's not fair."

"He's very clever. It's wonderful," Mimmer says.

Slud is crippled. He wears a shoe with a built-up heel to balance himself.

"Ah, Slud," I say, "I've seen him run."

"He has beaten the horses in the park. It's very beautiful," Slud says.

"He's handsome, isn't he, Clob?" Clob looks contagious, radioactive. He has severe acne. He is ugly *under* his acne.

"He gets the girls," Clob says.

He gets *everything*, I think. But I'm alone in my envy, awash in my lust. It's as if I were a prophet to the deaf. Schnooks, schnooks, I want to scream, dopes and settlers. What good does his smile do you, of what use is his good heart?

The other day I did something stupid. I went to the cafeteria and shoved a boy out of the way and took his place in the line. It was foolish, but their fear is almost all gone and I felt I had to show the flag. The boy only grinned and let me pass. Then someone called my name. It was *him*. I turned to face him. "Push," he said, "you forgot your silver." He handed it to a girl in front of him and she gave it to the boy in front of her and it came to me down the long line.

I plot, I scheme. Snares, I think; tricks and traps. I remember the old days when there were ways to snap fingers, crush toes, ways to pull noses, twist heads and punch arms—the old-timey Flinch Law I used to impose, the gone bully magic of deceit. But nothing works against him, I think. How does he know so much? He is bully-prepared, that one, not to be trusted.

It is worse and worse.

In the cafeteria he eats with Frank. "You don't want those potatoes," he tells him. "Not the ice cream, Frank. One sandwich, remember. You lost three pounds last week." The fat boy smiles his fat love at him. John Williams puts his arm around him. He seems to squeeze him thin.

He's helping Mimmer to study. He goes over his lessons and

teaches him tricks, short cuts. "I want you up there with me on the Honor Roll, Mimmer."

I see him with Slud the cripple. They go to the gym. I watch from the balcony. "Let's develop those arms, my friend." They work out with weights. Slud's muscles grow, they bloom from his bones.

I lean over the rail. I shout down, "He can bend iron bars. Can he peddle a bike? Can he walk on rough ground? Can he climb up a hill? Can he wait on a line? Can he dance with a girl? Can he go up a ladder or jump from a chair?"

Beneath me the rapt Slud sits on a bench and raises a weight. He holds it at arm's length, level with his chest. He moves it high, higher. It rises above his shoulders, his throat, his head. He bends back his neck to see what he's done. If the weight should fall now it would crush his throat. I stare down into his smile.

I see Eugene in the halls. I stop him. "Eugene, what's he done for you?" I ask. He smiles—he never did this—and I see his mouth's flood. "High tide," I say with satisfaction.

Williams has introduced Clob to a girl. They have double-dated.

A week ago John Williams came to my house to see me! I wouldn't let him in.

"Please open the door, Push. I'd like to chat with you. Will you open the door? Push? I think we ought to talk. I think I can help you to be happier."

I was furious. I didn't know what to say to him. "I don't want to be happier. Go way." It was what little kids used to say to me.

"*Please* let me help you."

"*Please* let me—" I begin to echo. "Please let me alone."

"We ought to be friends, Push."

"No deals." I am choking, I am close to tears. What can I do? *What?* I want to kill him.

I double-lock the door and retreat to my room. He is still out there. I have tried to live my life so that I could keep always the lamb from my door.

He has gone too far this time; and I think sadly, I will have to fight him, I will have to fight him. Push pushed. I think sadly of the pain. Push pushed. I will have to fight him. Not to preserve honor but its opposite. Each time I see him I will have to fight him. And then I think—*of course!* And *I* smile. He has done *me* a favor. I know it at once. If he fights me he fails. He fails if he fights me. *Push pushed pushes!* It's physics! Natural law! I know he'll beat me, but I won't prepare, I won't train, I won't use the tricks I know. It's strength against strength, and my strength is as the strength of ten because my jaw is glass! *He doesn't know everything, not everything he doesn't.* And I think, I could go out now, he's still there, I could hit him in the hall, but I think, No, I want them to see, I want *them* to see!

The next day I am very excited. I look for Williams. He's not in the halls. I miss him in the cafeteria. Afterward I look for him in the schoolyard where I first saw him. (He has them organized now. He teaches them games of Tibet, games of Japan; he gets them to play lost sports of the dead.) He does not disappoint me. He is there in the yard, a circle around him, a ring of the loyal.

I join the ring. I shove in between two kids I have known. They try to change places; they murmur and fret.

Williams sees me and waves. His smile could grow flowers. "Boys," he says, "boys, make room for Push. Join hands, boys." They welcome me to the circle. One takes my hand, then another. I give to each calmly.

I wait. *He doesn't know everything.*

"Boys," he begins, "today we're going to learn a game that the knights of the lords and kings of old France used to play in another century. Now you may not realize it, boys, because today when we think of a knight we think, too, of his fine charger, but the fact is that a horse was a rare animal—not a domestic European animal at all, but Asian. In western Europe, for example, there was no such thing as a work horse until the eighth century.

Your horse was just too expensive to be put to heavy labor in the fields. (This explains, incidentally, the prevalence of famine in western Europe, whereas famine is unrecorded in Asia until the ninth century, when Euro-Asian horse trading was at its height.) It wasn't only expensive to purchase a horse, it was expensive to keep one. A cheap fodder wasn't developed in Europe until the tenth century. Then, of course, when you consider the terrific risks that the warrior horse of a knight naturally had to run, you begin to appreciate how expensive it would have been for the lord—unless he was extremely rich—to provide all his knights with horses. He'd want to make pretty certain that the knights who got them knew how to handle a horse. (Only your knights errant—an elite, crack corps—ever had horses. We don't realize that most knights were *home* knights; *chevalier chez* they were called.)

"This game, then, was devised to let the lord, or king, see which of his knights had the skill and strength in his hands to control a horse. Without moving your feet, you must try to jerk the one next to you off balance. Each man has two opponents, so it's very difficult. If a man falls, or if his knee touches the ground, he's out. The circle is diminished but must close up again immediately. Now, once for practice only—"

"Just a minute," I interrupt.

"Yes, Push?"

I leave the circle and walk forward and hit him as hard as I can in the face.

He stumbles backward. The boys groan. He recovers. He rubs his jaw and smiles. I think he is going to let me hit him again. I am prepared for this. He knows what I'm up to and will use his passivity. Either way I win, but I am determined he shall hit me. I am ready to kick him, but as my foot comes up he grabs my ankle and turns it forcefully. I spin in the air. He lets go and I fall heavily on my back. I am surprised at how easy it was, but am content if they understand. I get up and am walking away, but there is an arm on my shoulder. He pulls me around roughly. He hits me.

"*Sic semper tyrannus*," he exults.

"Where's your other cheek?" I ask, falling backward.

"One cheek for tyrants," he shouts. He pounces on me and raises his fist and I cringe. His anger is terrific. I do not want to be hit again.

"You see? You see?" I scream at the kids, but I have lost the train of my former reasoning. I have in no way beaten him. I can't remember now what I had intended.

He lowers his fist and gets off my chest and they cheer. "Hurrah," they yell. "Hurrah, hurrah." The word seems funny to me.

He offers his hand when I try to rise. It is so difficult to know what to do. Oh God, it is so difficult to know which gesture is the right one. I don't even know this. He knows everything, and I don't even know this. I am a fool on the ground, one hand behind me pushing up, the other not yet extended but itching in the palm where the need is. It is better to give than receive, surely. It is best not to need at all.

Appalled, guessing what I miss, I rise alone.

"Friends?" he asks. He offers to shake.

"Take it, Push." It's Eugene's voice.

"Go ahead, Push." Slud limps forward.

"Push, hatred's so ugly," Clob says, his face shining.

"You'll feel better, Push," Frank, thinner, taller, urges softly.

"Push, don't be foolish," Mimmer says.

I shake my head. I may be wrong. I am probably wrong. All I know at last is what feels good. "Nothing doing," I growl. "No deals." I begin to talk, to spray my hatred at them. They are not an easy target even now. "Only your knights errant—your crack corps—ever have horses. Slud may dance and Clob may kiss but they'll never be good at it. *Push is no service animal.* No. *No.* Can you hear that, Williams? There isn't any magic, but your no is still stronger than your yes, and distrust is where I put my faith." I turn to the boys. "What have you settled for? Only your knights errant ever have horses. *What have you settled for?* Will Mimmer do sums in his head? How do you like your lousy hunger, thin boy? Slud, you can break me but you can't catch me. And Clob will never shave without pain, and ugly, let me tell you, is *still* in the eye of the beholder!"

John Williams mourns for me. He grieves his gamy grief. No one has everything—not even John Williams. He doesn't have *me*. He'll never have me, I think. If my life were only to deny him that, it would almost be enough. I could do his voice now if I wanted. His corruption began when he lost me. "You," I shout, rubbing it in, "*indulger*, dispense me no dispensations. Push the bully hates your heart!"

"Shut him up, somebody," Eugene cries. His saliva spills from his mouth when he speaks.

"Swallow! *Pig, swallow!*"

He rushes toward me.

Suddenly I raise my arms and he stops. I feel a power in me. I am Push, Push the bully, God of the Neighborhood, its incarnation of envy and jealousy and need. I vie, strive, emulate, compete, a contender in every event there is. I didn't make myself. I probably can't save myself, but maybe that's the only need I don't have. I taste my lack and that's how I win—by having nothing to lose. It's not good enough! I want and I want and I will die wanting, but first I will have something. This time I will have something. I say it aloud. "This time I will have something." I step toward them. The power makes me dizzy. It is enormous. They feel it. They back away. They crouch in the shadow of my outstretched wings. It isn't deceit this time but the real magic at last, the genuine thing: the cabala of my hate, of my irreconcilableness.

Logic is nothing. Desire is stronger.

I move toward Eugene. "*I will have something*," I roar.

"Stand back," he shrieks, "I'll spit in your eye."

"*I will have something.* I will have terror. I will have drought.

I bring the dearth. Famine's contagious. Also is thirst. Privation, privation, barrenness, void. I dry up your glands, I poison your well."

He is choking, gasping, chewing furiously. He opens his mouth. It is dry. His throat is parched. There is sand on his tongue.

They moan. They are terrified, but they move up to see. We are thrown together. Slud, Frank, Clob, Mimmer, the others, John Williams, myself. I will not be reconciled, or halve my hate. *It's* what I have, all I can keep. My bully's sour solace. It's enough, I'll make do.

I can't stand them near me. I move against them. I shove them away. I force them off. I press them, thrust them aside. *I push through.*

COUSIN
POOR LESLEY
AND
THE
LOUSY
PEOPLE

I went home to see my mother and to visit with the lousy people.

My mother showed me a photograph. It was of myself, my cousin Lesley and Lesley's sister, taken when we were kids. I hadn't seen Lesley for years but I had no trouble recognizing him. There he was, in the picture, inevitably its center, looking directly into the camera, staring at it—as he stared at everything—as though perhaps he did not understand what he was looking at, as though the camera were some strange object which could be stared into comprehension. His eyes wide, the expression vaguely blank, troubled, the thick dry lips of the mouth breather slightly parted, his face suggested that there was danger an unspecified number of feet in front of it. The big body, not heavy but giving the impression of bloat, was at an awkward, stiff attention, and his arm, partially extended like a patrol boy's at an intersection, shielded his huge-breasted sister—perhaps from the forgotten photographer. He looked like someone standing at the edge of a jungle clearing staring into brush which had suddenly moved. The picture had been taken years before when we had visited Lesley's family in Chicago.

"Poor Lesley," I said.

"A good boy," my mother said.

"I heard his sister is engaged."

"Maybe engaged. Maybe not engaged," my mother said.

Of course I did not see them often—they lived in Chicago, too far from The Bronx—but there had been a time when I saw Lesley's sister a lot. We went to the same Midwestern university. Her brother had been at the university before her and she was there, I think, because he had been there. She took a room in a place next to Lesley's old boarding house, and this proximity, and the knowledge that there were still people at the school who had known Lesley, must have been a comfort to her, like the arm in the photograph.

She used to come over to talk about her brother. She would sit on the couch across the room from me, her posture stiff, uncompromising, and tell me, trusting mistakenly in my interest, of Lesley's life. Always in the purse which she held primly in her lap was some long letter of Lesley's from which she could quote endless passages of brotherly sententiae. He called her Sister and advised her in clinically sensuous terms of the baseness in men's hearts. The letters were absolutely pornographic.

Less embarrassing, but duller, were our talks when Lesley's sister returned to school after a vacation at home. She had total recall about her brother and she would come, her mind brimming with anecdotes of Lesley, to tell me of some new suit he'd bought, of what humorless thing he had said to the clerk when they went together to shop for it. She spoke of Lesley's disappointment in the advertising agency he'd taken a job with after graduation, of vague plans he had to return to school to study law, of his new girl friend who was always, in his sister's description of her, not beautiful, but *sensible*. Sometimes she would offer a picture of an anonymous, almost featureless girl in health shoes. Invariably the girls looked feckless, tired.

What bothered me most in all this was the picture I got of Lesley's horribly distorted picture of himself. I knew him to be completely without humor, massively stolid, as though the imagination were a finite organ which he, somehow, had been born without. Yet his view of himself as revealed to me through his sister was romantic—there is no other word for it—cavalier. Advertising. Law. In his letters to his sister, Lord Chesterfield.

Then, in her last year at the university, his sister came to tell me that Lesley had joined the Marines. I was astonished. Our family, not even counting Lesley, is not what you could call a United States Marine family. Ours is more a Certified Public Accountant family. We seem to have been born between wars. For Lesley deliberately to seek out the Marines struck me as an incredible gesture, almost heroic, a declaration that though it would cost him dearly, he must assert ultimately and irrevocably what he had long and mistakenly felt himself to be. For the Marines to accept him was no less impressive. It seemed crazily reciprocal, and in the instant that his sister told me about it I had a senseless vision of two forces—expansive, drunkenly generous.

After this, Lesley's sister came to me even oftener, but the tone of the visits and of her manner changed.

Before, she had been enthusiastic, quickened with optimism at her brother's impossible plans for himself. Now she was clearly not so sure, saddened, and though she still carried Lesley's letters in the clumsy pocketbook which self-consciously she held, guarding herself, against her foolishly large breasts (once I said to her, "What *have* you got there anyway?"), she no longer quoted directly from the letters, but instead gave long rambling résumés of what he had written. I got the impression that he must have been very lonely. Once she showed me a picture of Lesley in his Marine uniform. He looked startled, bewildered, like someone who had gotten lost while swimming.

When she spoke of her brother now she always prefaced his name with the adjective "poor." "In Chicago I saw a movie with my parents," she'd say. "Poor Lesley would have liked it. One thing about the service though, poor Lesley says they get all the latest pictures. Even before downtown." Or, "Poor Lesley's in Tokyo now. He says there's a place he can get kosher food whenever he wants. He says there are lots of Japanese Jewish people who eat lox and rolls and they've got this delicatessen on the Ginza Strip. Poor Lesley says you have to take your shoes off when you go inside." I got the idea that she used the word super-stitiously, as though by openly insisting on Lesley's helplessness nothing would come of it.

I even had a theory about the orgin of that word. I think that sometime, on one of her holidays in Chicago, she and her mother and her father and her grandfather who lived with them must have sat down to dinner. The maid must have brought in the main dish. I like to think it was chicken. On its steaming platter, set down at the center of the table, the golden chicken, snug in its brown-potatoed insularity, luxurious as old gold against the thick white cloth, glowed like a household god in the awed silence. Someone, perhaps the grandfather, must have said, "Such chicken! Poor Lesley would have liked such chicken."

I was reminded, on my visit home, when my mother showed me the photograph, of my feelings as a boy in high school when I learned that Lesley and his family were coming to The Bronx for a visit.

I remember my fears of introducing Lesley to my friends—the lousy people. They would kill him, I thought. They would take my cousin, that stiff-necked wonder, and destroy him.

What I have to say is very hard. My crowd—and I don't mean that old gang of mine, kids with holes in their gym shoes—my friends had a *thing*. I don't know if I had it too. All I had, I think, was a feeling for this thing. But they had it, whatever it terribly was—an esprit de corps beyond rationality, or a sense of neighborhood run riot, or merely a kind of fatal intuition—and it made them wild. I'm not talking about delinquency. They didn't steal. There was nothing to steal. There was no one to steal it from. What they already had was all they needed. What they had was—there's no *real* name for it—*personality*, out-sized, grotesque, collective. Look, they didn't have jobs with a future; they didn't date girls; they didn't *apply* themselves; they didn't know anybody's line-up, and they didn't care. They weren't rooters. In all that crowd there wasn't one flat, half-hearted cheer between them. But anything could break them up. There was this little girl who'd come into the candy store at exactly the same time every afternoon and say to Fein, the owner, "Mr. Fein, my mother please wants a package of Chesterfield cigarettes and that you should put away a late edition of a *World-Telegram* which my brother will pick it up later," and one of my friends would start laughing. And pretty soon they'd all be laughing, myself too. I don't know why it was funny. It was, though.

But they were wild, and even dangerous, flashing out with sudden viciousness at passing, solemn strangers or at each other. I don't know, it was as though they sensed something terrible about the world.

When Lesley came I introduced him around.

"How come you're so fat?" Danny Lubell asked him.

Lesley answered as though this were a perfectly normal question, one asked him frequently. "I'm not fat," he said. "I'm big-boned."

"You're monstrous-boned," Danny said, "but you're fat too."

Lesley looked at him without smiling or even seeming to realize that he had been insulted. Often something would happen to Lesley—in college he might fail a course; a girl would rebuff him—and you thought, now, *now* he will question himself, now he's going to realize what he is. But he never did.

We were in front of the candy store and just then a stray cat, looking ill at ease in the street, as though it had drunkenly wandered from its alley home, and now, sober, could not find it, sulked by.

"Hey, Lesley, there's my cat. Did you ever see my pussy cat?" Danny said. ·

"Is that really your cat?" Lesley asked, mildly put off by its unkemptness.

"Sure it's my cat. Whose cat do you suppose it is? You see the special scientific color of the fur? That's years of careful breeding. The cat books call that 'Scientific Colored Pussy-Cat Fur.'

That's some cat, ain't it, Belgium?" He had turned to Joey Stowka, a refugee kid Danny called Belgium.

Joey blushed and did not answer.

Danny reached down suddenly and grabbed the cat, catching it skillfully around its belly. Its claws burst from the furred paws, its face contorted in rage. Danny made a feint with the cat, as if he were going to throw it at Lesley. Lesley stood stolidly, not even throwing up his hands in reflex.

"All right, all right," Danny said to the cat, calming it. He turned to Lesley. "Want to stroke its special pussy-cat fur?"

"What's special about it? It's ordinary cat fur," Lesley said.

"Why's it special, Belgium? Tell him."

"Because," Belgium said shyly.

"Go ahead. Tell Lesley why," Danny said gently.

"Because," he said again.

"Because it feels like the hair . . ." Danny said, inciting Belgium's imagination.

"Because it feels like the hair . . ."

"On . . ." Danny said softly.

"On . . ." Belgium repeated.

"On . . ."

"On my mother," Belgium shouted.

Danny dropped the cat and hugged Belgium. "*Creep,*" he roared, hugging him, kissing him. "Creep. Foreigner. Creep."

Danny Lubell was not so much our leader as he was a polarity about whom we gathered. He had a job in a gas station which paid him only enough to keep him in egg creams. These, as far as I could see, sustained him. The job also kept him in stolen gasoline for his long black 1933 Packard. What ventures we made beyond the horizons of the neighborhood were made in Danny's car, which Ox Hersh, another member of our group, drove because Danny didn't know how. These trips, rare because somehow we were uncomfortable in other sections of the city, were expeditions really, halting and tentative as steps into cold, deep water. Once Ox, sent to another borough on some special

mission for Danny, told us on coming back, unfeigned sadness in
his face, "There's nothing out there. There's really nothing out
there."

I have said that Danny was a polarity, but this is inexact, at
least incomplete. He was our taste-maker. There are night clubs
—sometimes we went to them in the Village to insult the queers
—where they cater to the demented, where for money they tap
the private lusts of the diseased and crippled. In a way, Danny
was like the owners of these clubs. He could never, as they were,
have been in it for the money, however; he encouraged aberra-
tion for its own sake. He drew it out of you. Whatever secrets
you kept—awful things—you could not keep, could not hide
from him. He pulled them out of you, and then he'd laugh at
them, making them such a good joke that you were almost glad
you were the way you were.

But all of them—pervert Belgium; Ox Hersh; Rabbi Old Guy,
a crazy Yeshiva kid who told us he liked to spit in the *shul* because he was mad at God for Hitler; Shelly Malkin; all of them
—had this private thing which turned into a public thing around
Danny Lubell. This is the point. I had no thing, and Danny left
me alone. I mean, I had no thing except the thing I had for my
friends. For a year after I graduated from high school I didn't
go to college. I just wanted to be around the boys, wanted to
stay in the neighborhood to see what was going to happen to
them. I mean, you've got to see how they must have been to make
me want to do that. Fun's fun, but who delays his life just so he
can hang around with his pals?

Sometimes we'd go out with girls. Not *with* them, but where
they were. Shelly Malkin, who went to C.C.N.Y. night school,
was our social chairman. The girls were always ugly. After one
of his parties he'd apologize. "Gee, I'm sorry," he'd say. "It's a
night school. They never turn on the lights." We didn't care
what they looked like. We liked to sit around and tell them filthy
stories.

Or we liked to listen to Ox Hersh talk to a girl. Ox was a

giant. He shouldered out of his small suits in a way that gave you the impression you were actually watching him grow. His voice disturbed the peace. Listening to him used to break us up. He was wonderful with girls. We could hear him across the room. He'd be sitting on this couch and you could see he was straining not to put all his weight down on it—he had a way of sitting on tiptoe—and he'd let his huge head hang down, or roll it around on his chest or stick it in the girl's lap as though it were the trunk of some curious elephant. He would talk very slowly, drawing out each word as though there were a danger that the girl did not understand English.

"Oh, you go to col-lege? You are a col-lege girl? Education is a beauti-ful thing. I have a cousin who lives in Brooklyn who is planning on going to college. Maybe you will . . . meet . . . him there . . . one day. What do you study at your col-lege, miss? Do you study so-ci-ol-o-gy? I am sure that must be terribly difficult. Is it not, miss?"

"You get used to it," she'd say, clearing her throat.

Ox would think about this for a while in silence, his big head shaking up and down. "I think you are being modest, miss," he'd say finally. "I think you must be very brilliant in col-lege." He'd pause and start the business with the head again, rolling it around as though it had to be wound up every time he wanted to say something. "I think your pro-*fess*-ors must be very proud to have such a . . . brilliant girl in their col-lege . . . What is so-ci-ol-o-gy?" he would ask her suddenly. By now her own head would be unconsciously tracing the splendid arcs made by Ox's and he would take it in his big hands and steady it. "Better get your head fixed, miss," he would say.

Maybe afterward we'd be feeling so good we'd go out to a cafeteria on the Grand Concourse, where each of us would do his imitation of Ox and the girl. We might arrive just when the movies were letting out, and Ox would storm into the place and start throwing people out of the line. We'd be right behind him. "Excuse me," Ox told them, "ain't ate today yet," and little Belgium, stepping on his heels, ferociously pumping his tiny legs to keep up with the Ox's long strides, would shout his favorite joke in his piping voice, "Excuse us, excuse us, got to feed an Ox. Out of the way please. Got an Ox here to feed." It's funny the way people relinquished their rights in the line. They always thought somebody was going to hit them. Not violent themselves, they thought they lived in a world of violence. People get hurt only by accident, but they don't know that.

Only Belgium and the Ox seemed to have a kind of extra-group relationship. The rest of us were each other's friends and seemed to be able to let it go at that, but with Belgium and the Ox it was different. I don't know if it was affection or hate Belgium felt for the Ox. Sometimes he'd whine to Danny, "Come on, Danny. Let's get in your car and leave the big fat Ox. I drive it for you, Danny. Ox too fat to drive, Danny. Come on. I have to sit next to him and he's so fat he squeezes me. Let's leave the bastard." But whenever all of us were together Belgium wouldn't let the Ox out of his sight. In the cafeteria he'd run up behind the Ox, who was beginning to pile things on his tray, and he'd yell at him, "How come you always first in line and not me? How come? Why I'm always second? Why is that?"

Ox would turn around to him, and not bothering to modulate his dangerous voice, tell him, "Cause you're a midget, that's why. You're a little midget, you midget."

We were a tight-knit group, but no closed corporation. Eventually we got to know almost every nut in The Bronx.

There was one guy named Eugene Lepransky. Eugene was much older than the rest of us, about twenty, I guess, at the time of Pearl Harbor, the turning point in Eugene's life. He was huge, bigger even than the Ox. Something was wrong with Eugene, of course, which was why we took such delight in him, but what it was, even a psychiatrist couldn't have told you. Except for us he was an insulated individual. He lived with his mother, and she never let him out of the neighborhood. He couldn't cross streets, so he never had a job. When you asked him he said he was "self-employed." This was true in a unique way. He got ten dollars a week for walking his mother's dog, and this was more than enough for Eugene to buy one copy of each comic book and flashy crime magazine in Fein's candy store. But Eugene took Pearl Harbor as a personal insult and for weeks raged against "the day of infamy." Soon afterward he told us he was going into the "services." From that day until V-J Day none of us saw Eugene again, and we thought, fantastically, that perhaps some branch of service *had* accepted him. I think it was 1943 before we found out that he had simply hidden himself in his apartment.

Eugene lived in an apartment on the second floor, and sure enough, not long after he went upstairs a flag with a blue star on it was popped into the window by his mother. After we learned what it meant we used to stand below that window with the blue star and look up at it, prouder of Eugene's blue star than of any on the block. On V-J Day he came downstairs for the first time in four years.

He couldn't have been more than twenty-four but he looked much older. The war had aged him.

"Hello, Eugene," Danny said to him.

"Hello, fellows," Eugene said, and he told us of an experience we soon knew by heart. In all the long war he had killed, he said, only one German. Eugene variously described the circumstances which led up to it. Sometimes Eugene was a soldier, sometimes a naval officer on loan to the army for a special mission—one gathered, to kill this German—and sometimes a pilot forced to land in enemy territory, but the final act, the killing, was always the same. Eugene had been forced to kill him at close range with his M-1. "He was so young," Eugene would say. "But I had to do it. Him or me. You know how it is in a war. He asked for a cigarette when he was dying, and I didn't even have one to give him. I would have given him, but I didn't even have one." Then he'd add sadly, "He was young. Just a kid."

The rest of us would look down, pretending to be embarrassed. Finally somebody would say, "Aw, you would have given him, Eugene. You would have given him the whole pack if you'd had it."

Anyway, after the war Eugene gradually brightened. He had gotten an Ike jacket somewhere and like many people in those days that was all you ever saw on his back. "Got to get a job," he'd say. "Got to make up for the years I lost. Got to get a job from one of those dirty-rat black marketeers who cleaned up during the war safe at home. Got to get an angle."

He was never really one of us, you understand. He was older and crazier and seemed not at all amused by his idiosyncracies, as though he suffered because of them even though he didn't know it. But we were all keen on him. When he came by—walking so fast that you didn't think he saw you, not walking his mother's dog but pulling it behind him, its feet locked stiff, the neck resisting, the paws grinding along the cement sidewalk, until suddenly he was abreast of you and he stopped and turned quickly and said what he had to say about the black marketeers and then started again, yanking the dog along—Danny Lubell would say, "I admire him. I respect him. One thing about Eugene. He don't stand still. Most nuts, they bury themselves in the sand. But not Eugene. Eugene moves along with the times. There's a war, Eugene fights it in his bedroom. Peacetime, he's a regular veteran worrying to get an angle. You got to give it to a man like that. He don't stand still. He moves right along with the times."

One night when he came by, Danny called to him, "Hey, Eugene, Eugene, where you been?"

He walked up close to examine us. He was wearing torn slacks and a dirty T-shirt. "Found an angle," he said mysteriously. "Busy now, can't talk much. Tell you quick and get along. Lots of details, lots to do. Sitting in the Roxy watching the picture. Next to me's this beautiful babe. I think maybe she's a movie star.

" 'Ain't you Eugene Lepransky from The Bronx?' she says.
" 'It's me,' I says.
" 'After the picture we'll go to my place up the Hudson, I got a few friends coming over, we'll dance,' she says. Well, I'm trying to figure out how to get there on the subway, but when the picture's over this big limousine pulls up, it's a block long. It's 'Miss' this and 'Miss' that from the chauffeur and I can see this is a fancy dame. We get in the car. Drive to this place up the Hudson. A palace! We go in. Butler at the door. 'Hello there,' he says. 'Hello there, miss.' What a place!
" 'You wait here, Eugene,' she says. 'I got to change into my beautiful ball gown. Then we'll dance.' So I'm waitin' for her and she comes down, she's got on this beautiful ball gown and we go into this ballroom. Chandeliers. Guys in tuxedos. We walk in right away everybody stops dancing and she nods to the guys in the band and she nods to me and we start to dance in the center all these people."

"In your *T-shirt?*" Danny asked him.

Eugene doesn't pay any attention to him. "So we're dancin' along and I give her the nod. How long can a guy dance, you know? We go off in her car, me and her and this other couple. We're in the back seat necking and up in front is the mayor and his girl. Just the four of us. Me and her and the mayor of the City of New York and his date. Necking."

"Eugene, the mayor was there?" Danny asked.

"Sure. Very horny man, the mayor. So later on she tells the chauffeur to drive me home and that's where I get the angle. Turns out the chauffeur is Black Matt."

"Who?"

"Black Matt, the pirate. He fills me in on the angle. We're going down the Amazon River on Black Matt's boat to find the mysterious black pearls."

"Eugene, Eugene," Danny says, "you can't cross streets."

"Only Black Matt knows where they are. Dangerous. Very

dangerous. We'll be millionaires. Only thing, they got these jaguars that they jump on the boat they try to rip you up. Black Matt wants me to shoot the jaguars on account he heard how I'm a good shot from the War Department. I'm going to shoot the jaguars and the Pygmies that protect the black pearls on account they think they're special holy eggs. Goddamn stupid Pygmies. Stupidest guy in the world is a stupid Pygmy. Lot of them in my outfit during the war. He's got movies. Black Matt's got movies. He showed me. Pearls as big as your fist. Black. You want to come along? I tell Black Matt you're good shots he'll probably take you. Need guys to lift the pearls. Heavy."

"Would you do that for us, Eugene?" Danny asked him.

"Got to ask Black Matt. His boat."

"Would we meet him?"

"Sure. Take you tomorrow."

The next day we were out in front again and Eugene came along pulling his mother's dog.

Danny called him over. "Eugene," he asked him, "when are we going to meet Black Matt?"

Eugene looked angrily at Danny, then at the rest of us. We didn't often try to trap him. Ox Hersh moved up in case there was trouble.

"Deal's off," Eugene said. "Black Matt died."

In 1949 Eugene went after his mother with a knife and they had to take him away. Shortly afterward—this was in the summer—I decided I'd better start school. I went around to the gas station and told Danny about it.

"Sure," he said. "Do that."

"Danny," I said, "I have to go to school."

"Sure," he said. "Look, I'm busy. Write me a letter."

After that I didn't see much of Danny and in a few weeks I went away to school.

I turned to my mother, who was still holding the photograph.

"I guess I'll go downstairs," I said.

"All right," she said.

"What was all that about Lesley's sister? You said maybe she's engaged, maybe she's not engaged."

"They got a telegram Lesley was killed on one of those games they play like it was war."

"Maneuvers?"

"Yeah. Maneuvers. Your cousin Lesley was killed on them."

We were never close; we didn't see each other often. He was just a fat, humorless cousin I had I used to run across once in a while, but his death was a shock to me. After a while I thought, Poor Lesley, unconsciously eulogizing him with the gag name with which I had come to associate him. Poor Lesley, foolish Lesley, who should have died in bed, somebody's fat and aged uncle, somebody's loyal, uninspired employee in honor of whom maybe the office was closed a couple of hours the day of the funeral. And now he was dead who had this silly, lethal vision of himself, which was, ultimately, the correct vision, the true one, however ridiculous or inappropriate. Now my cousin was a dead Marine, killed in a war game which was no game, outmaneuvered. Poor Lesley, I thought. He played it straight. A straight man.

I went downstairs to the candy store. I wanted to cry. Fein was an old man, his candy was stale and hard, his egg creams without life. "My cousin died," I told him.

"Condolences," he said. I wondered if he remembered me.

"Where is everybody?" I asked him.

He shrugged. "Where are the lousy people?" I asked him.

Some recognition came into his face.

"In a little while Belgium comes in to make his phone calls."

"Belgium's around? Good old Belgium. What phone calls, Mr. Fein?"

"He sells a policy. Between you and me, the policy is in *drerd*. You pay for sixty years, collect nothing. But he calls up people on the telephone. They buy from him sometime. Falls he sells football-parlay cards to school kids."

I sat down on a stool to wait. It was getting dark. About seven-thirty Belgium came in. He gave Fein a dollar and Fein gave him a bunch of dimes. He went into the booth. I went up to the booth and hammered on it. Inside, he jumped as though he was very scared. "Just a minute," he squeaked in his effeminate, pugnacious voice. Then he recognized me. He scooped up the dimes he had laid on the ledge and burst out of the phone booth. "Pal," he shouted. "Pal, it's you? No crap, it's you?"

"Sure it's me," I said. "How've you been, Belgium?" I shook his little hand.

"Never better. Never better. You want to buy a policy? I sell policies. I'm in insurance. I'm an insurance man. You still go to school?"

"No more, Belgium. All through," I said.

"Moving back? You moving back?"

"No," I said. "Where are the lousy people?"

"No more lousy people," he said. "Just me. All gone away. Want to buy some insurance? Fire? Comprehensive? Automobile? Accident? I got it. I got every kind of insurance. You need some? Shake hands. I show you fancy way I shake hands. In business world very important. Shake." He pulled my hand toward him and began to pump it with ornate, mystical gestures. "In business world very important. Rockefeller. Vanderbilt. J. P. Morgan. Baruch. Those boys knew how to shake hands. Want to buy some insurance?"

"No. No insurance. I heard about your lousy insurance." He looked hurt. "What do you mean all gone? Where'd they go?"

"Gone away," he said impatiently.

"Old Guy?"

"Ain't seen Old Guy three, four years. Upstate somewhere. Somewhere upstate," he said, waving his hand vaguely.

"Shelly Malkin?"

Belgium shrugged.

"The Ox? Ox Hersh?"

"The Ox? The lousy Ox? Don't speak to me about that *mumser.*

Don't say his name. He wrestles carnivals. Travels. Remember in the old days when I'd want to leave the bastard? Well, he left me. Travels all over the country, wrestles carnivals. Big bastard. I got a clipping from the paper where he broke a guy's neck in Jersey. I got a clipping. You think they'd arrest the rat? No. Jersey's crooked. You can break a guy's neck in Jersey they don't do a thing to you. How come he always gets away with it? How come? The Ox is married. Married a woman."

"Belgium, where's Danny? Where's Danny Lubell?"

Belgium grinned. "You want to hear something about my pal Danny? Remember that car of his? Now you know well as me a thing like that got no right on the streets. I mean, it's fun to play with, but it ain't a car. It's a toy. But I go up to him in all good faith after I become a businessman and I tell him, 'Danny, for old times' sake I get you coverage on the car.' He looks at me like I'm nuts and says, 'Look what happens. Look who all of a sudden is doing the protecting.' That's a hell of a thing to say to a pal, right? I try to tell him, 'Danny, you got to provide, you got to provide,' but you might as well talk to a wall. Well, the thing is, after the fat Ox started wrestling carnivals there was nobody to drive the car, so Danny takes it out himself. Well, don't you think he smashed it up?" Belgium was grinning broadly now. "*He* smashed it up. It looked like a smashed can he got through with it. No insurance, nothing. He didn't know how to provide."

"Was he hurt?"

"Hurt? He was damn near killed. Hospital for a month."

"He's home now?"

"Yeah, he's home. He's home. He's *in* a home, that's where he is."

I asked Belgium what he was talking about, but without Danny, or without the Ox, or maybe without even me there to watch him, Belgium had become just another self-centered nut. It was hard to get a straight answer out of him. He kept asking me if I wanted some of his insurance, and when I told him no, finally with real severity, he wanted to shake hands again. He kept saying that it was very important in the business world and that he was surprised I didn't realize this and buy some insurance. Finally he told me that Danny had had what Belgium called a "nerve breakdown" and that he was a real nut now, and that this was all you could expect from a guy who didn't know how to provide.

"You ever been up to visit him?" I asked Belgium.

"That nut?" Belgium asked with real outrage. "I ain't got no time to be a fool. I give him good years. What I got to show? Ox breaking guys' necks over in Jersey, Old Guy upstate somewheres, Danny in a home. I got a business to look after."

I asked Belgium for the name of the place where Danny was. He told me he didn't have it written down but that he thought it was on Long Island and that if he saw the name he might remember. Finally we got it from the operator. I told Belgium I was going to go out to see Danny and I asked him if he wanted to come with me. He said Sundays were his best days for making contacts and I didn't press him. I saw that in a screwy way he was providing.

I said, "So long, Belgium," and he looked at me shamefaced for a moment. I thought he was feeling guilty about Danny, but finally he said to me that he was in business now, and that if I could remember I should call him by his real name. "It looks better," he said, " you know what I mean?"

When I left the candy store I gave him my hand to shake, but he must have been thinking of something else. He merely took it and pumped it mechanically. There was no art.

On Sunday it rained but I went downtown and caught a train going out to Long Island.

There is something faintly disreputable and sad about people using public transportation on a Sunday. They are so obviously people on "outings," desperately counted-on holidays complicated by train and bus schedules, or they are cautious visitors, stiffly carrying their inexpensive boxes of candy to luckier people than themselves. I had written down the name of Danny's home on a slip of paper and beneath the name I had printed the address. On the train I showed this to a fellow passenger. Handing him the paper, I felt inexplicably sad and depressed, like a foreigner who does not know the language, or like an orphan shipped to relatives across the country with a tag pinned to his overcoat. It was as though I had no business going to Long Island by myself at all. I deliberately chose to ask directions of a well-dressed man, and as I handed him the slip I regretted having written down the name of what was so obviously an asylum. I almost told him it was a friend I intended to visit, just an old friend who had not taken care of himself.

The man was not positive, but he named a bus he thought I could take, and I did not check with any of the other passengers.

At my stop I got on the wrong bus. I should have asked the driver.

Waiting in the rain for a bus to take me back to where I had started, I thought for a moment that maybe the years with my friends had finally made me irresponsible too. Finally I got a cab and gave the driver the address. It cost me two dollars.

The home where Danny was seemed friendly enough, even in the rain. It was an old, sprawling, wooden building, but there were a lot of flowers, plenty of shade trees. It could have been a lot of places. I remember going to a funeral parlor not long ago. I had been apprehensive that the arrangements might be too stagey, but I was surprised to find I was really quite comfortable.

I told the volunteer I wanted to see Danny Lubell. She had to look up his name in her card file, and I guessed that not many people came to visit him. She called an attendant, who took me to the door of Danny's room and then turned to leave.

"Shouldn't you go in and tell him I'm here?"

"Don't he know you?"

"I haven't seen him in a long time. He doesn't expect me."

"It'll be all right. He's safe."

I knocked softly, then with more force.

Danny opened the door. He was dressed in a suit. Except for

the times we went to parties I couldn't remember Danny in a suit.

"Hello, Danny," I said.

"I'm nuts," he said.

"You always were," I said, and we went into the room. He stood by the door. "You afraid for me to close this or anything?" he asked.

"No, of course not," I said quickly.

"I don't like people peering in at me. They visit their relatives and look into every damned room along the way."

He seemed all right. The Sunday papers were sprawled out on the neatly made bed. Danny had probably been sitting in the chair by the window when I knocked.

"Back in town, hey?" he said.

"I'm visiting my mother."

"Way it goes," he said.

"Danny, you probably don't remember, you only met him once. My cousin Lesley? He was killed."

"The Marine?"

I nodded.

"Fat guy, shy around pussy-cat fur, joined the Marines. You told me about him. I remember. He was a beauty. The lousy people could have used a man like that. Yeah, I remember. Killed? Killed in the Marines?"

"He was on maneuvers."

"Son of a bitch," he said.

He went over and sat down on the bed on the papers. He looked at me for a long while.

"Bet you never thought you'd be seeing me in a place like this."

"Belgium told me," I said.

"*That* creep," he said.

"Joey Stowka. He told me to call him Joey Stowka."

"Joey Belgium Creep. Insurance Representative. Sometimes I think I'm pretty well off in here, but if people buy insurance from

Insurance Representative Joey Belgium Creep I'm sort of sorry I'm not out there. There must be a whole new crop of beauties roaming around loose."

I laughed. I started to laugh hard.

"Hey, cut it out, cut it out. They'll think it's me. They'll come in and feel the bumps on my head."

"Hey, Danny," I said, "what's it all about? I mean, you seem fine. How long—you know—will you have to be here?"

"I ain't made my mind up," he said.

"You can get out when you want?"

"You hear about Ox?" Danny said.

"From Belgium."

"How's your school? They taking care of you?"

"I'm through with school, Danny."

"But they took care of you okay? They kept you busy?"

"What do you mean?"

"You never did nothing but look, you know that?"

"I was crazy about you people."

"Sure, sure you were. But you never did nothing but look."

"You look too."

"I look *harder*. I strained my *eyes* I looked so hard. Not you."

"That's what I was there for," I said.

"Sure," he said.

"I was supposed to look."

"That's right, chief."

"I'm sorry."

"It's okay. You tried to give us your jerky cousin Lesley. Poor Lesley, now he's dead."

"What's that?"

"He's dead too, your jerky cousin."

"That's right."

"It's a pile of crap," he said. "It's no deal at all."

"Oh, Danny," I said, my heart tearing.

"It's no damn deal at all. It's a pile of crap."

He didn't say anything else. He sat there, on the bed, but

wouldn't talk to me. I tried to tell him I was sorry, but he didn't answer me. After a while I stopped talking and we just sat there together. I sat with him half an hour, then I had to get out of there. "I've got to catch my bus," I said.

"I've got to get started, Danny. Danny?" He looked up at me when I stood, but he didn't say anything. I walked toward the door slowly, wanting him to say good-by. There was nothing but my own footsteps going to the door. I turned around to look at him for the last time.

Still he said nothing, but I did not miss the broad wink in the wild and knowing eye.

PERLMUTTER
AT
THE
EAST
POLE

"It's absurd," Morty was saying to the chief, "three times around the world, attendance in eighty-two national capitals, fourteen days at one pole, eleven at the other—which reminds me: Did you know, you savage, there are *four* poles? Well, certainly. Read my write-up: 'East Pole, West Pole.' I got the idea from a popular song. That's where the ideas are. I tell them and I tell them. Read my write-up. There's a reprint in my knapsack. Anyway, it's ridiculous, the basic paradox of my life: *The places I've been.* In the knapsack—you saw yourself: seventeen hand-drawn maps of unexplored territory. You know those white areas on globes—no, of course not; how would you—well, Morty Perlmutter's been to most of them. Milonka? Check. Los Pappas, check. Frigtoony, check. Bishtumba, check. Bishtumba, check two times, once in summer, then in spring for the hatching of the slugs. It's nothing, incidentally. Nature is nothing. Here it's better. Wildnesses, *wildnesses!* Your Festival of Birth for example —those marvelous two weeks in Zum, our January, when all your women come to the clearing to have their babies in formation. Marvelous."

"You must stay," the chief said in Pragmatii, "for Lorp, your April."

"I can't. I *can't*. It's what I've been saying. I've been to Gish-lunt, to Kakos, to Schwatl, but never to New York City."

"*Fa na batoogie* New York City?" the chief asked absently, stringing another eye on the live-forever-have-fine-sons-win-many-noses necklace.

"A great city in my homeland, Chief, and I've never been there. Well, it's easily understood. California, where I'm from, has its own ports, and then even with my patrimony there's my terrific expenses and I'm always looking for bargain bays— Texas City, Texas; Tampa—No, no, not the turtle foot next to the *pig* ear, man. *There*, the *gland*, that should go with the finger. Forgive me, but I understand these things. For three months I studied with the greatest jeweler in the Baktivian jungle."

"We have our own ways," the chief said shyly.

"There it is—that's the curse—*that's* it. Relativism. When are you people going to learn there's only one truth?"

The next day Perlmutter pitched camp by the river and waited for the immunization boat. There was always an immunization boat. One of the ways he chose his jungles was by first learning of the prevalent diseases there and then finding out if there were serums to combat them. If there were, there would be an immunization boat somewhere in the woodpile and that solved his transportation problem.

He had to wait five weeks, and each night the chief came to his camp at the edge of the jungle to say good-by. Perlmutter was embarrassed one evening when the chief gave him the necklace he had seen him working on. Perlmutter gave the chief a reprint, but saw that the shy man was disappointed.

"Read it after I'm gone and make three wishes," he told the chief.

On the afternoon the boat came Morty hailed it from the shore. "Take me to where I get the mule," he shouted.

He wasted another day while the doctors immunized the natives.

As they were pulling away he heard a chorus of strange sighs from the direction of the clearing. Morty had never heard anything like it before.

"First of Lorp, must be," the captain said to the doctor.

It took three weeks to get to where the mule was and two after that before the sandy beginnings of the highway. It was another six days from there in the jeep to the port. In ten days there was a boat that could take him to a place where the cook thought there might be a ship for Vancouver, British Columbia.

Morty worked on his book along the way. It was, he felt, his best effort in his lifelong struggle to synthesize the universe. Still, something was missing.

In the evenings he listened to the songs of the sailors. He took them down and translated them into English, but there was nothing new to be gleaned from them.

From Vancouver he made his way across Canada and entered the United States at International Falls, Minnesota. It was fitting, he thought, that he should approach New York from the West. He was, after all, a Westerner. New York he had saved for last. It was no use fooling himself. It *would* be last. He had a million diseases; a polyglot death worked in him—there's your synthesis, he thought sadly—and as he made his way toward the East Pole he was troubled by his timing. He would be there in the final margins of his health and mind and resources, but it couldn't be helped. He had come as one only *could* come: prepared, knowing a trillion things, having seen everything else. As though New York were the land and everything else the sea—so great was his hope—and he were some sea changeling swimming from western depths, out of all the old places, toward a drier fate. He did not know what to expect, but it would be tremendous.

. . .

"No standing," the driver said.

"I have to see this."

"No standing till the bus stops."

Morty sat down in the front seat, over the wheel, and leaned far forward. He stared past the green-tinted glass, looking for light. Through the open window he heard the subaqueous roar. Under the water the bus hissed through the tiled tunnel. *And then light.* And then ramps. They spiraled toward a passageway. The bus went up and through and stopped.

"What is this place?" Morty asked.

"It's the Port of New York Authority," the driver said.

"Ah," Morty said, "*authority.*"

In a phone booth, with a tool he took from his knapsack, he severed the chain that held the Yellow Pages to the narrow shelf. He buried the thick book in the depths of the knapsack.

He was exhausted from his journey.

"Where are rooms?" he asked the woman in the Travelers' Aid booth. "I require a bed, a chair, a desk and light-housekeeping privileges. I can pay one hundred dollars a month for a good central location."

"This isn't that kind of agency," the woman said.

"But you know a good deal about this city?"

"Yes," the woman said, "we have to."

Morty reached inside his shirt and slyly palmed the Haitian Sleep Stone he wore on a chain around his neck. He brought it out and hypnotized the woman. She said she'd call a friend who had a place on West 70th Street.

"I'm done with all that," Morty said. "*East* 70th Street."

"Not . . . for . . . a . . . hundred doll . . . ars," the woman spoke soddenly from her trance.

Morty sat propped up in bed. Behind his head was the bulging knapsack he used for a pillow. He read the Yellow Pages until two in the morning and had just finished TAXIS when he had the inspiration. He went to Eighth Avenue and 164th Street, to the Manhattan garage of the largest cab company in the city. He chose one ramp and followed it down until he came to an enormous room where there were more cabs than he had ever seen. I could have used one of these in the jungle, he thought absently. Despite the vastness of the room and the dim light, the yellow machinery lent a kind of brightness to the place. Everywhere there were drivers, alone or in groups, writing up log sheets or talking together. Men stood in line in front of the coffee machines along the wall. Inside some of the cabs, the doors open wide on their hinges, Morty could see drivers reading newspapers. He heard the steadily registering bells on the gas pumps. It was three-thirty in the morning.

Morty walked toward the center of the cavernous room and climbed up on top of a cab.

"Hey, what's the matter with you? Get down from there," a man yelled.

"New York cab drivers are world famous," Morty shouted from the roof of the cab, "for their compassion and their oracular wisdom. I am Morty Perlmutter, fifty-seven years old, fifty-seven-time loser of the Nobel Prize for Everything, and I'm here to find out what you know." They stared up at him, astonished. "I got the idea from the Yellow Pages," he added sweetly.

"That's my cab that nut is up on," a driver said. "Come on, nut, off and out."

"I challenge you to a debate, sir," Morty shouted. "I challenge *all* of you to a debate. Let's go, every man on his taxicab." He watched them carefully. Someone moved forward threateningly but stopped, still several feet away from the taxi on which Morty stood. It was the Perlmutter Dipsy Doodle, the dependable mock madness, one of his most useful techniques. He told them that frankly. He told them to their faces. He didn't hold back a thing.

"It's a known fact," he said. "People have a lot of respect for insanity. Madmen are among the least persecuted members of any society. It's because they're not a *part* of society. They're *strangers.* The Greco-Persian ethic of hospitality lies behind that. Listen, I didn't read *Hamlet* until I was forty-two years old, but I learned the lesson. When does Hamlet die? *During the single moment in the play he's completely sane,* that's when! Figure it out." He folded his arms and hugged himself and did a little dance on the roof. He was completely safe. "Come on, up on your cabs. Everybody."

A man laughed and put a knee on his fender. "What the hell," he said, "I'm a sport. A sport's a sport." He scrambled onto the hood and made his way over the windshield to the roof of the cab and stood up uncertainly. "Hey," he said, "you guys look goofy down there."

Morty applauded, and below him the drivers were grinning and pointing up at the two of them. Soon others were climbing over their cabs, and in a few minutes only the man whose roof Morty had taken was without a cab to stand on. He seemed disappointed. Morty shrugged.

Perlmutter waited until the others stopped giggling and became accustomed to their strange positions. "All right," he said. "You men have lived in this city all your lives, most of you. What do you know? Tell me." He pointed to a fat driver on a taxicab across from him, but the man looked back blankly and smiled helplessly. Morty waited for one of the others to speak. At last a tall driver in a green cap started to say something.

"Louder, sir," Morty shouted. "It's hard to hear pronouncements in this cave."

"I was just saying that if you want I could talk about what's wrong with the traffic in this town."

The drivers groaned. Morty joined them. "Small-time," he said, "but that's an interesting demonstration of the limited world view. Thank you."

"I'll tell you how I give up smoking," another driver said.

"Why did you?"

"I went out and bought a whole carton and dipped them in the

old lady's chicken soup and let them dry out on the radiator overnight. Then when I'd go for a smoke—"
"Why did you give it up?" Morty interrupted him.
". . . you can imagine for yourself. They tasted—"
"I asked *why*. Why did you give it up?"
The driver stared at him. "Well, who needs the aggravation of
a lung cancer?" he said. "I got a brother-in-law in Queens he's got
three dry-cleaning plants, a daughter away at school. Forty-eight
years old he gets this cough he can't get rid of it."
"Self-preservation," Morty said, bored. "Nothing. *Nothing.*"
The man sat down on the roof of his cab. "Look," Morty said,
"I'm asking the meaning of life. This one says traffic congestion,
that one lung congestion. I won't be sidetracked." Morty wiped
his forehead. "New Yorkers, Cab Drivers, Big Mouths: I'm
Morton Perlmutter from the world's cities and jungles and seas
and poles. I come, a genius, but humble, willing to learn, you
understand, to the largest city in the world—that's crap about
London: they count everybody from Scotland to Surrey; Tokyo
the same—*the largest city in the world*, a capstone of the planet,
melting pot for the tired, the poor, the huddled masses, the not so
huddled, the works. And if anyone should know, *you* should
know. What's the meaning of life?"
Morty watched a driver cup his hands against his mouth and
he saw it coming.
"Life?" the driver shouted. "Life's a fountain."
"Yeah, yeah," Morty said, getting down from the cab. "I know
that one too."

He had been disturbed by his experience with the cab drivers. He
had meant, he supposed, to get the lay of the land, a maneuver
familiar enough, but, finally, deflective. Science itself was deflective, he thought. What did he care, after all, about hypotheses,
procedures, experiments? He needed answers. He was weary of
his endless preparations. He reminded himself of someone for-

ever adjusting his body in a bed, shifting, turning, raising, lifting, punching pillows, as though comfort was available only in
some future displacement. He knew that his endless making
ready would have to give way sometime to a final making do. But
for all he seemed to the contrary, Morty was an essentially cautious man and he knew that before moving in on the truth he
would have to make additional preparations. He would know
where to look when he had to, but until then he needed to lay the
groundwork.

He began his researches.

On successive weekends he attended representative churches
and synagogues. He read the newspapers, including the Harlem
papers and all forty-eight foreign-language weeklies and dailies.
He read only the local news and the letters to the editor. In the
New York Public Library he went through the newspaper files
for the years 1947 through 1962, collating the subjects of these
letters and classifying them according to their tones and literary
styles. (By 1952 beautiful patterns began to emerge, though
1958 puzzled him until he saw how 1960 explained away the
apparent discrepancy.) Once he spent a week in a branch library
on Staten Island studying the loan rate of thirty-five key books on
a list Morty had prepared himself. He walked through Central
Park and studied the litter. (Also he went through the garbage
dumps. What people threw away was frequently as significant as
what they kept, he felt.) He haunted hospital corridors and waiting rooms, observing the attitudes of a sick man's relatives and
friends. He crashed weddings and bar mitzvahs and confirma-
tions and baptisms and wakes. He watched the lines outside mo-
tion-picture houses and eavesdropped on the intermission conversations of theatergoers. He studied the menus in restaurants and
spoke to salad men and short-order cooks to learn what New
Yorkers were eating, and then used the information to work out
interesting metabolic calculations. He observed the crowds at
sporting events, deliberately inciting bets among the spectators.
(You could tell a lot about human courage if you knew the odds

men gave each other.) And he listened. Always he listened: to children, to hoodlums, to the old, the strong, to people in trouble and people who would never be in trouble.

In the second year something happened to interrupt Morty's researches.

"I'm a scientist," Morty explained suddenly to the woman next to him. This was his third day underground. "I'm trying to get the feel of the earth," he said. "Last night I was on the Broadway-7th Avenue local and I got out at 14th Street and walked along the tracks through the tunnel to 8th Street. Exhilarating, *marvelous*." The train had broken from its tunnel and begun to climb The Bronx. He glanced casually along the woman's bosom and down at Jerome Avenue. He looked back at the woman. She was a blue-haired lady of about fifty-three, heavy, probably powerful. He had seen the type before, in London, in Buenos Aires, in Paris, in Chicago. He saw in her a sort of *bahlabustuh*-cum-duchess who would survive her husband by twenty years. Perlmutter was attracted to such women; something atavistic in him responded while his heart said no. He imagined them around bridge tables, or playing poker in their dining rooms. He saw them giving daughters away in hotel ballrooms, and ordering meat from the butcher over the telephone, and in girdles in the fitting rooms of department stores. He had seen thousands of these women since coming to New York, recognizing in them from the days of some Ur-Morty (as if he had known them in the sea) old, vital aunts. She troubled him. He was responding, he supposed, to the *science* in her, to the solid certainty she gave off like a scent, to what he guessed might be in her an almost Newtonian *suspicion*, and to what he knew would be her fierce loyalty. Recognizing what he really wanted—it was to seduce one of these women—he had to laugh. The Morty Perlmutter who had known African Amazons and snuggled beneath arctic skins with Eskimo girls, who had loved queens of the circus and lady pearl divers—was this a Morty Perlmutter who could be stymied in

The Bronx? (Because he understood that he would probably never make it with her. He sighed.) A scientist *tries*, he told himself, and tried.

"Excuse me, my dear," he said. "I'm very clumsy at this sort of thing, but I find myself extraordinarily attracted to you. Will you have a drink with me?"

The woman would have changed her seat right then, but she was by the window and Morty had her penned in.

"I'll call the guard," she said.

"Now, now," Morty said. "What's in the bag?" he said. "Some little pretty for yourself?" he asked brightly. "Or is it for your husband?"

"None of your business. Let me out, you pervert, or I'll yell."

Morty stood up quickly. She seemed genuinely frightened and he leaned down to reassure her. "I am no punk molester of women," he said. "I speak from respectable need. Of course, if you insist on making a scene I'll have to leave you alone, but yours is a rare type with a rarer appeal. It is precisely my perversion, as you call it, which makes you attractive to me. Don't knock success, lady. When was the last time someone not your husband wanted to have a drink with you? I do not count the one time in the Catskills ten years ago when the guests waited on the waiters and the band played on. This I write off. Or when you danced with the college bus boy and he kissed you for the tip. *This* I write off."

She stared at him for a moment with an astonished respect, and Morty sat down again. He contemplated using the Haitian Sleep Stone but decided it would be immoral. "All right, I'm Morton Perlmutter and I'm here in the final phase of my search for synthesis. More later over cocktails."

"I'm married," she said, out of breath.

"Of course you are. Don't I know that? You think your kind of character is possible otherwise? It's sacrifice and single-mindedness that does that. It's years of love love love. You'll have to tell me all about yourself. I'm dying to kiss you. Where does your boy intern?"

"We have no children," she said shyly.

He wanted to take her hand. It was unscientific, but there it was. He wondered, too, if he might not make a cozy confidante of this woman. He knew what it meant, of course. Why not? He knew everything. All that was nonsense about the vital aunts. Morty was King Oedipus. He shrugged. I am what I am. Nothing bothers me, he thought lightly. This is my finest hour. One of them. It's all been swell.

"Let me have your number," he told her.

She shook her head.

"Let me have your phone number."

"No," she said, frightened again.

He used the Sleep Stone.

"I . . . am . . . Rose . . . Gold. You . . . can . . . usually . . . reach . . . me . . . at Klondike 5- . . . 6 . . . 7 . . . 4 . . . 3. Tuesdays I . . . play . . . mahjongg. Wednesdays I at . . . tend matinees."

He brought her out of it quickly. "Now about that drink . . ." Morty said.

"No. Leave me alone. You're a strange man."

"I am what I am," he said.

"This is my stop," she said, getting up. "Don't try to follow me. You'll be arrested. I'm warning you."

When she had called him a strange man, she had meant something unpleasant. His shock value had worn off. That often happened to him now. He equated it with the dying sense of wonder in the world. TV has done that, he thought absently, mass communication has. It made him angry. He followed her to the platform.

She turned quickly and faced him. "I meant what I said."

"I've got *your* number, Rose Gold," he said passionately. She started to walk away and Morty ran after her. "Listen to Perlmutter's curse," he commanded darkly. "May your neighborhood change!" She was running along the platform now. "May the fares to Miami be trebled! May your chicken soup freeze over!" She was going down the stairs now and he rushed after her. "*May your fur coats explode!*" he roared.

Just for the hell of it he went to the Chase Manhattan and asked to see the director. (He had to use the Sleep Stone on two tellers, one vice-president and three secretaries. This made him uneasy. You could wear it out—like anything else.)

"Been overseas," Morty explained to the director. "I'm thinking of moving my plant to New York City."

"That's wonderful, Mr. Perlmutter, but you'll have to forgive me—I don't think I'm familiar with your operation. If you could fill me in and then explain what it is you require of us—"

"Not so fast," Morty said, "not so very fast there. There are some things *I* need to know."

"I don't understand why our Mr. Johnson—" he said speculatively. And then cheerfully to Morty: "Of course, if I can help you."

"How's the water supply?" Morty demanded.

"How's that?"

"The water supply. Plants need water."

The director blinked and Morty went on. "I don't expect you to have all this stuff at the tip of your fingertips, you understand, but what is your labor situation in the area? Are the workers organized?" He thought of the natives back in the Pragmatii jungle. "Would there be women for my men?" he asked slyly. "These lads haven't seen white girls in years."

The director moved his chair back.

"Is there any culture?" Morty asked. "What about transportation facilities? How are the hospitals? In short, Mr. Director, what has New York City to offer me?"

The director had not heard the last few questions. He was

mumbling into an emergency intercom in his water carafe. Morty offered the Sleep Stone but the man wouldn't look.

He sat down in the Russian Tea Room on West 57th Street and addressed the waiter in Russian. "We are a long way from Lubsk, hah, cousin?" he said.

The waiter didn't answer and went immediately for the manager. The manager came over to Morty's table.

"It is miles to Pinfh, is it not, little Russian brother?" Morty said.

The manager glared at him. "You're one of those FBI guys, right?" he asked. "Sure, pal, I been expecting you." He turned to the waiter. "I never seen it fail. Every four months one of these FBI guys comes around and tries to talk Russian to my waiters." He looked back at Morty scornfully. "When are you boys going to wake up? You're looking for spies, go learn Albanian and eat at one of their places."

"Everybody is under arrest," Morty said weakly, his heart not in it. "I hadn't really meant to make my move just yet, but I was in the neighborhood."

On the fifth ring a man answered.

"Let me speak to Rose Gold, please," Morty said politely.

"Rose is next door," the man said. "Who's this calling?"

"My business is with Rose Gold," he said firmly.

"Is this a tradesman? It's almost midnight. Is this a tradesman?"

"I am Rose's friend," Morty said. "We used to travel together."

"Oh. To Philadelphia. The man who used to take Rose in his car to visit her sister? Why didn't you say so? Just a minute."

"Hello," a woman said in a little while. "What is it, Mr. Shintler?"

"It's me," Morty said, "it's Morty Perlmutter. Last month. The subway. I wanted to buy you a drink."

"How did you get this number?" Rose asked angrily. "Did you follow me?"

"No, no, listen to me. I'm very low tonight."

"Why did you tell my husband you were Mr. Shintler?"

"Can I see you?"

"No. Of course not."

"I'm very low," Morty said again. "I've been thinking about you a lot. Today's my fifty-ninth birthday. I haven't got any friends, any family. My money is almost gone. My health stinks. I'm restless. Also I'm worried about the synthesis."

"The what? What are you talking about?"

"I'm fifty-nine years old." He felt his heart turn over. He couldn't talk.

"You . . ." Rose Gold said. "*You*. Are you still there? What is this?"

"Don't hang up," Morty said.

"Look, I don't hang up on people," she said. "So. You've been thinking about me, have you? Well, I'm very flattered. I'm very flattered a fifty-nine-year-old man with no friends and no family and who rides the subway and bothers women has been thinking about me."

"I had to talk to somebody."

"Say, wait a minute," Rose Gold said. "You're *retired*. Am I right? And you're not fifty-nine, you're past sixty-five. Is that right? And you're out of business now and you're a widower and your children have moved away and you don't know what to do with yourself. Am I wrong or right?"

"It's nothing like that," Morty said.

"Of course it is," Rose Gold said. "Listen, I remember you too. You're basically a very decent-looking man, presentable, clean, I'll give you some advice. Move to Florida."

"Move to *Florida?*"

"Certainly."

"That's your advice?"

"Or California. Or Phoenix, Arizona. Wherever there's sun. Old people need the sun. It cheers them up."

Okay for you, Fatso, Morty thought. "Listen," he said, "I haven't any time. I think Shintler just came in. If he hears me my life isn't worth a nickel. He's coming after you when your husband goes to work tomorrow. He's got this powerful new car, and he's going to abduct you. He knows a place in Philadel—No, Shintler, I swear, I'm just sending out for pizza."

Morty couldn't sleep. It was hot in the room, and however he moved his head against his knapsack he could not get into a comfortable position. Also, as he had told Rose Gold a few nights before, he was very low.

He knew what the trouble was. For weeks now he had been statistically oriented—filled in, filled up. He was in a position now to move in on the truth. Then what? Where other men often experienced the vague emptiness of anticlimax, Morty was depressed by *ante*climax. It was what he called his "Moses Syndrome." (It was Morty's hypothesis that Moses hadn't died at the edge of the wilderness, and could have, had he chosen, entered the Promised Land with the other children of Israel, but that he had probably experienced, as Morty did now, an anteclimax and had turned back at the last minute. He had written it up. There was a reprint in his knapsack.) That's what happens to you, Morty thought. He punched the knapsack a few more times and finally gave up.

He called Rose Gold and told her he thought he'd go over to Central Park and try to get some sleep there. He asked her if she'd meet him, and she said no and not to call her any more.

In the park Morty propped his knapsack against a tree and lighted his South American Rain Forest Lamp. He set it beside him and lay down in the grass. He decided to browse through the Yellow Pages until he became tired enough to sleep.

He was studying RESTAURANT EQUIPMENT REPAIRING when he saw the boys.

His hand closed around his blowpipe. "That's close enough," he said.

"Who you supposed to be, man," the largest boy said, "Jungle Jim?"

Morty took careful aim and sank a poison dart directly into the center of the kid's T-shirt. The boy sat down solemnly. A second boy kneeled beside him and looked at Morty in terror.

"You killed my brother," he said.

"No, no," Morty explained, "he's not dying. I used Opiola. It just takes some of the fight out of them."

"Jeez," the oldest boy—probably the leader—said respectfully.

"You boys muggers?" Morty asked. "What do you generally clear on a night like this?"

"Hey, man," the boy on the ground said suddenly, "I feel great. He turned me on, I think."

"Yeah?" the leader asked, interested.

"Yeah. No crud, man, it's very, very great. I see interesting things. Thanks, mister."

Morty smiled.

"Mister?" the leader said.

"What is it?"

"Shoot me and my friend with the blowgun, hey."

"You boys muggers?" Morty asked again.

"No, man," the leader said, "we like to camp out."

"What do you do," Morty asked, "go after old ladies, old men, what?"

"Tell him, Ramon," the boy on the ground said, "maybe he'll shoot you." He lay spread-eagled in Central Park and looked up at the stars. "I never been so high," he whispered reverently.

Ramon looked down at his friend and then turned to Morty. "Sure," Ramon said, "that's right. We're muggers. My friend here hits them low and my other buddy hits them high and I grab their purse and clip them a little." He looked at Morty for approval. "We're dropouts," he added.

"I see," Morty said.

"Poison me," Ramon said hungrily.

The boy on the ground hummed *The Star-Spangled Banner.*
"That's a beautiful song," he said. "I never realized what a beautiful song that is."

"What do you make out of it?" Morty asked the leader.

"Depends," he said. "Hot weather, a lot of people in the park, maybe a hundred, a hundred-fifty a week."

"Wow," the kid on the ground said. "Wow! *Wow!*"

"But you have to divide that between you," Morty said.

"That's right," Ramon said impatiently, "between us. Go ahead, mister. Don't miss."

"Listen," Morty said, "do yourselves a favor." He took a memo pad from his breast pocket and tore off a notation and handed it to Ramon. "Here are the names and addresses of six organizations looking for boys. I took them out of tonight's paper. You'll make a lot more money and I understand there's a real opportunity for advancement."

"Okay," Ramon said, "in the morning. I promise. Shoot us."

"Why should I shoot you? You're rehabilitated."

"Don't waste time talking, man," the wounded boy's brother told Ramon. "Let's close in on him. He'll have to shoot."

"Yeah," the leader said, "yeah, that's right."

They moved toward Morty.

"It actually gets better," the boy on the ground said.

"No closer," Morty said.

"Come on, Ramon, jump him."

"No closer," Morty warned.

Ramon moved to spring at Morty, and at close range Morty pumped a dart into his stomach. The boy fell writhing to the ground.

"How is it, Ramon? Is it as great as George says?" the boy's brother asked.

"It hurts," Ramon said.

"It doesn't hurt," George said. "It's great."

"It hurts," Ramon said. "I think I'm dying."

"It doesn't hurt, man. It's very pleasant," George said.

"No," Ramon said, "it hurts."

"Ramon is right," Morty explained expertly. "I'm out of Opiola. I didn't kill him, but he'll have the pain for seven years."

Morty called Rose Gold.

"I'm terrified of you," she told him.

"No," he said, saddened. "No, Rose."

"I am. Terrified. You have our name, our number. Probably you have our address. I'm terrified."

"No, Rose," Morty said, "that's awful. Why should you be afraid?"

"Listen," Rose Gold said, "I've given the police a full description. You can't get away with frightening people."

"You're being too soft with him," a man's voice suddenly broke in. "I've hired private detectives. They've got important clues. You'll be brought to justice, don't you worry about that."

"Who is that?" Morty asked. "Who's there?"

"This is Rose Gold's husband," the man said. "I hear everything you say to my wife."

"Why are you talking to me like this?" Morty demanded. "What are you talking about clues? You want clues, I'll give you clues. I never had a secret in my life. I live at 205 West 70th Street. Come get me. What do you think this is?"

"Did you hear that, Rose?" the man asked, excited. "Did you get the address? All right, you," he said, "what do you want from Rose? Why do you keep calling her?"

"I don't have to tell you a thing," Morty said, "but as it happens, I have no secrets. In each society I visit I try to find somebody I can talk to. Then they pass on what I tell them. It's the oral tradition. When we finally met for that drink, I was going to share everything with Rose."

"Share everything? Share what?"

"Just the meaning of things, that's all," Morty said.

"Baloney the meaning of things," Gold said.

"Jerk," Morty said, "you don't think there is one? There is one, there is one. I have an astonished heart. Life is immense. Don't you know that?"

The man laughed. "Okay, Mr. Philosopher," he said, "you find out the meaning of things and you call us up at a decent hour and you let us know—but no drinks. No meetings and no drinks. We have your address. We can put our hands on you whenever we have to."

"No threats, please," Morty said quietly.

"This man is crazy, Rose," Gold said.

"Let me talk to your wife now, if you don't mind," Morty said.

"Sure," Gold said, laughing, "talk to her. Rose."

"Rose?"

"Yes? What is it?"

"Is he still there?"

"He's watching television. I guarantee you. What is it?"

"I'm very sorry, Rose. I didn't know how awful it was for you."

"He's a good provider," Rose Gold said.

"Don't patronize me," Morty said, raising his voice. "Don't hang up. I'm sorry I yelled. Listen, I think I can help you. In my knapsack I have a special soap. Its lather brings understanding. It won't give wisdom, but it opens the mind to the wisdom of others. Do you think you could get him to bathe?"

"Is that what you wanted to say to me?" Rose asked angrily.

"No. Listen. Tomorrow."

"Tomorrow?"

"Yes, tomorrow. I move up. I close in on the truth. Frankly, I've been putting it off. I'm a little nervous about it."

"Well sure, a big thing like that."

"I told you, Rose, I don't permit people to patronize me," Morty said, controlling himself. "Now," he said, calm again, "this thing tomorrow will be tremendous. I'm qualified for it to be. Before no—now yes. I told them in 1934, when I refused the doctorate. That was a speech. *That* was. What was I in 1934? A small, marked man, thin as a warrior, passionate in the guts but unripe as next week. Still, I told them. 'Doctors Lopus and Moore and Stitt and Frane,' I said, 'I decline to be examined. What of music, gentlemen? What of medicine and history and physics and literature? What of military strategy and folk dancing and astronomy and law? I know nothing, doctors. Good-by.' "

"Good-by," Rose Gold said.

"Not you. It's what I said. So now I'm prepared. Listen, it wasn't easy. These aren't the old-timey German-beer-garden days when all you had to do for knowledge was sell your soul. It's a buyer's market now. It probably always was. Anyway, it hasn't been easy. Those damned jungles, that creepy food, those redundant world capitals—all that lousy note-taking and collating and waiting for boats and keeping your ears off their bloody necklaces. Phooey, Rose. But—you prepare and you're prepared. Tomorrow."

"Hah!" Rose Gold's husband shouted. "Hah! You see? The man's a fool. He's crazy. Tomorrow is Sunday. *Everything's closed!*"

"*Tomorrow!*"

He left his room and went downstairs and crossed Amsterdam Avenue and walked the two blocks to the park. He entered and turned right, walking south along the western margins of Central Park, crossing intricate foot and bridle paths, raising his stout stick to greet the few early morning riders, cutting through greensward where the wet grass swished against his cuffs. He was grateful it was cool, for his knapsack was heavy and he had a long way to go. From time to time, from a hilly rise, he could see the fine apartments across the avenue, and once, down a wide, plunging street, the hazy green of Jersey like something at the bottom of a moated hill. Then the road—there was barely any traffic—swung next to him and he moved along narrower and narrower grassy plots out into Columbus Circle. "Oh, brave new world," he said, and caught his breath, and looked for a moment at the stunning marble brightness of the Coliseum. All around him were the city's new museums, theaters, concert, and exhibition halls. "This is it," they boasted to him. This ain't it, he thought, and shoved the knapsack higher, lifting it as one would push up on the buttocks of a piggybacking child.

He crossed the wide street and walked past the expensive hotels toward the Grand Army Plaza, seeing his face, like something on fire, in the brassy medallion plates of the Essex and Hampshire Houses and the Barbizon-Plaza and the St. Moritz and Plaza hotels. *And this ain't it*, he thought, catching a dim fragrance of open luggage, cuff links on the rug, melting ice.

He headed south on Fifth Avenue past the fine stores, their clean enormous windows reminding him of nativity scenes, glassed, moneyed crèches. He paused for a moment before a window, looking past his reflection into the cool, tweedy depths of the scene, and admired the horsey, intelligent dummies, a season ahead in a different time zone and climate, in some heaven off earth, standing, awkwardly graceful, self-conscious and chosen in front of the precious furniture and rare books. He caught a scent of the turning wheels inside Swiss watches. "This ain't it," he sniffed. "It's only the way it ought to be."

A policeman moved up behind him. Morty could feel the cop's eyes on his back. "I'm no revolutionary, Officer," he said without turning. "The thought of smashing this thick glass makes me shudder. I only wish I could afford some of this stuff."

"You a peace marcher?" the cop asked.

"Too old," Morty said. "Truth walker."

He crossed the street to look into the window of F.A.O. Schwarz and stared in amazement at the toys for the emperor's children, the king's kids, and then went down 56th Street toward Madison Avenue. In the distance, on both sides of the street, he could see the striped, fringed canopies and bright pennants of

French and Italian restaurants. They looked like the gay tents of ancient, opposing armies. Knights could have appeared under the awnings, buckling armor.

He turned down Madison Avenue and smelled electric-typewriter ribbons. At Abercrombie & Fitch on 45th Street, Morty stopped, startled. There in the window was a manikin, burdened as Morty himself was by a knapsack, but pith-helmeted, superbly, masculinely bloused, with clever canvas loops for his shells running like intricate braid across his handsome shirt, his field marshal's jodhpurs flowing like twin, wind-whipped flags into the rich leather boots. He marched proudly through his air-cooled, Platonized jungle, his eyes like jeweler's crystal, toward the grand bull koodoo of creation somewhere behind Morty's back. Morty was not put off. "No, this ain't it either, is it, oh, wax brother?" he said and moved east along 45th Street past Park, where the banks were and the new office buildings like upended trays of ice cubes.

He went on to Lexington, walking abreast of the stocky, Greeky splendor of the Grand Central Terminal, still idle and almost cabless this early on a Sunday morning. He followed the big building, like a stone roadblock, around two corners and came out at 42nd Street.

He moved toward Broadway. Now he could smell dollar-nine-cent steaks. He could smell publishers' remainders, paperback books, lenses, tripods, leatherette camera cases, record albums, little Statues of Liberty, transistorized tape recorders—plastic. Overwhelmingly he could smell plastic. "This ain't it, and this ain't even the way it ought to be," he said.

At Times Square he looked north into the great valley of Broadway. Slogans, the names of movie stars, trademarks, colossal painted labels stuck flat to the buildings like ripped shards of poster on a kiosk. In the wilderness of unkempt, unlit tubing scribbled across signs, he could just make out glassy, ghost traces of airplanes, fountain pens, the complicated wing movements of birds.

"Pretty wonderful, ain't it?" a man with a thick New York accent said to him.

"Sure is, hick," Morty said.

He turned around and walked down Broadway. Once he left Times Square and was into the Thirties he felt more comfortable, but he was very tired. He walked into the little square at 32nd Street and sat down on a bench to rest. An old woman in a dark cloth coat too warm for the day was across from him. She had on black, broken, high-heeled shoes and white bobbysocks, and sat feeding pigeons from a deep paper sack.

"Good morning there, mother," Morty said.

"Good morning there, tramp," the woman said.

Morty sat contentedly, looking from the great complex of department stores to the jerky thrusts of pigeon neck. "I am a traveler from the West who has come a long journey," he said after a while. "Can you tell me the meaning of life?"

She looked up and squinted at him, her squeezed eyes enormous and burning behind her rimless, sun-reflecting glasses.

"I can but I won't," she said.

He stood up, wiping his forehead. "In that case I must be moving on, hi ho Silver."

On his right as he went out was a statue of Horace Greeley. "*You* go West," he told the statue. The nerve of that guy, he thought.

He walked down Broadway.

In the garment district he looked up at the huge windows, enjoying the familial, personal poetry of the names of the firms lettered there.

Broadway moved into the East Side at 23rd Street, and he began to walk faster. Now he no longer looked around him but moved quickly, excited and urgent and nervous.

At 17th Street he rushed to the picket railing around the square and closed his hands tightly about two iron-dark spears. His heart pumped violently. The muscles in his throat, contracting, gagged him. *He entered Union Square Park.*

• • •

It was an open-air forum, the last in New York, one of the last in the world.

Morty had known about Union Square but until now had stayed away from it, saving it, savoring the idea of it. It would not be like Hyde Park in London, where a man would take your picture on a soapbox for money. It would not be like the Bughouse Square in Chicago, where the high-school boys, smug, mock innocence like jam on their faces, came to bully the speaker, to grab at his pants from behind. This was different. This was serious.

There were no boxes. *That* made the difference. It kept the exhibitionists away. He remembered Kachoa, where the king had no throne. He met you at eye level. There the laws were wise, complex fiats issuing as naturally as rote morning salutations between friends. He knew where he would have to come to hear truth when he read about a New York City ordinance that permitted speech-making in the park so long as the speakers were level with their hearers.

It was not yet eleven, but already the men had begun to gather. They were men just past middle age, in blue work shirts, or tieless in white short-sleeved shirts, the collars spread neat and wide as bibs over the lapels of their jackets. They lounged on benches with newspapers in their laps or sticking out of wide, slack side pockets in their suit coats. It alarmed him to hear them question each other about absent speakers and to see their smiles as each name invoked some old-cronied recognition. If they knew the truth, why, he wondered, would they come back? Then he thought: Why, to *relish* it; they return to relish it, like old men warmed by any familiar, mutual memory.

Men continued to gather. They came into the park and waved at acquaintances or stopped to chat with friends with the odd, dignified courtesy of legislators in a cloakroom. There was about the place—in addition to expectancy, which was what Morty brought there—a sort of placidity: an air among them of having shared together something immense and final and incorruptible. Though he had never seen any of these men before, he could almost tell which of them had been labor agitators in the thirties, which had been hit by policemen, or been cellmates, or conspired together in basements.

An hour had passed and still no one had begun formally to address the crowds. Just after noon Morty leaned toward the man next to him on the bench.

"When does everything begin?" he asked.

The man didn't look at him when he answered. "Too many regulars," he said out of the side of his mouth. "Somebody who's never heard it has to be around to listen. Otherwise it'd be like trees falling in the forest. Is a sound made?"

I've never heard it, Morty thought.

People continued to come into the square. Morty imagined them to be, like the men already there before he had asked his question, fellow connoisseurs.

Suddenly, and apparently at no signal, a man sprang up from a bench. He was already talking by the time he gained his feet.

"Ladies and gentlemen," the man was saying, "in the City of New York last year two hundred forty-three people were burned to death in fires. Now, that does not take in Westchester County or Newark in New Jersey or the burned populations of Chicago or Montana or any other place on the face of this flammable globe. That's the City of New York alone. Two hundred forty-three. How many of them husbands, fathers, kids, mothers, wives? And that's *death* I'm talking about. How many singed children or limbs burned permanently useless?"

People moved up to him. Some were smiling.

"What's the earth? How did it get here? The earth is the sun. The earth is a spinning fragment of the exploded sun. And I tell you that it is the natural function of the sun to burn. And I tell you that just as the acorn does not fall far from the tree, so too will the earth ever combust from here to eternity.

"Do not be deceived, my friends, by the notion of a 'cooling earth.' That's nothing but the cant phrase of sophist scientists—"

"You tell 'em, Smoky Joe," a man called good-naturedly from the crowd.

The speaker ignored him.

". . . *the cant phrase of sophist scientists.* Don't be lulled by it. As the one million people destroyed on the slopes of Etna were lulled. As the thousands charred beneath Vesuvius were lulled."

"Smoky Joe thinks the Empire State Building will erupt one day," a man shouted.

"Or as the natives of Chicago were lulled. Or Hiroshima. Or any of a hundred other places I could name." He turned to the heckler. "Wise guy. It will. One day it will. What do you think? Do you know what the combined total of fire-insurance premiums *is* on the Empire State Building each year? One million . . ."

". . . six hundred and ninety thousand," the crowd joined him, familiar with the figure, "four hundred seventy-two dollars . . ."

". . . fourteen cents," the speaker said, finishing just behind the crowd.

"Let him speak," Morty shouted.

"Thank you, sir," the speaker said, "but they don't bother me. Those bums don't bother me. All right. What do you think? Those guys know what they're doing they shell out like that. Everything burns. Where are your houses of yesteryear? Where are they? Gone. Burned down. What are your majestic ruins of Rome and Athens? *Burned buildings!* I've inspected them. I've been there and inspected them and they make me sick.

"The kindling point of human flesh is fifty-five degrees lower than the kindling point of a varnished hardwood floor, did you know that?"

"We know it, Smoky Joe," said a man through cupped hands. "You told us last week." Others near him grinned and clapped him on the back.

"What are we thinking about, friends? What are we thinking about to let this holocaust continue? And it *will* continue. Mark my words. It *will* continue. *What's the answer?*" Smoky Joe made himself taller as he challenged them. He grinned.

"It's not a case of fighting fire *with* fire, let me tell you," he said, and Morty, sick, knew it was a joke he had made a hundred times before. The speaker stooped for a moment and drew something out of a large cardboard file near his feet. Standing, he held out a mat on which had been mounted half a dozen box-camera photographs. They appeared to be views of a rather strange-looking house. He thumped the photographs with a thick finger. "The Fire Commissioner knows the answer. The Real Estate Board knows the answer. The construction interests know the answer," he said, building to a climax. "And Smoky Joe has lived in the answer . . ."

". . . *twenty-four years*," the crowd yelled, anticipating him.

". . . -four years," Smoky Joe echoed. "And what *is* the answer? It's processed tin. Processed-tin walls. Processed-tin floors. Processed-tin doors and ceilings. Simple? Yes. Fallible? Yes. I'm very frank. It'll burn. Everything will. But—after you've all been charred, marred and scarred in those Japanesey parchment-and-paper-dolls' houses you call homes, the chances are a million to one that old Smoky Joe will be sitting back, high, dry and cool in his processed-tin strongbox!" He pounded his photographs again.

"Cool you'll be," a man said, "—in *winter*."

"I already said it's not infallible. But suppose there *is* a fire. Now, it can't start in those processed-tin floors, walls, ceilings or doors, but let's suppose for the sake of argument that you've gone to bed and your wife is still up reading in the living room and she's smoking a cigarette, and she gets sleepy and her burning cigarette falls on her housecoat and starts a fire. Well, you're sound asleep, but you smell the smoke and you get up to see what's what, and you see all the furniture in the living room is burning. That could happen. Well, what do you do? *All you do is go back into your bedroom and slam the processed-tin door and forget about it!"*

"What about your wife, Smoky?"

"My wife is dead in a fire. Don't make jokes about my wife."

"Oh no," Morty said softly. "Oh no."

"He always uses the same example," a man explained. "He always uses the same example, and that guy always asks the same question."

Morty shouldered his way out of the crowd, seeing, suddenly projected on the grass, his shadow, the knapsack making a kind of hump on his back.

While he had been listening to the man who believed in fire, other groups had formed.

A dozen voices competed against each other, and Morty moved along the curving cement walks behind the backs of the crowds. It was like a holiday. Small children climbed over benches or darted in and out of groups, like dwarfs with messages.

In the crowds, constricted, clumsy under his knapsack, he brushed against the shoulders of other men and felt a queer, muffled shock, as though someone had stepped on an artificial leg he used, or struck him in a glass eye. He shoved against people— collecting randomly now, drawn to the speakers by some curious abeyance of the will, as men pause before one booth rather than another at a fair. He stepped over a low iron railing onto a soft no-man's-land of grass. A policeman waved him away. He moved back into the voices.

He stopped to listen to a man with a beard, and it struck him that the man appeared not so much to address those men already listening to him as the others—those passing by in low-geared, imposed shuffle, or already settled in small, thickish bands around other speakers. He did not speak or persuade so much as *call* his oration, the ideas strangely shouted in an unthinking excitement, like someone with another's umbrella rushing to a doorway to call after the guest who has left it behind.

"People waste time," the man shouted. "They're fools. It's simple. I never ask questions. Notice that. No one's ever heard me ask a question. The most perfidious instrument in all human language is the question.

"Look at your great teachers. 'Verily I *say* unto you,' Christ says. The Ten Commandments are not questions. Not one sentence in the Declaration of Independence is a question. No valuable literature or great human or divine instrument is ever interrogative. *Sermons! Declarations! Commandments! Marvelous!*

"There is no room or time in life for questions. Questions are the breeding ground of dissension, atheistic pestilence and war. I tell you that when I hear men talking together and one man asks another a question, I want to go up and shake that man!

"Look at your tragic secular literature: Faust is punished for asking questions. Oedipus is. Hell is a questioner's answer. Nature's sinuous and hideous serpent forms a question mark as he writhes along the ground. So did he in Paradise! So does he in Hades!

"Ask me no questions I'll tell you no lies, the poet says. No one has ever heard me ask questions."

"What do you do when you're lost?" a man asked.

"Who gets lost?" the bearded man roared.

Morty pulled away, turning carefully, conscious again of the heavy pack, feeling clumsy.

"When do *you* speak?" a boy said, coming up to him. He was young, vaguely tough. "I been here a hundred times. I never heard you speak."

He pushed past the boy.

Five men stood casually before a lamppost. One, jacketless, his bare arms slackly ribbed with long, stretched veins, addressed the others in a husky, conversational tone. Morty could not be sure whether he was a speaker or someone who had come there to chat with the others.

"Forty years I had a store in The Bronx," he said, "and I tell you the important thing is the right mark-up."

Another interrupted him. "That's all very well. Of course, mark-up is important—"

"The *right* mark-up, I said."

"All right, the *right* mark-up, but more important is knowing how *much* of an item to stock."

"No, no," a third said, "it's the timing, knowing when to sell what. You got to understand the needs of the neighborhood."

"Display. Display is everything," a fourth joined in. "In the proper package you could sell a rat on a stick."

"I don't know," the last man said. "I think good will. Good will is very important."

Morty left them and went toward a tall, gray-haired woman a few yards away.

"The salvation of the world," she said calmly, "can only lie in the successful efforts of our organization to bring to bear as a practical, major influence in all the underdeveloped nations, as well as in all the presently constituted world powers, free and iron curtain, the noble principles of the universal Republican party!"

When he turned away he saw the boy who had asked when he would speak. A friend was with him, and the two of them pointed to Perlmutter. The boy who had spoken nudged his friend expectantly.

Morty went toward the largest group he had yet seen, the people standing in a sort of deep, shapeless huddle. They shifted from foot to foot like people dancing in place and craned their necks back and forth nervously, endlessly, evidently trying to obtain some momentary view of the speaker hidden amongst them. They reminded Morty of the pigeons he had seen the old lady feeding in the park. Maybe this time, he thought, and moved closer. From where he stood, still at the perimeter of the crowd, he couldn't hear the speaker. He would have moved away, but just then, out of the corner of his eye, he saw that the two boys were still following him. To get away from them he pushed harshly against the people straining to get a look at the speaker. When they saw he wore a knapsack they dropped back, intimidated and docile, and then closed around him again as though pouring in to fill up an imaginary wake.

Now he was surrounded, and apparently no closer to the speaker he still could not hear. He lunged forward, the canvas hump climbing unsmoothly on his back, and pushed through the final ring of people. There, in the center of the crowd, was a tiny man, shirtless, bald, explaining, in a thin, wavering voice pitched like a whisper, the tattoos that completely covered his torso and arms and hands and face and skull. It was as if he had been impossibly wrapped in a tight, shiny oriental rug. He raised his left arm and pointed with a tattooed finger to tattooed hair etched into his shaved armpit.

Morty stumbled past him without looking and, arms extended, reached into the crowd behind the man, jabbing at them stiffly to make them move.

When he emerged, the boys were waiting for him. Now there were four of them.

One came forward as if to speak to him, and another reached out to touch the pack on his back. Morty jerked violently away. Somewhere he had lost his stick. He only realized it now that he meant to strike them with it. They continued to trail him in a sort of sneering casualness, and he turned on them.

"I am not defenseless," he said. "Stop following me."

"It's a free park, ain't it?" one said. "When are you going to speak? Are you going to speak or ain't you?"

"People must . . ." a voice said suddenly, clearly. "That's what I've been trying to tell you." So abruptly had the voice broken into all their consciousnesses that even the boys looked away to see its source.

"It's the Professor," someone at the edge of one of the groups said, and Morty could see the sudden turning of a dozen heads, faces slamming alert.

"Where?" one asked.

"There. It's the Professor. The Professor is going to speak."

The groups dissolved, the speakers around whom they had been standing suddenly abandoned in mid-sentence, their mouths still open in stunned discouragement. Thirty feet away Morty saw the tattooed man appear as the crowd around him broke up. He had put on a hat and was buttoning his shirt.

Morty stumbled after the rushing crowds, but his knapsack was an almost unbearable weight now and he could not keep up. Already the crowds had re-formed into a single mass. Morty caught up and tried to push through but they shoved him back, his assertiveness, even his knapsack, no longer seeming to have any effect on them.

"People must serve . . ." the voice sang out, hopelessly hidden from Morty. He was struck by its precision and strength and clarity, by the wholesome sweetness of its range and timbre. He could not really tell if it was the voice of a man or a woman. It could even have been a child's.

"It's what I've been trying to tell you, trying to say," it went on.

This would be it, Morty thought, alarmed and startled and pleased. This would be it and it would be worth it. That was the incredible thing. For a moment he regretted the ordinance that forbade platforms, but then he realized it made no difference that he couldn't see the speaker.

"People must serve . . ." the voice said again, very slowly. "It's what I've been trying to say, to make you understand, it's what you must learn for the guilt . . . it's the only thing that will help it, the guilt . . . help the guilt— People must serve . . ."

The splendid beauty of the voice thrilled him. Even the others were hushed. Far away, against a tree, the policeman leaned, his face as rapt as any there. The man who believed in fire and the man who never asked questions stood together, staring toward the voice, their faces, like Morty's own, waiting, calm.

"People must serve—" the voice said, tired now, strained with the effort of mouthing the first premise of the universe "—must serve their necessity. People must serve their necessity—knuckle under to their necessity."

Morty waited for the voice to go on. In the silence that followed the last pronouncement he and everyone else—there were hundreds now, it seemed, perhaps thousands—stood in thick, sedative patience.

They waited like that for five minutes, perhaps ten. Then someone shrugged. And another did. And a man sighed. And a fourth coughed. And someone else was the first to turn around and walk away. And then, in a distant corner of the square, a rough voice began a new address. And then Morty could not see where the people had stood to listen to the voice. "Tch, tch," Morty said sadly. "Tch tch tch." It was the beginning of his compassion.

They had no preparation, no facts, no languages, no questions, no years behind them of jungle and pole and city and sex, no totems, no tokens, none of the trillion knowledges, none of the patience that Morty brought there. What would they have heard, what could they have made of it? To them it had been babble, less than nonsense. He had prepared, and everything had been made good. Redeemed, he thought. He was excited as he had never been excited. No. Yes. Once, he thought. When he had first conceived of what his life must be.

He had begun to tremble. A man, passing him, stared. "What's eating that one?" he heard him say to his wife.

Morty slipped the straps of his knapsack off his shoulders and down over his arms and let it fall behind him. He turned and climbed on it, standing slowly, awkwardly, striving violently for balance on the soft, uncertain perch.

"Ladies and gentlemen," Morty Perlmutter began. He was glad the weather was warm. He would have weeks of it yet. In the fall the nights would be cool, but there were the big, folded

Cajawohl heat leaves in his knapsack. If he was careful the Sambatlian total-food berries might last half a year. "Ladies and gentlemen," he repeated. "Ladies and gentlemen and Rose Gold . . ."

AFTERWORD:
STANLEY ELKIN,
THE STORY MAN

This is about Stanley Elkin and this book of *stories*.

The story — well, the long story, the novella, the short story and the very short story — constitute a genre troubling and difficult to write, troubling and difficult to write about; difficult to analyse and review, difficult to get a grip on in terms of teaching or learning, a problem technically.

The genre of short prose fictions of a certain length (the definition proposed by Henry James) has puzzled critics since its inception. Writing courses in this country have made it the genre of entry into the profession of writing. And the ways it is taught — as a form of confession, as a form of emotional philosophizing, as diary-keeping-cum-joke-telling (American autobiography plus attitude) or as a branch of letter-writing (in terms of a more sophisticated recounting of what are essentially anecdotes) — make the reality of the genre still more puzzling. Writing courses teach kinds of prose — kinds varying from course to course — that have as much to do with learning to think, while keeping a record of that thinking, as they have to do with propitiating some god or goddess who bestows inspiration, or with literary merit.

The modern story, or novella, is *not* book length. It lacks some principle of independence as a publishing unit — a principle that has to do with meaning, I think — and so it remains a journalistic genre largely identified as *not* being a journalistic (or biographical) anecdote, while existing under the constraint of always having to be considered as something more suited to publication in a periodical than to publication as itself alone, as a pamphlet or a book.

Meaning and length. The matter of *length* is probably the most important element in the genre technically, and in such important other ways as the length of time it takes to read it and the length of time it takes to write it and then the amount of actual time it purports to represent. So that someone who writes passable stories, and passably good stories, and very good stories, and very very very good ones (the category Stanley Elkin is in) can be discussed in terms of his or her regard for and intelligent use of length in this genre — length and scale, length and duration; the kind of attention that is asked for, the kinds of characterization of places, people, actions that are used in the account.

This is not the place to discuss the relation of journalism to art, that is to say, the relation of journalistic accounts to amusement, instruction, catharsis, and significance. Or the roles that story and character play (and don't play) in various cultures.

One might mention, however, that in a journalistic account of an event two stories are automatically present, that of the event and that of how the information was gotten, written, and presented — and that in journalism, any extensive study of either of the two stories is called *news analysis*. News story and journalistic history and commentary are like text and biographical study and critical analysis.

So far, in the history of the modern story, stories that are too journalistic have not done well in the course of time in terms of popular and critical judgment. Journalism is perhaps a horrendous but essential and valid and *moral* (sometimes) simplification of life — useful within reason and, of course, very dangerous, as a basis for immediate judgment — while *art*, to use a maddening term, when it is capable of holding the attention of an audience over long stretches of historical time, is not a simplification of any significance: it does not philosophically or morally simplify.

In a story, the formal resources of ancient emphasis — soliloquy, interlocking accounts, dramatic revelations — interrupt it, usually. Perhaps it can be said a story is a study in the simplification of emphases and in uninterrupted, or steady, attention. When you read a good story, you mostly don't rest your attention until you finish. Generally, in its apparent invention of a sort of narrative time (and of a public time and public place of auctorial speech to a reader), the story uses techniques and devices (tricks) to convey ideas and to generate feelings. It's probably all right to call this *significance*: the reason for reading it, the reason for writing it. The pattern of significance in a story of any length is unlike that of a news story and is unlike that of events in actual time. It usually gives to readers a sense of conclusion and of concision but not of complete conclusion, not of completeness, not of true finality.

The presence of often stale significance is taken as simplification, but, except in terms of study time, staleness is not simplification: it is emptiness. Concision is a matter of the weight of meaning per word, phrase, sentence, paragraph, and piece: How much padding is there? How much dubious or pseudo meaning is present? How much dubious maundering?

Concision has nothing to do with simplicity. It relates to something often called *density*. Density is not often praised, particularly by readers who want to feel emptiness is concision. Anyway, in *art*, concision is a complex matter. It is partly a matter of courtesy toward time — but not in terms of the time it may take to absorb what is concisely said when what is said is worth saying. It asks something of a reader: it asks for sophisticated comprehension.

But here is where biography enters in: For a long period of

time after something is written, it can ask for comprehension only as sophisticated as that of the author.

It can be argued that a novel should be more accessible than a story of any length because the novel is less concise, less driven by considerations of concision, and of codification, and so is more accessible than a story. There is more time to learn the writer's language. The writer gives more evidence for his opinions. One has more time to use what one learns about comprehending the procedures of significance in the course of reading so many pages by one author. Strenuous forms of emphasis can be used. It should be taken for granted that the reader's attention will vary; the reader's mind will wander; her or his attention will even stop at times.

On the whole, the greater the significance for us, the less we notice the concision as we read. And the harder it is to define the concision. And the less the significance, the easier it is to discuss concision, and even to see it.

After all, on one level concision is a convenient trick having to do with publicity — with journalism. *Veni, vidi, vici* is showy fun that has stayed amusing for two thousand years in its concision, but it is not of the same order of meaning as *ripeness is all*, although it uses the same number of words.

Elkin is of the *ripeness is all* school of writers.

Journalism, because of its nature, must be self-righteously conventional. It deals in clichés because of the constraint it is under to be current and to be read with appropriate quickness. It informs a reader: it does not train her or him in the use of language of the description of feeling and of event and in the actuality of character.

It deals in changeable clichés of no great age.

A news story — a newsy account of a love affair as part of a murder scandal, say — is a shrewdly worded account that deals in quick responses and in a quick transparency of *apparent* comprehension. And it is meant for large numbers of people, an audience larger than any single congregation addressed by a single voice, than any audience limited in size by considerations of any actually physical architecture, than any audience for traditional art.

Good stories, I think, very often correct journalism. Thus, the stories in this collection.

If these stories of Stanley Elkin's are art — and it is more than merely likely that they are — then they convey significance which is not simple; and they are not journalistic or familiar in form (or in intent), and we must approach them — and here is the paradox of the genres — in a spirit entirely unlike that in which we open the magazine or journal in which they might appear.

And this is a problem . . . Where does one find the context in oneself? It is easy to say that a good story is worth six or sixteen or six hundred bad novels, but reading sixteen bad novels — and six hundred news stories — is a preparation for reading that is not much like the act of reading these stories.

What is our experience in reading *good* stories? If one is an absolute-absolutist, one says that doesn't matter. Truth is truth. Excellence is excellence. And so on.

But if one is a sensible relativist, one says that one ought to know a bit about post-modernism, about Davenport and Gass and Barth and, also, about Bellow and Bach; but it is also true that nowadays education is more diverse than it used to be. Reality — not the reality of the realists but the reality of the philosophers and the scientists and of some writers — reality invites pluralism in discourses, in approach, and in perceptions: reality rests on diversity.

Old-fashioned flat remarks are not very useful: they never were, really.

I say the presence of art means a greater degree of truth than is possible with journalistic simplifications, and that one approaches good stories like these as one approaches a semi-secret assignation with someone, one's tie to whom is a correction of one's ordinary attitudes, habits, self-denial, hiddenness.

But the modern short story and the onset of mass literacy (or nearly mass literacy) go hand in hand. And many of the attributes of the story have to do with mass literacy and not with privacy and some semi-illicit nakedness or secrecy of response. The attributes of modern literacy that fathered that which turned into the popular novel and the popular movie — whether that fathering is stylistically disguised or not — inevitably play with the idea and reality of media fame as if fame were the princess in a legend or the happy ending that replaced the happy endings of the large-scale chronicle novels of the last century.

And famous stories exist — there are stories that have a mass media existence.

But I would still want to argue (even if a figure of speech is not quite an argument) that good stories mostly exist in people's talk and in individual minds, and that in settling down to read them one is as if going to a rendezvous.

Two writers in the past, great and journalistic (and in English), are Defoe and Dickens; and much of their work can be broken into units of linked stories. And their sense of diction at a rendezvous has stayed modern.

A writer has a great many ancestors, and a great many sources for their work; in Elkin's case, rightly or wrongly, I see a line of descent from Defoe and Dickens.

Some people equate Jews with mass literacy but let's not discuss that here except to say that elements of that question inflect Elkin's work. His literacy is enormous — verging on enormity. The literacy of the Jews in his stories, the verbal dexterity, is rarely less than extreme. His characters are not victims, like Wozzeck, because of ignorance or verbal inadequacy. And moral questions for them are not hovering and inexpressible — are not implied — but are present, expressible — and expressed. This is a form of clarity, not of simplicity.

And it comes as something of a shock, the extent and ways

they are articulate. And then, too, American writing this articulate is rare.

Some people associate Jews with the death of Christian social classes (mass literacy and mass moralism destroys the distinctions between the old social classes which were set by differences in literacy and illiteracy and by consequent differences in moral outlook), and Jewish literate classlessness happens to be an element in Elkin's writing as well. The absence of social distinctions of the usual Christian social sort found in the canonical novels and the stories written by famous novelists may obscure the accuracy in these tales of the sense of actual predicament and of actual character, shown by linguistic means here, and the degree of "realistic" but more often "stylized" social observation.

The short and long story, as we know it, took shape in the nineteenth century as a result and concomitant of revolutions: the American, the French, the industrial, and then the Decembrists, 1848, the Paris Commune, on and on . . . The creation of a large, monied middle class — the *responsible* class in modern times (*pace* Marx), but new, ill-informed, untraditional, with no great moral claim except as *responsible* — changed our sense of language. In fact, in one sense the new class deconstructed all prior uses of language and all later deconstructions unwittingly mimic that and are, I think, willy-nilly middle-class movements no matter how disguised as radicalism.

Part of what grew up in that deconstruction was a new hierarchy of *literacy*, which, tendentiously, I would like to describe as consisting of rich men's and protected women's art novels, and of the popular novel (and drama), and of the quite low-ranked but extremely important journalistic story. These three ranks of the New Literacy are highly aware of one another. Some of the effect of beauty in Elkin's work (as in Chekhov's) is the combination — the conflation — of elements of the three ranks.

The new class needed daily or weekly or monthly information because the newly formed industrial world moved rapidly and, also, partly because the new class did not have methods and systems and traditions of its own and was improvising as it went along and needed quick, up-to-date advice about a great many things.

Such mass information (and the consequent social arrangements and social organisms or *mechanisms* perhaps) formed the spine of its existence, and the grounds of its superiority to the lower classes and to the hereditary aristocracy, and was the grounds of its power, its efficiency, its efficacy, its ugliness, and its many obvious failures.

The line between this as a search for a sort of Baconian truth of daily existence and the corruption of this information as *propaganda* was always, in actual practice, uncertain.

And that moves over into art where it becomes a question in the works of Wagner and in nineteenth century philosophy and early twentieth century philosophy, in general; and in our country, it becomes a central issue in Thoreau, Melville, Dickinson, and the rest—and, currently, Elkin, Gass, Davenport, and others . . . I mean the refusal to accept mass information is overtly central in their work.

The games, the strength and dexterity of language, and the sometimes appalling truthfulness of these stories of Elkin's— their having a very large truth-element as art, not journalism — makes them important; but it is not an importance that can be dealt with by the reviewers, academic or popular, who deal with such matters, unless they are willing to be students of his and to recognize their own defects—their thinness of conventional response in the light of the largeness of *his* response, the depth of technique, the subversive game of new emphases that he plays and the games with length, speed of narration, concision (and unconcision), and so on.

Conventionalized discourse and false and true revolutions lie at the center of what I think of as the melodrama of the spread of a form that depends on length of attention and subdued emphasis as the main elements in its formal arrangements. I think you can see this in these stories — a war with conventionalized discourse and a recurring surrender to it — and the characters caught up in false and true revolutions of attitude, of outlook.

Chekhov began by writing for a newspaper, as did Dickens, and as did George Eliot (in a somewhat different form). The movement into book length by the latter two is more than roughly equivalent to Chekhov's movement into longer sentences, longer tales, and, generally, more complex forms of concision and less simplified significance as he grew older (and more famous).

In his case, one guesses, he did not intend to write in the shadow of Tolstoy. He avoided the genres Tolstoy had exploited. One can see in Nabokov's silliness and frequent absence of significance how crippling Tolstoy's shadow was. One can also see in a number of Nabokov's novels the presence of long stories, which are more truly what if they are they are considered separately as stories than if they are considered to be parts of novels. Often, excerpts from those books are considerably better, are more artful, are more matters of art, than are the books themselves.

Elkin bathes these matters of inherited forms and of commonly held information and banal but also real revolutionariness (if I can say that) with a kind of bottom-of-the-heap Jewish lyrical snottiness and direct and inverted skepticism that has amazing reverberations (I don't mean Elkin personally, but the persona that stands behind the voice of many of these stories).

Length, not requirements of narrative, determines the scale of things in a story. The reader supplies much of the story. If you consider that Poe and Sir Walter Scott and Lord Byron are roughly coeval, you can see that Poe expected his readers to know that other sort of adventurous narrative with its usually happy ending. De Maupassant expected his readers to be familiar with nineteenth century French narrative, Hugo and Balzac. But Henry James and Chekhov seem to me to rely much more on readers knowing journalism, not novels.

They are opposed to and yet derived from journalism.

The blowsiness of novelists is no accident nor is the marvelous use of not going on at length by story writers of merit.

Chekhov, now taken to be the greatest master of the form, wrote paragraphs and sections of stories that are clearly *novelistic* in their use of length; but he and other short story writers of the (currently) highest rank have been so far more clearly artful and restrained in form than their novel-writing counterparts have been.

Not De Maupassant, who was trained by, and who was considerably less artful than, Flaubert. And sometimes a coeval short story writer and novelist are nearly equal in their sense of formal restraint, as in the cases of Katherine Mansfield and Virginia Woolf (but the latter includes more and has emerged as the writer of greater formal interest). Chekhov did, ably, place a great many novelistic paragraphs in sequence — he did it with care and usually with some punctuation of unnovelistic paragraphs. The more novelistic a story writer is, the sloppier in matters of length and shape and in matters of characterization; but these ace writers make it work.

The matters of length and shape should be paramount in any study of stories, long or short. But that is lousy work — hard, vague, unvocabularied, really bad work for beginners.

In our century, which now is ending, the line of good and very good short story writers splits into three categories. One is public and very popular: O. Henry and Damon Runyan. (And some novelists chose to do similar work in popular and not so popular novels: one thinks of Jack London and of Nathanael West.)

A second category is of the intense and rather odd. This category includes Katherine Mansfield and Saki and W.W. Jacobs. And Sherwood Anderson. Borges. Kafka. Babel.

But the third category is that of the quite serious and effective and valid but not actually short works, not actually stories. This category is occupied by able novelists such as Lawrence, Joyce, Faulkner, Mann.

So far as I know and judge, no writer has written with equal success in two of the categories; so far, it has always been one or the other.

None of the three categories can be taught — and none is reducible to formula. One can say the chief difference, if one thinks of the symptomology of stories, is in the nature of significance: there is no real significance in a story of the first sort, merely a sensation of pleasure, and perhaps a sentiment.

The significance in the stories of the second type is primarily solipsistic: it is rarely, if ever, a matter of character, no matter the pretenses of the story. Good stories of this sort, as of the first sort, match one of the Bahktinian categories — that of subversion of official language — but cannot produce a plurality of voices.

The significance of the third sort of stories has not been written about much. The assumption has been that the writers did it better in their novels. But one can notice that the stories in this category are subversive and do, usually, offer more than one valid voice.

Stanley Elkin, but not with great firmness, is in the last category; but it would seem that at moments he tries to be a writer of stories in the second category.

Good for him.

One notices the rhythms of the opening of a story — the rhythms of individual sentences and the successive rhythms of the first five sentences, say, including the rhythms of the presentation of the emergency, of the reason for writing this story, for relating it (two different things), and of what is offered you as an inducement to read the story. The density of the concision, of ideas and of events — indeed, if you will permit me, the presence of the absence of no-meaning — is at once recognizable as the context for the rest of the story.

And the matter of length, the length of time devoted to a character, to an action, to an idea, is apparent in every sentence, every phrase, every reference. This is why good stories of the first and second type, and many of the very best stories of the third type suggest they are a form of poetry and of poetic drama, and do not seem to be directly related to novelistic prose or to the prose of memoirs and of letters.

The length of a sentence, of a paragraph, of a scene in a story is a showy matter as it is in popular music. As it is in classical music in concert halls. It should not be a matter of such importance in a novel — and in the good ones, it isn't.

The history of length, if I can say it like this, is partly the history of seriousness; and in every public and popular form it is something an audience knows about. Art of this sort, a public sort, widely known about, is always micro-historical — as are sports.

But melody and orchestral color and mood in a piece of music are all subsumed under length or are aspects of length in a short story and in a long short story and in a very long story and in a novella. The length of a riff, of a speech, of a scene is the melody, the orchestration, the public mood in the stories in this collection. The matter of length can be so showy a matter that one might say it can supply a basis for dealing with the question of significance — the brevity or extension of a moment, a scene, a phrase, a sentence, an observation, a joke.

That is, as the central element length (and its opposite, extreme quickness) can supply a beginning and provable (or almost provable) ground for one's efforts at interpretation and analysis of "The Dead" or of "Criers and Kibitzers, Kibitzers and Criers" or of Kafka's parables or of Chekhov's tales.

For instance, in the title story of this book, it is the presence and portrayal of the work day that underlies almost all the uses of length and concision. Or rather, the effect of Elkin's uses of length and concision portray the day so that it might be the case that it is the work day that is the hero, and the hero is simply the human creature whose work day it is. Here is a work day gone through despite grief—grief not simplified, not lied about, not sentimentalized.

Oh, it's art.

And one can see various things then. One can see how the use of length (rather than emphasis or storytelling) gives stories of this third sort their human dimension, their humane music.

But one can also see that as the chief formal determinant, this sort of gardening of attention imposes an almost impossible strain of meaning and presence on the language used—almost an inhuman strain. One can see how a very very good story is always in competition, oddly, with poetry in this regard. One can see how the language must carry meaning at all times, and must not be stale language used sentimentally and trashily and popularly—except as a joke or as an expression of pain. That is to say, the language of the thing, like the language of a review or of a news story, carries the burden of displaying the morality of workmanship, while the overall meaning or significance of the story carries a more public burden of topical meaning and significance—which, however, it can't convey without the help of language, unlike the novel, which can function in regard to meaning without disciplined language (cf. Dreiser, Zola, early Solzhenitsyn, many current Americans).

So, you have two kinds of dexterity going at once in a good story such as Elkin's, one having to do with the duration and nature of attention and its extension or its rhythmic curtness, and the other having to do with language similarly attached to duration and the nature of attention and used with considerable extension or with considerable rhythmic curtness.

It's a juggling act. It's W.C. Fields doing ballet, sort of. Once you get on this horrible-wonderful treadmill or merry-go-round of the length-determined modern forms, not only must the sentences interrelate in terms of event and of technique, but the tone must be sequential, and the narrative or progression of meaning must be consequential. And in a country devoted to shrewdness and to confidence tricks, to a steady middling sort of decent lying you're supposed to be sharp-witted about — in a country of mass-produced cars and nearly universal considerations of the prices of real estate — this means producing a piece of work that is like a hand-produced sports car which a limited number of people can afford and a limited number of people can drive well, can deal with, can be unintimidated by with regard to the significance and excellence of the thing.

The great historical switch to the political preponderance of the middle class has in it a double element — a defense of the merits and abilities of ordinary people, but also of the rights of the mediocre. When ancient states were wrecked by the mediocrity of their rulers, it was not always considered mediocrity, but fate — which may or may not be considered tactful.

Elkin's central thematic preoccupations have to do with ordinariness, with mediocrity, but with human merit as well, and fate; but these are considered in the light of the fatal injustice, and of individual merit and individual feelings, and of individuals and their actions as good or evil.

Elkin is primarily known as a novelist, but notice that his preoccupations as a short story writer seem to match the form, and the history of the form as well. He is a novelist who seems to have been born partly to write stories.

In the nineteenth century, mediocrity took on its modern meaning and was named as the enemy, but not in the best stories (Chekhov's, for instance), and mediocrity was praised in socialism and in lousy stories and was courted by the media. One can see the literary history of the century as a Napoleonic one, a recurrent attempt by artists to enlist mediocrity or to come to terms with it or to embody it as part of a campaign for the conquest of history.

Echoes of this survive in Elkin but he is more than modern; he is post-modern, and was even before he knew it. The bitter skepticism and newness of attitude in these stories matches something that was happening historically among writers. Elkin was born during the same era in which Kafka did not publish much in his lifetime. Babel was silenced once it became apparent just how good a writer he was. Joyce was considered difficult. An existing great translation of Proust into English was held to require simplification — and was ruined.

That is to say, the truest art, or some of it anyway, is felt to be anti-Napoleonic, honorably unseductive, and perhaps not recognizably art at all.

Art becomes recessive, inverted, teasing — it becomes incoherent in regard to mediocrity and fate.

More than a good novel, a good, or very good, or very very good story challenges mediocrity, our marvelously vicious and successful emperor, but it does so in a sort of privacy of un-media-overseen intimacy.

That means, given democracy or socialism, given any dictatorship, a good story challenges the social world.

Stanley Elkin, being a very good writer, does just that, paragraph after paragraph in his books and stories, but he is also a practical man. In him is the longing to be a popular writer of the cliché-ridden, calculating sort; the solipsistic, trashy, self-loving sort. It is almost part of his aesthetic — almost a love affair. Each of Stanley Elkin's stories here shows a tendency now and then to escape from itself and enter another category, often at a lower level. Modesty and greed peek out, but meanwhile, almost ferociously, the story resumes its own wayward grace, which is to say that Stanley Elkin, the poor tortured creature, gets on with producing his art.

Most of his characters — perhaps all — are Jews. (I admired and enjoyed the stories too much to take notes, to look for exceptions). In the story form, if even a single phrase has an obvious flabbiness of meaning, that absence of significance tends to signal the unimportance of the story — the writer doesn't care. It often takes the form of *shtick* or of romanticizing the reader's experience as the reader knows it in whatever verbal form he knows it; that is, in its use of *kitsch* and *shtick* as elements of a display of social virtuousness: he's a good guy, one of us, and so on. You can study this in translations of Chekhov when the translation is no good. You can tell it's no good because even Chekhov is no good if the translation is flabby, no matter its claims of accuracy — if it lacks a certain energy of progression and a certain deep cleverness about the uses of length as a formal element, and a certain sense, a certainty of significance being present. Those elements determine which translations of Chekhov are acceptable.

The presence of the openly journalistic (the journalistically formulaic) means, flatly, that the story is not worth one's time. One might enjoy that, however. The feeling of superiority to the writer is one of the democratic pleasures.

It is impossible, I think, to find much that is journalistic in these stories. For the moment, let us call that a flaw. But I don't think it is a flaw at all. It is impossible to feel superior to Elkin. He is too good a writer. He thinks and feels too profoundly. He is modest and human and down-to-earth and all that, but he is too good at what he does: he's a little scarey.

Some stories that appear in print and win prizes are quite wonderful on first reading. They may be a high form of journalism, and of a quality that keeps them readable for a decade — but not two. One ought not to make time to return to them.

And many stories are useful as training devices: to train one's attention, give one experience at decoding narrative progressions; and they ought not awe the reader too much, or she or he will be too awed to learn. It is like tennis: one should play with people not too greatly superior to oneself.

But such stories are not really of enough merit to read with one's full attention. They are good for purposes that have little to do with actual reading. Reading is a dangerous act. One mustn't be misled by the usefulness of teachable stories into thinking they are any good. They have the same relation to merit (and the real thing) that examples of business letters given in textbooks written a decade or two decades earlier than one's time have to raw business letters in a time of economic emergency — letters that affect your destiny and that of others, lying letters, truthful letters, letters in the real world.

Elkin-on-the-page is too immediate, too large, too good to try to learn from. One tends to be a bystander — except humanly, except as a man, say; then one is a student always, I suppose. But as a writer Elkin is not imitable, which means he is not for classroom teaching except of an elevated sort. These are good stories.

Elkin is often a marvel. His language is often splendid, often low, always supple, dextrous, frequently inspired. It is never without meaning. It is true his use of length is a bit uncertain, but that is true of all the writers in the third category when they write stories. They know too much. They are too experienced in other forms which don't use length in that way. So they are all unreliable, no matter how good they are.

As an American, Elkin is a bit shy about being an artist. He clearly is one, but he is too playful and he puts in things to show he is a good guy. He dilutes effects. He has the self-sufficiency, the sense of order, the near-madness of a major figure. He plays with the Chekhovian sufficiency notion that in a story everything must be part of the story, must be usefully part of the creation of the overall effect, the meaning — but then he plays with that by going too far, by being too much. (May I use those idioms here?) He is a bit like a dolphin playing in an aquarium pool. He stands comedy and meaning, pain and compassion, Jewish realities, and terror on his dolphinlike nose—so to speak—and on *their* noses, and he sets them dancing, often upside down. And then he says or implies that the things he is playing with are logical and not at all playful in themselves, and that their obstinacy as fate in reality wins out. And often, then, my heart is broken.

At moments he is as good a stylist as Bellow and at times he is as funny as Roth—funnier and more passionate sometimes. He has never written a short piece as magical as Bellow's translation of Singer's "Gimpel the Fool," and is never as seductive as Salinger or ever as brilliant at farce or at editorializing as Roth. But he is wider and wilder in attitude and in subject matter than all of them, and far more reliable in moral judgment than Ozick. He is unlike anyone else; and in certain ways, he is superior to all of us—I mean, in his unremitting seriousness (even when he's trying to sell out), and in his concentration and the consequent energy, and in the wit of his narrations in relation to significance. He is much bitterer than we are, and a better delineator of character and of the consequences of specific actions on human affairs (and feelings). He is more serious than anyone now alive, which may mean he is at times a better writer than anyone. Time will judge these matters for us. Later readers playing with the danger inherent in reading anything will have their turn at voting and judging all of us now alive.

But what I want to say is that he is never a journalist, and that the stories in this book will curl your hair, inform your mind, instruct and terrify your heart, and make you laugh and make you wish you knew him and that he would live forever and write more and more and more and more.

HAROLD BRODKEY
1990